The Adventures Of Captain Horn

by

Frank R. Stockton

Double9
BOOKS

The Adventures Of Captain Horn
by Frank R. Stockton

ISBN: 978-93-59953-28-1

Published by

DOUBLE 9 BOOKS

2/13-B, Ansari Road
Daryaganj, New Delhi – 110002
info@double9books.com
www.double9books.com
Tel. 011-40042856

ABOUT THE AUTHOR

Frank Richard Stockton was an American author and humorist who lived from April 5, 1834, to April 20, 1902. He is best known for a set of unique children's fairy tales that were very popular in the last few decades of the 1800s. Stockton was born in Philadelphia in 1834. His father was a famous Methodist preacher who told him he shouldn't become a writer. He and his wife went to Burlington, New Jersey, after getting married to Mary Ann Edwards Tuttle. That's where he wrote some of his first books. They then moved to New Jersey's Nutley. He worked as a wood carver for many years until his father died in 1860. He went back to Philadelphia in 1867 to work as a writer for a newspaper that his brother had started. His first fairy tale, "Ting-a-ling," came out in The Riverside Magazine that same year. In 1870, he released his first collection of stories. In the early 1870s, he was also the editor of the magazine Hearth and Home. He went to Charles Town, West Virginia, around 1899. He died of a brain bleed in Washington, DC, on April 20, 1902. He is buried at The Woodlands in Philadelphia.

CONTENTS

CHAPTER I
AN INTRODUCTORY DISASTER

Early in the spring of the year 1884 the three-masted schooner *Castor*, from San Francisco to Valparaiso, was struck by a tornado off the coast of Peru. The storm, which rose with frightful suddenness, was of short duration, but it left the *Castor* a helpless wreck. Her masts had snapped off and gone overboard, her rudder-post had been shattered by falling wreckage, and she was rolling in the trough of the sea, with her floating masts and spars thumping and bumping her sides.

The *Castor* was an American merchant-vessel, commanded by Captain Philip Horn, an experienced navigator of about thirty-five years of age. Besides a valuable cargo, she carried three passengers—two ladies and a boy. One of these, Mrs. William Cliff, a lady past middle age, was going to Valparaiso to settle some business affairs of her late husband, a New England merchant. The other lady was Miss Edna Markham, a school-teacher who had just passed her twenty-fifth year, although she looked older. She was on her way to Valparaiso to take an important position in an American seminary. Ralph, a boy of fifteen, was her brother, and she was taking him with her simply because she did not want to leave him alone in San Francisco. These two had no near relations, and the education of the brother depended upon the exertions of the sister. Valparaiso was not the place she would have selected for a boy's education, but there they could be together, and, under the circumstances, that was a point of prime importance.

But when the storm had passed, and the sky was clear, and the mad waves had subsided into a rolling swell, there seemed no reason to believe that any one on board the *Castor* would ever reach Valparaiso. The vessel had been badly strained by the wrenching of the masts, her sides had been battered by the floating wreckage, and she was taking in water rapidly. Fortunately, no one had been injured by the storm, and although the captain found it would be a useless waste of time and labor to attempt to work the pumps, he was convinced, after a careful examination, that the ship would float some hours, and that there would, therefore, be time for those on board to make an effort to save not only their lives, but some of their property.

All the boats had been blown from their davits, but one of them was floating, apparently uninjured, a short distance to leeward, one of the heavy blocks by which it had been suspended having caught in the cordage of the topmast, so that it was securely moored. Another boat, a small one, was seen, bottom upward, about an eighth of a mile to leeward. Two seamen, each pushing an oar before him, swam out to the nearest boat, and having got on board of her, and freed her from her entanglements, they rowed out to the capsized boat, and towed it to the schooner. When this boat had been righted and bailed out, it was found to be in good condition.

The sea had become almost quiet, and there was time enough to do everything orderly and properly, and in less than three hours after the vessel had been struck, the two boats, containing all the crew and the passengers, besides a goodly quantity of provisions and water, and such valuables, clothing, rugs, and wraps as room could be found for, were pulling away from the wreck.

The captain, who, with his passengers, was in the larger boat, was aware that he was off the coast of Peru, but that was all he certainly knew of his position. The storm had struck the ship in the morning, before he had taken his daily observation, and his room, which was on deck, had been carried away, as well as every nautical instrument on board. He did not believe that the storm had taken him far out of his course, but of this he could not be sure. All that he knew with certainty was that to the eastward lay the land, and eastward, therefore, they pulled, a little compass attached to the captain's watch-guard being their only guide.

For the rest of that day and that night, and the next day and the next night, the two boats moved eastward, the people on board suffering but little inconvenience, except from the labor of continuous rowing, at which everybody, excepting the two ladies, took part, even Ralph Markham being willing to show how much of a man he could be with an oar in his hand.

The weather was fine, and the sea was almost smooth, and as the captain had rigged up in his boat a tent-like covering of canvas for the ladies, they were, as they repeatedly declared, far more comfortable than they had any right to expect. They were both women of resource and courage. Mrs. Cliff, tall, thin in face, with her gray hair brushed plainly over her temples, was a woman of strong frame, who would have been perfectly willing to take an oar, had it been necessary. To Miss Markham this boat trip would have been a positive pleasure, had it not been for the unfortunate circumstances which made it necessary.

On the morning of the third day land was sighted, but it was afternoon before they reached it. Here they found themselves on a portion of the coast where the foot-hills of the great mountains stretch themselves almost down to the edge of the ocean. To all appearances, the shore was barren and uninhabited.

The two boats rowed along the coast a mile or two to the southward, but could find no good landing-place, but reaching a spot less encumbered with rocks than any other portion of the coast they had seen, Captain Horn determined to try to beach his boat there. The landing was accomplished in safety, although with some difficulty, and that night was passed in a little encampment in the shelter of some rocks scarcely a hundred yards from the sea.

The next morning Captain Horn took counsel with his mates, and considered the situation. They were on an uninhabited portion of the coast, and it was not believed that there was any town or settlement near enough to be reached by walking over such wild country, especially with ladies in the party. It was, therefore, determined to seek succor by means of the sea. They might be near one of the towns or villages along the coast of Peru, and, in any case, a boat manned by the best oarsmen of the party, and loaded as lightly as possible, might hope, in the course of a day or two, to reach some port from which a vessel might be sent out to take off the remainder of the party.

But first Captain Horn ordered a thorough investigation to be made of the surrounding country, and in an hour or two a place was found which he believed would answer very well for a camping-ground until assistance should arrive. This was on a little plateau about a quarter of a mile back from the ocean, and surrounded on three sides by precipices, and on the side toward the sea the ground sloped gradually downward. To this camping-ground all of the provisions and goods were carried, excepting what would be needed by the boating party.

When this work had been accomplished, Captain Horn appointed his first mate to command the expedition, deciding to remain himself in the camp. When volunteers were called for, it astonished the captain to see how many of the sailors desired to go.

The larger boat pulled six oars, and seven men, besides the mate Rynders, were selected to go in her. As soon as she could be made ready she was launched and started southward on her voyage of discovery, the mate having first taken such good observation of the landmarks that he felt sure he would have no difficulty in finding the spot where he left his companions. The people in the little camp on the bluff now consisted of Captain Horn, the two ladies, the boy Ralph, three sailors,—one an Englishman, and the other two Americans from Cape Cod,—and a jet-black native African, known as Maka.

Captain Horn had not cared to keep many men with him in the camp, because there they would have little to do, and all the strong arms that could be spared would be needed in the boat. The three sailors he had retained were men of intelligence, on whom he believed he could rely in case of emergency, and Maka was kept because he was a cook. He had been one of the cargo of a slave-ship which had been captured by a British cruiser several years before, when on its way to Cuba, and the unfortunate negroes had been landed in British Guiana. It was impossible to return them to Africa, because none of them could speak English, or in any way give an idea as to what tribes they belonged, and if they should be landed anywhere in Africa except among their friends, they would be immediately reënslaved. For some years they lived in Guiana, in a little colony by themselves, and then, a few of them having learned some English, they made their way to Panama, where they obtained employment as laborers on the great canal. Maka, who was possessed of better intelligence than most of his fellows, improved a good deal in his English, and learned to cook very well, and having wandered to San Francisco, had been employed for two or three voyages by Captain Horn. Maka was a faithful and willing servant, and if he had been able to express himself more intelligibly, his merits might have been better appreciated.

CHAPTER II
A NEW FACE IN CAMP

The morning after the departure of the boat, Captain Horn, in company with the Englishman Davis, each armed with a gun, set out on a tour of investigation, hoping to be able to ascend the rocky hills at the back of the camp, and find some elevated point commanding a view over the ocean. After a good deal of hard climbing they reached such a point, but the captain found that the main object was really out of his reach. He could now plainly see that a high rocky point to the southward, which stretched some distance out to sea, would cut off all view of the approach of rescuers coming from that direction, until they were within a mile or two of his landing-place. Back from the sea the hills grew higher, until they blended into the lofty stretches of the Andes, this being one of the few points where the hilly country extends to the ocean.

The coast to the north curved a little oceanward, so that a much more extended view could be had in that direction, but as far as he could see by means of a little pocket-glass which the boy Ralph had lent him, the captain could discover no signs of habitation, and in this direction the land seemed to be a flat desert. When he returned to camp, about noon, he had made up his mind that the proper thing to do was to make himself and his companions as comfortable as possible and patiently await the return of his mate with succor.

Captain Horn was very well satisfied with his present place of encampment. Although rain is unknown in this western portion of Peru, which is, therefore, in general desolate and barren, there are parts of the country that are irrigated by streams which flow from the snow-capped peaks of the Andes, and one of these fertile spots the captain seemed to have happened upon. On the plateau there grew a few bushes, while the face of the rock in places was entirely covered by hanging vines. This fertility greatly puzzled Captain Horn, for nowhere was to be seen any stream of water, or signs of there ever having been any. But they had with them water enough to last for several days, and provisions for a much longer time, and the captain felt little concern on this account.

As for lodgings, there were none excepting the small tent which he had put up for the ladies, but a few nights in the open air in that dry climate would not hurt the male portion of the party.

In the course of the afternoon, the two American sailors came to Captain Horn and asked permission to go to look for game. The captain had small hopes of their finding anything suitable for food, but feeling sure that if they should be successful, every one would be glad of a little fresh meat, he gave his permission, at the same time requesting the men to do their best in the way of observation, if they should get up high enough to survey the country, and discover some signs of habitation, if such existed in that barren region. It would be a great relief to the captain to feel that there was some spot of refuge to which, by land or water, his party might make its way in case the water and provisions gave out before the return of the mate.

As to the men who went off in the boat, the captain expected to see but a few of them again. One or two might return with the mate, in such vessel as he should obtain in which to come for them, but the most of them, if they reached a seaport, would scatter, after the manner of seamen.

The two sailors departed, promising, if they could not bring back fish or fowl, to return before dark, with a report of the lay of the land.

It was very well that Maka did not have to depend on these hunters for the evening meal, for night came without them, and the next morning they had not returned. The captain was very much troubled. The men must be lost, or they had met with some accident. There could be no other reason for their continued absence. They had each a gun, and plenty of powder and shot, but they had taken only provisions enough for a single meal.

Davis offered to go up the hills to look for the missing men. He had lived for some years in the bush in Australia, and he thought that there was a good chance of his discovering their tracks. But the captain shook his head.

"You are just as likely to get lost, or to fall over a rock, as anybody else," he said, "and it is better to have two men lost than three. But there is one thing that you can do. You can go down to the beach, and make your way southward as far as possible. There you can find your way back, and if you take a gun, and fire it every now and then, you may attract the attention of Shirley and Burke, if they are on the hills above, and perhaps they may even be able to see you as you walk along. If they are alive, they will probably see or hear you, and fire in answer. It is a very strange thing that we have not heard a shot from them."

Ralph begged to accompany the Englishman, for he was getting very restless, and longed for a ramble and scramble. But neither the captain nor his sister would consent to this, and Davis started off alone.

"If you can round the point down there," said the captain to him, "do it, for you may see a town or houses not far away on the other side. But don't take any risks. At all events, make your calculations so that you will be back here before dark."

The captain and Ralph assisted the two ladies to a ledge of rock near the camp from which they could watch the Englishman on his way. They saw him reach the beach, and after going on a short distance he fired his gun, after which he pressed forward, now and then stopping to fire again. Even from their inconsiderable elevation they could see him until he must have been more than a mile away, and he soon after vanished from their view.

As on the previous day darkness came without the two American sailors, so now it came without the Englishman, and in the morning he had not returned. Of course, every mind was filled with anxiety in regard to the three sailors, but Captain Horn's soul was racked with apprehensions of which he did not speak. The conviction forced itself upon him that the men had been killed by wild beasts. He could imagine no other reason why Davis should not have returned. He had been ordered not to leave the beach, and, therefore, could not lose his way. He was a wary, careful man, used to exploring rough country, and he was not likely to take any chances of disabling himself by a fall while on such an expedition.

Although he knew that the great jaguar was found in Peru, as well as the puma and black bear, the captain had not supposed it likely that any of these creatures frequented the barren western slopes of the mountains, but he now reflected that there were lions in the deserts of Africa, and that the beasts of prey in South America might also be found in its deserts.

A great responsibility now rested upon Captain Horn. He was the only man left in camp who could be depended upon as a defender,—for Maka was known to be a coward, and Ralph was only a boy,—and it was with a shrinking of the heart that he asked himself what would be the consequences if a couple of jaguars or other ferocious beasts were to appear upon that unprotected plateau in the night, or even in the daytime. He had two guns, but he was only one man. These thoughts were not cheerful, but the captain's face showed no signs of alarm, or even unusual anxiety, and, with a smile on his handsome brown countenance, he bade the ladies good morning as if he were saluting them upon a quarter-deck.

"I have been thinking all night about those three men," said Miss Markham, "and I have imagined something which may have happened. Isn't it possible that they may have discovered at a distance some inland settlement which could not be seen by the party in the boat, and that they thought it their duty to push their way to it, and so get assistance for us? In that case, you know, they would probably be a long time coming back."

"That is possible," said the captain, glad to hear a hopeful supposition, but in his heart he had no faith in it whatever. If Davis had seen a village, or even a house, he would have come back to report it, and if the others had found human habitation, they would have had ample time to return, either by land or by sea.

The restless Ralph, who had chafed a good deal because he had not been allowed to leave the plateau in search of adventure, now found a vent for his surplus energy, for the captain appointed him fire-maker. The camp fuel was not abundant, consisting of nothing but some dead branches and twigs from the few bushes in the neighborhood. These Ralph collected with great energy, and Maka had nothing to complain of in regard to fuel for his cooking.

Toward the end of that afternoon, Ralph prepared to make a fire for the supper, and he determined to change the position of the fireplace and bring it nearer the rocks, where he thought it would burn better. It did burn better—so well, indeed, that some of the dry leaves of the vines that there covered the face of the rocks took fire. Ralph watched with interest the dry leaves blaze and the green ones splutter, and then he thought it would be a pity to scorch those vines, which were among the few green things about them, and he tried to put out the fire. But this he could not do, and, when he called Maka, the negro was not able to help him. The fire had worked its way back of the green vines, and seemed to have found good fuel, for it was soon crackling away at a great rate, attracting the rest of the party.

"Can't we put it out?" cried Miss Markham. "It is a pity to ruin those beautiful vines."

The captain smiled and shook his head. "We cannot waste our valuable water on that conflagration," said he. "There is probably a great mass of dead vines behind the green outside. How it crackles and roars! That dead stuff must be several feet thick. All we can do is to let it burn. It cannot hurt us. It cannot reach your tent, for there are no vines over there."

The fire continued to roar and blaze, and to leap up the face of the rock.

"It is wonderful," said Mrs. Cliff, "to think how those vines must have been growing and dying, and new ones growing and dying, year after year, nobody knows how many ages."

"What is most wonderful to me," said the captain, "is that the vines ever grew there at all, or that these bushes should be here. Nothing can grow in this region, unless it is watered by a stream from the mountains, and there is no stream here."

Miss Markham was about to offer a supposition to the effect that perhaps the precipitous wall of rock which surrounded the little plateau, and shielded it from the eastern sun, might have had a good effect upon the vegetation, when suddenly Ralph, who had a ship's biscuit on the end of a sharp stick, and was toasting it in the embers of a portion of the burnt vines, sprang back with a shout.

"Look out!" he cried. "The whole thing's coming down!" And, sure enough, in a moment a large portion of the vines, which had been clinging to the rock, fell upon the ground in a burning mass. A cloud of smoke and dust arose, and when it had cleared away the captain and his party saw upon the perpendicular side of the rock, which was now revealed to them as if a veil had been torn away from in front of it, an enormous face cut out of the solid stone.

CHAPTER III
A CHANGE OF LODGINGS

The great face stared down upon the little party gathered beneath it. Its chin was about eight feet above the ground, and its stony countenance extended at least that distance up the cliff. Its features were in low relief, but clear and distinct, and a smoke-blackened patch beneath one of its eyes gave it a sinister appearance. From its wide-stretching mouth a bit of half-burnt vine hung, trembling in the heated air, and this element of motion produced the impression on several of the party that the creature was about to open its lips.

Mrs. Cliff gave a little scream,—she could not help it,—and Maka sank down on his knees, his back to the rock, and covered his face with his hands. Ralph was the first to speak.

"There have been heathen around here," he said. "That's a regular idol."

"You are right," said the captain. "That is a bit of old-time work. That face was cut by the original natives."

The two ladies were so interested, and even excited, that they seized each other by the hands. Here before their faces was a piece of sculpture doubtless done by the people of ancient Peru, that people who were discovered by Pizarro; and this great idol, or whatever it was, had perhaps never before been seen by civilized eyes. It was wonderful, and in the conjecture and exclamation of the next half-hour everything else was forgotten, even the three sailors.

Because the captain was the captain, it was natural that every one should look to him for some suggestion as to why this great stone face should have been carved here on this lonely and desolate rock. But he shook his head.

"I have no ideas about it," he said, "except that it must have been some sort of a landmark. It looks out toward the sea, and perhaps the ancient inhabitants put it there so that people in ships, coming near enough to the coast, should know where they were. Perhaps it was intended to act as a lighthouse to warn seamen off a dangerous coast. But I must say that I do not see how it could do that, for they would have had to come pretty close to the shore to see it, unless they had better glasses than we have."

The sun was now near the horizon, and Maka was lifted to his feet by the captain, and ordered to stop groaning in African, and go to work to get supper on the glowing embers of the vines. He obeyed, of course, but never did he turn his face upward to that gaunt countenance, which grinned and winked and frowned whenever a bit of twig blazed up, or the coals were stirred by the trembling negro.

After supper and until the light had nearly faded from the western sky, the two ladies sat and watched that vast face upon the rocks, its features growing more and more solemn as the light decreased.

"I wish I had a long-handled broom," said Mrs. Cliff, "for if the dust and smoke and ashes of burnt leaves were brushed from off its nose and eyebrows, I believe it would have a rather gracious expression."

As for the captain, he went walking about on the outlying portion of the plateau, listening and watching. But it was not stone faces he was thinking of. That night he did not sleep at all, but sat until day-break, with a loaded gun across his knees, and another one lying on the ground beside him.

When Miss Markham emerged from the rude tent the next morning, and came out into the bright light of day, the first thing she saw was her brother Ralph, who looked as if he had been sweeping a chimney or cleaning out an ash-hole.

"What on earth has happened to you!" she cried. "How did you get yourself so covered with dirt and ashes?"

"I got up ever so long ago," he replied, "and as the captain is asleep over there, and there was nobody to talk to, I thought I would go and try to find the back of his head"—pointing to the stone face above them. "But he hasn't any. He is a sham."

"What do you mean?" asked his sister.

"You see, Edna," said the boy, "I thought I would try if I could find any more faces, and so I got a bit of stone, and scratched away some of the burnt vines that had not fallen, and there I found an open place in the rock on this side of the face. Step this way, and you can see it. It's like a narrow doorway. I went and looked into it, and saw that it led back of the big face, and I went in to see what was there."

"You should never have done that, Ralph," cried his sister. "There might have been snakes in that place, or precipices, or nobody knows what. What could you expect to see in the dark?"

"It wasn't so dark as you might think," said he. "After my eyes got used to the place I could see very well. But there was nothing to see—just walls on each side. There was more of the passageway ahead of me, but I began to think of snakes myself, and as I did not have a club or anything to kill them with, I concluded I wouldn't go any farther. It isn't so very dirty in there. Most of this I got on myself scraping down the burnt vines. Here comes the captain. He doesn't generally oversleep himself like this. If he will go with me, we will explore that crack."

When Captain Horn heard of the passage into the rock, he was much more interested than Ralph had expected him to be, and, without loss of time, he lighted a lantern and, with the boy behind him, set out to investigate it. But before entering the cleft, the captain stationed Maka at a place where he could view all the approaches to the plateau, and told him if he saw any snakes or other dangerous things approaching, to run to the opening and call him. Now, snakes were among the few things that Maka was not afraid of, and so long as he thought these were the enemies to be watched, he would make a most efficient sentinel.

When Captain Horn had cautiously advanced a couple of yards into the interior of the rock, he stopped, raised his lantern, and looked about him. The passage was about two feet wide, the floor somewhat lower than the ground outside, and the roof but a few feet above his head. It was plainly the work of man, and not a natural crevice in the rocks. Then the captain put the lantern behind him, and stared into the gloom ahead of them. As Ralph had said, it was not so dark as might have been expected. In fact, about twenty feet forward there was a dim light on the right-hand wall.

The captain, still followed by Ralph, now moved on until they came to this lighted place, and found it was an open doorway. Both heads together, they peeped in, and saw it was an opening like a doorway into a chamber about fifteen feet square and with very high walls. They scarcely needed the lantern to examine it, for a jagged opening in the roof let in a good deal of light.

Passing into this chamber, keeping a good watch out for pitfalls as he moved on, and forgetting, in his excitement, that he might go so far that he could not hear Maka, should he call, the captain saw to the right another open doorway, on the other side of which was another chamber, about the size of the one they had first entered. One side of this was a good deal broken away, and through a fracture three or four feet wide the light entered freely, as if from the open air. But when the two explorers peered through the ragged aperture, they did not look into the open air, but into another chamber, very much larger than the others, with high, irregular walls, but with scarcely any roof, almost the whole of the upper part being open to the sky.

A mass of broken rocks on the floor of this apartment showed that the roof had fallen in. The captain entered it and carefully examined it. A portion of the floor was level and unobstructed by rocks, and in the walls there was not the slightest sign of a doorway, except the one by which he had entered from the adjoining chamber.

"Hurrah!" cried Ralph. "Here is a suite of rooms. Isn't this grand? You and I can have that first one, Maka can sleep in the hall to keep out burglars, and Edna and Mrs. Cliff can have the middle room, and this open place here can be their garden, where they can take tea and sew. These rocks will make splendid tables and chairs."

The captain stood, breathing hard, a sense of relief coming over him like the warmth of fire. He had thought of what Ralph had said before the boy had spoken. Here was safety from wild beasts—here was immunity from the only danger he could imagine to those under his charge. It might be days yet before the mate returned,—he knew the probable difficulties of obtaining a vessel, even when a port should be reached,—but they would be safe here from the attacks of ferocious animals, principally to be feared in the night. They might well be thankful for such a good place as this in which to await the arrival of succor, if succor came before their water gave out. There were biscuits, salt meat, tea, and other things enough to supply their wants for perhaps a week longer, provided the three sailors did not return, but the supply of water, although they were very economical of it, must give out in a day or two. "But," thought the captain, "Rynders may be back before that, and, on the other hand, a family of jaguars might scent us out to-night."

"You are right, my boy," said he, speaking to Ralph. "Here is a suite of rooms, and we will occupy them just as you have said. They are dry and airy, and it will be far better for us to sleep here than out of doors."

As they returned, Ralph was full of talk about the grand find. But the captain made no answers to his remarks—his mind was busy contriving some means of barricading the narrow entrance at night.

When breakfast was over, and the entrance to the rocks had been made cleaner and easier by the efforts of Maka and Ralph, the ladies were conducted to the suite of rooms which Ralph had described in such glowing terms. Both were filled with curiosity to see these apartments, especially Miss Markham, who was fairly well read in the history of South America, and who had already imagined that the vast mass of rock by which they had camped might be in reality a temple of the ancient Peruvians, to which the stone face was a sacred sentinel. But when the three apartments had been thoroughly explored she was disappointed.

"There is not a sign or architectural adornment, or anything that seems to have the least religious significance, or significance of any sort," she said. "These are nothing but three stone rooms, with their roofs more or less broken in. They do not even suggest dungeons."

As for Mrs. Cliff, she did not hesitate to say that she should prefer to sleep in the open air.

"It would be dreadful," she said, "to awaken in the night and think of those great stone walls about me."

Even Ralph remarked that, on second thought, he believed he would rather sleep out of doors, for he liked to look up and see the stars before he went to sleep.

At first the captain was a little annoyed to find that this place of safety, the discovery of which had given him such satisfaction and relief, was looked upon with such disfavor by those who needed it so very much, but then the thought came to him, "Why should they care about a place of safety, when they have no idea of danger?" He did not now hesitate to settle the matter in the most straightforward and honest way. Having a place of refuge to offer, the time had come to speak of the danger. And so, standing in the larger apartment, and addressing his party, he told them of the fate he feared had overtaken the three sailors, and how anxious he had been lest the same fate should come upon some one or all of them.

Now vanished every spark of opposition to the captain's proffered lodgings.

"If we should be here but one night longer," cried Mrs. Cliff, echoing the captain's thought, "let us be safe."

In the course of the day the two rooms were made as comfortable as circumstances would allow with the blankets, shawls, and canvas which had been brought on shore, and that night they all slept in the rock chambers, the captain having made a barricade for the opening of the narrow passage with the four oars, which he brought up from the boat. Even should these be broken down by some wild beast, Captain Horn felt that, with his two guns at the end of the narrow passage, he might defend his party from the attacks of any of the savage animals of the country.

The captain slept soundly that night, for he had had but a nap of an hour or two on the previous morning, and, with Maka stretched in the passage outside the door of his room, he knew that he would have timely warning of danger, should any come. But Mrs. Cliff did not sleep well, spending a large part of the night imagining the descent of active carnivora down the lofty and perpendicular walls of the large adjoining apartment.

The next day was passed rather wearily by most of the party in looking out for signs of a vessel with the returning mate. Ralph had made a flag which he could wave from a high point near by, in case he should see a sail, for it would be a great misfortune should Mr. Rynders pass them without knowing it.

To the captain, however, came a new and terrible anxiety. He had looked into the water-keg, and saw that it held but a few quarts. It had not lasted as long as he had expected, for this was a thirsty climate.

The next night Mrs. Cliff slept, having been convinced that not even a cat could come down those walls. The captain woke very early, and when he went out he found, to his amazement, that the barricade had been removed, and he could not see Maka. He thought at first that perhaps the negro had gone down to the sea-shore to get some water for washing purposes, but an hour passed, and Maka did not return. The whole party went down to the beach, for the captain insisted upon all keeping together. They shouted, they called, they did whatever they could to discover the lost African, but all without success.

They returned to camp, disheartened and depressed. This new loss had something terrible in it. What it meant no one could conjecture. There was no reason why Maka should run away, for there was no place to run to, and it was impossible that any wild beast should have removed the oars and carried off the negro.

CHAPTER IV
ANOTHER NEW FACE

As the cook had gone, Mrs. Cliff and Miss Markham prepared breakfast, and then they discovered how little water there was.

There was something mysterious about the successive losses of his men which pressed heavily upon the soul of Captain Horn, but the want of water pressed still more heavily. Ralph had just asked his permission to go down to the beach and bathe in the sea, saying that as he could not have all the water he wanted to drink, it might make him feel better to take a swim in plenty of water. The boy was not allowed to go so far from camp by himself, but the captain could not help thinking how this poor fellow would probably feel the next day if help had not arrived, and of the sufferings of the others, which, by that time, would have begun. Still, as before, he spoke hopefully, and the two women, as brave as he, kept up good spirits, and although they each thought of the waterless morrow, they said nothing about it.

As for Ralph, he confidently expected the return of the men in the course of the day, as he had done in the course of each preceding day, and two or three times an hour he was at his post of observation, ready to wave his flag.

Even had he supposed that it would be of any use to go to look for Maka, a certain superstitious feeling would have prevented the captain from doing so. If he should go out, and not return, there would be little hope for those two women and the boy. But he could not help feeling that beyond the rocky plateau which stretched out into the sea to the southward, and which must be at least two miles away, there might be seen some signs of habitation, and, consequently, of a stream. If anything of the sort could be seen, it might become absolutely necessary for the party to make their way toward it, either by land or sea, no matter how great the fatigue or the danger, and without regard to the fate of those who had left camp before them.

About half an hour afterwards, when the captain had mounted some rocks near by, from which he thought he might get a view of the flat region to the north on which he might discover the missing negro, Ralph, who was looking seaward, gave a start, and then hurriedly called to his sister and Mrs. Cliff, and pointed to the beach. There was the figure of a man which might well be Maka, but, to their amazement and consternation, he was running, followed, not far behind, by another man. The figures rapidly approached, and it was soon seen that the first man was Maka, but that the second figure was not one of the sailors who had left them. Could he be pursuing Maka? What on earth did it mean?

For some moments Ralph stood dumfounded, and then ran in the direction in which the captain had gone, and called to him.

At the sound of his voice the second figure stopped and turned as if he were about to run, but Maka—they were sure it was Maka—seized him by the arm and held him. Therefore this newcomer could not be pursuing their man. As the two now came forward, Maka hurrying the other on, Ralph and his two companions were amazed to see that this second man was also an African, a negro very much like Maka, and as they drew nearer, the two looked as if they might have been brothers.

The captain had wandered farther than he had intended, but after several shouts from Ralph he came running back, and reached the campground just as the two negroes arrived.

At the sight of this tall man bounding toward him the strange negro appeared to be seized with a wild terror. He broke away from Maka, and ran first in this direction and then in that, and perceiving the cleft in the face of the rock, he blindly rushed into it, as a rat would rush into a hole. Instantly Maka was after him, and the two were lost to view.

When the captain had been told of the strange thing which had happened, he stood without a word. Another African! This was a puzzle too great for his brain.

"Are you sure it was not a native of these parts?" said he, directly. "You know, they are very dark."

"No!" exclaimed Mrs. Cliff and her companions almost in the same breath, "it was an African, exactly like Maka."

At this moment a wild yell was heard from the interior of the rocks, then another and another. Without waiting to consider anything, or hear any more, the captain dashed into the narrow passage, Ralph close behind him. They ran into the room in which they had slept. They looked on all sides, but saw nothing. Again, far away, they heard another yell, and they ran out again into the passage.

This narrow entry, as the investigating Ralph had already discovered, continued for a dozen yards past the doorway which led to the chambers, but there it ended in a rocky wall about five feet high. Above this was an aperture extending to the roof of the passage, but Ralph, having a wholesome fear of snakes, had not cared to climb over the wall to see what was beyond.

When the captain and Ralph had reached the end of the passage, they heard another cry, and there could be no doubt that it came through the aperture by which they stood. Instantly Ralph scrambled to the top of the wall, pushed himself head foremost through the opening, and came down on the other side, partly on his hands and partly on his feet. Had the captain been first, he would not have made such a rash leap, but now he did not hesitate a second. He instantly followed the boy, taking care, however, to let himself down on his feet.

The passage on the other side of the dividing wall seemed to be the same as that they had just left, although perhaps a little lighter. After pushing on for a short distance, they found that the passage made a turn to the right, and then in a few moments the captain and Ralph emerged into open space. What sort of space it was they could not comprehend.

"It seemed to me," said Ralph, afterwards, "as if I had fallen into the sky at night. I was afraid to move, for fear I should tumble into astronomical distances."

The captain stared about him, apparently as much confounded by the situation as was the boy. But his mind was quickly brought to the consideration of things which he could understand. Almost at his feet was Maka, lying on his face, his arms and head over the edge of what might be a bank or a bottomless precipice, and yelling piteously. Making a step toward him, the captain saw that he had hold of another man, several feet below him, and that he could not pull him up.

"Hold on tight, Maka," he cried, and then, taking hold of the African's shoulders, he gave one mighty heave, lifted both men, and set them on their feet beside him.

Ralph would have willingly sacrificed the rest of his school-days to be able to perform such a feat as that. But the Africans were small, and the captain was wildly excited.

Well might he be excited. He was wet! The strange man whom he had pulled up had stumbled against him, and he was dripping with water. Ralph was by the captain, tightly gripping his arm, and, without speaking, they both stood gazing before them and around them.

At their feet, stretching away in one direction, farther than they could see, and what at first sight they had taken to be air, was a body of water—a lake! Above them were rocks, and, as far as they could see to the right, the water seemed to be overhung by a cavernous roof. But in front of them, on the other side of the lake, which here did not seem to be more than a hundred feet wide, there was a great upright opening in the side of the cave, through which they could see the distant mountains and a portion of the sky.

"Water!" said Ralph, in a low tone, as if he had been speaking in church, and then, letting go of the captain's arm, he began to examine the ledge, but five or six feet wide, on which they stood. At his feet the water was at least a yard below them, but a little distance on he saw that the ledge shelved down to the surface of the lake, and in a moment he had reached this spot, and, throwing himself down on his breast, he plunged his face into the water and began drinking like a thirsty horse. Presently he rose to his knees with a great sigh of satisfaction.

"Oh, captain," he cried, "it is cold and delicious. I believe that in one hour more I should have died of thirst."

But the captain did not answer, nor did he move from the spot where he stood. His thoughts whirled around in his mind like chaff in a winnowing-machine. Water! A lake in the bosom of the rocks! Half an hour ago he must have been standing over it as he scrambled up the hillside. Visions that he had had of the morrow, when all their eyes should be standing out of their faces, like the eyes of shipwrecked sailors he had seen in boats, came back to him, and other visions of his mate and his men toiling southward for perhaps a hundred miles without reaching a port or a landing, and then the long, long delay before a vessel could be procured. And here was water!

Ralph stood beside him for an instant. "Captain," he cried, "I am going to get a pail, and take some to Edna and Mrs. Cliff." And then he was gone.

Recalled thus to the present, the captain stepped back. He must do something—he must speak to some one. He must take some advantage of this wonderful, this overpowering discovery. But before he could bring his mind down to its practical workings, Maka had clutched him by the coat.

"Cap'n," he said, "I must tell you. I must speak it. I must tell you now, quick. Wait! Don't go!"

CHAPTER V
THE RACKBIRDS

The new African was sitting on the ground, as far back from the edge of the ledge as he could get, shivering and shaking, for the water was cold. He had apparently reached the culmination and termination of his fright. After his tumble into the water, which had happened because he had been unable to stop in his mad flight, he had not nerve enough left to do anything more, no matter what should appear to scare him, and there was really no reason why he should be afraid of this big white man, who did not even look at him or give him a thought.

Maka's tale, which he told so rapidly and incoherently that he was frequently obliged to repeat portions of it, was to the following effect: He had thought a great deal about the scarcity of water, and it had troubled him so that he could not sleep. What a dreadful thing it would be for those poor ladies and the captain and the boy to die because they had no water! His recollections of experiences in his native land made him well understand that streams of water are to be looked for between high ridges, and the idea forced itself upon him very strongly that on the other side of the ridge to the south there might be a stream. He knew the captain would not allow him to leave the camp if he asked permission, and so he rose very early, even before it was light, and going down to the shore, made his way along the beach—on the same route, in fact, that the Englishman Davis had taken. He was a good deal frightened sometimes, he said, by the waves, which dashed up as if they would pull him into the water. When he reached the point of the rocky ridge, he had no difficulty whatever in getting round it, as he could easily keep away from the water by climbing over the rocks.

He found that the land on the other side began to recede from the ocean, and that there was a small sandy beach below him. This widened until it reached another and smaller point of rock, and beyond this Maka believed he would find the stream for which he was searching. And while he was considering whether he should climb over it or wade around it, suddenly a man jumped down from the rock, almost on top of him. This man fell down on his back, and was at first so frightened that he did not try to move.

Maka's wits entirely deserted him, he said, and he did not know anything, except that most likely he was going to die.

But on looking at the man on the ground, he saw that he was an African like himself, and in a moment he recognized him as one of his fellow-slaves, with whom he had worked in Guiana, and also for a short time on the Panama Canal. This made him think that perhaps he was not going to die, and he went up to the other man and spoke to him. Then the other man thought perhaps he was not going to die, and he sat up and spoke.

When the other man told his tale, Maka agreed with him that it would be far better to die of thirst than to go on any farther to look for water, and, turning, he ran back, followed by the other, and they never stopped to speak to each other until they had rounded the great bluff, and were making their way along the beach toward the camp. Then his fellow-African told Maka a great deal more, and Maka told everything to the captain.

The substance of the tale was this: A mile farther up the bay than Maka had gone, there was a little stream that ran down the ravine. About a quarter of a mile up this stream there was a spot where, it appeared from the account, there must be a little level ground suitable for habitations. Here were five or six huts, almost entirely surrounded by rocks, and in these lived a dozen of the most dreadful men in the whole world. This Maka assured the captain, his eyes wet with tears as he spoke. It must truly be so, because the other African had told him things which proved it.

A little farther up the stream, on the other side of the ravine, there was a cave, a very small one, and so high up in the face of the rock that it could only be reached by a ladder. In this lived five black men, members of the company of slaves who had gone from Guiana to the isthmus, and who had been brought down there about a year before by two wicked men, who had promised them well-paid work in a lovely country. They had, however, been made actual slaves in this barren and doleful place, and had since worked for the cruel men who had beguiled them into a captivity worse than the slavery to which they had been originally destined.

Eight of them had come down from the isthmus, but, at various times since, three of them had been killed by accident, or shot while trying to run away. The hardships of these poor fellows were very great, and Maka's voice shook as he spoke of them. They were kept in the cave all the time, except when they were wanted for some sort of work, when a ladder was put up by the side of the rock, and such as were required were called to come down. Without a ladder no one could get in or out of the cave. One man who had tried to slip down at night fell and broke his neck.

The Africans were employed in cooking and other rough domestic or menial services, and sometimes all of them were taken down to the shore of the bay, where they saw small vessels, and they were employed in carrying goods from one of these to another, and were also obliged to carry provisions and heavy kegs up the ravine to the houses of the wicked men. The one whom he had brought with him, Maka said, had that day escaped from his captors. One of the Rackbirds, whom in some way the negro had offended, had sworn to kill him before night, and feeling sure that this threat would be carried out, the poor fellow had determined to run away, no matter what the consequences. He had chosen the way by the ocean, in order that he might jump in and drown himself if he found that he was likely to be overtaken, but apparently his escape had not yet been discovered.

Maka was going on to tell something more about the wicked men, when the captain interrupted him. "Can this friend of yours speak English?" he asked.

"Only one, two words," replied Maka.

"Ask him if he knows the name of that band of men."

"Yes," said Maka, presently, "he know, but he no can speak it."

"Are they called the Rackbirds?" asked Captain Horn.

The shivering negro had been listening attentively, and now half rose and nodded his head violently, and then began to speak rapidly in African.

"Yes," said Maka, "he says that is name they are called."

At this moment Ralph appeared upon the scene, and the second African, whose name was something like Mok, sprang to his feet as if he were about to flee for his life. But as there was no place to flee to, except into the water or into the arms of Ralph, he stood still, trembling. A few feet to the left the shelf ended in a precipitous rock, and on the right, as has been said, it gradually descended into the water, the space on which the party stood not being more than twenty feet long and five or six feet wide. When he saw Ralph, the captain suddenly stopped the question he was about to ask, and said in an undertone to Maka:

"Not a word to the boy. I will tell."

"Oh," cried Ralph, "you do not know what a lively couple there is out there. I found that my sister and Mrs. Cliff had made up their minds that they would perish in about two days, and Mrs. Cliff had been making her will with a lead-pencil, and now they are just as high up as they were low down before. They would not let me come to get them some water, though I kept telling them they never tasted anything like it in their whole lives, because they wanted to hear everything about everything. My sister will be wild to come to this lake before long, even if Mrs. Cliff does not care to try it. And when you are ready to come to them, and bring Maka, they want to know who that other colored man is, and how Maka happened to find him. I truly believe their curiosity goes ahead of their thirst." And so saying he went down to the lake to fill a pail he had brought with him.

The captain told Ralph to hurry back to the ladies, and that he would be there in a few minutes. Captain Horn knew a great deal about the Rackbirds. They were a band of desperadoes, many of them outlaws and criminals. They had all come down from the isthmus, to which they had been attracted by the great canal works, and after committing various outrages and crimes, they had managed to get away without being shot or hung. Captain Horn had frequently heard of them in the past year or two, and it was generally supposed that they had some sort of rendezvous or refuge on this coast, but there had been no effort made to seek them out. He had frequently heard of crimes committed by them at points along the coast, which showed that they had in their possession some sort of vessel. At one time, when he had stopped at Lima, he had heard that there was talk of the government's sending out a police or military expedition against these outlaws, but he had never known of anything of the sort being done.

Everything that, from time to time, had been told Captain Horn about the Rackbirds showed that they surpassed in cruelty and utter vileness any other bandits, or even savages, of whom he had ever heard. Among other news, he had been told that the former leader of the band, which was supposed to be composed of men of many nationalities, was a French Canadian, who had been murdered by his companions because, while robbing a plantation in the interior,—they had frequently been known to cross the desert and the mountains,—he had forborne to kill an old man because as the trembling graybeard looked up at him he had reminded him of his father. Some of the leading demons of the band determined that they could not have such a fool as this for their leader, and he was killed while asleep.

Now the band was headed by a Spaniard, whose fiendishness was of a sufficiently high order to satisfy the most exacting of his fellows. These and other bits of news about the Rackbirds had been told by one of the band who had escaped to Panama after the murder of the captain, fearing that his own talents for baseness did not reach the average necessary for a Rackbird.

When he had made his landing from the wreck, Captain Horn never gave a thought to the existence of this band of scoundrels. In fact, he had supposed, when he had thought of the matter, that their rendezvous must be far south of this point.

But now, standing on that shelf of rock, with his eyes fixed on the water without seeing it, he knew that the abode of this gang of wretches was within a comparatively short distance of this spot in which he and his companions had taken refuge, and he knew, too, that there was every reason to suppose that some of them would soon be in pursuit of the negro who had run away.

Suddenly another dreadful thought struck him. Wild beasts, indeed!

He turned quickly to Maka. "Does that man know anything about Davis and the two sailors? Were they killed?" he asked.

Maka shook his head and said that he had already asked his companion that question, but Mok had said that he did not know. All he knew was that those wicked men killed everybody they could kill.

The captain shut his teeth tightly together. "That was it," he said. "I could not see how it could be jaguars, although I could think of nothing else. But these bloodthirsty human beasts! I see it now." He moved toward the passage. "If that dirty wretch had not run away," he thought, "we might have stayed undiscovered here until a vessel came. But they will track his footsteps upon the sand—they are bound to do that."

CHAPTER VI
THREE WILD BEASTS

When the captain joined the two ladies and the boy, who were impatiently waiting for him on the plateau, he had made up his mind to tell them the bad news. Terrible as was the necessity, it could not be helped. It was very hard for him to meet those three radiant faces, and to hear them talk about the water that had been discovered.

"Now," said Mrs. Cliff, "I see no reason why we should not live here in peace and comfort until Mr. Rynders chooses to come back for us. And I have been thinking, captain, that if somebody—and I am sure Ralph would be very good at it—could catch some fish, it would help out very much. We are getting a little short of meat, but as for the other things, we have enough to last for days and days. But we won't talk of that now. We want to hear where that other colored man came from. Just look at him as he sits there with Maka by those embers. One might think he would shiver himself to pieces. Was he cast ashore from a wreck?"

The captain stood silent for a moment, and then, briefly but plainly, and glossing over the horrors of the situation as much as he could, he told them about the Rackbirds. Not one of the little party interrupted the captain's story, but their faces grew paler and paler as he proceeded.

When he had finished, Mrs. Cliff burst into tears. "Captain," she cried, "let us take the boat and row away from this dreadful place. We should not lose a minute. Let us go now!"

But the captain shook his head. "That would not do," he said. "On this open sea they could easily see us. They have boats, and could row much faster than we could."

"Then," exclaimed the excited woman, "we could turn over the boat, and all sink to the bottom together."

To this the captain made no answer. "You must all get inside as quickly as you can," he said. "Maka, you and that other fellow carry in everything that has been left out here. Be quick. Go up, Ralph, and take the flag down, and then run in."

When the others had entered the narrow passage, the captain followed. Fortunately, he had two guns, each double-barrelled, and if but a few of the Rackbirds came in pursuit of the escaped negro, he might be a match for them in that narrow passage.

Shortly after the party had retired within the rocks, Miss Markham came to the captain, who was standing at the door of the first apartment. "Captain Horn," said she, "Mrs. Cliff is in a state of nervous fear, and I have been trying to quiet her. Can you say anything that might give her a little courage? Do you really think there is any chance of our escape from this new danger?"

"Yes," said the captain, "there is a chance. Rynders may come back before the Rackbirds discover us, and even if two or three of them find out our retreat, I may be able to dispose of them, and thus give us a little more time. That is our only ground of hope. Those men are bound to come here sooner or later, and everything depends upon the return of Rynders."

"But," urged Miss Markham, "perhaps they may not come so far as this to look for the runaway. The waves may have washed out his footsteps upon the sand. There may be no reason why they should come up to this plateau."

The captain smiled a very sombre smile. "If any of them should come this way," he said, "it is possible that they might not think it worth while to cease their search along the beach and come up to this particular spot, were it not that our boat is down there. That is the same thing as if we had put out a sign to tell them where we are. The boat is hauled up on shore, but they could not fail to see it."

"Captain," said Miss Markham, "do you think those Rackbirds killed the three sailors?"

"I am very much afraid of it," he answered. "If they did, they must have known that these poor fellows were survivors of a shipwreck, and I suppose they stole up behind them and shot them down or stabbed them. If that were so, I wonder why they have not sooner been this way, looking for the wreck, or, at least, for other unfortunates who may have reached shore. I suppose, if they are making this sort of a search, they went southward. But all that, of course, depends upon whether they really saw Davis and the two other men. If they did not, they could have no reason for supposing there were any shipwrecked people on the coast."

"But that thought is of no use to us," said Miss Markham, her eyes upon the ground, "for, of course, they will be coming after the black man. Captain," she continued quickly, "is there anything I can do? I can fire a gun."

He looked at her for a moment. "That will not be necessary," he said. "But there is something you can do. Have you a pistol?"

"Yes," said she, "I have. I put it in my pocket as soon as I came into the cave. Here it is."

The captain took the pistol from her hands and examined it. "Five chambers," he said, "all charged. Be very careful of it," —handing it back to her. "I will put your brother and Mrs. Cliff in your charge. At the slightest hint of danger, you must keep together in the middle room. I will stand between you and the rascals as long as I can, but if I am killed, you must do what you think best."

"I will," said she, and she put the pistol back in her pocket.

The captain was very much encouraged by the brave talk of this young woman, and it really seemed as if he now had some one to stand by him, some one with whom he could even consult.

"I have carefully examined this cavern," said the captain, after a moment's pause, "and there are only two ways by which those men could possibly get in. You need not be afraid that any one can scramble down the walls of that farthest apartment. That could not be done, though they might be able to fire upon any one in it. But in the middle room you will be perfectly secure from gunshots. I shall keep Maka on guard a little back from the entrance to the passage. He will lie on the ground, and can hear footsteps long before they reach us. It is barely possible that some of them might enter by the great cleft in the cave on the other side of the lake, but in that case they would have to swim across, and I shall station that new African on the ledge of which you have heard, and if he sees any of them coming in that direction, I know he will give very quick warning. I hardly think, though, that they would trust themselves to be picked off while swimming."

"And you?" said she.

"Oh, I shall keep my eyes on all points," said he, "as far as I can. I begin to feel a spirit of fight rising up within me. If I thought I could keep them off until Rynders gets here, I almost wish they would then come. I would like to kill a lot of them."

"Suppose," said Edna Markham, after a moment's reflection, "that they should see Mr. Rynders coming back, and should attack him."

"I hardly think they would do that," replied the captain. "He will probably come in a good-sized vessel, and I don't think they are the kind of men for open battle. They are midnight sneaks and assassins. Now, I advise all of you to go and get something to eat. It would be better for us not to try to do any cooking, and so make a smoke."

The captain did not wish to talk any more. Miss Markham's last remark had put a new fear into his mind. Suppose the Rackbirds had lured Rynders and his men on shore? Those sailors had but few arms among them. They had not thought, when they left, that there would be any necessity for defence against their fellow-beings.

When Edna Markham told Mrs. Cliff what the captain had said about their chances, and what he intended to do for their protection, the older woman brightened up a good deal.

"I have great faith in the captain," she declared, "and if he thinks it is worth while to make a fight, I believe he will make a good one. If they should be firing, and Mr. Rynders is approaching the coast, even if it should be night, he would lose no time in getting to us."

Toward the close of that afternoon three wild beasts came around the point of the bluff and made their way northward along the beach. They were ferocious creatures with shaggy hair and beards. Two of them carried guns, and each of them had a knife in his belt. When they came to a broad bit of beach above the reach of the waves, they were very much surprised at some footsteps they saw. They were the tracks of two men, instead of those of the one they were looking for. This discovery made them very cautious. They were eager to kill the escaped African before he got far enough away to give information of their retreat, for they knew not at what time an armed force in search of them might approach the coast. But they were very wary about running into danger. There was somebody with that black fellow— somebody who wore boots.

After a time they came to the boat. The minute they saw this, each miscreant crouched suddenly upon the sand, and, with cocked guns, they listened. Then, hearing nothing, they carefully examined the boat. It was empty—there were not even oars in it.

Looking about them, they saw a hollow behind some rocks. To this they ran, crouching close to the ground, and there they sat and consulted.

It was between two and three o'clock the next morning that Maka's eyes, which had not closed for more than twenty hours, refused to keep open any longer, and with his head on the hard, rocky ground of the passage in which he lay, the poor African slept soundly. On the shelf at the edge of the lake, the other African, Mok, sat crouched on his heels, his eyes wide open. Whether he was asleep or not it would have been difficult to determine, but if any one had appeared in the great cleft on the other side of the lake, he would have sprung to his feet with a yell—his fear of the Rackbirds was always awake.

Inside the first apartment was Captain Horn, fast asleep, his two guns by his side. He had kept watch until an hour before, but Ralph had insisted upon taking his turn, and, as the captain knew he could not keep awake always, he allowed the boy to take a short watch. But now Ralph was leaning back against one of the walls, snoring evenly and steadily. In the next room sat Edna Markham, wide awake. She knew of the arrangement made with Ralph, and she knew the boy's healthy, sleepy nature, so that when he went on watch she went on watch.

Outside of the cave were three wild beasts. One of them was crouching on the farther end of the plateau. Another, on the lower ground a little below, stood, gun in hand, and barely visible in the starlight. A third, barefooted, and in garments dingy as the night, and armed only with a knife, crept softly toward the entrance of the cave. There he stopped and listened. He could plainly hear the breathing of the sleepers. He tried to separate these sounds one from another, so that he should be able to determine how many persons were sleeping inside, but this he could not do. Then his cat-like eyes, becoming more and more accustomed to the darkness within the entrance, saw the round head of Maka close upon the ground.

The soul of the listening fiend laughed within him. "Pretty watchers they are," he said to himself. "Not three hours after midnight, and they are all snoring!" Then, as stealthily and as slowly as he had come, he slipped away, and joining the others, they all glided through the darkness down to the beach, and then set off at their best speed back to their rendezvous.

After they had discovered that there were people in the cave, they had not thought of entering. They were not fully armed, and they did not know how many persons were inside. But they knew one thing, and that was that these shipwrecked people—for that was what they must be—kept a very poor watch, and if the whole band came on the following night, the affair would probably be settled with but very little trouble, no matter how large the party in the cave might be. It was not necessary to look any further for the escaped negro. Of course, he had been picked up by these people.

The three beasts reached their camp about daybreak, and everybody was soon awakened and the tale was told.

"It is a comfort," said the leader, lighting the stump of a black pipe which he thrust under his great mustache, and speaking in his native tongue, which some of them understood, and others did not, "to know that to-night's work is all cut out for us. Now we can take it easy to-day, and rest our bones. The order of the day is to keep close. No straggling, nor wandering. Keep those four niggers up in the pigeonhole. We will do our own cooking to-day, for we can't afford to run after any more of them. Lucky the fellow who got away can't speak English, for he can't tell anything about us, any more than if he was an ape. So snooze to-day, if you want to. I will give you work to do for to-night."

CHAPTER VII
GONE!

That morning, when the party in the cavern had had their breakfast, with some hot tea made on a spiritlamp which Mrs. Cliff had brought, and had looked cautiously out at the sunlit landscape, and the sea beyond, without seeing any signs or hearing any sound of wicked men, there came a feeling of relief. There was, indeed, no great ground for such a feeling, but as the Rackbirds had not come the day before nor during the night, perhaps they would not come at all. It might be they did not care whether the black man ran away or not. But Captain Horn did not relax his precautions. He would take no chances, and would keep up a watch day and night.

When, on the night before, the time had come for Ralph's watch to end, his sister had awakened him, and when the captain, in his turn, was aroused, he had not known that it was not the boy who had kept watch during his sleep.

In the course of the morning Mrs. Cliff and Edna, having been filled with an intense desire to see the wonderful subterranean lake, had been helped over the rocky barrier, and had stood at the edge of the water, looking over to where it was lighted by the great chasm in the side of the rocks, and endeavoring to peer into the solemn, cavernous distance into which it extended on the right. Edna said nothing, but stood gazing at the wonderful scene—the dark, mysterious waters before her, the arched cavern above her, and the picture of the bright sky and the tops of the distant mountains, framed by the sides of the great opening which stretched itself upward like a cathedral window on the other side of the lake.

"It frightens me," said Mrs. Cliff. "To be sure, this water was our salvation, for we should have been dead by this time, pirates or no pirates, if we had not found it. But it is terrifying, for all that. We do not know how far it stretches out into the blackness, and we do not know how far down it goes. It may be thousands of feet deep, for all we know. Don't go so near the edge, Ralph. It makes me shudder."

When the little party had returned to the cavern, the captain and the two ladies had a long talk about the lake. They all agreed that the existence of this great reservoir of water was sufficient to account for the greenness and fertility of the little plateau outside. Even if no considerable amount of water trickled through the cracks in the rocks, the moisture which arose from the surface of the water found its way out into the surrounding atmosphere, and had nourished the bushes and vines.

For some time they discussed their new-found water-supply, and they were all glad to have something to think about and talk about besides the great danger which overhung them.

"If it could only have been the lake without the Rackbirds," said Mrs. Cliff.

"Let us consider that that is the state of the case," remarked Edna. "We have the lake, and so far we have not had any Rackbirds."

It was now nearly noon, and the captain looked around for Ralph, but did not see him. He went to search for him, and finding that the boy had not passed Maka, who was on watch, he concluded he must have gone to the lake. There was no reason why the restless youth should not seek to enliven his captivity by change of scene, but Captain Horn felt unwilling to have any one in his charge out of sight for any length of time, so he went to look for Ralph.

He found no one on the rocky shelf. As there had been little reason to expect a water attack at this hour, Mok had been relieved from guard for a meal and a nap. But as Ralph was not here, where could he be? A second glance, however, showed the captain the boy's clothes lying close by, against the upright side of the rock, and at that moment he heard a cry. His eyes flashed out toward the sound. There on the other side of the water, sitting on a bit of projecting rock not far from the great opening in the cave, he saw Ralph. At first the captain stood dumb with amazement, and he was just about to call out, when Ralph shouted again.

"I swam over," he said, "but I can't get back. I've got the cramps. Can't you make some sort of a raft, and come over to me! The water's awfully cold."

Raft, indeed! There was no material or time for anything of the kind. If the boy dropped off that bit of rock, he would be drowned, and the captain did not hesitate a moment. Throwing aside his jacket and slipping off his shoes, he let himself down into the water and struck out in Ralph's direction.

The water was, indeed, very cold, but the captain was a strong swimmer, and it would not take him very long to cross the lake at this point, where its width was not much more than a hundred feet. As he neared the other side he did not make immediately for Ralph. He thought it would be wise to rest a little before attempting to take the boy back, and so he made for another point of rock, a little nearer the opening, urging the boy, as he neared him, to sit firmly and keep up a good heart.

"All right," said Ralph. "I see what you are after. That is a better place than this, and if you land there I think I can scramble over to you."

"Don't move," said the captain. "Sit where you are until I tell you what to do."

The captain had not made more than two or three strokes after speaking when his right hand struck against something hard, just below the surface of the water. He involuntarily grasped it. It was immovable, and it felt like a tree, a few inches in diameter, standing perpendicularly in the lake. Wondering what this could be, he took hold of it with his other hand, and finding that it supported him, he let his feet drop, when, to his surprise, he found that they rested on something with a rounded surface, and the idea instantly came into his mind that it was a submerged tree, the trunk lying horizontally, from which this upright branch projected. This might be as good a resting-place as the rock to which he had been going, and standing on it, with his head well out of the water, he turned to speak to Ralph. At that moment his feet slipped from the slimy object on which he stood, and he fell backward into the water, still grasping, however, his upright support. But this did not remain upright more than an instant, but yielded to his weight, and the end of it which he held went down with him. As he sank, the captain, in his first bewilderment, did not loosen his grasp upon what had been his support, and which still prevented him from sinking rapidly. But in a moment his senses came to him, he let go, and a few downward strokes brought him to the surface of the water. Then he struck out for the point of rock for which he had been aiming, and he was soon mounted upon it.

"Hi!" shouted Ralph, who had been so frightened by the captain's sudden sinking that he nearly fell off his narrow seat, "I thought something had pulled you down."

The captain did not explain. He was spluttering a little after his involuntary dive, and he wanted to get back as soon as possible, and so wasted no breath in words. In a few minutes he felt himself ready for the return trip, and getting into the water, he swam to Ralph. Following the directions given him, the boy let himself down into the water behind the captain, and placed his hands upon the latter's hips, firmly grasping the waistband of his trousers. Then urging the boy not to change his position, nor attempt to take hold of him in any other way, the captain struck out across the lake, Ralph easily floating behind him.

When they stood upon the shelf on the other side, and Ralph, having rubbed himself down with the captain's jacket, put on his clothes, Captain Horn rather sternly inquired of him how he came to do such a foolish and wicked thing as to run the risk of drowning himself in the lake at a time when his sister and his friends had already trouble enough on their minds.

Ralph was sorry, of course, that the captain had to come after him, and get himself wet, but he explained that he wanted to do something for the good of the party, and it had struck him that it would be a very sensible thing to investigate the opening on the other side of the lake. If he could get out of that great gap, he might find some way of climbing out over the top of the rocks and get to the place where his flag was, and then, if he saw Mr. Rynders coming, he could wave it. It would be a great thing if the people in the vessel which they all expected should see that flag the moment they came in sight of the coast. They might get to shore an hour or two sooner than if they had not seen it.

"If the cramp in this leg had kept off five minutes longer," he said, "I would have reached that big hole, and then, if I could have climbed over the top of the rocks, I could have come down on the other side to the front door, and asked Maka to get me my clothes, so I would not have had to swim back at all."

"That will do," said the captain. "And now that you are dressed, you can go inside and get me that woollen shirt and trousers that I use for a pillow, for I must take off these wet things."

When the boy came back with the clothes, the captain told him that he need not say anything to his sister or Mrs. Cliff about the great danger he had been in, but before he had finished his injunction Ralph interrupted him.

"Oh, I have told them that already," said he. "They wanted to know where I had been, and it did not take a minute to tell them what a splendid swimmer you are, and how you came over after me without taking as much as two seconds to think about it. And I let them know, too, that it was a mighty dangerous thing for you to do. If I had been one of those fellows who were not used to the water, and who would grab hold of any one who came to save them, we might both have gone to the bottom together."

The captain smiled grimly. "It is hard to get ahead of a boy," he said to himself.

It was late that afternoon when Captain Horn, with Ralph and the two ladies, were standing on the rocks in the inner apartment, trying to persuade themselves that they were having a cosey cup of tea together, when suddenly a scrambling sound of footsteps was heard, and Maka dashed through the two adjoining apartments and appeared before them. Instantly the captain was on his feet, his gun, which had been lying beside him, in his hand. Up sprang the others, mute, with surprise and fear on their faces. Maka, who was in a state of great excitement, and seemed unable to speak, gasped out the one word, "Gone!"

"What do you mean?" cried the captain.

Maka ran back toward the passage, and pointed inward. Instantly the captain conjectured what he meant. Mok, the second African, had been stationed to watch the lake approach, and he had deserted! Now the hot thought flashed upon the captain that the rascal had been a spy. The Rackbirds had known that there were shipwrecked people in these caves. How could they help knowing it, if they had killed Davis and the others? But, cowardly hounds as they were, they had been afraid to attack the place until they knew how many people were in it, what arms they had, and in what way the place could best be assailed. This Mok had found out everything. If the boy could swim across the lake, that black man could do it, and he had gone out through the cleft, and was probably now making his report to the gang.

All this flashed through the captain's brain in a few seconds. He set his teeth together. He was ashamed that he had allowed himself to be so tricked. That African, probably one of the gang, and able to speak English, should have been kept a prisoner. What a fool he had been to treat the black-hearted and black-bodied wretch as one of themselves, and actually to put him on guard!

Of course, it was of no use to go to look for him, and the captain had put down his gun, and was just about to turn to speak to the others, when Maka seized him by the coat. The negro seemed wildly excited and still unable to speak. But it was plain that he wanted the captain to follow him along the passage. There was no use in asking questions, and the captain followed, and behind him came Ralph, Edna, and Mrs. Cliff.

Maka was about to climb over the rocky partition which divided the passage, but the captain stopped him. "Stay here," said he, "and watch the passage. I will see what is the matter over there." And then he and Ralph jumped over and hurried to the lake. As they came out on the little platform of rock, on which the evening light, coming through the great; cleft, still rendered objects visible, they saw Mok crouching on his heels, his eyes wide open as usual.

The captain was stupefied. That African not gone! If it were not he, who had gone?

Then the captain felt a tight clutch upon his arm, and Ralph pulled him around. Casting eyes outward, the captain saw that it was the lake that had gone!

As he and Ralph stood there, stupefied and staring, they saw, by the dim light which came through the opening on the other side of the cavern, a great empty rocky basin. The bottom of this, some fifteen or twenty feet below them, wet and shining, with pools of water here and there, was plainly visible in the space between them and the open cleft, but farther on all was dark. There was every reason to suppose, however, that all the water had gone from the lake. Why or how this had happened, they did not even ask themselves. They simply stood and stared.

In a few minutes they were joined by Edna, who had become so anxious at their absence and silence that she had clambered over the wall, and came running to them. By the time she reached them it was much darker than when they had arrived, but she could see that the lake had gone. That was enough.

"What do you suppose it means?" she said presently. "Are we over some awful subterranean cavern in which things sink out of sight in an instant?"

"It is absolutely unaccountable," said the captain. "But we must go back to Mrs. Cliff. I hear her calling. And if Maka has come to his senses, perhaps he can tell us something."

But Maka had very little to tell. To the captain's questions he could only say that a little while before, Mok had come running to him, and told him that, being thirsty, he had gone down to the edge of the lake to get a drink, and found that there was no water, only a great hole, and then he had run to tell Maka, and when Maka had gone back with him, so greatly surprised that he had deserted his post without thinking about it, he found that what

Mok had said was true, and that there was nothing there but a great black hole. Mok must have been asleep when the water went away, but it was gone, and that was all he knew about it.

There was something so weird and mysterious about this absolute and sudden disappearance of this great body of water that Mrs. Cliff became very nervous and frightened.

"This is a temple of the devil," she said, "and that is his face outside. You do not know what may happen next. This rocky floor on which we stand may give way, and we may all go down into unknown depths. I can't think of staying here another minute. It is dark now. Let us slip away down to the beach, and take the boat, and row away from this horrible region where human devils and every other kind seem to own the country."

"Oh, no," said the captain, "we can't consider such wild schemes as that. I have been thinking that perhaps there may be some sort of a tide in this lake, and in the morning we may find the water just as it was. And, at any rate, it has not entirely deserted us, for in these pools at the bottom we can find water enough for us to drink."

"I suppose I would not mind such things so much," said Mrs. Cliff, "if they happened out of doors. But being shut up in this cave with magical lakes, and expecting every minute to see a lot of bloodthirsty pirates bursting in upon us, is enough to shake the nerves of anybody."

"Captain," said Ralph, "I suppose you will not now object to letting me go in the morning to explore that opening. I can walk across the bottom of the lake without any danger, you know."

"Don't you try to do anything of the kind," said the captain, "without my permission."

"No, indeed!" exclaimed Mrs. Cliff. "Supposing the water were to suddenly rise just as you were half-way across. Now that I think of it, there are springs and bodies of water which rise and fall this way, some of them in our own Western country, but none of them are as large as this. What if it should rise in the night and flood the cave while we are asleep?"

"Why, dear Mrs. Cliff," said Edna, "I am not afraid of the water's rising or of the earth's sinking. Don't let us frighten ourselves with imaginations like that. Perhaps there may not even be any real thing to be afraid of, but if there should be, let us keep courage for that."

The disappearance of the lake gave the captain an uneasiness of which the others had not thought. He saw it would be comparatively easy for the Rackbirds to gain access to the place through the cleft in the eastern wall of the lake cavern. If they should discover that aperture, the cavern might be attacked from the rear and the front at the same time, and then the captain feared his guns would not much avail.

Of course, during the darkness which would soon prevail there was no reason to expect a rear attack, and the captain satisfied himself with leaving Mok at his former post, with instructions to give the alarm if he heard the slightest sound, and put Maka, as before, in the outer passage. As for himself, he took an early nap in the evening, because at the very first break of dawn it would be necessary for him to be on the alert.

He did not know how much he had depended upon the lake as a barrier of defence, but now that it had gone, he felt that the dangers which threatened them from the Rackbirds were doubled.

CHAPTER VIII
THE ALARM

It was still dark when the captain woke, and he struck a match to look at his watch. It was three o'clock.

"Is that you, captain?" said a voice from the next room. "Is it time for you to begin watch again?"

"Yes," said the captain, "it is about time. How do you happen to be awake, Miss Markham? Ralph! I believe the boy is snoring."

"Of course he is," said Edna, speaking in a low voice. "We cannot expect such a boy to keep awake, and so I have been on watch. It was easy enough for me to keep my eyes open."

"It is too bad," said the captain, and then, listening for a moment, he said: "I truly believe that Maka is snoring, too, and as for that black fellow over there, I suspect that he sleeps all the time. Miss Markham, you have been the only person awake."

"Why shouldn't I be?" said she. "I am sure that a woman is just as good as a man for keeping watch."

"If they should come," thought the captain, as he again sat in the dark, "I must not try to fight them in the passage. That would have been my best chance, but now some of them might pick me off from behind. No, I must fight them in this chamber. I can put everybody else in the middle apartment. Perhaps before to-morrow night it might be well to bring some of those loose rocks here and build a barricade. I wish I had thought of that before."

The captain sat and listened and thought. His listening brought him no return, and his thinking brought him too much. The most mournful ideas of what might happen if more than two or three of the desperadoes attacked the place crowded into his mind. If they came, they came to rob, and they were men who left behind them no living witnesses of their whereabouts or their crimes. And if two or three should come, and be repulsed, it would not be long before the rest would arrive. In fact, the only real hope they had was founded on the early return of Rynders—that is, if Rynders and his men were living.

The captain waited and listened, but nothing came but daylight. As soon as he was able to discern objects outside the opening on the plateau, he awoke Maka, and, leaving him on guard, he made his way to the lake cavern.

Here the light was beginning to come freely through the chasm which faced nearly east. Mok was sitting with his eyes open, and showed that he was alive by a little grunt when the captain approached. If there were such a thing here as a subterranean tide, it had not risen. There was no water where the lake had been.

Gazing across the empty basin, the captain felt a strong desire to go over, climb up to the opening, and discover whether or not the cavern was accessible on that side. It would be very important for him to know this, and it would not take long for him to make an investigation. One side of the rocky shelf which has been before mentioned sloped down to the lake, and the captain was just about to descend this when he heard a cry from the passage, and, at the same moment, a shout from Mok which seemed to be in answer to it. Instantly the captain turned and dashed into the passage, and, leaping over the barrier, found Maka standing near the entrance.

As soon as the negro saw him, he began to beckon wildly for him to come on. But there was no need now of keeping quiet and beckoning. The first shout had aroused everybody inside, and the two ladies and Ralph were already in the passage. The captain, however, made them keep back, while he and Maka, on their hands and knees, crawled toward the outer opening. From this point one could see over the plateau, and the uneven ground beyond, down to the beach and the sea; but there was still so little light upon this western slope that at first the captain could not see anything noticeable in the direction in which Maka was pointing. But in a few moments his mariner eyes asserted themselves, and he saw some black spots on the strip of beach, which seemed to move. Then he knew they were moving, and moving toward him—coming up to the cave! They were men!

"Sit here," said the captain to Maka, and then, with his gun in his hand, he rushed back to the rest of the party.

"They seem to be coming," said he, speaking as calmly as he could, "but we have discovered them in good time, and I shall have some shots at them before they reach here. Let us hope that they will never get here at all. You two," said he to Mrs. Cliff and Ralph, "are to be under command of

Miss Markham. You must do exactly what she tells you to." Then, turning to Edna, he said, "You have your pistol ready?"

"Yes," said she, "I am ready."

Without another word, the captain took his other gun and all his ammunition, and went back into the passage. Here he found Mok, who had come to see what was the matter. Motioning the negro to go back to his post, the captain, with his loaded guns, went again to the entrance. Looking out, he could now plainly see the men. There were four of them. It was lighter down toward the sea, for the rocks still threw a heavy shadow over the plateau. The sight sent a thrill of brave excitement through the captain.

"If they come in squads of four," thought he, "I may be a match for them. They can't see me, and I can see them. If I could trust Maka to load a gun, I would have a better chance, but if I could pick off two, or even one, that might stop the others and give me time to reload. Come on, you black-hearted scoundrels," he muttered through his teeth, as he knelt outside the cave, one gun partly raised, and the other on the ground beside him. "If I could only know that none of your band could come in at that hole in the back of the cave, I'd call the odds even."

The dawn grew brighter, and the four men drew nearer. They came slowly, one considerably ahead of the others. Two or three times they stopped and appeared to be consulting, and then again moved slowly forward straight toward the plateau.

When the leading man was nearly within gunshot, the captain's face began to burn, and his pulses to throb hard and fast.

"The sooner I pick off the head one," he thought, "the better chance I have at the others."

He brought his gun to his shoulder, and was slowly lowering the barrel to the line of aim, when suddenly something like a great black beast rushed past him, pushing up his arm and nearly toppling him over. It came from the cave, and in a second it was out on the plateau. Then it gave a leap upward, and rushed down toward the sea. Utterly astounded, the captain steadied himself and turned to Maka.

"What was that?" he exclaimed.

The African was on his feet, his body bent forward, his eyes peering out into the distance.

"Mok!" said he. "Look! Look!"

It was Mok who had rushed out of the cave. He was running toward the four men. He reached them, he threw up his arms, he sprang upon the first man. Then he left him, and jumped upon the others. Then Maka gave a little cry and sprang forward, but in the same instant the captain seized him.

"Stop!" he cried. "What is it?"

The African shouted: "Mok's people! Mok knowed them. Look! Look—see! Mok!"

The party was now near enough and the day was bright enough for the captain to see that on the lower ground beyond the plateau there were five black men in a state of mad excitement. He could hear them jabbering away at a great rate. So far as he could discover, they were all unarmed, and as they stood there gesticulating, the captain might have shot them down in a bunch, if he had chosen.

"Go," said he to Maka, "go down there and see what it all means."

The captain now stepped back into the passage. He could see Miss Markham and Ralph peering out of the doorway of the first compartment.

"There does not seem to be any danger so far," said he. "Some more Africans have turned up. Maka has gone to meet them. We shall find out about them in a few minutes," and he turned back to the entrance.

He saw that the six black fellows were coming toward him, and, as he had thought, they carried no guns.

CHAPTER IX
AN AMAZING NARRATION

When the captain had gone out again into the open air, he was followed by the rest of the party, for, if there were no danger, they all wanted to see what was to be seen. What they saw was a party of six black men on the plateau, Maka in the lead. There could be no doubt that the newcomers were the remainder of the party of Africans who had been enslaved by the Rackbirds, and the desire of the captain and his companions to know how they had got away, and what news they brought, was most intense.

Maka now hurried forward, leading one of the strangers. "Great things they tell," said he. "This Cheditafa. He speak English good as me. He tell you."

"The first thing I want," cried the captain, "is some news of those Rackbirds. Have they found we are here? Will they be coming after these men, or have they gone off somewhere else? Tell me this, and be quick."

"Oh, yes," cried Maka, "they found out we here. But Cheditafa tell you—he tell you everything. Great things!"

"Very well, then," said the captain. "Let him begin and be quick about it."

The appearance of Cheditafa was quite as miserable as that of poor Mok, but his countenance was much more intelligent, and his English, although very much broken, was better even than Maka's, and he was able to make himself perfectly understood. He spoke briefly, and this is the substance of his story:

About the middle of the afternoon of the day before, a wonderful thing happened. The Rackbirds had had their dinner, which they had cooked themselves, and they were all lying down in their huts or in the shadows of the rocks, either asleep, or smoking and telling stories. Cheditafa knew why they were resting. The Rackbirds had no idea that he understood English, for he had been careful to keep this fact from them after he found out what sort of men they were,—and this knowledge had come very soon to him,—and they spoke freely before him. He had heard some of the men who had been out looking for Mok, and who had come back early that morning, tell about some shipwrecked people in a cave up the coast, and had heard all the plans which had been made for the attack upon them during the night. He also knew why he and his fellows had been cooped up in the cave in the rock in which they lived, all that day, and had not been allowed to come down and do any work.

They were lying huddled in their little cave, feeling very hungry and miserable, and whispering together,—for if they spoke out or made any noise, one of the men below would be likely to fire a load of shot at them,—when suddenly a strange thing happened.

They heard a great roar like a thousand bulls, which came from the higher part of the ravine, and peeping out, they saw what seemed like a wall of rock stretching across the little valley. But in a second they saw it was not rock—it was water, and before they could take two breaths it had reached them. Then it passed on, and they saw only the surface of a furious and raging stream, the waves curling and dashing over each other, and reaching almost up to the floor of their cave.

They were so frightened that they pressed back as far as they could get, and even tried to climb up the sides of the rocky cavity, so fearful were they that the water would dash in upon them. But the raging flood roared and surged outside, and none of it came into their cave. Then the sound of it became not quite so loud, and grew less and less. But still Cheditafa and his companions were so frightened and so startled by this awful thing, happening so suddenly, as if it had been magic, that it was some time— he did not know how long—before they lifted their faces from the rocks against which they were pressing them.

Then Cheditafa crept forward and looked out. The great waves and the roaring water were gone. There was no water to be seen, except the brook which always ran at the bottom of the ravine, and which now seemed not very much bigger than it had been that morning.

But the little brook was all there was in the ravine, except the bare rocks, wet and glistening. There were no huts, no Rackbirds, nothing. Even the vines and bushes which had been growing up the sides of the stream were all gone. Not a weed, not a stick, not a clod of earth, was left—nothing but a great, rocky ravine, washed bare and clean.

Edna Markham stepped suddenly forward and seized the captain by the arm.
"It was the lake," she cried. "The lake swept down that ravine!"

"Yes," said the captain, "it must have been. But listen—let us hear more. Go on," he said to Cheditafa, who proceeded to tell how he and his companions looked out for a long time, but they saw nor heard nothing of any living creature. It would be easy enough for anybody to come back up the ravine, but nobody came.

They had now grown so hungry that they could have almost eaten each other. They felt they must get out of the cave and go to look for food. It would be better to be shot than to sit there and starve.

Then they devised a plan by which they could get down. The smallest man got out of the cave and let himself hang, holding to the outer edge of the floor with his hands. Then another man put his feet over the edge of the rock, and let the hanging man take hold of them. The other two each seized an arm of the second man, and lowered the two down as far as they could reach. When they had done this, the bottom man dropped, and did not hurt himself. Then they had to pull up the second man, for the fall would have been too great for him.

After that they had to wait a long time, while the man who had got out went to look for something by which the others could help themselves down—the ladder they had used having been carried away with everything else. After going a good way down the ravine to a place where it grew much wider, with the walls lower, he found things that had been thrown up on the sides, and among these was the trunk of a young tree, which, after a great deal of hard work, he brought back to the cave, and by the help of this they all scrambled down.

They hurried down the ravine, and as they approached the lower part, where it became wider before opening into the little bay into which the stream ran, they found that the flood, as it had grown shallower and spread itself out, had left here and there various things which it had brought down from the camp—bits of the huts, articles of clothing, and after a while they came to a Rackbird, quite dead, and hanging upon a point of projecting rock. Farther on they found two or three more bodies stranded, and later in the day some Rackbirds who had been washed out to sea came back with the tide, and were found upon the beach. It was impossible, Cheditafa said, for any of them to have escaped from that raging torrent, which hurled them against the rocks as it carried them down to the sea.

But the little party of hungry Africans did not stop to examine anything which had been left. What they wanted was something to eat, and they knew where to get it. About a quarter of a mile back from the beach was the storehouse of the Rackbirds, a sort of cellar which they had made in a sand-hill. As the Africans had carried the stores over from the vessel which had brought them, and had afterwards taken to the camp such supplies as were needed from time to time, of course they knew where to find them, and they lost no time in making a hearty meal.

According to Cheditafa's earnest assertions, they had never eaten as they had eaten then. He believed that the reason they had been left without food was that the Rackbirds were too proud to wait on black men, and had concluded to let them suffer until they had returned from their expedition, and the negroes could be let down to attend to their own wants.

After they had eaten, the Africans went to a spot which commanded a view up the ravine, as well as the whole of the bay, and there they hid themselves, and watched as long as it was daylight, so that if any of the Rackbirds had escaped they could see them. But they saw nothing, and being very anxious to find good white people who would take care of them, they started out before dawn that morning to look for the shipwrecked party about whom Cheditafa had heard the Rackbirds talking, and with whom they hoped to find their companion Mok, and thus it was that they were here.

"And those men were coming to attack us last night?" asked the captain. "You are sure of that?"

"Yes," said Cheditafa, "it was last night. They not know how many you are, and all were coming."

"And some of them had already been here?"

"Yes," replied the African. "One day before, three went out to look for Mok, and they found his track and more track, and they waited in the black darkness, and then came here, and they heard you all sleep and snore that night. They were to come again, and if they—"

"And yesterday afternoon the lake came down and swept them out of existence!" exclaimed Mrs. Cliff.

CHAPTER X
THE CAPTAIN EXPLORES

Captain Horn had heard the story of Cheditafa, he walked away from the rest of the party, and stood, his eyes upon the ground, still mechanically holding his gun. He now knew that the great danger he had feared had been a real one, and far greater than he had imagined. A systematic attack by all the Rackbirds would have swept away his single resistance as the waters had swept them and their camp away. As to parley or compromise with those wretches, he knew that it would have been useless to think of it. They allowed no one to go forth from their hands to reveal the place of their rendezvous.

But although he was able to appreciate at its full force the danger with which they had been threatened, his soul could not immediately adjust itself to the new conditions. It had been pressed down so far that it could not easily rise again. He felt that he must make himself believe in the relief which had come to them, and, turning sharply, he called out to Cheditafa:

"Man, since you have been in this part of the country, have you ever seen or heard of any wild beasts here? Are there any jaguars or pumas?"

The African shook his head. "No, no," said he, "no wild beasts. Everybody sleep out of doors. No think of beasts—no snakes."

The captain dropped his gun upon the ground. "Miss Markham!" he exclaimed. "Mrs. Cliff! I truly believe we are out of all danger—that we—"

But the two ladies had gone inside, and heard him not. They appreciated to the full the danger from which they had been delivered. Ralph, too, had gone. The captain saw him on his post of observation, jamming the end of his flagpole down between two rocks.

"Hello!" cried the boy, seeing the captain looking up at him, "we might as well have this flying here all the time. There is nobody to hurt us now, and we want people to know where we are."

The captain walked by the little group of Africans, who were sitting on the ground, talking in their native tongue, and entered the passage. He climbed over the barrier, and went to the lake. He did not wish to talk to anybody, but he felt that he must do something, and now was a good time to carry out his previous intention to cross over the empty bed of the lake and to look out of the opening on the other side. There was no need now to do this for purposes of vigilance, but he thought that if he could get out on the other side of the cave he might discover some clew to the disappearance of the lake.

He had nearly crossed the lake bottom, when suddenly he stopped, gazing at something which stood before him, and which was doubtless the object he had struck when swimming. The sun was now high and the cave well lighted, and with a most eager interest the captain examined the slimy and curious object on which his feet had rested when it was submerged, and from which he had fallen. It was not the horizontal trunk of a tree with a branch projecting from it at right angles. It was nothing that was natural or had grown. It was plainly the work of man. It was a machine.

At first the captain thought it was made of wood, but afterwards he believed it to be of metal of some sort. The horizontal portion of it was a great cylinder, so near the bottom of the lake that he could almost touch it with his hands, and it was supported by a massive framework. From this projected a long limb or bar, which was now almost horizontal, but which the captain believed to be the thick rod which had stood upright when he clutched it, and which had yielded to his weight and had gone down with him. He knew now what it was: it was a handle that had turned.

He hurried to the other end of the huge machine, where it rested against the rocky wall of the cavern. There he saw in the shadow, but plain enough now that he was near it, a circular aperture, a yard or more in diameter. Inside of this was something which looked like a solid wheel, very thick, and standing upright in the opening. It was a valve. The captain stepped back and gazed for some minutes at this great machine which the disappearance of the water had revealed. It was easy for him to comprehend it now.

"When I slipped and sank," he said to himself, "I pulled down that lever, and I opened the water-gate and let out the lake."

The captain was a man whose mind was perfectly capable of appreciating novel and strange impressions, but with him such impressions always connected themselves, in one way or another, with action: he could not stand and wonder at the wonderful which had happened—it always suggested something he must do. What he now wanted to do was to climb up to the great aperture which lighted the cavern, and see what was outside. He could not understand how the lake could have gone from its basin without the sound of the rushing waters being heard by any one of the party.

With some difficulty, he climbed up to the cleft and got outside. Here he had a much better view of the topography of the place than he had yet been able to obtain. So far as he had explored, his view toward the interior of the country had been impeded by rocks and hills. Here he had a clear view from the mountains to the sea, and the ridge which he had before seen to the southward he could now examine to greater advantage. It was this long chain of rocks which had concealed them from their enemies, and on the other side of which must be the ravine in which the Rackbirds had made their camp.

Immediately below the captain was a little gorge, not very deep nor wide, and from its general trend toward the east and south the captain was sure that it formed the upper part of the ravine of the Rackbirds. At the bottom of it there trickled a little stream. To the northeast ran another line of low rock, which lost itself in the distance before it blended into the mountains, and at the foot of this must run the stream which had fed the lake.

In their search for water, game, or fellow-beings, no one had climbed these desolate rocks, apparently dry and barren. But still the captain was puzzled as to the way the water had gone out of the lake. He did not believe that it had flowed through the ravine below. There were no signs that there had been a flood down there. Little vines and plants were growing in chinks of the rocks close to the water. And, moreover, had a vast deluge rushed out almost beneath the opening which lighted the cave, it must have been heard by some of the party. He concluded, therefore, that the water had escaped through a subterranean channel below the rocks from which he looked down.

He climbed down the sides of the gorge, and walked along its bottom for two or three hundred yards, until around a jutting point of rock he saw that the sides of the defile separated for a considerable distance, and then, coming together again below, formed a sort of amphitheatre. The bottom of this was a considerable distance below him, and he did not descend into it, but he saw plainly that it had recently contained water, for pools and puddles were to be seen everywhere.

At the other end of it, where the rocks again approached each other, was probably a precipice. After a few minutes' cogitation, Captain Horn felt sure that he understood the whole matter: a subway from the lake led to this amphitheatre, and thus there had been no audible rush of the waters until they reached this point, where they poured in and filled this great basin, the lower end of which was probably stopped up by accumulations of sand and deposits, which even in that country of scant vegetation had accumulated in the course of years. When the waters of the lake had rushed into the amphitheatre, this natural dam had held them for a while, but then, giving way before the great pressure, the whole body of water had suddenly rushed down the ravine to the sea.

"Yes," said the captain, "now I understand how it happened that although I opened the valve at noon, the water did not reach the Rackbirds until some hours later, and then it came suddenly and all at once, which would not have been the case had it flowed steadily from the beginning through the outlet made for it."

When the captain had returned and reported his discoveries, and he and his party had finished their noonday meal, which they ate outside on the plateau, with the fire burning and six servants to wait on them, Mrs. Cliff said:

"And now, captain, what are we going to do? Now that our danger is past, I suppose the best thing for us is to stay here in quiet and thankfulness, and wait for Mr. Rynders. But, with the provisions we have, we can't wait very long. When there were but five of us, we might have made the food hold out for a day or two longer, but now that we are ten, we shall soon be without anything to eat."

"I have been talking to Maka about that," said the captain, "and he says that Cheditafa reports all sorts of necessary things in the Rackbirds' storehouse, and he proposes that he and the rest of the black fellows go down there and bring us some supplies. They are used to carrying these stores, and six of them can bring us enough to last a good while. Now that everything is safe over there, I can see that Maka is very anxious to go, and, in fact, I would like to go myself. But although there doesn't seem to be any danger at present, I do not want to leave you."

"As for me," said Miss Markham, "I want to go there. There is nothing I like better than exploring."

"That's to my taste, too," said the captain, "but it will be better for us to wait here and see what Maka has to say when he gets back. Perhaps, if Mr. Rynders doesn't turn up pretty soon, we will all make a trip down there. Where is Ralph? I don't want him to go with the men."

"He is up there on his lookout, as he calls it," said his sister, "with his spy-glass."

"Very good," said the captain. "I will send the men off immediately. Maka wants to go now, and they can come back by the light of the young moon. When they have loads to carry, they like to travel at night. We shall have to get our own supper, and that will give Ralph something to do."

The party of Africans had not gone half-way from the plateau to the beach before they were discovered by the boy on the outlook rock, and he came rushing down to report that the darkies were running away. When he was told the business on which they had gone, he was very much disappointed that he was not allowed to go with them, and, considerably out of temper, retired to his post of observation, where, as it appeared, he was dividing his time between the discovery of distant specks on the horizon line of the ocean and imaginary jaguars and pumas on the foot-hills.

CHAPTER XI
A NEW HEMISPHERE

With a tin pail in his hand, the captain now went to the cavern of the lake. He wished very much to procure some better water than the last that had been brought, and which Mok must have dipped up from a very shallow puddle. It was possible, the captain thought, that by going farther into the cavern he might find a deeper pool in which water still stood, and if he could not do this, he could get water from the little stream in the ravine. More than this, the captain wished very much to take another look at the machine by which he had let out the water. His mind had been so thoroughly charged with the sense of danger that, until this had faded away, he had not been able to take the interest in the artificial character of the lake which it deserved.

As the captain advanced into the dimmer recesses of the cavern, he soon found a pool of water a foot or more in depth, and having filled his pail at this, he set it down and walked on to see what was beyond. His eyes having now conformed themselves to the duskiness of the place, he saw that the cavern soon made a turn to the left, and gazing beyond him, he judged that the cave was very much wider here, and he also thought that the roof was higher. But he did not pay much attention to the dimensions of the cavern, for he began to discern, at first dimly and then quite plainly, a large object which rose from the bottom of the basin. He advanced eagerly, peering at what seemed to be a sort of dome-like formation of a lighter color than the rocks about him, and apparently about ten feet high.

Carefully feeling his way for fear of pitfalls, the captain drew close to the object, and placed his hand upon it. He believed it to be of stone, and moving his hand over it, he thought he could feel joints of masonry. It was clearly a structure built by men. Captain Horn searched his pockets for a match, but found none, and he hastened back to the cave to get the lantern, passing, without noticing it, the pail which he had filled with water. He would have brought the lantern with him when he first came, but they had no oil except what it contained, and this they had husbanded for emergencies. But now the captain wanted light—he cared not what might happen afterwards. In a very short time, with the lantern in his hand, which lighted up the cave for a considerable distance about him, the captain again stood at the foot of the subterranean dome.

He walked around it. He raised and lowered his lantern, and examined it from top to bottom. It was one half a sphere of masonry, built in a most careful manner, and, to all appearances, as solid as a great stone ball, half sunken in the ground. Its surface was smooth, excepting for two lines of protuberances, each a few inches in height, and about a foot from each other. These rows of little humps were on opposite sides of the dome, and from the bottom nearly to the top. It was plain they were intended to serve as rude ladders by which the top of the mound could be gained.

The captain stepped back, held up his lantern, and gazed in every direction. He could now see the roof of the cavern, and immediately above him he perceived what he was sure were regular joints of masonry, but on the sides of the cave he saw nothing of the sort. For some minutes he stood and reflected, his brain in a whirl. Presently he exclaimed:

"Yes, this cave is man's work! I am sure of it. It is not natural. I wondered how there could be such a cave on the top of a hill. It was originally a gorge, and they have roofed it over, and the bottom of the basin has been cut out to make it deeper. It was made so that it could be filled up with water, and roofed over so that nobody should know there was any water here, unless they came on it by means of the passage from our caves. That passage must have been blocked up. As for the great opening in the side of the cave, the rocks have fallen in there—that is easy enough to see. Yes, men made this cave and filled it with water, and if the water were high enough to cover the handle of that machine, as it was when I struck it, it must also have been high enough to cover up this stone mound. The lake was intended to cover and hide that mound. And then, to make the hiding of it doubly sure, the men who built all this totally covered up the lake so that nobody would know it was here. And then they built that valve apparatus, which was also submerged, so that they could let out the water when they wanted to get at this stone thing, whatever it is. What a scheme to hide anything! Even if anybody discovered the lake, which would not be likely until some part of the cave fell in, they would not know it was anything but a lake when they did see it. And as for letting off the water, nobody but the people who knew about it could possibly do that, unless somebody was fool enough to take the cold bath I was obliged to take, and even then it would have been one chance in a hundred that he found the lever, and would know how to turn it when he did find it. This whole thing is the work of the ancient South Americans, and I imagine that this stone mound is the tomb of one of their kings."

At this moment the captain heard something, and turned to listen. It was a voice—the voice of a boy. It was Ralph calling to him. Instantly the captain turned and hurried away, and as he went he extinguished his lantern. When he reached his pail of water he picked it up, and was very soon joined by Ralph, who was coming to meet him over the bottom of the lake.

"I have been looking for you everywhere, captain," said he. "What have you been after? More water? And you took a lantern to find it, eh? And you have been ever so far into the cave. Why didn't you call me? Let me have the lantern. I want to go to explore."

But the captain did not give him the lantern, nor did he allow him to go to explore.

"No, sir," said he. "What we've got to do is to hurry outside and help get supper. We must wait on ourselves to-night."

When supper was over, that evening, and the little party was sitting out on the plateau, gazing over the ocean at the sunlit sky, Mrs. Cliff declared that she wished they could bring their bedding and spread it on the ground out there, and sleep.

"It is dry enough," she said, "and warm enough, and if there is really nothing to fear from animals or men, I don't want ever to go inside of those caves again. I had such horrible fears and ideas when I was sitting trembling in those dismal vaults, expecting a horde of human devils to burst in upon us at any moment, that the whole place is horrible to me. Anyway, if I knew that I had to be killed, I would rather be killed out here."

The captain smiled. "I don't think we will give up the caves just yet. I, for one, most certainly want to go in there again." And then he told the story of the stone mound which he had discovered.

"And you believe," cried Mrs. Cliff, leaning forward, "that it is really the tomb of an ancient king?"

"If it isn't that, I don't know what it can be," said the captain.

"The grave of a king!" cried Ralph. "A mummy! With inscriptions and paintings! Oh, captain, let's go open it this minute, before those blackies get back."

The captain shook his head. "Don't be in such a hurry," he said. "It will not be an easy job to open that mound, and we shall need the help of the blackies, as you call them, if we do it at all."

"Do it at all!" cried Ralph. "I'll never leave this place until I do it myself, if there is nobody else to help."

Miss Markham sat silent. She was the only one of the company who had studied the history of South America, and she did not believe that the ancient inhabitants of that country buried their kings in stone tombs, or felt it necessary to preserve their remains in phenomenal secrecy and security. She had read things, however, about the ancient peoples of this country which now made her eyes sparkle and her heart beat quickly. But she did not say anything. This was a case in which it would be better to wait to see what would happen.

"Captain!" cried Ralph, "let's go to see the thing. What is the use of waiting? Edna and Mrs. Cliff won't mind staying here while you take me to see it. We can go in ten minutes."

"No," said Mrs. Cliff, "there may be no danger, but I am not going to be left here with the sun almost down, and you two out of sight and hearing."

"Let us all go," said Edna.

The captain considered for a moment. "Yes," said he, "let us all go. As we shall have to take a lantern anyway, this is as good a time as another."

It was not an easy thing for the two ladies to get over the wall at the end of the passage, and to make their way over the rough and slippery bottom of the lake basin, now lighted only by the lantern which the captain carried. But in the course of time, with a good deal of help from their companions, they reached the turning of the cave and stood before the stone mound.

"Hurrah!" cried Ralph. "Why, captain, you are like Columbus! You have discovered a new hemisphere."

"It is like one of the great ant-hills of Africa," said Mrs. Cliff, "but, of course, this was not built by ants I wonder if it is possible that it can be the abode of water-snakes."

Edna stood silent for a few moments, and then she said, "Captain, do you suppose that this dome was entirely covered by water when the lake was full?"

"I think so," said he. "Judging from what I know of the depth of the lake, I am almost sure of it."

"Ralph!" suddenly cried Mrs. Cliff, "don't try to do that. The thing may break under you, and nobody knows what you would fall into. Come down."

But Ralph paid no attention to her words. He was half-way up the side of the mound when she began to speak, and on its top when she had finished.

"Captain," he cried, "hand me up the lantern. I want to see if there is a trap-door into this affair. Don't be afraid, Mrs. Cliff. It's as solid as a rock."

The captain did not hand up the lantern, but holding it carefully in one hand, he ascended the dome by means of the row of protuberances on the other side, and crouched down beside Ralph on the top of it.

"Oh, ho!" said he, as he moved the lantern this way and that, "here is a square slab fitted into the very top."

"Yes," said Ralph, "and it's got different mortar around the edges."

"That is not mortar," said the captain. "I believe it is some sort of resin. Here, hold the lantern, and be careful of it." The captain took his jack-knife out of his pocket, and with the large blade began to dig into the substance which filled the joint around the slab, which was about eighteen inches square. "It is resin," said he, "or something like it, and it comes out very easily. This slab is intended to be moved."

"Indeed it is!" exclaimed Ralph, "and we're intended to move it. Here, captain, I'll help you. I've got a knife. Let's dig out that stuff and lift up the lid before the darkies come back. If we find any dead bodies inside this tomb, they will frighten those fellows to death, if they catch sight of them."

"Very good," said the captain. "I shall be only too glad to get this slab up, if I can, but I am afraid we shall want a crowbar and more help. It's a heavy piece of stone, and I see no way of getting at it."

"This isn't stone in the middle of the slab," said Ralph. "It's a lot more resinous stuff. I had the lantern over it and did not see it. Let's take it out."

There was a circular space in the centre of the stone, about eight inches in diameter, which seemed to be covered with resin. After a few minutes' work with the jack-knives this substance was loosened and came out in two parts, showing a bowl-like depression in the slab, which had been so cut as to leave a little bar running from side to side of it.

"A handle!" cried Ralph.

"That is what it is," said Captain Horn. "If it is intended to be lifted, I ought to be able to do it. Move down a little with the lantern, and give me room."

The captain now stood on the top of the mound, with the slab between his feet, and stooping down, he took hold of the handle with both hands. He was a powerful man, but he could not lift the stone. His first effort, however, loosened it, and then he began to move it from side to side, still pulling upward, until at last he could feel it rising. Then, with a great heave, he lifted it entirely out of the square aperture in which it had been fitted, and set it on one side.

In an instant, Ralph, lantern in hand, was gazing down into the opening. "Hello!" he cried, "there is something on fire in there. Oh, no," he added quickly, correcting himself, "it's only the reflection from our light."

CHAPTER XII
A TRADITION AND A WAISTCOAT

Captain Horn, his face red with exertion and excitement, stood gazing down into the square aperture at his feet. On the other edge of the opening knelt Ralph, holding the lantern so that it would throw its light into the hole. In a moment, before the boy had time to form a question, he was pushed gently to one side, and his sister Edna, who had clambered up the side of the mound, knelt beside him. She peered down into the depths beneath, and then she drew back and looked up at the captain. His whole soul was in his downward gaze, and he did not even see her.

Then there came a voice from below. "What is it?" cried Mrs. Cliff. "What are you all looking at! Do tell me."

With half-shut eyes, Edna let herself down the side of the mound, and when her feet touched the ground, she made a few tottering steps toward Mrs. Cliff, and placing her two hands on her companion's shoulders, she whispered, "I thought it was. It is gold! It is the gold of the Incas." And then she sank senseless at the feet of the older woman.

Mrs. Cliff did not know that Miss Markham had fainted. She simply stood still and exclaimed, "Gold! What does it mean?"

"What is it all about?" exclaimed Ralph. "It looks like petrified honey. This never could have been a beehive."

Without answering, Captain Horn knelt at the edge of the aperture, and taking the lantern from the boy, he let it down as far as it would go, which was only a foot or two.

"Ralph," he said hoarsely, as he drew himself back, "hold this lantern and get down out of my way. I must cover this up, quick." And seizing the stone slab by the handle, he lifted it as if it had been a pot-lid, and let it down into its place. "Now," said he, "get down, and let us all go away from this place. Those negroes may be back at any moment."

When Ralph found that his sister had fainted, and that Mrs. Cliff did not know it, there was a little commotion at the foot of the mound. But some water in a pool near by soon revived Edna, and in ten minutes the party was on the plateau outside the caverns. The new moon was just beginning to peep over the rocks behind them, and the two ladies had seated themselves on the ground. Ralph was pouring out question after question, to which nobody paid any attention, and Captain Horn, his hands thrust into his pockets, walked backward and forward, his face flushed and his breath coming heavily, and, with his eyes upon the ground, he seemed to think himself entirely alone among those desolate crags.

"Can any of you tell me what it means?" cried Mrs. Cliff. "Edna, do you understand it? Tell me quickly, some of you!"

"I believe I know what it means," said Edna, her voice trembling as she spoke. "I thought I knew as soon as I heard of the mound covered up by the lake, but I did not dare to say anything, because if my opinion should be correct it would be so wonderful, so astounding, my mind could hardly take hold of it."

"But what is it?" cried Mrs. Cliff and Ralph, almost in one breath.

"I scarcely know what to say," said Edna, "my mind is in such a whirl about it, but I will tell you something of what I have read of the ancient history of Peru, and then you will understand my fancies about this stone mound. When the Spaniards, under Pizarro, came to this country, their main object, as we all know, was booty. They especially wished to get hold of the wonderful treasures of the Incas, the ancient rulers of Peru. This was the reason of almost all the cruelties and wickedness of the invaders. The Incas tried various ways of preserving their treasures from the clutch of the Spaniards, and I have read of a tradition that they drained a lake, probably near Cuzco, the ancient capital, and made a strong cellar, or mound, at the bottom of it in which to hide their gold. They then let the water in again, and the tradition also says that this mound has never been discovered."

"Do you believe," cried the captain, "that the mound back there in the cavern is the place where the Incas stored their gold?"

"I do not believe it is the place I read about," said Miss Markham, "for that, as I said, must have been near Cuzco. But there is no reason why there should not have been other places of concealment. This was far away from the capital, but that would make the treasure so much the safer. The Spaniards would never have thought of going to such a lonely, deserted place as this, and the Incas would not have spared any time or trouble necessary to securely hide their treasures."

"If you are right," cried the captain, "this is, indeed, astounding! Treasure in a mound of stone—a mound covered by water, which could be let off! The whole shut up in a cave which must have originally been as dark as pitch! When we come to think of it," he continued excitedly, "it is an amazing hiding-place, no matter what was put into the mound."

"And do you mean," almost screamed Mrs. Cliff, "that that stone thing down there is filled with the wealth of the Incas!—the fabulous gold we read about?"

"I do not know what else it can be," replied Edna. "What I saw when I looked down into the hole was surely gold."

"Yes," said the captain, "it was gold—gold in small bars."

"Why didn't you get a piece, captain?" asked Ralph. "Then we could be sure about it. If that thing is nearly filled, there must be tons of it."

"I did not think," said the captain. "I could not think. I was afraid somebody would come."

"And now tell me this," cried Mrs. Cliff. "Whom does this gold belong to? That is what I want to know. Whose is if?"

"Come, come!" said the captain, "let us stop talking about this thing, and thinking about it. We shall all be maniacs if we don't quiet ourselves a little, and, besides, it cannot be long before those black fellows come back, and we do not want to be speaking about it then. To-morrow we will examine the mound and see what it is we have discovered. In the meantime, let us quiet our minds and get a good night's sleep, if we can. This whole affair is astounding, but we must not let it make us crazy before we understand it."

Miss Markham was a young woman very capable of controlling herself. It was true she had been more affected in consequence of the opening of the mound than any of the others, but that was because she understood, or thought she understood, what the discovery meant, and to the others it was something which at first they could not appreciate. Now she saw the good common sense of the captain's remarks, and said no more that evening on the subject of the stone mound.

But Mrs. Cliff and Ralph could not be quiet. They must talk, and as the captain walked away that they might not speak to him, they talked to each other.

It was nearly an hour after this that Captain Horn, standing on the outer end of the plateau, saw some black dots moving on the moonlit beach. They moved very slowly, and it was a long time—at least, it seemed so to the captain—before Maka and his companions reached the plateau.

The negroes were heavily loaded with bags and packages, and they were glad to deposit their burdens on the ground.

"Hi!" cried the captain, who spoke as if he had been drinking champagne, "you brought a good cargo, Maka, and now don't let us hear any tales of what you have seen until we have had supper—supper for everybody. You know what you have got, Maka. Let us have the best things, and let every one of you take a hand in making a fire and cooking. What we want is a first-class feast."

"I got 'em," said Maka, who understood English a good deal better than he could speak it,—"ham, cheese, lots things. All want supper—good supper."

While the meal was being prepared, Captain Horn walked over to Mrs. Cliff and Ralph. "Now, I beg of you," he said, "don't let these men know we have found anything. This is a very important matter. Don't talk about it, and if you can't keep down your excitement, let them think it is the prospect of good victuals, and plenty of them, that has excited you."

After supper Maka and Cheditafa were called upon to tell their story, but they said very little. They had gone to the place where the Rackbirds had kept their stores, and had selected what Maka considered would be most desirable, including some oil for the lantern, and had brought away as much as they could carry. This was all.

When the rest of his party had gone inside, hoping to get their minds quiet enough to sleep, and the captain was preparing to follow them, Maka arose from the spot on the open plateau where the tired negroes had stretched themselves for the night, and said:

"Got something tell you alone. Come out here."

When the two had gone to a spot a little distance from the cavern entrance, where the light of the moon, now nearly set, enabled objects to be seen with some distinctness, Maka took from inside his shirt a small piece of clothing. "Look here," said he. "This belong to Davis."

The captain took the garment in his hand. It was a waistcoat made of plaid cloth, yellow, green, and red, and most striking in pattern, and Captain Horn instantly recognized it as the waistcoat of Davis, the Englishman.

"He dead," said Maka, simply.

The captain nodded. He had no doubt of it.

"Where did you find it?" he asked.

"Sticking on rock," said the African. "Lots things down there. Some one place, some another place. Didn't know other things, but know this. Davis' waistcoat. No mistake that. Him wear it all time."

"You are a good fellow, Maka," said the captain, "not to speak of this before the ladies. Now go and sleep. There is no need of a guard to-night."

The captain went inside, procured his gun, and seated himself outside, with his back against a rock. There he sat all night, without once closing his eyes. He was not afraid that anything would come to molest them, but it was just as well to have the gun. As for sleeping, that was impossible. He had heard and seen too much that day.

CHAPTER XIII
"MINE!"

Captain Horn and his party sat down together the next morning on the plateau to drink their hot coffee and eat their biscuit and bacon, and it was plain that the two ladies, as well as the captain, had had little sleep the night before. Ralph declared that he had been awake ever so long, endeavoring to calculate how many cubic feet of gold there would be in that mound if it were filled with the precious metal. "But as I did not know how much a cubic foot of gold is worth," said he, "and as we might find, after all, that there is only a layer of gold on top, and that all the rest is Incas' bones, I gave it up."

The captain was very grave—graver, Miss Markham thought, than the discovery of gold ought to make a man.

"We won't worry ourselves with calculations," said he. "As soon as I can get rid of those black fellows, we will go to see what is really in that tomb, or storehouse, or whatever it is. We will make a thorough investigation this time."

When the men had finished eating, the captain sent them all down to look for driftwood. The stock of wood on the plateau was almost exhausted, and he was glad to think of some reasonable work which would take them away from the cavern.

As soon as they had gone, the captain rose to get the lantern, and called Ralph to accompany him to the mound.

When they were left alone, Edna said to Mrs. Cliff, "Let us go over there to that shady rock, where we can look out for a ship with Mr. Rynders in it, and let us talk about our neighbors in America. Let us try to forget, for a time, all about what the captain is going to investigate. If we keep on thinking and talking of it, our minds will not be in a fit condition to hear what he will have to tell us. It may all come to nothing, you know, and no matter what it comes to, let us keep quiet, and give our nerves a little rest."

"That is excellent advice," said Mrs. Cliff. But when they were comfortably seated in the shade, she said: "I have been thinking, Edna, that the possession of vast treasures did not weaken the minds of those Incas, I supposed, until yesterday, that the caverns here were intended for some sort of temple for religious ceremonies, and that the great face on the rock out here was an idol. But now I do not believe that. All openings into the cave must once have been closed up, but it would not do to hide the place so that no one could ever find it again, so they carved that great head on the rocks. Nobody, except those who had hid the treasure, would know what the face meant."

Edna gave a little smile and sighed. "I see it is of no use to try to get that mound out of our minds," she said.

"Out of our minds!" exclaimed Mrs. Cliff. "If one of the Rothschilds were to hand you a check for the whole of his fortune, would you expect to get that out of your mind?"

"Such a check," said Edna, "would be a certain fortune. We have not heard yet what this is."

"I think we are the two meekest and humblest people in the whole world!" exclaimed Mrs. Cliff, walking up and down the sand. "I don't believe any other two persons would be content to wait here until somebody should come and tell them whether they were millionaires or not. But, of course, somebody must stay outside to keep those colored people from swarming into the cave when they come back."

It was not long after this that Mrs. Cliff and Edna heard the sound of quickly advancing feet, and in a few moments they were joined by Ralph and the captain.

"Your faces shine like gold," cried Edna. "What have you found?"

"Found!" cried Ralph. "Why, Edna, we've got—"

"Be quiet, Ralph," exclaimed Edna. "I want to hear what the captain has to say. Captain, what is in the mound?"

"We went to the mound," said he, speaking very rapidly, "and when we got to the top and lifted off that stone lid—upon my soul, ladies, I believe there is gold enough in that thing to ballast a ship. It isn't filled quite up to the top, and, of course, I could not find out how deep the gold goes down; but I worked a hole in it as far down as my arm would reach, and found nothing but gold bars like this." Then, glancing around to see that none of the Africans were returning, he took from his pocket a yellow object about three inches in length and an inch in diameter, shaped like a rough prism, cast in a rudely constructed mortar or mould. "I brought away just one of them," he said, "and then I shut down the lid, and we came away."

"And is this gold?" exclaimed Edna, eagerly seizing the bar. "Are you sure of it, captain?"

"I am as sure of it as I am that I have a head on my shoulders," said he, "although when I was diving down into that pile I was not quite sure of that. No one would ever put anything but gold in such a hiding-place. And then, anybody can see it is gold. Look here: I scraped that spot with my knife. I wanted to test it before I showed it to you. See how it shines! I could easily cut into it. I believe it is virgin gold, not hardened with any alloy."

"And that mound full of it!" cried Mrs. Cliff.

"I can't say about that," said the captain. "But if the gold is no deeper than my arm went down into it, and all pure metal at that, why—bless my soul!—it would make anybody crazy to try to calculate how much it is worth."

"Now, then," exclaimed Mrs. Cliff, "whom does all this gold belong to? We have found it, but whose is it?"

"That is a point to be considered," said the captain. "What is your opinion?"

"I have been thinking and thinking and thinking about it," said Mrs. Cliff. "Of course, that would have been all wasted, though, if it had turned out to be nothing but brass, but then, I could not help it, and this is the conclusion I have come to: In the first place, it does not belong to the people who govern Peru now. They are descendants of the very Spaniards that the Incas hid their treasure from, and it would be a shame and a wickedness to let them have it. It would better stay there shut up for more centuries. Then, again, it would not be right to give it to the Indians, or whatever they call themselves, though they are descendants of the ancient inhabitants, for the people of Spanish blood would not let them keep it one minute, and they would get it, after all. And, besides, how could such treasures be properly divided among a race of wretched savages? It would be preposterous, even if they should be allowed to keep it. They would drink themselves to death, and it would bring nothing but misery upon them. The Incas, in their way, were good, civilized people, and it stands to reason that the treasure they hid away should go to other good, civilized people when the Incas had departed from the face of the earth. Think of the good that could be done with such wealth, should it fall into the proper hands! Think of the good to the poor people of Peru, with the right kind of mission work done among them! I tell you all that the responsibility of this discovery is as great as its value in dollars. What do you think about it, Edna?"

"I think this," said Miss Markham: "so far as any of us have anything to do with it, it belongs to Captain Horn. He discovered it, and it is his."

"The whole of it?" cried Ralph.

"Yes," said his sister, firmly, "the whole of it, so far as we are concerned. What he chooses to do with it is his affair, and whether he gets every bar of gold, or only a reward from the Peruvian government, it is his, to do what he pleases with it."

"Now, Edna, I am amazed to hear you speak of the Peruvian government," cried Mrs. Cliff. "It would be nothing less than a crime to let them have it, or even know of it."

"What do you think, captain?" asked Edna.

"I am exactly of your opinion, Miss Markham," he said. "That treasure belongs to me. I discovered it, and it is for me to decide what is to be done with it."

"Now, then," exclaimed Ralph, his face very red, "I differ with you! We are all partners in this business, and it isn't fair for any one to have everything."

"And I am not so sure, either," said Mrs. Cliff, "that the captain ought to decide what is to be done with this treasure. Each of us should have a voice."

"Mrs. Cliff, Miss Markham, and Ralph," said the captain, "I have a few words to say to you, and I must say them quickly, for I see those black fellows coming. That treasure in the stone mound is mine. I discovered the mound, and no matter what might have been in it, the contents would have been mine. All that gold is just as much mine as if I dug it in a gold-mine in California, and we won't discuss that question any further. What I want to say particularly is that it may seem very selfish in me to claim the whole of that treasure, but I assure you that that is the only thing to be done. I know you will all agree to that when you see the matter in the proper light, and I have told you my plans about it. I intended to claim all that treasure, if it turned out to be treasure. I made up my mind to that last night, and I am very glad Miss Markham told me her opinion of the rights of the thing before I mentioned it. Now, I have just got time to say a few words more. If there should be any discussion about the ownership of this gold and the way it ought to be divided, there would be trouble, and perhaps bloody trouble. There are those black fellows coming up here, and two of them speak English. Eight of my men went away in a boat, and they may come back at any time. And then, there were those two Cape Cod men, who went off first. They may have reached the other side of the mountains, and may bring us assistance overland. As for Davis, I know he will never come back. Maka brought me positive proof that he was killed by the Rackbirds. Now, you see my point. That treasure is mine. I have a right to it, and I stand by that right. There must be no talk as to what is to be done with it. I shall decide what is right, and I shall do it, and no man shall have a word to say about it. In a case like this there must be a head, and I am the head."

The captain had been speaking rapidly and very earnestly, but now his manner changed a little. Placing his hand on Ralph's shoulder, he said: "Now don't be afraid, my boy, that you and your sister or Mrs. Cliff will be left in the lurch. If there were only us four, there would be no trouble at all, but if there is any talk of dividing, there may be a lot of men to deal with, and a hard lot, too. And now, not a word before these men.—Maka, that is a fine lot of fire-wood you have brought. It will last us a long time."

The African shrugged his shoulders. "Hope not," he said. "Hope Mr. Rynders come soon. Don't want make many fires."

As Captain Horn walked away toward Ralph's lookout, he could not account to himself for the strange and unnatural state of his feelings. He ought to have been very happy because he had discovered vast treasures. Instead of that his mind was troubled and he was anxious and fearful. One reason for his state of mind was his positive knowledge of the death of Davis. He had believed him dead because he had not come back, but now that he knew the truth, the shock seemed as great as if he had not suspected it. He had liked the Englishman better than any of his seamen, and he was a man he would have been glad to have had with him now. The Cape Cod men had been with him but a short time, and he was not well acquainted with them. It was likely, too, that they were dead also, for they had not taken provisions with them. But so long as he did not really know this, the probability could not lower his spirits.

But when he came to analyze his feelings, which he did with the vigorous directness natural to him, he knew what was the source of his anxiety and disquietude. He actually feared the return of Rynders and his men! This feeling annoyed and troubled him. He felt that it was unworthy of him. He knew that he ought to long for the arrival of his mate, for in no other way could the party expect help, and if help did not arrive before the provisions of the Rackbirds were exhausted, the whole party would most likely perish. Moreover, when Rynders and his men came back, they would come to rare good fortune, for there was enough gold for all of them.

But, in spite of these reasonable conclusions, the captain was afraid that Rynders and his men would return.

"If they come here," he said to himself, "they will know of that gold, for I cannot expect to keep such fellows out of the cavern, and if they know of it, it will be their gold, not mine. I know men, especially those men, well enough for that."

And so, fearing that he might see them before he was ready for them, — and how he was going to make himself ready for them he did not know, — he stood on the lookout and scanned the ocean for Rynders and his men.

CHAPTER XIV
A PILE OF FUEL

Four days had passed, and nothing had happened. The stone mound in the lake had not been visited, for there had been no reason for sending the black men away, and with one of them nearer than a mile the captain would not even look at his treasure. There was no danger that they would discover the mound, for they were not allowed to take the lantern, and no one of them would care to wander into the dark, sombre depths of the cavern without a light.

The four white people, who, with a fair habitation in the rocks, with plenty of plain food to eat, with six servants to wait on them, and a climate which was continuously delightful, except in the middle of the day, and with all fear of danger from man or beast removed from their minds, would have been content to remain here a week or two longer and await the arrival of a vessel to take them away, were now in a restless and impatient condition of mind. They were all eager to escape from the place. Three of them longed for the return of Rynders, but the other one steadily hoped that they might get away before his men came back.

How to do this, or how to take with him the treasure of the Incas, was a puzzling question with which the captain racked his brains by day and by night. At last he bethought himself of the Rackbirds' vessel. He remembered that Maka had told him that provisions were brought to them by a vessel, and there was every reason to suppose that when these miscreants went on some of their marauding expeditions they travelled by sea. Day by day he had thought that he would go and visit the Rackbirds' storehouse and the neighborhood thereabout, but day by day he had been afraid that in his absence Rynders might arrive, and when he came he wanted to be there to meet him.

But now the idea of the boat made him brave this possible contingency, and early one morning, with Cheditafa and two other of the black fellows, he set off along the beach for the mouth of the little stream which, rising somewhere in the mountains, ran down to the cavern where it had once widened and deepened into a lake, and then through the ravine of the Rackbirds on to the sea. When he reached his destination, Captain Horn saw a great deal to interest him.

Just beyond the second ridge of rock which Maka had discovered, the stream ran into a little bay, and the shores near its mouth showed evident signs that they had recently been washed by a flood. On points of rock and against the sides of the sand mounds, he saw bits of debris from the Rackbirds' camp. Here were sticks which had formed the timbers of their huts; there were pieces of clothing and cooking-utensils; and here and there, partly buried by the shifting sands, were seen the bodies of Rackbirds, already desiccated by the dry air and the hot sun of the region. But the captain saw no vessel.

"Dat up here," said Cheditafa. "Dey hide dat well. Come 'long, captain."

Following his black guide, the captain skirted a little promontory of rocks, and behind it found a cove in which, well concealed, lay the Rackbirds' vessel. It was a sloop of about twenty tons, and from the ocean, or even from the beach, it could not be seen. But as the captain stood and gazed upon this craft his heart sank. It had no masts nor sails, and it was a vessel that could not be propelled by oars.

Wading through the shallow water,—for it was now low tide,—the captain climbed on board. The deck was bare, without a sign of spar or sail, and when, with Cheditafa's help, he had forced the entrance of the little companionway, and had gone below, he found that the vessel had been entirely stripped of everything that could be carried away, and when he went on deck again he saw that even the rudder had been unshipped and removed. Cheditafa could give him no information upon this state of things, but after a little while Captain Horn imagined the cause for this dismantled condition of the sloop. The Rackbirds' captain could not trust his men, he said to himself, and he made it impossible for any of them to escape or set out on an expedition for themselves. It was likely that the masts and sails had been carried up to the camp, from which place it would have been impossible to remove them without the leader knowing it.

When he spoke to Cheditafa on the subject, the negro told him that after the little ship came in from one of its voyages he and his companions had always carried the masts, sails, and a lot of other things up to the camp. But there was nothing of the sort there now. Every spar and sail must have been carried out to sea by the flood, for if they had been left on the shores of the stream the captain would have seen them.

This was hard lines for Captain Horn. If the Rackbirds' vessel had been in sailing condition, everything would have been very simple and easy for him. He could have taken on board not only his own party, but a large portion of the treasure, and could have sailed away as free as a bird, without reference to the return of Rynders and his men. A note tied to a pole set up in a conspicuous place on the beach would have informed Mr. Rynders of their escape from the place, and it was not likely that any of the party would have thought it worth while to go farther on shore. But it was of no use to think of getting away in this vessel. In its present condition it was absolutely useless.

While the captain had been thinking and considering the matter, Cheditafa had been wandering about the coast exploring. Presently Captain Horn saw him running toward him, accompanied by the two other negroes.

"'Nother boat over there," cried Cheditafa, as the captain approached him,—"'nother boat, but badder than this. No good. Cook with it, that's all."

The captain followed Cheditafa across the little stream, and a hundred yards or so along the shore, and over out of reach of the tide, piled against a low sand mound, he saw a quantity of wood, all broken into small pieces, and apparently prepared, as Cheditafa had suggested, for cooking-fires. It was also easy to see that these pieces of wood had once been part of a boat, perhaps of a wreck thrown up on shore. The captain approached the pile of wood and picked up some of the pieces. As he held in his hand a bit of gunwale, not much more than a foot in length, his eyes began to glisten and his breath came quickly. Hastily pulling out several pieces from the mass of debris, he examined them thoroughly. Then he stepped back, and let the piece of rudder he was holding drop to the sand.

"Cheditafa," said he, speaking huskily, "this is one of the Castor's boats. This is a piece of the boat in which Rynders and the men set out."

The negro looked at the captain and seemed frightened by the expression on his face. For a moment he did not speak, and then in a trembling voice he asked, "Where all them now?"

The captain shook his head, but said nothing. That pile of fragments was telling him a tale which gradually became plainer and plainer to him, and which he believed as if Rynders himself had been telling it to him. His ship's boat, with its eight occupants, had never gone farther south than the mouth of the little stream. That they had been driven on shore by the stress of weather the captain did not believe. There had been no high winds or storms since their departure. Most likely they had been induced to land by seeing some of the Rackbirds on shore, and they had naturally rowed into the little cove, for assistance from their fellow-beings was what they were in search of. But no matter how they happened to land, the Rackbirds would never let them go away again to carry news of the whereabouts of their camp. Almost unarmed, these sailors must have fallen easy victims to the Rackbirds.

It was not unlikely that the men had been shot down from ambush without having had any intercourse or conversation with the cruel monsters to whom they had come to seek relief, for had there been any talk between them, Rynders would have told of his companions left on shore, and these would have been speedily visited by the desperadoes. For the destruction of the boat there was reason enough: the captain of the Rackbirds gave his men no chance to get away from him.

With a heart of lead, Captain Horn turned to look at his negro companions, and saw them all sitting together on the sands, chattering earnestly, and holding up their hands with one or more fingers extended, as if they were counting. Cheditafa came forward.

"When all your men go away from you?" he asked.

The captain reflected a moment, and then answered, "About two weeks ago."

"That's right! That's right!" exclaimed the negro, nodding violently as he spoke. "We talk about that. We count days. It's just ten days and three days, and Rackbirds go 'way, and leave us high up in rock-hole, with no ladder. After a while we hear guns, guns, guns. Long time guns shooting. When they come back, it almost dark, and they want supper bad. All time they eat supper, they talk 'bout shooting sharks. Shot lots sharks, and chuck them into the water. Sharks in water already before they is shot. We say then it no sharks they shot. Now we say it must been—"

The captain turned away. He did not want to hear any more. There was no possible escape from the belief that Rynders and all his men had been shot down, and robbed, if they had anything worth taking, and then their bodies carried out to sea, most likely in their own boat, and thrown overboard.

There was nothing more at this dreadful place that Captain Horn wished to see, to consider, or to do, and calling the negroes to follow him, he set out on his return.

During the dreary walk along the beach the captain's depression of spirits was increased by the recollection of his thoughts about the sailors and the treasure. He had hoped that these men would not come back in time to interfere with his disposal, in his own way, of the gold he had found. They would not come back now, but the thought did not lighten his heart. But before he reached the caves, he had determined to throw off the gloom and sadness which had come upon him. Under the circumstances, grief for what had happened was out of place. He must keep up a good heart, and help his companions to keep up good hearts. Now he must do something, and, like a soldier in battle, he must not think of the comrade who had fallen beside him, but of the enemy in front of him.

When he reached the caves he found supper ready, and that evening he said nothing to his companions of the important discoveries he had made, contenting himself with a general statement of the proofs that the Rackbirds and their camp had been utterly destroyed by the flood.

CHAPTER XV
THE CLIFF-MAKA SCHEME

The next morning Captain Horn arose with a plan of action in his mind, and he was now ready, not only to tell the two ladies and Ralph everything he had discovered, but also what he was going to do. The announcement of the almost certain fate of Rynders and his men filled his hearers with horror, and the statement of the captain's plans did not tend to raise their spirits.

"You see," said he, "there is nothing now for us to wait for here. As to being taken off by a passing vessel, there is no chance of that whatever. We have gone over that matter before. Nor can we get away overland, for some of us would die on the way. As to that little boat down there, we cannot all go to sea in her, but in it I must go out and seek for help."

"And leave us here!" cried Mrs. Cliff. "Do not think of that, captain! Whatever happens, let us all keep together."

"That cannot be," he said. "I must go because I am the only seaman among you, and I will take four of those black fellows with me. I do not apprehend any danger unless we have to make a surf landing, and even then they can all swim like fishes, while I am very well able to take care of myself in the water. I shall sail down the coast until I come to a port, and there put in. Then I will get a vessel of some sort and come back for you. I shall leave with you two of these negroes—Cheditafa, who seems to be a highly respectable old person, and can speak English, and Mok, who, although he can't talk to you, can understand a great deal that is said to him. Apart from his being such an abject coward, he seems to be a good, quiet fellow, willing to do what he is told. On the whole, I think he has the best disposition of the four black dummies, begging their pardons. I will take the three others, with Maka as head man and interpreter. If I should be cast on shore by a storm, I could swim through the surf to the dry land, but I could not undertake to save any one else. If this misfortune should happen, we could make our way on foot down the coast."

"But suppose you should meet some Rackbirds?" cried Ralph.

"I have no fear of that," answered the captain. "I do not believe there is another set of such scoundrels on this hemisphere. So, as soon as I can get that boat in order, and rig up a mast and a sail for her, I shall provision her well and set out. Of course, I do not want to leave you all here, but there is no help for it, and I don't believe you need have the slightest fear of harm. Later, we will plan what is to be done by you and by me, and get everything clear and straight. The first thing is to get the boat ready, and I shall go to work on that to-day. I will also take some of the negroes down to the Rackbirds' camp, and bring away more stores."

"Oh, let me go!" cried Ralph. "It is the cruellest thing in the world to keep me cooped up here. I never go anywhere, and never do anything."

But the captain shook his head. "I am sorry, my boy," said he, "to keep you back so much, but it cannot be helped. When I go away, I shall make it a positive condition that you do not leave your sister and Mrs. Cliff, and I do not want you to begin now." A half-hour afterwards, when the captain and his party had set out, Ralph came to his sister and sat down by her.

"Do you know," said he, "what I think of Captain Horn? I think he is a brave man, and a man who knows what to do when things turn up suddenly, but, for all that, I think he is a tyrant. He does what he pleases, and he makes other people do what he pleases, and consults nobody."

"My dear Ralph," said Edna, "if you knew how glad I am we have such a man to manage things, you would not think in that way. A tyrant is just what we want in our situation, provided he knows what ought to be done, and I think that Captain Horn does know."

"That's just like a woman," said Ralph. "I might have expected it."

During the rest of that day and the morning of the next, everybody in the camp worked hard and did what could be done to help the captain prepare for his voyage, and even Ralph, figuratively speaking, put his hand to the oar.

The boat was provisioned for a long voyage, though the captain hoped to make a short one, and at noon he announced that he would set out late that afternoon.

"It will be flood-tide, and I can get away from the coast better then than if the tide were coming in."

"How glad I should be to hear you speak in that way," said Mrs. Cliff, "if we were only going with you! But to be left here seems like a death sentence all around. You may be lost at sea while we perish on shore."

"I do not expect anything of the sort!" exclaimed Edna. "With Ralph and two men to defend us, we can stay here a long time. As for the captain's being lost, I do not think of it for a moment. He knows how to manage a boat too well for that."

"I don't like it at all! I don't like it at all!" exclaimed Mrs. Cliff. "I don't expect misfortunes any more than other people do, but our common sense tells us they may come, and we ought to be prepared for them. Of course, you are a good sailor, captain, but if it should happen that you should never come back, or even if it should be a very long time before you come back, how are we going to know what we ought to do? As far as I know the party you leave behind you, we would all be of different opinions if any emergency arose. As long as you are with us, I feel that, no matter what happens, the right thing will be done. But if you are away—"

At this moment Mrs. Cliff was interrupted by the approach of Maka, who wished very much to speak to the captain. As the negro was not a man who would be likely to interrupt a conversation except for an important reason, the captain followed him to a little distance. There he found, to his surprise, that although he had left one person to speak to another, the subject was not changed.

"Cap'n," said Maka, "when you go 'way, who's boss?"

The captain frowned, and yet he could not help feeling interested in this anxiety regarding his successor. "Why do you ask that?" he said. "What difference does it make who gives you your orders when I am gone?"

Maka shook his head. "Big difference," he said. "Cheditafa don' like boy for boss. He wan' me tell you, if boy is boss, he don' wan' stay. He wan' go 'long you."

"You can tell Cheditafa," said the captain, quickly, "that if I want him to stay he'll stay, and if I want him to go he'll go. He has nothing to say about that. So much for him. Now, what do you think?"

"Like boy," said Maka, "but not for boss."

The captain was silent for a moment. Here was a matter which really needed to be settled. If he had felt that he had authority to do as he pleased, he would have settled it in a moment.

"Cap'n big man. He know everyt'ing," said Maka. "But when cap'n go 'way, boy t'ink he big man. Boy know nothin'. Better have woman for boss."

Captain Horn could not help being amused. "Which woman?" he asked.

"I say old one. Cheditafa say young one."

The captain was not a man who would readily discuss his affairs with any one, especially with such a man as Maka; but now the circumstances were peculiar, and he wanted to know the opinions of these men he was about to leave behind him.

"What made you and Cheditafa think that way?" he asked.

"I t'ink old one know more," replied the negro, "and Cheditafa t'ink wife make bes' boss when cap'n gone, and young one make bes' wife."

"You impertinent black scoundrels!" exclaimed the captain, taking a step toward Maka, who bounced backward a couple of yards. "What do you mean by talking about Miss Markham and me in that way? I'll—" But there he paused. It would not be convenient to knock the heads off these men at this time. "Cheditafa must be a very great fool," said he, speaking more quietly. "Does he suppose I could call anybody my wife just for the sake of giving you two men a boss?"

"Oh, Cheditafa know!" exclaimed Maka, but without coming any nearer the captain. "He know many, many t'ings, but he 'fraid come tell you hisself."

"I should think he would be," replied the captain, "and I wonder you are not afraid, too."

"Oh, I is, I is," said Maka. "I's all w'ite inside. But somebody got speak boss 'fore he go 'way. If nobody speak, den you go 'way—no boss. All crooked. Nobody b'long to anybody. Den maybe men come down from mountain, or maybe come in boat, and dey say, 'Who's all you people? Who you b'long to?' Den dey say dey don' b'long nobody but demselves. Den, mos' like, de w'ite ones gets killed for dey clothes and dey money. And Cheditafa and me we gets tuck somew'ere to be slaves. But if we say, 'Dat lady big Cap'n Horn's wife—all de t'ings and de people b'long to big he'—hi! dey men hands off—dey shake in de legs. Everybody know big Cap'n Horn."

The captain could not help laughing. "I believe you are as big a fool as Cheditafa," said he. "Don't you know I can't make a woman my wife just by calling her so?"

"Don' mean dat!" exclaimed Maka. "Cheditafa don' mean dat. He make all right. He priest in he own country. He marry people. He marry you 'fore you go, all right. He talk 'bout dat mos' all night, but 'fraid come tell cap'n."

The absurdity of this statement was so great that it made the captain laugh instead of making him angry; but before he could say anything more to Maka, Mrs. Cliff approached him. "You must excuse me, captain," she said, "but really the time is very short, and I have a great deal to say to you, and if you have finished joking with that colored man, I wish you would talk with me."

"You will laugh, too," said the captain, "when you hear what he said to me." And in a few words he told her what Maka had proposed.

Instead of laughing, Mrs. Cliff stood staring at him in silent amazement.

"I see I have shocked you," said the captain, "but you must remember that that is only a poor heathen's ignorant vagary. Please say nothing about it, especially to Miss Markham."

"Say nothing about it!" exclaimed Mrs. Cliff. "I wish I had a thousand tongues to talk of it. Captain, do you really believe that Cheddy man is a priest, or what goes for one in his own country? If he is, he ought to marry you and Edna."

The captain frowned, with an air of angry impatience. "I could excuse that poor negro, madam," he said, "when he made such a proposition to me, but I must say I did not expect anything of the kind from you. Do you think, even if we had a bishop with us, that I would propose to marry any woman in the world for the sake of making her what that fellow called the 'boss' of this party?"

It was now Mrs. Cliff's turn to be impatient. "That boss business is a very small matter," she replied, "although, of course, somebody must be head while you are gone, and it was about this that I came to see you. But after hearing what that colored man said, I want to speak of something far more important, which I have been thinking and thinking about, and to which I could see no head or tail until a minute ago. Before I go on, I want you to answer me this question: If you are lost at sea, and never come back, what is to become of that treasure? It is yours now, as you let us know plainly enough, but whose will it be if you should die? It may seem like a selfish and sordid thing for me to talk to you in this way just before you start on such an expedition, but I am a business woman,—since my husband's death I have been obliged to be that,—and I look at things with a business eye. Have you considered this matter?"

"Yes, I have," answered the captain, "very seriously."

"And so have I," said Mrs. Cliff. "Whether Edna has or not I don't know, for she has said nothing to me. Now, we are not related to you, and, of course, have no claim upon you in that way, but I do think that, as we have all suffered together, and gone through dangers together, we all ought to share, in some degree at least, in good things as well as bad ones."

"Mrs. Cliff," said the captain, speaking very earnestly, "you need not say anything more on that subject. I have taken possession of that treasure, and I intend to hold it, in order that I may manage things in my own way, and avoid troublesome disputes. But I have not the slightest idea of keeping it all for myself. I intend that everybody who has had any concern in this expedition shall have a share in it. I have thought over the matter a great deal, and intended, before I left, to tell you and Miss Markham what I have decided upon. Here is a paper I have drawn up. It is my will. It is written in lead-pencil and may not be legal, but it is the best I can do. I have no relatives, except a few second cousins somewhere out in the Northwest, and I don't want them to have anything to do directly with my property, for they would be sure to make trouble. Here, as you see, I leave to you, Miss Markham, and Ralph all the property, of every kind and description, of which I may die possessed. This, of course, would cover all treasure you may be able to take away from this place, and which, without this will, might be claimed by some of my distant relatives, if they should ever chance to hear the story of my discovery.

"Besides this, I have written here, on another page of this note-book, a few private directions as to how I want the treasure disposed of. I say nothing definite, and mention no exact sums, but, in a general way, I have left everything in the hands of you two ladies. I know that you will make a perfectly just and generous disposition of what you may get."

"That is all very kind and good of you," said Mrs. Cliff, "but I cannot believe that such a will would be of much service. If you have relatives you are afraid of,—and I see you have,—if Edna Markham were your widow, then by law she would get a good part of it, even if she did not get it all, and if Edna got it, we would be perfectly satisfied."

"It is rather a grim business to talk about Miss Markham being my widow," said the captain, "especially under such circumstances. It strikes me that the kind of marriage you propose would be a good deal flimsier than this will."

"It does not strike me so," said she. "A mere confession before witnesses by a man and woman that they are willing to take each other for husband and wife is often a legal ceremony, and if there is any kind of a religious person present to perform the ceremony, it helps, and in a case like this no stone should be left unturned. You see, you have assumed a great deal of responsibility about this. You have stated—and if we were called upon to testify, Miss Markham and I would have to acknowledge that you have so stated—that you claimed this treasure as your discovery, and that it all belonged to you. So, you see, if we keep our consciences clear,—and no matter what happens, we are going to do that,—we might be obliged to testify every cent of it away from ourselves. But if Edna were your wife, it would be all right."

The captain stood silent for a few moments, his hands thrust into his pockets, and a queer smile on his face. "Mrs. Cliff," said he, presently, "do you expect me to go to Miss Markham and gravely propose this scheme which you and that half-tamed African have concocted?"

"I think it would be better," said Mrs. Cliff, "if I were to prepare her mind for it. I will go speak to her now."

"No," said he, quickly, "don't you do that. If the crazy idea is to be mentioned to her at all, I want to do it myself, and in my own way. I will go to her now. I have had my talk with you, and I must have one with her."

CHAPTER XVI
ON A BUSINESS BASIS

Captain Horn found Edna at the entrance to the caves, busily employed in filling one of the Rackbirds' boxes with ship-biscuit.

"Miss Markham," said he, "I wish to have a little business talk with you before I leave. Where is Ralph?"

"He is down at the boat," she answered.

"Very good," said he. "Will you step this way?"

When they were seated together in the shade of some rocks, he stated to Edna what he had planned in case he should lose his life in his intended expedition, and showed her the will he had made, and also the directions for herself and Mrs. Cliff. Edna listened very attentively, occasionally asking for an explanation, but offering no opinion. When he had finished, she was about to say something, but he interrupted her.

"Of course, I want to know your opinion about all this," he said, "but not yet. I have more to say. There has been a business plan proposed by two members of our party which concerns me, and when anything is told concerning me, I want to know how it is told, or, if possible, tell it myself."

And then, as concisely as possible, he related to her Maka's anxiety in regard to the boss question, and his method of disposing of the difficulty, and afterwards Mrs. Cliff's anxiety about the property, in case of accident to himself, and her method of meeting the contingency.

During this recital Edna Markham said not one word. To portions of the narrative she listened with an eager interest; then her expression became hard, almost stern; and finally her cheeks grew red, but whether with anger or some other emotion the captain did not know. When he had finished, she looked steadily at him for a few moments, and then she said:

"Captain Horn, what you have told me are the plans and opinions of others. It seems to me that you are now called upon to say something for yourself."

"I am quite ready to do that," he answered. "A half-hour ago I had never thought of such a scheme as I have laid before you. When I heard it, I considered it absurd, and mentioned it to you only because I was afraid I would be misrepresented. But since putting the matter to you, even while I have been just now talking, I have grown to be entirely in favor of it. But I want you to thoroughly understand my views on the subject. If this marriage is to be performed, it will be strictly a business affair, entered into for the purpose of securing to you and others a fortune, large or small, which, without this marriage, might be taken from you. In other words," said he, "you are to be looked upon in this affair in the light of my prospective widow."

For a moment the flush on the face of the young woman faded away, but it quickly returned. Apparently involuntarily, she rose to her feet. Turning to the captain, who also rose, she said:

"But there is another way in which the affair would have to be looked at. Suppose I should not become your widow? Suppose you should not be lost at sea, and should come back safely?"

The captain drew a deep breath, and folded his arms upon his chest. "Miss Markham," said he, "if this marriage should take place, it would be entirely different from other marriages. If I should not return, and it should be considered legal, it may make you all rich and happy. If it should not hold good, we can only think we have done our best. But as to anything beyond this, or to any question of my return, or any other question in connection with the matter, our minds should be shut and locked. This matter is a business proposition, and as such I lay it before you. If we adopt it, we do so for certain reasons, and beyond those reasons neither of us is qualified to go. We should keep our eyes fixed upon the main point, and think of nothing else."

"Something else must be looked at," said Edna. "It is just as likely that you will come back as that you will be lost at sea."

"This plan is based entirely on the latter supposition," replied the captain. "It has nothing to do with the other. If we consider it at all, we must consider it in that light."

"But we must consider it in the other light," she said. She was now quite pale, and her face had a certain sternness about it.

"I positively refuse to do that," he said. "I will not think about it, or say one word about it. I will not even refer to any future settlement of that question. The plan I present rests entirely upon my non-return."

"But if you do return?" persisted Edna.

The captain smiled and shook his head. "You must excuse me," he said, "but I can say nothing about that."

She looked steadily at him for a few moments, and then she said: "Very well, we will say nothing about it. As to the plan which has been devised to give us, in case of accident to you, a sound claim to the treasure which has been found here, and to a part of which I consider I have a right, I consent to it. I do this believing that I should share in the wonderful treasures in that cave. I have formed prospects for my future which would make my life a thousand times better worth living than I ever supposed it would be, and I do not wish to interfere with those prospects. I want them to become realities. Therefore, I consent to your proposition, and I will marry you upon a business basis, before you leave."

"Your hand upon it," said the captain; and she gave him a hand so cold that it chilled his own. "Now I will go talk to Maka and Cheditafa," he said. "Of course, we understand that it may be of no advantage to have this coal-black heathen act as officiating clergyman, but it can do no harm, and we must take the chances. I have a good deal to do, and no time to lose if I am to get away on the flood-tide this afternoon. Will it suit you if I get everything ready to start, and we then have the ceremony?"

"Oh, certainly," replied Edna. "Any spare moment will suit me."

When he had gone, Edna Markham sat down on the rock again. With her hands clasped in her lap, she gazed at the sand at her feet.

"Without a minute to think of it," she said to herself, presently,— "without any consideration at all. And now it is done! It was not like me. I do not know myself. But yes!" she exclaimed, speaking so that any one near might have heard her, "I do know myself. I said it because I was afraid, if I did not say it then, I should never be able to say it."

If Captain Horn could have seen her then, a misty light, which no man can mistake, shining in her eyes as she gazed out over everything into nothing, he might not have been able to confine his proposition to a strictly business basis.

She sat a little longer, and then she hurried away to finish the work on which she had been engaged; but when Mrs. Cliff came to look for her, she did not find her packing provisions for the captain's cruise, but sitting alone in one of the inner caves.

"What, crying!" exclaimed Mrs. Cliff. "Now, let me tell you, my dear child, I do not feel in the least like crying. The captain has told me that everything is all right between you, and the more I think of it, the more firmly I believe that it is the grandest thing that could have happened. For some reason or other, and I am sure I cannot tell you why, I do not believe at all that the captain is going to be shipwrecked in that little boat. Before this I felt sure we should never see him again, but now I haven't a doubt that he will get somewhere all right, and that he will come back all right, and if he does it will be a grand match. Why, Edna child, if Captain Horn never gets away with a stick of that gold, it will be a most excellent match. Now, I believe in my heart," she continued, sitting down by Edna, "that when you accepted Captain Horn you expected him to come back. Tell me isn't that true?"

At that instant Miss Markham gave a little start. "Mrs. Cliff," she exclaimed, "there is Ralph calling me. Won't you go and tell him all about it? Hurry, before he comes in here."

When Ralph Markham heard what had happened while he was down at the beach, he grew so furiously angry that he could not find words in which to express himself.

"That Captain Horn," he cried, when speech came to him, "is the most despotic tyrant on the face of the earth! He tells people what they are to do, and they simply go and do it. The next thing he will do is to tell you to adopt me as a son. Marry Edna! My sister! And I not know it! And she, just because he asks her, must go and marry him. Well, that is just like a woman."

With savage strides he was about marching back to the beach, when Mrs. Cliff stopped him.

"Now, don't make everybody unhappy, Ralph," she said, "but just listen to me. I want to tell you all about this matter."

It took about a quarter of an hour to make clear to the ruffled mind of Ralph the powerful, and in Mrs. Cliffs eyes the imperative, reasons for the sudden and unpremeditated matrimonial arrangements of the morning. But before she had finished, the boy grew quieter, and there appeared upon his face some expressions of astute sagacity.

"Well," said he, "when you first put this business to me, it was tail side up, but now you've got heads up it looks a little different. He will be drowned, as like as not, and then I suppose we can call our souls our own, and if, besides that, we can call a lot of those chunks of gold our own, we ought not to grumble. All right. I won't forbid the banns. But, between you and me, I think the whole thing is stuff and nonsense. What ought I to call him? Brother Horn?"

"Now, don't say anything like that, Ralph," urged Mrs. Cliff, "and don't make yourself disagreeable in any way. This is a very serious time for all of us, and I am sure that you will not do anything which will hurt your sister's feelings."

"Oh, don't be afraid," said Ralph. "I'm not going to hurt anybody's feelings. But when I first meet that man, I hope I may be able to keep him from knowing what I think of him."

Five minutes later Ralph heard the voice of Captain Horn calling him. The voice came from the opening in the caves, and instantly Ralph turned and walked toward the beach. Again came the voice, louder than before: "Ralph, I want you." The boy stopped, put his hands in his pockets, and shrugged his shoulders, then he slowly turned.

"If I were bigger," he said to himself, "I'd thrash him on the spot. Then I'd feel easier in my mind, and things could go on as they pleased. But as I am not six feet high yet, I suppose I might as well go to see what he wants."

"Ralph," said the captain, as soon as the boy reached him, "I see Mrs. Cliff has been speaking to you, and so you know about the arrangements that have been made. But I have a great deal to do before I can start, and I want you to help me. I am now going to the mound in the cave to get out some of that gold, and I don't want anybody but you to go with me. I have just sent all the negroes down to the beach to carry things to the boat, and we must be quick about our business. You take this leather bag. It is Mrs. Cliff's, but I think it is strong enough. The lantern is lighted, so come on."

To dive into a treasure mound Ralph would have followed a much more ruthless tyrant than Captain Horn, and although he made no remarks, he went willingly enough. When they had climbed the mound, and the captain had lifted the stone from the opening in the top, Ralph held the lantern while the captain, reaching down into the interior, set himself to work to fill the bag with the golden ingots. As the boy gazed down upon the mass of dull gold, his heart swelled within him. His feeling of indignant resentment began to disappear rapidly before the growing consciousness that he was to be the brother-in-law of the owner of all that wealth. As soon as the bag was filled, the stone was replaced, and the two descended from the mound, the captain carefully holding the heavy bag under his arm, for he feared the weight might break the handle. Then, extinguishing the lantern as soon as they could see their way without it, they reached the innermost cave before any of the negroes returned. Neither Mrs. Cliff nor Edna was there, and the captain placed his burden behind a piece of rock.

"Captain," said the boy, his eyes glistening, "there must be a fortune in that bag!"

The captain laughed. "Oh, no," said he, "not a very large one. I have had a good deal of experience with gold in California, and I suppose each one of those little bars is worth from two hundred and fifty to three hundred dollars." What we have represents a good deal of money. But now, Ralph, I have something very important to say to you. I am going to appoint you sole guardian and keeper of that treasure. You are very young to have such a responsibility put upon you, but I know you will feel the importance of your duty, and that you will not be forgetful or negligent about it. The main thing is to keep those two negroes, and anybody who may happen to come here, away from the mound. Do what you can to prevent any one exploring the cave, and don't let the negroes go there for water. They now know the way over the rocks to the stream.

"If I should not come back, or a ship should come along and take you off before I return, you must all be as watchful as cats about that gold. Don't let anybody see a piece of it. You three must carry away with you as much as you can, but don't let any one know you are taking it. Of course, I expect to come back and attend to the whole business, but if I should not be heard from for a long time,—and if that is the case, you may be sure I am lost,—and you should get away, I will trust to your sister and you to get up an expedition to come back for it."

Ralph drew himself up as high as circumstances would permit. "Captain," said he, "you may count on me. I'll keep an eye on those black fellows, and on anybody else who may come here."

"Very good," said the captain. "I am sure you will never forget that you are the guardian of all our fortunes."

CHAPTER XVII
"A FINE THING, NO MATTER WHAT HAPPENS"

After the noonday meal, on the day of Captain Horn's departure, Mrs. Cliff went apart with Maka and Cheditafa, and there endeavored to find out, as best she might, the ideas and methods of the latter in regard to the matrimonial service. In spite of the combined efforts of the two, with their limited command of English, to make her understand how these things were done in the forests and wilds of the Dark Continent, she could not decide whether the forms of the Episcopal Church, those of the Baptists, or those of the Quakers, could be more easily assimilated with the previous notions of Cheditafa on the subject. But having been married herself, she thought she knew very well what was needed, and so, without endeavoring to persuade the negro priest that his opinions regarding the marriage rites were all wrong, or to make him understand what sort of a wedding she would have had if they had all been in their own land, she endeavored to impress upon his mind the forms and phrases of a very simple ceremony, which she believed would embody all that was necessary.

Cheditafa was a man of considerable intelligence, and the feeling that he was about to perform such an important ceremony for the benefit of such a great man as Captain Horn filled his soul with pride and a strong desire to acquit himself creditably in this honorable function, and he was able before very long to satisfy Mrs. Cliff that, with Maka's assistance as prompting clerk, he might be trusted to go through the ceremony without serious mistake.

She was strongly of the opinion that if she conducted the marriage ceremony it would be far better in every way than such a performance by a coal-black heathen; but as she knew that her offices would not count for anything in a civilized world, whereas the heathen ministry might be considered satisfactory, she accepted the situation, and kept her opinions to herself.

The wedding took place about six o'clock in the afternoon, on the plateau in front of the great stone face, at a spot where the projecting rocks cast a shade upon the heated ground. Cheditafa, attired in the best suit of clothes which could be made up from contributions from all his fellow-countrymen present, stood on the edge of the line of shadow, his hands clasped, his head slightly bowed, his bright eyes glancing from side to side, and his face filled with an expression of anxiety to observe everything and make no mistakes. Maka stood near him, and behind the two, in the brilliant sunlight, were grouped the other negroes, all very attentive and solemn, looking a little frightened, as if they were not quite sure that sacrifices were not customary on such occasions.

Captain Horn stood, tall and erect, his jacket a little torn, but with an air of earnest dignity upon his handsome, sunburnt features, which, with his full dark beard and rather long hair, gave him the appearance of an old-time chieftain about to embark upon some momentous enterprise. By his side was Edna Markham, pale, and dressed in the simple gown in which she had left the ship, but as beautiful, in the eyes of Mrs. Cliff, as if she had been arrayed in orange-blossoms and white satin.

Reverently the two answered the simple questions which were put to them, and made the necessary promises, and slowly and carefully, and in very good English, Cheditafa pronounced them man and wife. Mrs. Cliff then produced a marriage certificate, written with a pencil, as nearly as she could remember, in the words of her own document of that nature, on a leaf torn from the captain's note-book, and to this she signed Cheditafa's name, to which the African, under her directions, affixed his mark. Then Ralph and Mrs. Cliff signed as witnesses, and the certificate was delivered to Edna.

"Now," said the captain, "I will go aboard."

The whole party, Edna and the captain a little in the lead, walked down to the beach, where the boat lay, ready to be launched. During the short walk Captain Horn talked rapidly and earnestly to Edna, confining his remarks, however, to directions and advice as to what should be done until he returned, or, still more important, as to what should be done if he did not return at all.

When they reached the beach, the captain shook hands with Edna, Mrs. Cliff, and Ralph, and then, turning to Cheditafa, he informed him that that lady, pointing to Edna, was now the mistress of himself and Mok, and that every word of command she gave them must be obeyed exactly as if he had given it to them himself. He was shortly coming back, he said, and when he saw them again, their reward should depend entirely upon the reports he should receive of their conduct.

"But I know," said he, "that you are a good man, and that I can trust you, and I will hold you responsible for Mok."

This was the end of the leave-taking. The captain stepped into his boat and took the oars. Then the four negroes, two on a side, ran out the little craft as far as possible through the surf, and then, when they had scrambled on board, the captain pulled out into smooth water.

Hoisting his little sail, and seating himself in the stern, with the tiller in his hand, he brought the boat round to the wind. Once he turned toward shore and waved his hat, and then he sailed away toward the western sky.

Mrs. Cliff and Ralph walked together toward the caves, leaving Edna alone upon the beach.

"Well," said Ralph, "this is the first wedding I ever saw, but I must say it is rather different from my idea of that sort of thing. I thought that people always kissed at such affairs, and there was general jollification and cake, but this seemed more like a newfangled funeral, with the dear departed acting as his own Charon and steering himself across the Styx."

"He might have kissed her," said Mrs. Cliff, thoughtfully. "But you see, Ralph, everything had to be very different from ordinary weddings. It was a very peculiar case."

"I should hope so," said the boy, —"the uncommoner the better. In fact, I shouldn't call it a wedding at all. It seemed more like taking a first degree in widowhood."

"Ralph," said Mrs. Cliff, "that is horrible. Don't you ever say anything like that again. I hope you are not going to distress your sister with such remarks."

"You need not say anything about Edna!" he exclaimed. "I shall not worry her with any criticisms of the performance. The fact is, she will need cheering up, and if I can do it I will. She's captain now, and I'll stand up for her like a good fellow."

Edna stood on the beach, gazing out on the ocean illuminated by the rays of the setting sun, keeping her eyes fixed on the captain's boat until it became a mere speck. Then, when it had vanished entirely among the lights and shades of the evening sea, she still stood a little while and watched. Then she turned and slowly walked up to the plateau. Everything there was just as she had known it for weeks. The great stone face seemed to smile in the last rays of the setting sun. Mrs. Cliff came to meet her, her face glowing with smiles, and Ralph threw his arms around her neck and kissed her, without, however, saying a word about that sort of thing having been omitted in the ceremony of the afternoon.

"My dear Edna," exclaimed Mrs. Cliff, "from the bottom of my heart I congratulate you! No matter how we look at it, a rare piece of good fortune has come to you."

Edna gazed at her for a moment, and then she answered quietly, "Oh, yes, it was a fine thing, no matter what happens. If he does not come back, I shall make a bold stroke for widowhood; and if he does come back, he is bound, after all this, to give me a good share of that treasure. So, you see, we have done the best we can do to be rich and happy, if we are not so unlucky as to perish among these rocks and sand."

"She is almost as horrible as Ralph," thought Mrs. Cliff, "but she will get over it."

CHAPTER XVIII
MRS. CLIFF IS AMAZED

After the captain set sail in his little boat, the party which he left behind him lived on in an uneventful, uninteresting manner, which, gradually, day by day, threw a shadow over the spirits of each one of them.

Ralph, who always slept in the outer chamber of the caves, had been a very faithful guardian of the captain's treasure. No one, not even himself, had gone near it, and he never went up to the rocky promontory on which he had raised his signal-pole without knowing that the two negroes were at a distance from the caves, or within his sight.

For a day or two after the captain's departure Edna was very quiet, with a fancy for going off by herself. But she soon threw off this dangerous disposition, and took up her old profession of teacher, with Ralph as the scholar, and mathematics as the study. They had no books nor even paper, but the rules and principles of her specialty were fresh in her mind, and with a pointed stick on a smooth stretch of sand diagrams were drawn and problems worked out.

This occupation was a most excellent thing for Edna and her brother, but it did not help Mrs. Cliff to endure with patience the weary days of waiting. She had nothing to read, nothing to do, very often no one to talk to, and she would probably have fallen into a state of nervous melancholy had not Edna persuaded her to devote an hour or two each day to missionary work with Mok and Cheditafa. This Mrs. Cliff cheerfully undertook. She was a conscientious woman, and her methods of teaching were peculiar. She had an earnest desire to do the greatest amount of good with these poor, ignorant negroes, but, at the same time, she did not wish to do injury to any one else. The conviction forced itself upon her that if she absolutely converted Cheditafa from the errors of his native religion, she might in some way invalidate the marriage ceremony which he had performed.

"If he should truly come to believe," she said to herself, "that he had no right to marry the captain and Edna, his conscience might make him go back on the whole business, and everything that we have done would be undone. I don't want him to remain a heathen any longer than it can possibly be helped, but I must be careful not to set his priesthood entirely aside until Edna's position is fixed and settled. When the captain comes back, and we all get home, they must be married regularly; but if he never comes back, then I must try to make Cheditafa understand that the marriage is just as binding as any other kind, and that any change of religious opinion that he may undergo will have no effect upon it."

Accordingly, while she confined her religious teachings to very general principles, her moral teachings were founded upon the strictest code, and included cleanliness and all the household virtues, not excepting the proper care of such garments as an indigent human being in a tropical climate might happen to possess.

In spite, however, of this occupation, Mrs. Cliffs spirits were not buoyant. "I believe," she thought, "things would have been more cheerful if they had not married; but then, of course, we ought to be willing to sacrifice cheerfulness at present to future prosperity."

It was more than a month after the departure of the captain that Ralph, from his point of observation, perceived a sail upon the horizon. He had seen sails there before, but they never grew any larger, and generally soon disappeared, for it would lengthen the course of any coasting-vessel to approach this shore. But the sail that Ralph saw now grew larger and larger, and, with the aid of his little spy-glass, it was not long before he made up his mind that it was coming toward him. Then up went his signal-flag, and, with a loud hurrah, down went he to shout out the glad news.

Twenty minutes later it was evident to the anxiously peering eyes of every one of the party that the ship was actually approaching the shore, and in the heart of each one of them there was a bounding delight in the feeling that, after all these days of weary waiting, the captain was coming back.

As the ship drew nearer and nearer, she showed herself to be a large vessel—a handsome bark. About half a mile from the shore, she lay to, and very soon a boat was lowered.

Edna's heart beat rapidly and her face flushed as, with Ralph's spy-glass to her eyes, she scanned the people in the boat as it pulled away from the ship.

"Can you make out the captain?" cried Ralph, at her side.

She shook her head, and handed him the glass. For full five minutes the boy peered through it, and then he lowered the glass.

"Edna," said he, "he isn't in it."

"What!" exclaimed Mrs. Cliff, "do you mean to say that the captain is not in that boat?"

"I am sure of it," said Ralph. "And if he isn't in the boat, of course he is not on the ship. Perhaps he did not have anything to do with that vessel's coming here. It may have been tacking in this direction, and so come near enough for people to see my signal."

"Don't suppose things," said Edna, a little sharply. "Wait until the boat comes in, and then we will know all about it.—Here, Cheditafa," said she, "you and Mok go out into the water and help run that boat ashore as soon as it is near enough."

It was a large boat containing five men, and when it had been run up on the sand, and its occupants had stepped out, the man at the tiller, who proved to be the second mate of the bark, came forward and touched his hat. As he did so, no sensible person could have imagined that he had accidentally discovered them. His manner plainly showed that he had expected to find them there. The conviction that this was so made the blood run cold in Edna's veins. Why had not the captain come himself?

The man in command of the boat advanced toward the two ladies, looking from one to the other as he did so. Then, taking a letter from the pocket of his jacket, he presented it to Edna.

"Mrs. Horn, I believe," he said. "Here is a letter from your husband."

Now, it so happened that to Mrs. Cliff, to Edna, and to Ralph this recognition of matrimonial status seemed to possess more force and value than the marriage ceremony itself.

Edna's face grew as red as roses as she took the letter.

"From my husband," she said; and then, without further remark, she stepped aside to read it.

But Mrs. Cliff and Ralph could not wait for the reading of the letter. They closed upon the mate, and, each speaking at the same moment, demanded of him what had happened to Captain Horn, why he had not come himself, where he was now, was this ship to take them away, and a dozen similar questions. The good mariner smiled at their impatience, but could not wonder at it, and proceeded to tell them all he knew about Captain Horn and his plans.

The captain, he said, had arrived at Callao some time since, and immediately endeavored to get a vessel in which to go after the party he had left, but was unable to do so. There was nothing in port which answered his purpose. The captain seemed to be very particular about the craft in which he would be willing to trust his wife and the rest of the party.

"And after having seen Mrs. Horn," the mate politely added, "and you two, I don't wonder he was particular. When Captain Horn found that the bark out there, the Mary Bartlett, would sail in a week for Acapulco, Mexico, he induced the agents of the company owning her to allow her to stop to take off the shipwrecked party and carry them to that port, from which they could easily get to the United States."

"But why, in the name of common sense," almost screamed Mrs. Cliff, "didn't he come himself? Why should he stay behind, and send a ship to take us off?"

"That, madam," said the mate, "I do not know. I have met Captain Horn before, for he is well known on this coast, and I know he is a man who understands how to attend to his own business, and, therefore, I suppose he has good reasons for what he has done—which reasons, no doubt, he has mentioned in his letter to his wife. All I can tell you is that, after he had had a good deal of trouble with the agents, we were at last ordered to touch here. He could not give us the exact latitude and longitude of this spot, but as his boat kept on a straight westward course after he left here, he got a good idea of the latitude from the Mexican brig which he boarded three days afterwards. Then he gave us a plan of the coast, which helped us very much, and soon after we got within sight of land, our lookout spied that signal you put up. So here we are; and I have orders to take you all off just as soon as possible, for we must not lie here a minute longer than is necessary. I do not suppose that, under the circumstances, you have much baggage to take away with you, and I shall have to ask you to get ready to leave as soon as you can."

"All right," cried Ralph. "It won't take us long to get ready."

But Mrs. Cliff answered never a word. In fact, the injunction to prepare to leave had fallen unheeded upon her ear. Her mind was completely occupied entirely with one question: Why did not the captain come himself?

She hastened to Edna, who had finished reading the letter, and now stood silent, holding it in her hand.

"What does he say?" exclaimed Mrs. Cliff. "What are his reasons for staying away? What does he tell you about his plans? Read us the letter. You can leave out all the loving and confidential parts, but give us his explanations. I never was so anxious to know anything in all my life."

"I will read you the whole of it," said Edna. "Here, Ralph."

Her brother came running up. "That man is in an awful hurry to get away," he said. "We ought to go up to the caves and get our things."

"Stay just where you are," said Mrs. Cliff. "Before we do anything else, we must know what Captain Horn intends to do, and what he wants us to do."

"That's so!" cried Ralph, suddenly remembering his guardianship. "We ought to know what he says about leaving that mound. Read away, Edna."

The three stood at some little distance from the sailors, who were now talking with Cheditafa, and Edna read the letter aloud:

"Lima, May 14, 1884.

"MY DEAR WIFE: I reached this city about ten days ago. When I left you all I did not sail down the coast, but stood directly out to sea. My object was to reach a shipping-port, and to do this my best plan was to get into the track of coasting-vessels. This plan worked well, and in three days we were picked up by a Mexican guano brig, and were taken to Callao, which is the port of Lima. We all arrived in good health and condition.

"This letter will be brought to you by the bark Mary Bartlett, which vessel I have engaged to stop for you, and take you and the whole party to Acapulco, which is the port of the City of Mexico, from which place I advise you to go as soon as possible to San Francisco. I have paid the passage of all of you to Acapulco, and I inclose a draft for one thousand dollars for your expenses. I would advise you to go to the Palmetto Hotel, which is a good family house, and I will write to you there and send another draft. In fact, I expect you will find my letter when you arrive, for the mail-steamer will probably reach San Francisco before you do. Please write to me as soon as you get there, and address me here, care of Nasco, Parmley & Co."

An exclamation of impatience here escaped from Mrs. Cliff. In her opinion, the reasons for the non-appearance of the captain should, have been the first thing in the letter.

"When I reached Lima, which is six miles from Callao," the letter continued, "I disposed of some of the property I brought with me, and expect to sell it all before long. Being known as a Californian, I find no difficulty in disposing of my property, which is in demand here, and in a very short time I shall have turned the whole of it into drafts or cash. There is a vessel expected here shortly which I shall be able to charter, and as soon as I can do so I shall sail in her to attend to the disposition of the rest of my property. I shall write as frequently as possible, and keep you informed of my operations.

"Of course, you understand that I could not go on the Mary Bartlett to join you and accompany you to Acapulco, for that would have involved too great a loss of time. My business must be attended to without delay, and I can get the vessel I want here.

"The people of the *Mary Bartlett* will not want to wait any longer than can be helped, so you would all better get your baggage together as soon as possible and go on board. The two negroes will bring down your baggage, so there will be no need for any of the sailors to go up to the caves. Tell Ralph not to forget the charge I gave him if they do go up. When you have taken away your clothes, you can leave just as they are the cooking-utensils, the blankets, and *everything else*. I will write to you much more fully by mail. Cannot do so now. I hope you may all have a quick and safe voyage, and that I may hear from you immediately after you reach Acapulco. I hope most earnestly that you have all kept well, and that no misfortune has happened to any of you. I shall wait with anxiety your letter from Acapulco. Let Ralph write and make his report. I will ask you to stay in San Francisco until more letters have passed and plans are arranged. Until further notice, please give Mrs. Cliff one fourth of all moneys I send. I cannot insist, of course, upon her staying in San Francisco, but I would advise her to do so until things are more settled.

"In haste, your husband,

"Philip Horn."

"Upon my word!" ejaculated Mrs. Cliff, "a most remarkable letter! It might have been written to a clerk! No one would suppose it the first letter of a man to his bride! Excuse me, Edna, for speaking so plainly, but I must say I am shocked. He is very particular to call you his wife and say he is your husband, and in that way he makes the letter a valuable piece of testimony if he never turns up, but—well, no matter."

"He is mighty careful," said Ralph, "not to say anything about the gold. He speaks of his property as if it might be Panama stock or something like that. He is awfully wary."

"You see," said Edna, speaking in a low voice, "this letter was sent by private hands, and by people who were coming to the spot where his property is, and, of course, it would not do to say anything that would give any hint of the treasure here. When he writes by mail, he can speak more plainly."

"I hope he may speak more plainly in another way," said Mrs. Cliff. "And now let us go up and get our things together. I am a good deal more amazed by the letter than I was by the ship."

CHAPTER XIX
LEFT BEHIND

"Ralph," said Edna, as they were hurrying up to the caves, "you must do everything you can to keep those sailors from wandering into the lake basin. They are very different from the negroes, and will want to explore every part of it."

"Oh, I have thought of all that," said Ralph, "and I am now going to run ahead and smash the lantern. They won't be so likely to go poking around in the dark."

"But they may have candles or matches," said Edna. "We must try to keep them out of the big cave."

Ralph did not stop to answer, but ran as fast as his legs would carry him to the plateau. The rest of the party followed, Edna first, then the negroes, and after them Mrs. Cliff, who could not imagine why Edna should be in such a hurry. The sailors, having secured their boat, came straggling after the rest.

When Edna reached the entrance to the caves, she was met by her brother, so much out of breath that he could hardly speak.

"You needn't go to your room to get your things," he exclaimed. "I have gathered them all up, your bag, too, and I have tumbled them over the wall in the entrance back here. You must get over as quick as you can. That will be your room now, and I will tell the sailors, if they go poking around, that you are in there getting ready to leave, and then, of course, they can't pass along the passage."

"That is a fine idea," said Edna, as she followed him. "You are getting very sharp-witted, Ralph."

"Now, then," said he, as he helped her over the wall, "take just as long as you can to get your things ready."

"It can't take me very long," said Edna. "I have no clothes to change, and only a few things to put in my bag. I don't believe you have got them all, anyway."

"But you must make it take a long time," said he. "You must not get through until every sailor has gone. You and I must be the last ones to leave the caves."

"All right," said Edna, as she disappeared behind the wall.

When Mrs. Cliff arrived, she was met by Ralph, who explained the state of affairs, and although that lady was a good deal annoyed at the scattered condition in which she found her effects, she accepted the situation.

The mate and his men were much interested in the caves and the great stone face, and, as might have been expected, every one of them wanted to know where the narrow passage led. But as Ralph was on hand to inform them that it was the entrance to Mrs. Horn's apartment, they could do no more than look along its dusky length, and perhaps wonder why Mrs. Horn should have selected a cave which must be dark, when there were others which were well lighted.

Mrs. Cliff was soon ready, and explained to the inquiring mate her notion that these caves were used for religious purposes, and that the stone face was an ancient idol. In fact, the good lady believed this, but she did not state that she thought it likely that the sculptured countenance was a sort of a cashier idol, whose duty it was to protect treasure.

Edna, behind the stone barrier, had put her things in her bag, though she was not sure she had found all of them in the gloom, and she waited a long time, so it seemed to her, for Ralph's summons to come forth. But although the boy came to the wall several times, ostensibly to ask if she were not ready, yet he really told her to stay where she was, for the sailors were not yet gone. But at last he came with the welcome news that every one had departed, and they soon came out into the daylight.

"If anything is lost, charge it to me," said Ralph to Mrs. Cliff and his sister, as they hurried away. "I can tell you, if I had not thought of that way of keeping those sailors out of the passage, they would have swarmed over that lake bed, each one of them with a box of matches in his pocket; and if they had found that mound, I wouldn't give two cents for the gold they would have left in it. It wouldn't have been of any use to tell them it was the captain's property. They would have been there, and he wasn't, and I expect the mate would have been as bad as any of them."

"You are a good fellow, Ralph," said Mrs. Cliff, "and I hope you will grow up to be an administrator, or something of the kind. I don't suppose there was ever another boy in the world who had so much wealth in charge."

"You can't imagine," exclaimed Ralph, "how I hate to go away and leave it! There is no knowing when the captain will get here, nor who will drop in on the place before he does. I tell you, Edna, I believe it would be a good plan for me to stay here with those two black fellows, and wait for the captain. You two could go on the ship, and write to him. I am sure he would be glad to know I am keeping guard here, and I don't know any better fun than to be on hand when he unearths the treasure. There's no knowing what is at the bottom of that mound."

"Nonsense!" exclaimed Edna. "You can put that idea out of your head instantly. I would not think of going away and leaving you here. If the captain had wanted you to stay, he would have said so."

"If the captain wanted!" sarcastically exclaimed Ralph. "I am tired of hearing what the captain wants. I hope the time will soon come when those yellow bars of gold will be divided up, and then I can do what I like without considering what he likes."

Mrs. Cliff could not help a sigh. "Dear me!" said she, "I do most earnestly hope that time may come. But we are leaving it all behind us, and whether we will ever hear of it again nobody knows."

One hour after this Edna and Mrs. Cliff were standing on the deck of the Mary Bartlett, watching the plateau of the great stone face as it slowly sank into the horizon.

"Edna," said the elder lady, "I have liked you ever since I have known you, and I expect to like you as long as I live, but I must say that, for an intelligent person, you have the most colorless character I have ever seen. Whatever comes to pass, you receive it as quietly and calmly as if it were just what you expected and what you happened to want, and yet, as long as I have known you, you have not had anything you wanted."

"You are mistaken there," said Edna. "I have got something I want."

"And what may that be?" asked the other.

"Captain Horn," said Edna.

Mrs. Cliff laughed a little scornfully. "If you are ever going to get any color out of your possession of him," she said, "he's got to very much change the style of his letter-writing. He has given you his name and some of his money, and may give you more, but I must say I am very much disappointed in Captain Horn."

Edna turned suddenly upon her companion. "Color!" she exclaimed, but she did not finish her remark, for Ralph came running aft.

"A queer thing has happened," said he: "a sailor is missing, and he is one of the men who went on shore for us. They don't know what's become of him, for the mate is sure he brought all his men back with him, and so am I, for I counted them to see that there were no stragglers left, and all the people who were in that boat came on board. They think he may have fallen overboard after the ship sailed, but nobody heard a splash."

"Poor fellow!" exclaimed Mrs. Cliff, "and he was one of those who came to save us!"

At this moment a wet and bedraggled sailor, almost exhausted with a swim of nearly a mile, staggered upon the beach, and fell down upon the sand near the spot from which the Mary Bartlett's boat had recently been pushed off. When, an hour before, he had slipped down the side of the ship, he had swum under water as long as his breath held out, and had dived again as soon as he had filled his lungs. Then he had floated on his back, paddling along with little but his face above the surface of the waves, until he had thought it safe to turn over and strike out for land. It had been a long pull, and the surf had treated him badly, but he was safe on shore at last, and in a few minutes he was sound asleep, stretched upon the sand.

Toward the end of the afternoon he awoke and rose to his feet. The warm sand, the desiccating air, and the sun had dried his clothes, and his nap had refreshed him. He was a sharp-faced, quick-eyed man, a Scotchman, and the first thing he did was to shade his face with his hands and look out over the sea. Then he turned, with a shrug of his shoulders and a grunt.

"She's gone," said he, "and I will be up to them caves." After a dozen steps he gave another shrug. "Humph!" said he, "those fools! Do they think everybody is blind? They left victuals, they left cooking-things. Blasted careful they were to leave matches and candles in a tin box. I watched them. If everybody else was blind, I kenned they expected somebody was comin' back. That captain, that blasted captain, I'll wager! Wi' sae much business on his hands, he couldna sail wi' us to show us where his wife was stranded!"

For fifty yards more he plodded along, looking from side to side at the rocks and sand.

"A dreary place and lonely," thought he, "and I can peer out things at me ease. I'll find out what's at the end o' that dark alley. They were so fearsome that we'd go into her room. Her room, indeed! When the other woman had a big lighted cave! They expected somebody to come back, did they? Well, blast their eyes, he's here!"

CHAPTER XX
AT THE RACKBIRDS' COVE

It was about six weeks after the *Mary Bartlett* had sailed away from that desolate spot on the coast of Peru from which she had taken the shipwrecked party, that the great stone face might have seen, if its wide-open eyes had been capable of vision, a small schooner beating in toward shore. This vessel, which was manned by a Chilian captain, a mate, and four men, and was a somewhat dirty and altogether disagreeable craft, carried Captain Horn, his four negroes, and three hundred and thirty bags of guano.

In good truth the captain was coming back to get the gold, or as much of it as he could take away with him. But his apparent purpose was to establish on this desert coast a depot for which he would have nothing to pay for rent and storage, and where he would be able to deposit, from time to time, such guano as he had been able to purchase at a bargain at two of the guano islands, until he should have enough to make it worth while for a large vessel, trading with the United States or Mexico, to touch here and take on board his accumulated stock of odorous merchandise.

It would be difficult—in fact, almost impossible—to land a cargo at the point near the caves where the captain and his party first ran their boats ashore, nor did the captain in the least desire to establish his depot at a point so dangerously near the golden object of his undertaking. But the little bay which had been the harbor of the Rackbirds exactly suited his purpose, and here it was that he intended to land his bags of guano. He had brought with him on the vessel suitable timber with which to build a small pier, and he carried also a lighter, or a big scow, in which the cargo would be conveyed from the anchored schooner to the pier.

It seemed quite evident that the captain intended to establish himself in a somewhat permanent manner as a trader in guano. He had a small tent and a good stock of provisions, and, from the way he went to work and set his men to work, it was easy to see that he had thoroughly planned and arranged all the details of his enterprise.

It was nearly dark when the schooner dropped her anchor, and early the next morning all available hands were set to work to build the pier, and, when it was finished, the landing of the cargo was immediately begun. Some of the sailors wandered about a little, when they had odd moments to spare, but they had seen such dreary coasts before, and would rather rest than ramble. But wherever they did happen to go, not one of them ever got away from the eye of Captain Horn.

The negroes evinced no desire to visit the cave, and Maka had been ordered by the captain to say nothing about it to the sailors. There was no difficulty in obeying this order, for these rough fellows, as much landsmen as mariners, had a great contempt for the black men, and had little to do with them. As Captain Horn informed Maka, he had heard from his friends, who had arrived in safety at Acapulco; therefore there was no need for wasting time in visiting their old habitation.

In that dry and rainless region a roof to cover the captain's stock in trade was not necessary, and the bags were placed upon a level spot on the sands, in long double rows, each bag on end, gently leaning against its opposite neighbor, and between the double rows there was room to walk.

The Chilian captain was greatly pleased with this arrangement. "I see well," said he, in bad Spanish, "that this business is not new to you. A ship's crew can land and carry away these bags without tumbling over each other. It is a grand thing to have a storehouse with a floor as wide as many acres."

A portion of the bags, however, were arranged in a different manner. They were placed in a circle two bags deep, inclosing a space about ten feet in diameter. This, Captain Horn explained, he intended as a sort of little fort, in which the man left in charge could defend himself and the property, in case marauders should land upon the coast.

"You don't intend," exclaimed the Chilian captain, "that you will leave a guard here! Nobody would have cause to come near the spot from either land or sea, and you might well leave your guano here for a year or more, and come back and find it."

"No," said Captain Horn, "I can't trust to that. A coasting-vessel might put in here for water. Some of them may know that there is a stream here, and with this convenient pier, and a cargo ready to their hands, my guano would be in danger. No, sir. I intend to send you off to-morrow, if the wind is favorable, for the second cargo for which we have contracted, and I shall stay here and guard my warehouse."

"What!" exclaimed the Chilian, "alone?"

"Why not?" said Captain Horn. "Our force is small, and we can only spare one man. In loading the schooner on this trip, I would be the least useful man on board, and, besides, do you think there is any one among you who would volunteer to stay here instead of me?"

The Chilian laughed and shook his head. "But what can one man do," said he, "to defend all this, if there should be need?"

"Oh, I don't intend to defend it," said the other. "The point is to have somebody here to claim it in case a coaster should touch here. I don't expect to be murdered for the sake of a lot of guano. But I shall keep my two rifles and other arms inside that little fort, and if I should see any signs of rascality I shall jump inside and talk over the guano-bags, and I am a good shot."

The Chilian shrugged his shoulders. "If I stayed here alone," said he, "I should be afraid of nothing but the devil, and I am sure he would come to me, with all his angels. But you are different from me."

"Yes," said Captain Horn, "I don't mind the devil. I have often camped out by myself, and I have not seen him yet."

When Maka heard that the captain intended staying alone, he was greatly disturbed. If the captain had not built the little fort with the guano-bags, he would have begged to be allowed to remain with him, but those defensive works had greatly alarmed him, for they made him believe that the captain feared that some of the Rackbirds might come back. He had had a great deal of talk with the other negroes about those bandits, and he was fully impressed with their capacity for atrocity. It grieved his soul to think that the captain would stay here alone, but the captain was a man who could defend himself against half a dozen Rackbirds, while he knew very well that he would not be a match for half a one. With tears in his eyes, he begged Captain Horn not to stay, for Rackbirds would not steal guano, even if any of them should return.

But his entreaties were of no avail. Captain Horn explained the matter to him, and tried to make him understand that it was as a claimant, more than as a defender of his property, that he remained, and that there was not the smallest reason to suspect any Rackbirds or other source of danger. The negro saw that the captain had made up his mind, and mournfully joined his fellows. In half an hour, however, he came back to the captain and offered to stay with him until the schooner should return. If Captain Horn had known the terrible mental struggle which had preceded this offer, he would have been more grateful to Maka than he had ever yet been to any human being, but he did not know it, and declined the proposition pleasantly but firmly.

"You are wanted on the schooner," said he, "for none of the rest can cook, and you are not wanted here, so you must go with the others; and when you come back with the second load of guano, it will not be long before the ship which I have engaged to take away the guano will touch here, and then we will all go north together."

Maka smiled, and tried to be satisfied. He and the other negroes had been greatly grieved that the captain had not seen fit to go north from Callao, and take them with him. Their one desire was to get away from this region, so full of horrors to them, as soon as possible. But they had come to the conclusion that, as the captain had lost his ship, he must be poor, and that it was necessary for him to make a little money before he returned to the land of his home.

Fortune was on the captain's side the next day, for the wind was favorable, and the captain of the schooner was very willing to start. If that crew, with nothing to do, had been compelled by adverse weather to remain in that little cove for a day or more, it might have been very difficult indeed for Captain Horn to prevent them from wandering into the surrounding country, and what might have happened had they chanced to wander into the cave made the captain shudder to conjecture.

He had carefully considered this danger, and on the voyage he had made several plans by which he could keep the men at work, in case they were obliged to remain in the cove after the cargo had been landed. Happily, however, none of these schemes was necessary, and the next day, with a western wind, and at the beginning of the ebb-tide, the schooner sailed away for another island where Captain Horn had purchased guano, leaving him alone upon the sandy beach, apparently as calm and cool as usual, but actually filled with turbulent delight at seeing them depart.

CHAPTER XXI
IN THE GATES

When the topmasts of the Chilian schooner had disappeared below the horizon line, with no reason to suppose that the schooner would put back again, Captain Horn started for the caves. Had he obeyed his instincts, he would have begun to stroll along the beach as soon as the vessel had weighed anchor. But even now, as he hurried on, he walked prudently, keeping close to the water, so that the surf might wash out his footsteps as fast as he made them. He climbed over the two ridges to the north of Rackbirds' Cove, and then made his way along the stretch of sand which extended to the spot where the party had landed when he first reached this coast. He stopped and looked about him, and then, in fancy, he saw Edna standing upon the beach, her face pale, her eyes large and supernaturally dark, and behind her Mrs. Cliff and the boy and the two negroes. Not until this moment had he felt that he was alone. But now there came a great desire to speak and be spoken to, and yet that very morning he had spoken and listened as much as had suited him.

As he walked up the rising ground toward the caves, that ground he had traversed so often when this place had been, to all intents and purposes, his home, where there had been voices and movement and life, the sense of desertion grew upon him—not only desertion of the place, but of himself. When he had opened his eyes, that morning, his overpowering desire had been that not an hour of daylight should pass before he should be left alone, and yet now his heart sank at the feeling that he was here and no one was with him.

When the captain had approached within a few yards of the great stone face, his brows were slowly knitted.

"This is carelessness," he said to himself. "I did not expect it of them. I told them to leave the utensils, but I did not suppose that they would leave them outside. No matter how much they were hurried in going away, they should have put these things into the caves. A passing Indian might have been afraid to go into that dark hole, but to leave those tin things there is the same as hanging out a sign to show that people lived inside."

Instantly the captain gathered up the tin pan and tin plates, and looked about him to see if there was anything else which should be put out of sight. He did find something else. It was a little, short, black, wooden pipe which was lying on a stone. He picked it up in surprise. Neither Maka nor Cheditafa smoked, and it could not have belonged to the boy.

"Perhaps," thought the captain, "one of the sailors from the *Mary Bartlett* may have left it. Yes, that must have been the case. But sailors do not often leave their pipes behind them, nor should the officer in charge have allowed them to lounge about and smoke. But it must have been one of those sailors who left it here. I am glad I am the one to find these things."

The captain now entered the opening to the caves. Passing along until he reached the room which he had once occupied, there he saw his rough pallet on the ground, drawn close to the door, however.

The captain knew that the rest of his party had gone away in a great hurry, but to his orderly mariner's mind it seemed strange that they should have left things in such disorder.

He could not stop to consider these trifles now, however, and going to the end of the passage, he climbed over the low wall and entered the cave of the lake. When he lighted the lantern he had brought with him, he saw it as he had left it, dry, or even drier than before, for the few pools which had remained after the main body of water had run off had disappeared, probably evaporated. He hurried on toward the mound in the distant recess of the cave. On the way, his foot struck something which rattled, and holding down his lantern to see what it was, he perceived an old tin cup.

"Confound it!" he exclaimed. "This is too careless! Did the boy intend to make a regular trail from the outside entrance to the mound? I suppose he brought that cup here to dip up water, and forgot it. I must take it with me when I go back."

He went on, throwing the light of the lantern on the ground before him, for he had now reached a part of the cave which was entirely dark. Suddenly something on the ground attracted his attention. It was bright—it shone as if it were a little pale flame of a candle. He sprang toward it, he picked it up. It was one of the bars of gold he had seen in the mound.

"Could I have dropped this?" he ejaculated. He slipped the little bar into his pocket, and then, his heart beginning to beat rapidly, he advanced, with his lantern close to the rocky floor. Presently he saw two other pieces of gold, and then, a little farther on, the end of a candle, so small that it could scarcely have been held by the fingers. He picked up this and stared at it. It was a commonplace candle-end, but the sight of it sent a chill through him from head to foot. It must have been dropped by some one who could hold it no longer.

He pressed on, his light still sweeping the floor. He found no more gold nor pieces of candle, but here and there he perceived the ends of burnt wooden matches. Going on, he found more matches, two or three with the heads broken off and unburnt. In a few moments the mound loomed up out of the darkness like a spectral dome, and, looking no more upon the ground, the captain ran toward it. By means of the stony projections he quickly mounted to the top, and there the sight he saw almost made him drop his lantern. The great lid of the mound had been moved and was now awry, leaving about one half of the opening exposed.

In one great gasp the captain's breath seemed to leave him, but he was a man of strong nerves, and quickly recovered himself; but even then he did not lift his lantern so that he could look into the interior of the mound. For a few moments he shut his eyes. He did not dare even to look. But then his courage came back, and holding his lantern over the opening, he gazed down into the mound, and it seemed to his rapid glance that there was as much gold in it as when he last saw it.

The discovery that the treasure was still there had almost as much effect upon the captain as if he had found the mound empty. He grew so faint that he felt he could not maintain his hold upon the top of the mound, and quickly descended, half sliding, to the bottom. There he sat down, his lantern by his side. When his strength came back to him,—and he could not have told any one how long it was before this happened,—the first thing he did was to feel for his box of matches, and finding them safe in his waistcoat pocket, he extinguished the lantern. He must not be discovered, if there should be any one to discover him.

Now the captain began to think as fiercely and rapidly as a man's mind could be made to work. Some one had been there. Some one had taken away gold from that mound—how much or how little, it did not matter. Some one besides himself had had access to the treasure!

His suspicions fell upon Ralph, chiefly because his most earnest desire at that moment was that Ralph might be the offender. If he could have believed that he would have been happy. It must have been that the boy was not willing to go away and leave all that gold, feeling that perhaps he and his sister might never possess any of it, and that just before leaving he had made a hurried visit to the mound. But the more the captain thought of this, the less probable it became. He was almost sure that Ralph could not have lifted that great mass of stone which formed the lid covering the opening of the mound, for it had required all his own strength to do it; and then, if anything of this sort had really happened, the letters he had received from Edna and the boy must have been most carefully written with the intention to deceive him.

The letter from Edna, which in tone and style was a close imitation of his own to her, had been a strictly business communication. It told everything which happened after the arrival of the Mary Bartlett, and gave him no reason to suppose that any one could have had a chance to pillage the mound. Ralph's letter had been even more definite. It was constructed like an official report, and when the captain had read it, he had thought that the boy had probably taken great pride in its preparation. It was as guardian of the treasure mound that Ralph wrote, and his remarks were almost entirely confined to this important trust.

He briefly reported to the captain that, since his departure, no one had been in the recess of the cave where the mound was situated, and he described in detail the plan by which he had established Edna behind the wall in the passage, so as to prevent any of the sailors from the ship from making explorations. He also stated that everything had been left in as high a condition of safety as it was possible to leave it, but that, if his sister had been willing, he would most certainly have remained behind, with the two negroes, until the captain's return.

Much as he wished to think otherwise, Captain Horn could not prevail upon himself to believe that Ralph could have written such a letter after a dishonorable and reckless visit to the mound.

It was possible that one or both of the negroes had discovered the mound, but it was difficult to believe that they would have dared to venture into that awful cavern, even if the vigilance of Edna, Mrs. Cliff, and the boy had given them an opportunity, and Edna had written that the two men had always slept outside the caves, and had had no call to enter them. Furthermore, if Cheditafa had found the treasure, why should he keep it a secret? He would most probably have considered it an original discovery, and would have spoken of it to the others. Why should he be willing that they should all go away and leave so much wealth behind them? The chief danger, in case Cheditafa had found the treasure, was that he would talk about it in Mexico or the United States. But, in spite of the hazards to which such disclosures might expose his fortunes, the captain would have preferred that the black men should have been pilferers than that other men should have been discoverers. But who else could have discovered it? Who could have been there? Who could have gone away?

There was but one reasonable supposition, and that was that one or more of the Rackbirds, who had been away from their camp at the time when their fellow-miscreants were swept away by the flood, had come back, and in searching for their comrades, or some traces of them, had made their way to the caves. It was quite possible, and further it was quite probable, that the man or men who had found that mound might still be here or in the neighborhood. As soon as this idea came into the mind of the captain, he prepared for action. This was a question which must be resolved if he could do it, and without loss of time. Lighting his lantern,—for in that black darkness it was impossible for him to find his way without it, although it might make him a mark for some concealed foe,—the captain quickly made his way out of the lake cavern, and, leaving his lantern near the little wall, he proceeded, with a loaded pistol in his hand, to make an examination of the caves which he and his party had occupied.

He had already looked into the first compartment, but stopping at the pallet which lay almost at the passage of the doorway, he stood and regarded it. Then he stepped over it, and looked around the little room. The pallet of blankets and rugs which Ralph had used was not there. Then the captain stepped into the next room, and, to his surprise, he found this as bare of everything as if it had never been used as a sleeping-apartment. He now hurried back to the first room, and examined the pallet, which, when he had first been looking at it, he had thought to be somewhat different from what it had been when he had used it. He now found that it was composed of all the rugs and blankets which had previously made up the beds of all the party. The captain ground his teeth.

"There can be no doubt of it," he said. "Some one has been here since they left, and has slept in these caves."

At this moment he remembered the innermost cave, the large compartment which was roofless, and which, in his excitement, he had forgotten. Perhaps the man who slept on the pallet was in there at this minute. How reckless he had been! To what danger he had exposed himself! With his pistol cocked, the captain advanced cautiously toward the innermost compartment. Putting his head in at the doorway, he glanced up, down, and around. He called out, "Who's here?" and then he entered, and looked around, and behind each of the massive pieces of rock with which the floor was strewn. No one answered, and he saw no one. But he saw something which made him stare.

On the ground, at one side of the entrance to this compartment, were five or six pieces of rock about a foot high, placed in a small circle so that their tops came near enough together to support a tin kettle which was resting upon them. Under the kettle, in the centre of the rocks, was a pile of burnt leaves and sticks.

"Here he has cooked his meals," said the captain—for the pallet made up of all the others had convinced him that it had been one man who had been here after his party had left. "He stayed long enough to cook his meals and sleep," thought the captain. "I'll look into this provision business." Passing through the other rooms, he went to a deep niche in the wall of the entrance passage where his party had kept their stores, and where Edna had written him they had left provisions enough for the immediate use of himself and the men who should return. Here he found tin cans tumbled about at the bottom of the niche, and every one of them absolutely empty. On a little ledge stood a tin box in which they had kept the matches and candles. The box was open, but there was nothing in it. On the floor near by was a tin biscuit-box, crushed nearly flat, as if some one had stamped upon it.

"He has eaten everything that was left," said the captain, "and he has been starved out. Very likely, too, he got out of water, for, of course, those pools would dry up, and it is not likely he found the stream outside."

Now the captain let down the hammer of his revolver, and put it in his belt. He felt sure that the man was not here. Being out of provisions, he had to go away, but where he had gone to was useless to conjecture. Of another thing the captain was now convinced: the intruder had not been a Rackbird, for, while waiting for the disappearance of the Chilian schooner, he had gone over to the concealed storehouse of the bandits, and had found it just as he had left it on his last visit, with a considerable quantity of stores remaining in it. If the man had known of the Rackbirds' camp and this storehouse, it would not have been necessary for him to consume every crumb and vestige of food which had been left in these caves.

"No," said the captain, "it could not have been a Rackbird, but who he was, and where he has gone, is beyond my comprehension."

CHAPTER XXII
A PACK-MULE

When Captain Horn felt quite sure that it was not Ralph, that it was not Cheditafa, that it was not a Rackbird, who had visited the treasure mound, he stood and reflected. What had happened was a great misfortune,—possibly it was a great danger,—but it was no use standing there thinking about it. His reason could not help him; it had done for him all that it could, and it would be foolish to waste time in looking for the man, for it was plain enough that he had gone away. Of course, he had taken some gold with him, but that did not matter much. The danger was that he or others might come back for more, but this could not be prevented, and it was needless to consider it. The captain had come to this deserted shore for a purpose, and it was his duty, without loss of time, to go to work and carry out that purpose. If in any way he should be interfered with, he would meet that interference as well as he could, but until it came he would go on with his work. Having come to this conclusion, he got over the wall, lighted his lantern, and proceeded to the mound.

On his way he passed the tin cup, which he had forgotten to pick up, but now he merely kicked it out of the way. "If the man comes back," he thought, "he knows the way. There is no need of concealing anything."

When the captain had reached the top of the mound, he moved the stone lid so that the aperture was entirely uncovered. Then he looked down upon the mass of dull yellow bars. He could not perceive any apparent diminution of their numbers.

"He must have filled his pockets," the captain thought, "and so full that some of them dropped out. Well, let him go, and if he ventures back here, we shall have it out between us. In the meantime, I will do what I can."

The captain now took from the pocket of his jacket two small canvas bags, which he had had made for this purpose, and proceeded to fill one of them with the gold bars, lifting the bag, every now and then, to try its weight. When he thought it heavy enough, he tied up the end very firmly, and then packed the other, as nearly as possible, to the same extent. Then he got down, and laying one of the bags over each shoulder, he walked about to see if he could easily bear their weight.

"That is about right," he said to himself. "I will count them when I take them out." Then, putting them down, he went up for his lantern. He was about to close the lid of the mound, but he reflected that this would be of no use. It had been open nobody knew how long, and might as well remain so. He was coming back as often as he could, and it would be a tax upon his strength to lift that heavy lid every time. So he left the treasures of the Incas open to the air under the black roof of the cavern, and, with his lantern in his hand and a bag of gold on each shoulder, he left the cave of the lake, and then, concealing his lantern, he walked down to the sea.

Before he reached it he had thoroughly scanned the ocean, but not a sign of a ship could be seen. Walking along the sands, and keeping, as before, close to the curving line of water thrown up by the surf, he said to himself:

"I must have my eyes and ears open, but I am not going to be nervous or fidgety. I came here to be a pack-mule, and I intend to be a pack-mule until something stops me, and if that something is one man, he can look out for himself."

The bags were heavy and their contents were rough and galling to the shoulders, but the captain was strong and his muscles were tough, and as he walked he planned a pair of cushions which he would wear under his golden epaulets in his future marches.

When the captain had covered the two miles of beach and climbed the two rocky ridges, and reached his tent, it was long after noon, and throwing his two bags on the ground and covering them with a blanket, he proceeded to prepare his dinner. He laid out a complete working-plan, and one of the rules he had made was that, if possible, nothing should interfere with his regular meals and hours of sleep. The work he had set for himself was arduous in the extreme, and calculated to tax his energies to the utmost, and he must take very good care of his health and strength. In thinking over the matter, he had feared that the greed of gold might possess him, and that, in his anxiety to carry away as much as he could, he might break down, and everything be lost.

Even now he found himself calculating how much gold he had brought away in the two bags, and what would be its value in coined money, multiplying and estimating with his food untouched and his eyes fixed on the distant sea. Suddenly he clenched his fist and struck it on his knee.

"I must stop this," he said. "I shall be upset if I don't. I will not count the bars in those bags. I will not make any more estimates. A rough guess now and then I cannot help, but what I have to do is to bring away all the gold I can. It will be time enough to find out what it is worth when it is safe somewhere in North America."

When the captain had finished his meal, he went to his tent, and opened one of the trunks which he had brought with him, and which were supposed to contain the clothes and personal effects he had bought in Lima. This trunk, however, was entirely filled with rolls of cheap cotton cloth, coarse and strong, but not heavy. With a pair of shears he proceeded to cut from one of these some pieces, rather more than a foot square. Then, taking from his canvas bags as many of the gold bars as he thought would weigh twelve or fifteen pounds, trying not to count them as he did so, he made a little package of them, tying the corners of the cloth together with a strong cord. When five of these bundles had been prepared, his gold was exhausted, and then he carried the small bundles out to the guano-bags.

He had bought his guano in bulk, and it had been put into bags under his own supervision, for it was only in bags that the ship which was to take it north would receive it. The bags were new and good, and Captain Horn believed that each of them could be made twelve or fifteen pounds heavier without attracting the attention of those who might have to lift them, for they were very heavy as it was.

He now opened a bag of guano, and thrusting a stick down into its contents, he twisted it about until he had made a cavity which enabled him, with a little trouble, to thrust one of the packages of gold down into the centre of the bag. Then he pressed the guano down firmly, and sewed up the bag again, being provided with needles and an abundance of necessary cord. When this was done, the bag containing the gold did not differ in appearance from the others, and the captain again assured himself that the additional weight would not be noticed by a common stevedore, especially if all the bags were about the same weight. At this thought he stopped work and looked out toward the sea, his mind involuntarily leaping out toward calculations based upon the happy chance of his being able to load all the bags; but he checked himself. "Stop that," he said. "Go to work!"

Five guano-bags were packed, each with its bundle of gold, but the task was a disagreeable, almost a distressing, one, for the strong ammoniacal odor sometimes almost overpowered the captain, who had a great dislike for such smells. But he never drew back, except now and then to turn his head and take a breath of purer air. He was trying to make his fortune, and when men are doing that, their likes and dislikes must stand aside.

When this task was finished, the captain took up his two empty canvas bags and went back to the caves, returning late in the afternoon, loaded rather more heavily than before. From the experiences of the morning, he believed that, with some folded pieces of cloth on each shoulder, he could carry without discomfort a greater weight than his first ones. The gold he now brought was made up into six bundles, and then the captain rested from his labors. He felt that he could do a much better day's work than this, but this day had been very much broken up, and he was still somewhat awkward.

Day after day Captain Horn labored at his new occupation, and a toilsome occupation it was, which no one who did not possess great powers of endurance, and great hopes from the results of his work, could have undergone. In about a month the schooner was to be expected with another load of guano, and the captain felt that he must, if possible, finish his task before she came back. In a few days he found that, by practice and improvements in his system of work, he was able to make four trips a day between the cove of the Rackbirds and the caves. He rose very early in the morning, and made two trips before dinner. Sometimes he thought he might do more, but he restrained himself. It would not do for him to get back too tired to sleep.

During this time in which his body was so actively employed, his mind was almost as active, and went out on all sorts of excursions, some of them beneficial and some of them otherwise. Sometimes the thought came to him, as he plodded along bearing his heavy bags, that he was no more than a common thief, carrying away treasures which did not belong to him. Then, of course, he began to reason away these uncomfortable reflections. If this treasure did not belong to him, to whom did it belong? Certainly not to the descendants of those Spaniards from whom the original owners had striven so hard to conceal it. If the spirits of the Incas could speak, they would certainly declare in his favor over that of the children of the men who, in blood and torture, had obliterated them and their institutions. Sometimes such arguments entirely satisfied the captain; but if they did not entirely satisfy him, he put the whole matter aside, to be decided upon after he should safely reach the United States with such treasure as he might be able to take with him.

"Then," he thought, "we can do what we think is right. I shall listen to all that may be said by our party, and shall act justly. But what I do not take away with me has no chance whatever of ever falling into the proper hands."

But no matter how he might terminate such reflections, the captain always blamed himself for allowing his mind to occupy itself with them. He had fully decided that this treasure belonged to him, and there was no real reason for his thinking of such things, except that he had no one to talk to, and in such cases a man's thoughts are apt to run wild.

Often and often he wondered what the others were thinking about this affair, and whether or not they would all be able to keep the secret until he returned. He was somewhat afraid of Mrs. Cliff. He believed her to be an honorable woman who would not break her word, but still he did not know all her ideas in regard to her duty. She might think there was some one to whom she ought to confide what had happened, and what was expected to happen, and if she should do this, there was no reason why he should not, some day, descry a ship in the offing with treasure-hunters on board.

Ralph gave him no concern at all, except that he was young, and the captain could foretell the weather much better than the probable actions of a youth.

But these passing anxieties never amounted to suspicions. It was far better to believe in Mrs. Cliff and Ralph, and he would do it; and every time he thought of the two, he determined to believe in them. As to Edna, there was no question about believing in her. He did so without consideration for or against belief.

The captain did not like his solitary life. How happy he would have been if they could all have remained here; if the guano could have been brought without the crew of the schooner knowing that there were people in the caves; if the negroes could have carried the bags of gold; if every night, after having superintended their labors, he could have gone back to the caves, which, with the comforts he could have brought from Lima, would have made a very habitable home; if—But these were reflections which were always doomed to banishment as soon as the captain became aware of the enthralment of their charm, and sturdily onward, endeavoring to fix his mind upon some better sailor's knot with which to tie up his bundles, or to plant his feet where his tracks would soon be obliterated by the incoming waves, the strong man trudged, bearing bravely the burden of his golden hopes.

CHAPTER XXIII
HIS PRESENT SHARE

With four trips a day from the caves to the cove, taking time for rests, for regular meals, and for sleep, and not working on Sundays,—for he kept a diary and an account of days,—the captain succeeded in a little over three weeks in loading his bags of guano, each with a package of golden bars, some of which must have weighed as much as fifteen pounds.

When this work had been accomplished, he began to consider the return of the schooner. But he had no reason to expect her yet, and he determined to continue his work. Each day he brought eight canvas bags of gold from the caves, and making them up into small bundles, he buried them in the sand under his tent. When a full month had elapsed since the departure of the schooner, he began to be very prudent, keeping a careful lookout seaward, as he walked the beach, and never entering the caves without mounting a high point of the rocks and thoroughly scanning the ocean. If, when bearing his burden of gold, he should have seen a sail, he would have instantly stopped and buried his bags in the sand, wherever he might be.

Day after day passed, and larger and larger grew the treasure stored in the sands under the tent, but no sail appeared. Sometimes the captain could not prevent evil fancies coming to him. What if the ship should never come back? What if no vessel should touch here for a year or two? And why should a vessel ever touch? When the provisions he had brought and those left in the Rackbirds' storehouse had been exhausted, what could he do but lie down here and perish?—another victim added to the millions who had already perished from the thirst of gold. He thought of his little party in San Francisco. They surely would send in search of him, if he did not appear in a reasonable time. But he felt this hope was a vain one. In a letter to Edna, written from Lima, he had told her she must not expect to hear from him for a long time, for, while he was doing the work he contemplated, it would be impossible for him to communicate with her.

She would have no reason to suppose that he would start on such an expedition without making due arrangements for safety and support, and so would hesitate long before she would commission a vessel to touch at this point in search of him. If he should starve here, he would die months before any reasonable person, who knew as much of his affairs as did Edna, would think the time had arrived to send a relief expedition for him.

But he did not starve. Ten days overdue, at last the Chilian schooner appeared and anchored in the cove. She had now no white men on board but the captain and his mate, for the negroes had improved so much in seamanship that the economical captain had dispensed with his Chilian crew.

Captain Horn was delighted to be able to speak again to a fellow-being, and it pleased him far better to see Maka than any of the others.

"You no eat 'nough, cap'n," said the black man, as he anxiously scanned the countenance of Captain Horn, which, although the captain was in better physical condition than perhaps he had ever been in his life, was thinner than when Maka had seen it last. "When I cook for you, you not so long face," the negro continued. "Didn't us leave you 'nough to eat? Did you eat 'em raw?"

The captain laughed. "I have had plenty to eat," he said, "and I never felt better. If I had not taken exercise, you would have found me as fat as a porpoise."

The interview with the Chilian captain was not so cordial, for Captain Horn found that the Chilian had not brought him a full cargo of bags of guano, and, by searching questions, he discovered that this was due entirely to unnecessary delay in beginning to load the vessel. The Chilian declared he would have taken on board all the guano which Captain Horn had purchased at the smaller island, had he not begun to fear that Captain Horn would suffer if he did not soon return to him, and when he thought it was not safe to wait any longer, he had sailed with a partial cargo.

Captain Horn was very angry, for every bag of guano properly packed with gold bars meant, at a rough estimate, between two and three thousand dollars if it safely reached a gold-market, and now he found himself with at least one hundred bags less than he had expected to pack. There was no time to repair this loss, for the English vessel, the *Finland*, from Callao to Acapulco, which the captain had engaged to stop at this point on her next voyage northward, might be expected in two or three weeks, certainly sooner than the Chilian could get back to the guano island and return. In fact, there was barely time for that vessel to reach Callao before the departure of the *Finland*, on board of which the captain wished his negroes to be placed, that they might go home with him.

"If I had any men to work my vessel," said the Chilian, who had grown surly in consequence of the fault-finding, "I'd leave your negroes here, and cut loose from the whole business. I've had enough of it."

"That serves you right for discharging your own men in order that you might work your vessel with mine," said Captain Horn. He had intended to insist that the negroes should ship again with the Chilian, but he knew that it would be more difficult to find reasons for this than on the previous voyage, and he was really more than glad to find that the matter had thus arranged itself.

Talking with Captain Horn, the Chilian mate, who had had no responsibility in this affair, and who was, consequently, not out of humor, proposed that he should go back with them, and take the English vessel at Callao.

"I can't risk it," said Captain Horn. "If your schooner should meet with head winds or any other bad luck, and the *Finland* should leave before I got there, there would be a pretty kettle of fish, and if she touched here and found no one in charge, I don't believe she would take away a bag."

"Do you think they will be sure to touch here?" asked the mate. "Have they got the latitude and longitude? It didn't seem so bad before to leave you behind, because we were coming back, but now it strikes me it is rather a risky piece of business for you."

"No," said Captain Horn. "I am acquainted with the skipper of the *Finland*, and I left a letter for him telling him exactly how the matter stood, and he knows that I trust him to pick me up. I do not suppose he will expect to find me here all alone, but if he gives me the slip, I would be just as likely to starve to death if I had some men with me as if I were alone. The *Finland* will stop—I am sure of that."

With every reason for the schooner's reaching Callao as soon as possible, and very little reason, considering the uncordial relations of the two captains, for remaining in the cove, the Chilian set sail the morning after he had discharged his unsavory cargo. Maka had begged harder than before to be allowed to remain with Captain Horn, but the latter had made him understand, as well as he could, the absolute necessity of the schooner reaching Callao in good time, and the absolute impossibility of any vessel doing anything in good time without a cook. Therefore, after a personal inspection of the stores left behind, both in the tent and in the Rackbirds' storehouse, which latter place he visited with great secrecy, Maka, with a sad heart, was obliged to leave the only real friend he had on earth.

When, early the next morning, Captain Horn began to pack the newly arrived bags with the bundles of gold which he had buried in the sand, he found that the bags were not at all in the condition of those the filling of which he had supervised himself. Some of these were more heavily filled than others, and many were badly fastened up. This, of course, necessitated a good deal of extra work, but the captain sadly thought that probably he would have more time than he needed to do all that was necessary to get this second cargo into fair condition for transportation. He had checked off his little bundles as he had buried them, and there were nearly enough to fill all the bags. In fact, he had to make but three more trips in order to finish the business.

When the work was done, and everything was ready for the arrival of the *Finland*, the captain felt that he had good reason to curse the conscienceless Chilian whose laziness or carelessness had not only caused him the loss of perhaps a quarter of a million of dollars, but had given him days—how many he could not know—with nothing to do; and which of these two evils might prove the worse, the captain could not readily determine.

As Captain Horn walked up and down the long double rows of bags which contained what he hoped would become his fortune, he could not prevent a feeling of resentful disappointment when he thought of the small proportion borne by the gold in these bags to the treasure yet remaining in the mound. On his last visit to the mound he had carefully examined its interior, and although, of course, there was a great diminution in its contents, there was no reason to believe that the cavity of the mound did not extend downward to the floor of the cave, and that it remained packed with gold bars to the depth of several feet. It seemed silly, crazy, in fact, almost wicked, for him to sail away in the *Finland* and leave all that gold behind, and yet, how could he possibly take away any more of it?

He had with him a trunk nearly empty, in which he might pack some blankets and other stuff with some bags of gold stowed away between them, but more than fifty pounds added to the weight of the trunk and its contents would make it suspiciously heavy, and what was fifty pounds out of that vast mass? But although he puzzled his brains for the greater part of a day, trying to devise some method by which he could take away more gold without exciting the suspicions of the people on board the English vessel, there was no plan that entered his mind that did not contain elements of danger, and the danger was an appalling one. If the crew of the *Finland*, or the crew of any other vessel, should, on this desert coast, get scent of a treasure mound of gold ingots, he might as well attempt to reason with wild beasts as to try to make them understand that that treasure belonged to him. If he could get away with any of it, or even with his life, he ought to be thankful.

The captain was a man who, since he had come to an age of maturity, had been in the habit of turning his mind this way and that as he would turn the helm of his vessel, and of holding it to the course he had determined upon, no matter how strong the wind or wave, how dense the fog, or how black the night. But never had he stood to his helm as he now stood to a resolve.

"I will bring away a couple of bags," said he, "to put in my trunk, and then, I swear to myself, I will not think another minute about carrying away any more of that gold than what is packed in these guano-bags. If I can ever come back, I will come back, but what I have to do now is to get away with what I have already taken out of the mound, and also to get away with sound reason and steady nerves."

The next day there was not a sail on the far horizon, and the captain brought away two bags of gold. These, with some clothes, he packed in his empty trunk.

"Now," said he, "this is my present share. If I permit myself to think of taking another bar, I shall be committing a crime."

CHAPTER XXIV
HIS FORTUNE UNDER HIS FEET

Notwithstanding the fact that the captain had, for the present, closed his account with the treasure in the lake cave, and had determined not to give another thought to further drafts upon it, he could not prevent all sorts of vague and fragmentary plans for getting more of the gold from thrusting themselves upon him; but his hand was strong upon the tiller of his mind, and his course did not change a point. He now began to consider in what condition he should leave the caves. Once he thought he would go there and take away everything which might indicate that the caves had been inhabited, but this notion he discarded.

"There are a good many people," he thought, "who know that we lived there, and if that man who was there afterwards should come back, I would prefer that he should not notice any changes, unless, indeed," —and his eyes glistened as a thought darted into his mind,—"unless, indeed, he should find a lake where he left a dry cave. Good! I'll try it."

With his hands in his pockets, the captain stood a few moments and thought, and then he went to work. From the useless little vessel which, had belonged to the Rackbirds he gathered some bits of old rope, and having cut these into short pieces, he proceeded to pick them into what sailors call oakum.

Early the next morning, his two canvas bags filled with this, he started for the caves. When he reached the top of the mound, and was just about to hold his lantern so as to take a final glance into its interior, he suddenly turned away his head and shut his eyes.

"No," he said. "If I do that, it is ten to one I'll jump inside, and what might happen next nobody knows."

He put the lantern aside, lifted the great lid into its place, and then, with a hammer and a little chisel which he had brought with him from the tools which had been used for the building of the pier, he packed the crevices about the lid with oakum. With a mariner's skill he worked, and when his job was finished, it would have been difficult for a drop of water to have found its way into the dome, no matter if it rose high above it.

It was like leaving behind a kingdom and a throne, the command of armies and vast navies, the domination of power, of human happenings; but he came away.

When he reached the portion of the cave near the great gap which opened to the sky opposite the entrance to the outer caves, the captain walked across the dry floor to the place where was situated the outlet through which the waters of the lake had poured out into the Rackbirds' valley.

The machine which controlled this outlet was situated under the overhanging ledge of the cave, and was in darkness, so that the captain was obliged to use his lantern. He soon found the great lever which he had clutched when he had swum to the rescue of Ralph, and which had gone down with him and so opened the valve and permitted egress of the water, and which now lay with its ten feet or more of length horizontally near the ground. Near by was the great pipe, with its circular blackness leading into the depths below.

"That stream outside," said the captain, "must run in here somewhere, although I cannot see nor hear it, and it must be stopped off by this valve or another one connected with it, so that if I can get this lever up again, I should shut it off from the stream outside and turn it in here. Then, if that fellow comes back, he will have to swim to the mound, and run a good chance of getting drowned if he does it, and if anybody else comes here, I think it will be as safe as the ancient Peruvians once made it."

With this he took hold of the great lever and attempted to raise it. But he found the operation a very difficult one. The massive bar was of metal, but probably not iron, and although it was not likely that it had rusted, it was very hard to move in its socket. The captain's weight had brought it down easily, but this weight could not now be applied, and he could only attempt to lift it.

When it had first been raised, it was likely that a dozen slaves had seized it and forced it into an upright position. The captain pushed up bravely, and, a few inches at a time, he elevated the end of the great lever. Frequently he stopped to rest, and it was over an hour before the bar stood up as it had been when first he felt it under the water.

When this was done, he went into the other caves, looked about to see that everything was in the condition in which he had found it, and that he had left nothing behind him during his many visits. When he was satisfied on these points, he went back to the lake cave to see if any water had run in. He found everything as dry as when he had left it, nor could he hear any sound of running or dripping water. Considering the matter, however, he concluded that there might be some sort of an outside reservoir which must probably fill up before the water ran into the cave, and so he came away.

"I will give it time," he thought, "and come back to-morrow to see if it is flooded."

That night, as he lay on his little pallet, looking through the open front of his tent at the utter darkness of the night, the idea struck him that it was strange that he was not afraid to stay here alone. He was a brave man,—he knew that very well,—and yet it seemed odd to him that, under the circumstances, he should have so little fear. But his reason soon gave him a good answer. He had known times when he had been very much afraid, and among these stood preeminent the time when he had expected an attack from the Rackbirds. But then his fear was for others. When he was by himself it was a different matter. It was not often that he did not feel able to take care of his own safety. If there were any danger now, it was in the daytime, when some stray Rackbirds might come back, or the pilferer of the mound might return with companions. But if any such came, he had his little fort, two pistols, and a repeating rifle. At night he felt absolutely safe. There was no danger that could come by land or sea through the blackness of the night.

Suddenly he sat up. His forehead was moist with perspiration. A shiver ran through him, not of cold, but of fear. Never in his life had he been so thoroughly frightened; never before had he felt his hands and legs tremble. Involuntarily he rose and stood up in the tent. He was terrified, not by anything real, but by the thought of what might happen if that lake cave should fill up with water, and if the ancient valves, perhaps weakened by his moving them backward and forward, should give way under the great pressure, and, for a second time, a torrent of water should come pouring down the Rackbirds' ravine!

As the captain trembled with fear, it was not for himself, for he could listen for the sound of the rushing waters, and could dash away to the higher ground behind him; but it was for his treasure-bags, his fortune, his future! His soul quaked. His first impulse was to rush out and carry every bag to higher ground. But this idea was absurd. The night was too dark, and the bags too heavy and too many. Then he thought of hurrying away to the caves to see if the lake had risen high enough to be dangerous. But what could he do if it had? In his excitement, he could not stand still and do nothing. He took hold of one end of his trunk and pulled it out of his tent, and, stumbling and floundering over the inequalities of the ground, he at last got it to a place which he supposed would be out of reach of a sudden flood, and the difficulties of this little piece of work assured him of the utter futility of attempting to move the bags in the darkness. He had a lantern, but that would be of little service on such a night and for such a work.

He went back into his tent, and tried to prevail upon himself that he ought to go to sleep—that it was ridiculous to beset himself with imaginary dangers, and to suffer from them as much as if they had been real ones. But such reasoning was vain, and he sat up or walked about near his tent all night, listening and listening, and trying to think of the best thing to do if he should hear a coming flood.

As soon as it was light, he hurried to the caves, and when he reached the old bed of the lake, he found there was not a drop of water in it.

"The thing doesn't work!" he cried joyfully. "Fool that I am, I might have known that although a man might open a valve two or three centuries old, he should not expect to shut it up again. I suppose I smashed it utterly."

His revulsion of feeling was so great that he began to laugh at his own absurdity, and then he laughed at his merriment.

"If any one should see me now," he thought, "they would surely think I had gone crazy over my wealth. Well, there is no danger from a flood, but, to make all things more than safe, I will pull down this handle, if it will come. Anyway, I do not want it seen."

The great bar came down much easier than it had gone up, moving, in fact, the captain thought, as if some of its detachments were broken, and when it was down as far as it would go, he came away.

"Now," said he, "I have done with this cave for this trip. If possible, I shall think of it no more."

When he was getting some water from the stream to make some coffee for his breakfast, he stopped and clenched his fist. "I am more of a fool than I thought I was," he said. "This solitary business is not good for me. If I had thought last night of coming here to see if this little stream were still running, and kept its height, I need not have troubled myself about the lake in the cave. Of course, if the water were running into the caves, it would not be running here until the lake had filled. And, besides, it would take days for that great lake to fill. Well, I am glad that nobody but myself knows what an idiot I have been."

When he had finished his breakfast, Captain Horn went to work. There was to be no more thinking, no more plans, no more fanciful anxieties, no more hopes of doing something better than he had done. Work he would, and when one thing was done, he would find another. The first thing he set about was the improvement of the pier which had been built for the landing of the guano. There was a good deal of timber left unused, and he drove down new piles, nailed on new planking, and extended the little pier considerably farther into the waters of the cove. When this was done, he went to work on the lighter, which was leaky, and bailed it out, and calked the seams, taking plenty of time, and doing his work in the most thorough manner. He determined that after this was done, and he could find nothing better to do, he would split up the little vessel which the Rackbirds had left rudderless, mastless, and useless, and make kindling-wood of it.

But this was not necessary. He had barely finished his work on the lighter, when, one evening, he saw against the sun-lighted sky the topmasts of a vessel, and the next morning the *Finland* lay anchored off the cove, and two boats came ashore, out of one of which Maka was the first to jump.

In five hours the guano had been transferred to the ship, and, twenty minutes later, the *Finland*, with Captain Horn on board, had set sail for Acapulco. The captain might have been better pleased if his destination had been San Francisco, but, after all, it is doubtful if there could have been a man who was better pleased. He walked the deck of a good ship with a fellow-mariner with whom he could talk as much as he pleased, and under his feet were the bags containing the thousands of little bars for which he had worked so hard.

CHAPTER XXV
AT THE PALMETTO HOTEL

For about four months the persons who made up what might be considered as
Captain Horn's adopted family had resided in the Palmetto Hotel, in San Francisco. At the time we look upon them, however, Mrs. Cliff was not with them, having left San Francisco some weeks previously.

Edna was now a very different being from the young woman she had been. Her face was smoother and fuller, and her eyes seemed to have gained a richer brown. The dark masses of her hair appeared to have wonderfully grown and thickened, but this was due to the loose fashion in which it was coiled upon her head, and it would have been impossible for any one who had known her before not to perceive that she was greatly changed. The lines upon her forehead, which had come, not from age, but from earnest purpose and necessity of action, together with a certain intensity of expression which would naturally come to a young woman who had to make her way in the world, not only for herself, but for her young brother, and a seriousness born of some doubts, some anxieties, and some ambiguous hopes, had all entirely disappeared as if they had been morning mists rolling away from a summer landscape. Under the rays of a sun of fortune, shining, indeed, but mildly, she had ripened into a physical beauty which was her own by right of birth, but of which a few more years of struggling responsibility would have forever deprived her.

After the receipt of her second remittance, Edna and her party had taken the best apartments in the hotel. The captain had requested this, for he did not know how long they might remain there, and he wanted them to have every comfort. He had sent them as much money as he could spare from the sale, in Lima, of the gold he had carried with him when he first left the caves, but his expenses in hiring ships and buying guano were heavy. Edna, however, had received frequent remittances while the captain was at the Rackbirds' cove, through an agent in San Francisco. These, she supposed, came from further sales of gold, but, in fact, they had come from the sale of investments which the captain had made in the course of his fairly successful maritime career. In his last letter from Lima he had urged them all to live well on what he sent them, considering it as their share of the first division of the treasure in the mound. If his intended projects should succeed, the fortunes of all of them would be reconstructed upon a new basis as solid and as grand as any of them had ever had reason to hope for. But if he should fail, they, the party in San Francisco, would be as well off, or, perhaps, better circumstanced than when they had started for Valparaiso. He did not mention the fact that he himself would be poorer, for he had lost the *Castor*, in which he was part-owner, and had invested nearly all his share of the proceeds of the sale of the gold in ship hire, guano purchases, and other necessary expenses.

Edna was waiting in San Francisco to know what would be the next scene in the new drama of her life. Captain Horn had written before he sailed from Lima in the Chilian schooner for the guano islands and the Rackbirds' cove, and he had, to some extent, described his plans for carrying away treasure from the mound; but since that she had not heard from him until about ten days before, when he wrote from Acapulco, where he had arrived in safety with his bags of guano and their auriferous enrichments. He had written in high spirits, and had sent her a draft on San Francisco so large in amount that it had fairly startled her, for he wrote that he had merely disposed of some of the gold he had brought in his baggage, and had not yet done anything with that contained in the guano-bags. He had hired a storehouse, as if he were going regularly into business, and from which he would dispose of his stock of guano after he had restored it to its original condition. To do all this, and to convert the gold into negotiable bank deposits or money, would require time, prudence, and even diplomacy. He had already sold in the City of Mexico as much of the gold from his trunk as he could offer without giving rise to too many questions, and if he had not been known as a California trader, he might have found some difficulties even in that comparatively small transaction.

The captain had written that to do all he had to do he would be obliged to remain in Acapulco or the City of Mexico—how long he could not tell, for much of the treasure might have to be shipped to the United States, and his plans for all this business were not yet arranged.

Before this letter had been received, Mrs. Cliff had believed it to be undesirable to remain longer in San Francisco, and had gone to her home in a little town in Maine. With Edna and Ralph, she had waited and waited and waited, but at last had decided that Captain Horn was dead. In her mind, she had allowed him all the time that she thought was necessary to go to the caves, get gold, and come to San Francisco, and as that time had long elapsed, she had finally given him up as lost. She knew the captain was a brave man and an able sailor, but the adventure he had undertaken was strange and full of unknown perils, and if it should so happen that she should hear that he had gone to the bottom in a small boat overloaded with gold, she would not have been at all surprised.

Of course, she said nothing of these suspicions to Edna or Ralph, nor did she intend ever to mention them to any one. If Edna, who in so strange a way had been made a wife, should, in some manner perhaps equally extraordinary, be made a widow, she would come back to her, she would do everything she could to comfort her; but now she did not seem to be needed in San Francisco, and her New England home called to her through the many voices of her friends. As to the business which had taken Mrs. Cliff to South America, that must now be postponed, but it could not but be a satisfaction to her that she was going back with perhaps as much money as she would have had if her affairs in Valparaiso had been satisfactorily settled.

Edna and Ralph had come to be looked upon at the Palmetto Hotel as persons of distinction. They lived quietly, but they lived well, and their payments were always prompt. They were the wife and brother-in-law of Captain Philip Horn, who was known to be a successful man, and who might be a rich one. But what seemed more than anything else to distinguish them from the ordinary hotel guests was the fact that they were attended by two personal servants, who, although, of course, they could not be slaves, seemed to be bound to them as if they had been born into their service.

Cheditafa, in a highly respectable suit of clothes which might have been a cross between the habiliments of a Methodist minister and those of a butler, was a person of imposing aspect. Mrs. Cliff had insisted, when his new clothes were ordered, that there should be something in them which should indicate the clergyman, for the time might come when it would be necessary that he should be known in this character; and the butler element was added because it would harmonize in a degree with his duties as Edna's private attendant. The old negro, with his sober face, and woolly hair slightly touched with gray, was fully aware of the importance of his position as body-servant to Mrs. Horn, but his sense of the responsibility of that position far exceeded any other sentiments of which his mind was capable. Perhaps it was the fact that he had made Edna Mrs. Horn which gave him the feeling that he must never cease to watch over her and to serve her in every possible way. Had the hotel taken fire, he would have rushed through the flames to save her. Had robbers attacked her, they must have taken his life before they took her purse. When she drove out in the city or suburbs, he always sat by the side of the driver, and when she walked in the streets, he followed her at a respectful distance.

Proud as he was of the fact that he had been the officiating clergyman at the wedding of Captain Horn and this grand lady, he had never mentioned the matter to any one, for many times, and particularly just before she left San Francisco, Mrs. Cliff had told him, in her most impressive manner, that if he informed any one that he had married Captain Horn and Miss Markham, great trouble would come of it. What sort of trouble, it was not necessary to explain to him, but she was very earnest in assuring him that the marriage of a Christian by a heathen was something which was looked upon with great disfavor in this country, and unless Cheditafa could prove that he had a perfect right to perform the ceremony, it might be bad for him. When Captain Horn had settled his business affairs and should come back, everything would be made all right, and nobody need feel any more fear, but until then he must not speak of what he had done.

If Captain Horn should never come back, Mrs. Cliff thought that Edna would then be truly his widow, and his letters would prove it, but that she was really his wife until the two had marched off together to a regular clergyman, the good lady could not entirely admit. Her position was not logical, but she rested herself firmly upon it.

The other negro, Mok, could speak no more English than when we first met him, but he could understand some things which were said to him, and was very quick, indeed, to catch the meanings of signs, motions, and expressions of countenance. At first Edna did not know what to do with this negro, but Ralph solved the question by taking him as a valet, and day by day he became more useful to the youth, who often declared that he did not know how he used to get along without a valet. Mok was very fond of fine clothes, and Ralph liked to see him smartly dressed, and he frequently appeared of more importance than Cheditafa. He was devoted to his young master, and was so willing to serve him that Ralph often found great difficulty in finding him something to do.

Edna and Ralph had a private table, at which Cheditafa and Mok assisted in waiting, and Mrs. Cliff had taught both of them how to dust and keep rooms in order. Sometimes Ralph sent Mok to a circulating library. Having once been shown the place, and made to understand that he must deliver there the piece of paper and the books to be returned, he attended to the business as intelligently as if he had been a trained dog, and brought back the new books with a pride as great as if he had selected them. The fact that Mok was an absolute foreigner, having no knowledge whatever of English, and that he was possessed of an extraordinary activity, which enabled him, if the gate of the back yard of the hotel happened to be locked, to go over the eight-foot fence with the agility of a monkey, had a great effect in protecting him from impositions by other servants. When a black negro cannot speak English, but can bound like an india-rubber ball, it may not be safe to trifle with him. As for trifling with Cheditafa, no one would think of such a thing; his grave and reverend aspect was his most effectual protection.

As to Ralph, he had altered in appearance almost as much as his sister. His apparel no longer indicated the boy, and as he was tall and large for his years, the fashionable suit he wore, his gay scarf with its sparkling pin, and his brightly polished boots, did not appear out of place upon him. But Edna often declared that she had thought him a great deal better-looking in the scanty, well-worn, but more graceful garments in which he had disported himself on the sands of Peru.

CHAPTER XXVI
THE CAPTAIN'S LETTER

On a sofa in her well-furnished parlor reclined Edna, and on a table near by lay several sheets of closely written letter-paper. She had been reading, and now she was thinking—thinking very intently, which in these days was an unusual occupation with her. During her residence in San Francisco she had lived quietly but cheerfully. She had supplied herself abundantly with books, she had visited theatres and concerts, she had driven around the city, she had taken water excursions, she had visited interesting places in the neighborhood, and she had wandered among the shops, purchasing, in moderation, things that pleased her. For company she had relied chiefly on her own little party, although there had been calls from persons who knew Captain Horn. Some of these people were interesting, and some were not, but they all went away thinking that the captain was a wonderfully fortunate man.

One thing which used to be a pleasure to Edna she refrained from altogether, and that was the making of plans. She had put her past life entirely behind her. She was beginning a new existence—what sort of an existence she could not tell, but she was now living with the determinate purpose of getting the greatest good out of her life, whatever it might be.

Already she had had much, but in every respect her good fortunes were but preliminary to something else. Her marriage was but the raising of the curtain—the play had not yet begun. The money she was spending was but an earnest of something more expected. Her newly developed physical beauty, which she could not fail to appreciate, would fade away again, did it not continue to be nourished by that which gave it birth. But what she had, she had, and that she would enjoy. When Captain Horn should return, she would know what would happen next. This could not be a repetition of the life she was leading at the Palmetto Hotel, but whatever the new life might be, she would get from it all that it might contain for her. She did not in the least doubt the captain's return, for she believed in him so thoroughly that she felt—she knew—he would come back and tell her of his failure or his success, and what she was to do next. But now she was thinking. She could not help it, for her tranquil mind had been ruffled.

Her cogitations were interrupted by the entrance of Ralph.

"I say, Edna," said he, throwing himself into an easy-chair, and placing his hat upon another near by, "was that a returned manuscript that Cheditafa brought you this morning? You haven't been writing for the magazines, have you?"

"That was a letter from Captain Horn," she said.

"Whew!" he exclaimed. "It must be a whopper! What does he say? When is he coming here? Give me some of the points of it. But, by the way, Edna, before you begin, I will say that I think it is about time he should write. Since the letter in which he told about the guano-bags and sent you that lot of money—let me see, how long ago was that?"

"It was ten days ago," said his sister.

"Is that so? I thought it was longer than that. But no matter. Since that letter came, I have been completely upset. I want to know what I am to do, and, whatever I am to do, I want to get at it. From what the captain wrote, and from what I remember of the size and weight of those gold bars, he must have got away with more than a million dollars—perhaps a million and a half. Now, what part of that is mine? What am I to do with it? When am I to begin to prepare myself for the life I am to lead when I get it? All this I want to know, and, more than that, I want to know what you are going to do. Now, if I had got to Acapulco, or any other civilized spot, with a million dollars in solid gold, it would not have been ten days before I should have written to my family,—for I suppose that is what we are,—and should have told them what I was going to do, and how much they might count on. But I hope now that letter does tell?"

"The best thing to do," said Edna, taking up the letter from the table, "is to read it to you. But before I begin I want to say something, and that is that it is very wrong of you to get into these habits of calculating about what may come to you. What is to come will come, and you might as well wait for it without upsetting your mind by all sorts of wild anticipations; and, besides this, you must remember that you are not of age, and that I am your guardian, and whatever fortune may now come to you will be under my charge until you are twenty-one."

"Oh, I don't care about that," said Ralph. "We will have no trouble about agreeing what is the best thing for me to do. But now go ahead with the letter."

"'I am going to tell you'" (at the beginning of the second paragraph) "'of a very strange thing which happened to me since I last wrote. I will first state that after my guano-bags had all been safely stored in the warerooms I have hired, I had a heavy piece of work getting the packages of gold out of the bags, and in packing the bars in small, stout boxes I found in the City of Mexico and had sent down here. In looking around for boxes which would suit my purpose, I discovered these, which had been used for stereotype plates. They were stamped on the outside, and just what I wanted, being about as heavy after I packed them with gold as they were when they were filled with type-metal. This packing I had to do principally at night, when I was supposed to be working in a little office attached to the rooms. As soon as this was done, I sent all the boxes to a safe-deposit bank in Mexico, and there the greater part of them are yet. Some I have shipped to the mint in San Francisco, some have gone North, and I am getting rid of the rest as fast as I can.

"'The gold bars, cast in a form novel to all dealers, have excited a good deal of surprise and questioning, but for this I care very little. My main object is to get the gold separated as many miles as possible from the guano, for if the two should be connected in the mind of any one who knew where the guano was last shipped from, I might have cause for anxiety. But as the bars bear no sort of mark to indicate that they were cast by ancient Peruvians, and, so far as I can remember,—and I have visited several museums in South America,—these castings are not like any others that have come down to us from the times of the Incas, the gold must have been cast in this simple form merely for convenience in transportation and packing. Some people may think it is California gold, some may think it comes from South America, but, whatever they think, they know it is pure gold, and they have no right to doubt that it belongs to me. Of course, if I were a stranger it might be different, but wherever I have dealt I am known, or I send a good reference. And now I will come to the point of this letter.

"'Three days ago I was in my office, waiting to see a man to whom I hoped to sell my stock of guano, when a man came in,—but not the one I expected to see,—and if a ghost had appeared before me, I could not have been more surprised. I do not know whether or not you remember the two American sailors who were the first to go out prospecting, after Mr. Rynders and his men left us, and who did not return. This man was one of them— Edward Shirley by name.'"

"I remember him perfectly!" cried Ralph. "And the other fellow was George Burke. On board the *Castor* I used to talk to them more than to any of the other sailors."

"'But astonished as I was,'" Edna went on to read, "'Shirley did not seem at all surprised, but came forward and shook hands most heartily. He said he had read in a newspaper that I had been rescued, and was doing business in Acapulco, and he had come down on purpose to find me. I told him how we had given up him and his mate for lost, and then, as he had read a very slim account of our adventures, I told him the whole story, taking great care, as you may guess, not to say anything about the treasure mound. He did not ask any questions as to why I did not come back with the rest of you, but was greatly troubled when he heard of the murders of every man of our crew except himself and Burke and Maka.

"'When I had finished, he told me his story, which I will condense as much as possible. When he and Burke started out, they first began to make their way along the slope of the rocky ridge which ended in our caves, but they found this very hard work, so they soon went down to the sandy country to the north. Here they shot some little beast or other, and while they were hunting another one, up hill and down dale, they found night was coming on, and they were afraid to retrace their steps for fear they might come to trouble in the darkness. So they ate what they had with them, and camped, and the next morning the mountains to the east seemed to be so near them that they thought it much easier to push on instead of coming back to us. They thought that when they got to the fertile country they would find a settlement, and then they might be able to do something for the rest of the party, and it would be much wiser to go ahead than to turn back. But they found themselves greatly mistaken. Mountains in the distance, seen over a plain, appear very much nearer than they are, and these two poor fellows walked and walked, until they were pretty nearly dead. The story is a long one as Shirley told it to me, but just as they were about giving up entirely, they were found by a little party of natives, who had seen them from a long distance and had come to them.

"'After a great deal of trouble,—I believe they had to carry Burke a good part of the way,—the natives got them to their huts at the foot of the mountains, and took care of them. These people told Shirley—he knows a little Spanish—that it was a piece of rare good luck that they found them, for it was very seldom they went so far out into the desert.

"'In a day or two the two men went on to a little village in the mountains, and there they tried to get up an expedition to come to our assistance. They knew that we had food enough to last for a week or two, but after that we must be starved out. But nobody would do anything, and then they went on to another town to see what they could do there.'"

"Good fellows!" exclaimed Ralph.

"Indeed, they were," said Edna. "But wait until you hear what they did next.

"'Nobody in this small town,'" she read on, "'was willing to join Burke and Shirley in their proposed expedition, and no wonder; for crossing those deserts is a dangerous thing, and most people said it would be useless anyway, as it would be easier for us to get away by sea than by land. At this time Burke was taken sick, and for a week or two Shirley thought he was going to die. Of course, they had to stay where they were, and it was a long time before Burke was able to move about. Then they might have gone into the interior until they came to a railroad, and so have got away, for they had money with them, but Shirley told me they could not bear to do that without knowing what had become of us. They did not believe there was any hope for us, unless the mate had come back with assistance, and they had not much faith in that, for if a storm had come up, such as had wrecked the Castor, it would be all over with Mr. Rynders's boat.

"'But even if we had perished on that desolate coast, they wanted to know it and carry the news to our friends, and so they both determined, if the thing could be done, to get back to the coast and find out what had become of us. They went again to the little village where they had been taken by the natives who found them, and there, by promises of big pay,—at least, large for those poor Peruvians,—they induced six of them to join in an expedition to the caves. They did not think they had any reason to suppose they would find any one alive, but still, besides the provisions necessary for the party there and back, they carried something extra.

"'Well, they journeyed for two days, and then there came up a windstorm, hot and dry, filling the air with sand and dust, so that they could not see where they were going, and the natives said they ought all to go back, for it was dangerous to try to keep on in such a storm. But our two men would not give up so soon, and they made a camp in a sheltered place, and determined to press on in the morning, when they might expect the storm to be over. But in the morning they found that every native had deserted them. The wind had gone down, and the fellows must have started back before it was light. Then Shirley and Burke did not know what to do. They believed that they were nearer the coast than the mountains, and as they had plenty of provisions,—for the natives had left them nearly everything,—they thought they would try to push on, for a while at least.

"'There was a bit of rising ground to the east, and they thought if they could get on the top of that they might get a sight of the ocean, and then discover how far away it was. They reached the top of the rising ground, and they did not see the ocean, but a little ahead of them, in a smooth stretch of sand, was something which amazed them a good deal more than if it had been the sea. It was a pair of shoes sticking up out of the sand. They were an old pair, and appeared to have legs to them. They went to the spot, and found that these shoes belonged to a man who was entirely covered by sand, with the exception of his feet, and dead, of course. They got the sand off of him, and found he was a white man, in sailor's clothes. First they had thought he might be one of our party, but they soon perceived that this was a mistake, for they had never seen the man before. He was dried up until he was nothing but a skeleton with skin over it, but they could have recognized him if they had known him before. From what they had heard of the rainless climate of the Peruvian coast, and the way it had of drying up dead animals of all sorts, they imagined that this man might have been there for years. He was lying on his back, with his arms folded around a bundle, and when they tried to move this bundle, they found it was very heavy. It was something wrapped up in a blanket and tied with a cord, and when they opened the bundle, they were pretty nearly struck dumb; for they saw it held, as Shirley expressed it, about a peck of little hunks of gold.

"'They were utterly astounded by this discovery, and utterly unable to make head or tail of it. What that man, apparently an English sailor, had been doing out in the middle of this desert with a bundle of gold, and where he got it, and who he was, and where he was going to, and how long he had been dead, were things beyond their guessing. They dragged the body out of its burrow in the sand, and examined the pockets, but there was nothing in the trousers but an old knife. In the pocket of the shirt, however, were about a dozen matches, wrapped up in an old envelope. This was addressed, in a very bad hand, to A. McLeish, Callao, Peru, but they could not make out the date of the postmark. These things were all there was about the man that could possibly identify him, for his few clothes were such as any sailor would wear, and were very old and dirty.

"'But the gold was there. They examined it and scraped it, and they were sure it was pure gold. There was no doubt in their minds as to what they would do about this. They would certainly carry it away with them. But before they did so, Burke wanted to hunt around and see if they could not find more of it, for the mass of metal was so heavy he did not believe the sailor could have carried it very far. But after examining the country as far as the eye could reach, Shirley would not agree to this. They could see nothing but wide-stretching sands, and no place where it seemed worth while to risk their lives hunting for treasure. Their best plan was to get away with what they had found, and now the point was whether or not they should press on to the coast or go back; but as they could see no signs of the sea, they soon came to the conclusion that the best thing to do if they wanted to save their lives and their treasure was to get back to the mountains.

"'I forgot to say that as soon as Shirley began to talk about the dead man and his gold, I left the warehouse in charge of Maka, and took him to my hotel, where he told me the rest of his story in a room with the door locked. I must try to take as many reefs in what followed as I can. I don't believe that the finding of the gold made any difference in their plans, for, of course, it would have been foolish for them to try to get to us by themselves. They cut the blanket in half and made up the gold into two packages, and then they started back for the mountains, taking with them all the provisions they could carry in addition to the gold, and leaving their guns behind them. Shirley said their loads got heavier and heavier as they ploughed through the sand, and it took them three days to cover the ground they had gone over before in two. When they got to the village, they found scarcely a man in the place, for the fellows who had deserted them were frightened, and kept out of sight. They stayed there all night, and then they went on with their bundles to the next village, where they succeeded in getting a couple of travelling-bags, into which they put their gold, so that they might appear to be carrying their clothes.

"'After a good deal of travel they reached Callao, and there they made inquiries for A. McLeish, but nobody knew of him. Of course, he was a sailor who had had a letter sent there. They went up to Lima and sold a few pieces of the gold, but, before they did it, they got a heavy hammer and pounded them up, so that no one would know what their original shape was. Shirley said he could not say exactly why they did this, but that they thought, on the whole, it would be safer. Then they went to San Francisco on the first vessel that sailed. They must have had a good deal of talk on the voyage in regard to the gold, and it was in consequence of their discussions that Shirley wanted so much to find me. They had calculated, judging by the pieces they had sold, that the gold they had with them was worth about twelve thousand dollars, and they both thought they ought to do the right thing about it. In the first place, they tried in San Francisco to find out something about McLeish, but no one knew of such a man. They then began to consider some persons they did know about. They had heard in Lima that some of the people of the *Castor* had been rescued, and if any of them were hard up, as most likely they were, Shirley and Burke thought that by rights they ought to have some of the treasure that they had found. Shirley said at first they had gone on the idea that each of them would have six thousand dollars and could go into business for himself, but after a while they thought this would be a mean thing to do. They had all been shipwrecked together, and two of them had had a rare piece of good luck, and they thought it no more than honorable to share this good luck with the others, so they concluded the best thing to do was to see me about it. Burke left this business to Shirley, because he wanted to go to see his sister who lives in St. Louis.

"'They had not formed any fixed plan of division, but they believed that, as they had had the trouble, and, in fact, the danger, of getting the gold, they should have the main share, but they considered that they had enough to help out any of the original party who might be hard up for money." Of course, we must always remember," said Shirley, in finishing up his story, "that if we can find the heirs of McLeish, the money belongs to them. But, even in that case, Burke and I think we ought to keep a good share of it to pay us for getting it away from that beastly desert." Here I interrupted him. "Don't you trouble yourself any more about McLeish," I said. "That money did not belong to him. He stole it." "How do you know that, and who did he steal it from?" cried Shirley. "He stole it from me," said I.

"'At this point Shirley gave such a big jump backward that his chair broke beneath him, and he went crashing to the floor. He had made a start a good deal like that when I told him how the Rackbirds had been swept out of existence when I had opened the flood-gate that let out the waters of the lake, and I had heard the chair crack then. Now, while he had been telling me about his finding that man in the sand, with his load of gold, I had been listening, but I had also been thinking, and almost any man can think faster than another one can talk, and so by this time I had made up my mind what I was going to say to Shirley. I would tell him all about my finding the gold in the mound. It touched me to think that these poor fellows, who did all that they could to help us escape, and then, when they got safely home, started immediately to find us in order that they might give us some of that paltry twelve thousand dollars—give to us, who are actually millionaires, and who may be richer yet! It would not do to let any of the crew get ahead of their captain in fair dealing, and that was one reason why I determined to tell him. Then, there was another point. Ever since I have been here, selling and storing the gold I brought away, I have had a heavy load on my mind, and that was the thought of leaving all the rest of the gold in that mound for the next person who might come along and find it.

"'I devised plan after plan of getting more of it, but none of them would work. Two things were certain: One was that I could not get any more away by myself. I had already done the best I could and all I could in that line.

And the second thing was that if I should try for any more of the treasure, I must have people to help me. The plan that suited me best was to buy a small vessel, man it, go down there, load up with the gold, and sail away. There would be no reasonable chance that any one would be there to hinder me, and I would take in the cargo just as if it were guano, or anything else. Then I would go boldly to Europe. I have looked into the matter, and I have found that the best thing I can do, if I should get that gold, would be to transport it to Paris, where I could distribute it better than I could from any other point. But the trouble was, where could I get the crew to help me? I have four black men, and I think I could trust them, as far as honesty goes, but they would not be enough to work the ship, and I could not think of any white men with whom I would trust my life and that gold in the same vessel. But now they seemed to pop up right in front of me.

"'I knew Shirley and Burke pretty well when they were on the *Castor*, and after what Shirley told me I knew them better, and I believed they were my men. To be sure, they might fail me, for they are only human, but I had to have somebody to help me, and I did not believe there were any other two men who would be less likely to fail me. So by the time Shirley had finished his yarn I was ready to tell him the whole thing, and propose to him and Burke to join me in going down after the rest of the treasure and taking it to France.'"

At this point Ralph sprang to his feet, his eyes flashing. "Edna!" he cried, "I say that your Captain Horn is treating me shamefully. In the first place, he let me come up here to dawdle about, doing nothing, when I ought to have been down there helping him get more of that treasure. I fancy he might have trusted me, and if I had been with him, we should have brought away nearly twice as much gold, and at this minute we should be twice as well off as we are. But this last is a thousand times worse. Here he is, going off on one of the most glorious adventures of this century, and he leaves me out. What does he take me for? Does he think I am a girl? When he was thinking of somebody to go with him, why didn't he think of me, and why doesn't he think of me now? He has no right to leave me out!"

"I look at the matter in a different light," said his sister. "Captain Horn has no right to take you off on such a dangerous adventure, and, more than that, he has no right to take you from me, and leave me alone in the world. He once made you the guardian of all that treasure, and now he considers you as my guardian. You did not desert the first trust, and I am sorry to think you want to desert the other."

"That's all very fine," said Ralph. "You blow hot and you blow cold at the same time. When you want me to keep quiet and do what I am told, you tell me I am not of age, and that you are my guardian; and when you want me to stay here and make myself useful, you tell me I am wonderfully trusty, and that I must be your guardian."

Edna smiled. "That is pretty good reasoning," she said, "but there isn't any reasoning needed in this case. No matter what Captain Horn may say or do, I would not let you go away from me."

Ralph sat down again. "There is some sense in what you say," he said. "If the captain should come to grief, and I were with him, we would both be gone. Then you would have nobody left to you. But that does not entirely clear him. Even if he thought I ought not to go with him, he ought to have said something about it, and put in a word or so about his being sorry. Is there any more of the letter?"

"Yes," said Edna, "there is more of it," and she began to read again:

"'I intended to stop here and give you the rest of the matter in another letter, but now, as I have a good chance to write, I think it is better to keep on, although this letter is already as long as the pay-roll of the navy. When I told Shirley about the gold, he made a bounce pretty nearly as big as the others, but this time I had him in a stout arm-chair, and he did no damage. He had in his pocket one of the gold bars he spoke of, and I had one of mine in my trunk, and when we put them together they were as like as two peas. What I told him dazed him at first, and he did not seem properly to understand what it all meant, but, after a little, a fair view of it came to him, and for hours we talked over the matter. Who the man was who had gone there after we left did not matter, for he could never come back again.

"'We decided that what we should do was to go and get that gold as soon as possible, and Shirley agreed to go with me. He believed we could trust Burke to join us, and, with my four black men,—who have really become good sailors,—we would have a crew of seven men altogether, with which we could work a fair-sized brig to Havre or some other French port. Before he went away our business was settled. He agreed to go with me as first mate, to do his best to help me get that gold to France, to consider the whole treasure as mine, because I had discovered it,—I explained the reason to him, as I did to you,—and to accept as regular pay one hundred dollars a day, from then until we should land the cargo in a European port, and then to leave it to me how much more I would give him. I told him there were a lot of people to be considered, and I was going to try to make the division as fair as possible, and he said he was willing to trust it to me.

"'If we did not get the gold, he was to have eighteen dollars a month for the time he sailed with me, and if we got safely back, I would give him his share of what I had already secured. He was quite sure that Burke would make the same agreement, and we telegraphed him to come immediately. I am going to be very careful about Burke, however, and sound him well before I tell him anything.

"'Yesterday we found our vessel. She arrived in port a few days ago, and is now unloading. She is a small brig, and I think she will do; in fact, she has got to do. By the time Burke gets here I think we shall be ready to sail. Up to that time we shall be as busy as men can be, and it will be impossible for me to go to San Francisco. I must attend to the shipping of the treasure I have stored in the City of Mexico. I shall send some to one place and some to another, but want it all turned into coin or bonds before I start. Besides, I must be on hand to see Burke the moment he arrives. I am not yet quite sure about him, and if Shirley should let anything slip while I was away our looked-for fortune might be lost to us.'

"And that," said Edna, "is all of the letter that I need read, except that he tells me he expects to write again before he starts, and that his address after he sails will be Wraxton, Fuguet & Co., American bankers in Paris."

CHAPTER XXVII
EDNA MAKES HER PLANS

When she had finished reading the many pages of the letter, Edna leaned back on the sofa and closed her eyes. Ralph sat upright in his chair and gazed intently before him.

"So we are not to see the captain again," he said presently. "But I suppose that when a man has a thing to do, the best thing is to go and do it."

"Yes," said his sister, "that is the best thing."

"And what are we to do?"

"I am now trying to decide," she answered.

"Doesn't he say anything about it?"

"Not a word," replied Edna. "I suppose he considered he had made his letter long enough."

About an hour after this, when the two met again, Edna said: "I have been writing to Captain Horn, and am going to write to Mrs. Cliff. I have decided what we shall do. I am going to France."

"To France!" cried Ralph. "Both of us?"

"Yes, both of us. I made up my mind about this since I saw you."

"What are you going to France for?" he exclaimed. "Come, let us have it all—quick."

"I am going to France," said his sister, "because Captain Horn is going there, and when he arrives, I wish to be there to meet him. There is no reason for our staying here—"

"Indeed, there is not," interpolated Ralph, earnestly.

"If we must go anywhere to wait," continued his sister, "I should prefer Paris."

"Edna," cried Ralph, "you are a woman of solid sense, and if the captain wants his gold divided up, he should get you to do it. And now, when are we going, and is Mrs. Cliff to go? What are you going to do with the two darkies?"

"We shall start East as soon as the captain sails," replied his sister, "and I do not know what Mrs. Cliff will do until I hear from her, and as for Cheditafa and Mok, we shall take them with us."

"Hurrah!" cried Ralph. "Mok for my valet in Paris. That's the best thing I have got out of the caves yet."

Captain Horn was a strong man, prompt in action, and no one could know him long without being assured of these facts. But although Edna's outward personality was not apt to indicate quickness of decision and vigor of purpose, that quickness and vigor were hers quite as much as the captain's when occasion demanded, and occasion demanded them now. The captain had given no indication of what he would wish her to do during the time which would be occupied by his voyage to Peru, his work there, and his subsequent long cruise around South America to Europe. She expected that in his next letter he would say something about this, but she wished first to say something herself.

She did not know this bold sailor as well as she loved him, and she was not at all sure that the plans he might make for her during his absence would suit her disposition or her purposes. Consequently, she resolved to submit her plans to him before he should write again. Above everything else, she wished to be in that part of the world at which Captain Horn might be expected to arrive when his present adventure should be accomplished. She did not wish to be sent for to go to France. She did not wish to be told that he was coming to America. Wherever he might land, there she would be.

The point that he might be unsuccessful, and might never leave South America, did not enter into her consideration. She was acting on the basis that he was a man who was likely to succeed in his endeavors. If she should come to know that he had not succeeded, then her actions would be based upon the new circumstances.

Furthermore, she had now begun to make plans for her future life. She had been waiting for Captain Horn to come to her, and to find out what he intended to do. Now she knew he was not coming to her for a long time, and was aware of what he intended to do, and she made her own plans. Of course, she dealt only with the near future. All beyond that was vague, and she could not touch it even with her thoughts. When sending his remittances, the captain had written that she and Mrs. Cliff must consider the money he sent her as income to be expended, not as principal to be put away or invested. He had made provisions for the future of all of them, in case he should not succeed in his present project, and what he had not set aside with that view he had devoted to his own operations, and to the maintenance, for a year, of Edna, Ralph, and Mrs. Cliff, in such liberal and generous fashion as might please them, and he had apportioned the remittances in a way which he deemed suitable. As Edna disbursed the funds, she knew that this proportion was three quarters for herself and Ralph, and one quarter for Mrs. Cliff.

"He divides everything into four parts," she thought, "and gives me his share."

Acting on her principle of getting every good thing out of life that life could give her, and getting it while life was able to give it to her, there was no doubt in regard to her desires. Apart from her wish to go where the captain expected to go, she considered that every day now spent in America was a day lost. If her further good fortune should never arrive, and the money in hand should be gone, she wished, before that time came, to engraft upon her existence a period of life in Europe—life of such freedom and opportunity as never before she had had a right to dream of.

Across this golden outlook there came a shadow. If he had wished to come to her, she would have waited for him anywhere, or if he had wished her to go to him, she would have gone anywhere. But it seemed as if that mass of gold, which brought them together, must keep them apart, a long time certainly, perhaps always. Nothing that had happened had had any element of certainty about it, and the future was still less certain. If he had come to her before undertaking the perilous voyage now before him, there would have been a certainty in her life which would have satisfied her forever. But he did not come. It was plainly his intention to have nothing to do with the present until the future should be settled, so far as he could settle it.

In a few days after she had written to Captain Horn, informing him of the plans she had made to go to France, Edna received an answer which somewhat disappointed her. If the captain's concurrence in her proposed foreign sojourn had not been so unqualified and complete, if he had proposed even some slight modification, if he had said anything which would indicate that he felt he had authority to oppose her movements if he did not approve of them,—in fact, even if he had opposed her plan,—she would have been better pleased. But he wrote as if he were her financial agent, and nothing more. The tone of his letter was kind, the arrangements he said he had made in regard to the money deposited in San Francisco showed a careful concern for her pleasure and convenience, but nothing in his letter indicated that he believed himself possessed in any way of the slightest control over her actions. There was nothing like a sting in that kind and generous letter, but when she had read it, the great longing of Edna's heart turned and stung her. But she would give no sign of this wound. She was a brave woman, and could wait still longer.

The captain informed her that everything was going well with his enterprise—that Burke had arrived, and had agreed to take part in the expedition, and that he expected that his brig, the *Miranda*, would be ready in less than a week. He mentioned again that he was extremely busy with his operations, but he did not say that he was sorry he was unable to come to take leave of her. He detailed in full the arrangements he had made, and then placed in her hands the entire conduct of the financial affairs of the party until she should hear from him again. When he arrived in France, he would address her in care of his bankers, but in regard to two points only did he now say anything which seemed like a definite injunction or even request. He asked Edna to urge upon Mrs. Cliff the necessity of saying nothing about the discovery of the gold, for if it should become known anywhere from Greenland to Patagonia, he might find a steamer lying off the Rackbirds' cove when his slow sailing-vessel should arrive there. The other request was that Edna keep the two negroes with her if this would not prove inconvenient. But if this plan would at all trouble her, he asked that they be sent to him immediately.

In answer to this letter, Edna merely telegraphed the captain, informing him that she would remain in San Francisco until she had heard that he had sailed when she would immediately start for the East, and for France, with Ralph and the two negroes.

Three days after this she received a telegram from Captain Horn, stating that he would sail in an hour, and the next day she and her little party took a train for New York.

CHAPTER XXVIII
"HOME, SWEET HOME"

On the high-street of the little town of Plainton, Maine, stood the neat white house of Mrs. Cliff, with its green shutters, its porchless front door, its pretty bit of flower-garden at the front and side, and its neat back yard, sacred once a week to that virtue which is next to godliness.

Mrs. Cliff's husband had been the leading merchant in Plainton, and having saved some money, he had invested it in an enterprise of a friend who had gone into business in Valparaiso. On Mr. Cliff's death his widow had found herself with an income smaller than she had expected, and that it was necessary to change in a degree her style of living. The hospitalities of her table, once so well known throughout the circle of her friends, must be curtailed, and the spare bedroom must be less frequently occupied. The two cows and the horse were sold, and in every way possible the household was placed on a more economical basis. She had a good house, and an income on which, with care and prudence, she could live, but this was all.

In this condition of her finances it was not strange that Mrs. Cliff had thought a good deal about the investments in Valparaiso, from which she had not heard for a long time. Her husband had been dead for three years, and although she had written several times to Valparaiso, she had received no answer whatever, and being a woman of energy, she had finally made up her mind that the proper thing to do was to go down and see after her affairs. It had not been easy for her to get together the money for this long journey,—in fact, she had borrowed some of it,—and so, to lessen her expenses, she had taken passage in the *Castor* from San Francisco.

She was a housewife of high degree, and would not have thought of leaving—perhaps for months—her immaculate window-panes and her spotless floors and furniture, had she not also left some one to take care of them. A distant cousin, Miss Willy Croup, had lived with her since her husband's death, and though this lady was willing to stay during Mrs.

Cliff's absence, Mrs. Cliff considered her too quiet and inoffensive to be left in entire charge of her possessions, and Miss Betty Handshall, a worthy maiden of fifty, a little older than Willy, and a much more determined character, was asked to come and live in Mrs. Cliffs house until her return.

Betty was the only person in Plainton who lived on an annuity, and she was rather proud of her independent fortune, but as her annuity was very small, and as this invitation meant a considerable reduction in her expenses, she was very glad to accept it. Consequently, Mrs. Cliff had gone away feeling that she had left her house in the hands of two women almost as neat as herself and even more frugal.

When Mrs. Cliff left Edna and Ralph in San Francisco, and went home, nearly all the people in the little town who were worth considering gathered in and around her house to bid her welcome. They had heard of her shipwreck, but the details had been scanty and unsatisfactory, and the soul of the town throbbed with curiosity to know what had really happened to her. For the first few hours of her return Mrs. Cliff was in a state of heavenly ecstasy. Everything was so tidy, everything was so clean, every face beamed with such genial amity, her native air was so intoxicating, that she seemed to be in a sort of paradise. But when her friends and neighbors began to ask questions, she felt herself gradually descending into a region which, for all she knew, might resemble purgatory.

Of course, there was a great deal that was wonderful and startling to relate, and as Mrs. Cliff was a good story-teller, she thrilled the nerves of her hearers with her descriptions of the tornado at sea and the Rackbirds on land, and afterwards filled the eyes of many of the women with tears of relief as she told of their escapes, their quiet life at the caves, and their subsequent rescue by the *Mary Bartlett*. But it was the cross-examinations which caused the soul of the narrator to sink. Of course, she had been very careful to avoid all mention of the gold mound, but this omission in her narrative proved to be a defect which she had not anticipated. As she had told that she had lost everything except a few effects she had carried with her from the *Castor*, it was natural enough that people should want to know how she had been enabled to come home in such good fashion.

They had expected her to return in a shabby, or even needy, condition, and now they had stories of delightful weeks at a hotel in San Francisco, and beheld their poor shipwrecked neighbor dressed more handsomely than they had ever seen her, and with a new trunk standing in the lower hall which must contain something.

Mrs. Cliff began by telling the truth, and from this course she did not intend to depart. She said that the captain of the *Castor* was a just and generous man, and, as far as was in his power, he had reimbursed the unfortunate passengers for their losses. But as every one knows the richest steamship companies are seldom so generous to persons who may be cast away during transportation as to offer them long sojourns at hotels, with private parlors and private servants, and to send them home in drawing-room cars, with cloaks trimmed with real sealskin, the questions became more and more direct, and all Mrs. Cliff could do was to stand with her back against the captain's generosity, as if it had been a rock, and rely upon it for defence.

But when the neighbors had all gone home, and the trunk had to be opened, so that it could be lightened before being carried up-stairs, the remarks of Willy and Betty cut clean to the soul of the unfortunate possessor of its contents. Of course, the captain had not actually given her this thing, and that thing, and the other, or the next one, but he had allowed her a sum of money, and she had expended it according to her own discretion. How much that sum of money might have been, Willy and Betty did not dare to ask,—for there were limits to Mrs. Cliff's forbearance,—but when they went to bed, they consulted together.

If it had not been for the private parlor and the drawing-room car, they would have limited Captain Horn's generosity to one hundred dollars. But, under the circumstances, that sum would have been insufficient. It must have been nearly, if not quite, two hundred. As for Mrs. Cliff, she went to bed regretting that her reservations had not been more extended, and that she had not given the gold mound in the cave more company. She hated prevarications and concealments, but if she must conceal something, she should have concealed more. When the time came when she would be free to tell of her good fortune, even if it should be no more than she already possessed, then she would explain everything, and proudly demand of her friends and neighbors to put their fingers on a single untruth that she had told them.

For the next day or two, Mrs. Cliff's joy in living again in her own home banished all other feelings, and as she was careful to say nothing to provoke more questions, and as those which were still asked became uncertain of aim and scattering, her regrets at her want of reticence began to fade. But, no matter what she did, where she went, or what she looked at, Mrs. Cliff carried about with her a millstone. It did not hang from her neck, but it was in her pocket. It was not very heavy, but it was a burden to her. It was her money—which she wanted to spend, but dared not.

On leaving San Francisco, Edna had wished to give her the full amount which the captain had so far sent her, but Mrs. Cliff declined to receive the whole. She did not see any strong reason to believe that the captain would ever send any more, and as she had a home, and Ralph and Edna had not, she would not take all the money that was due her, feeling that they might come to need it more than she would. But even with this generous self-denial she found herself in Plainton with a balance of some thousands of dollars in her possession, and as much more in Edna's hands, which the latter had insisted that she would hold subject to order. What would the neighbors think of Captain Horn's abnormal bounteousness if they knew this?

With what a yearning, aching heart Mrs. Cliff looked upon the little picket-fence which ran across the front of her property! How beautiful that fence would be with a new coat of paint, and how perfectly well she could afford it! And there was the little shed that should be over the back door, which would keep the sun from the kitchen in summer, and in winter the snow. There was this in one room, and that in another. There were new dishes which could exist only in her mind. How much domestic gratification there was within her reach, but toward which she did not dare to stretch out her hand!

There was poor old Mrs. Bradley, who must shortly leave the home in which she had lived nearly all her life, because she could no longer afford to pay the rent. There had been an attempt to raise enough money by subscription to give the old lady her home for another year, but this had not been very successful. Mrs. Cliff could easily have supplied the deficit, and it would have given her real pleasure to do so,—for she had almost an affection for the old lady,—but when she asked to be allowed to subscribe, she did not dare to give more than one dollar, which was the largest sum upon the list, and even then Betty had said that, under the circumstances, she could not have been expected to give anything.

When she went out into the little barn at the rear of the house, and saw the empty cow-stable, how she longed for fresh cream, and butter of her own making! And when she gazed upon her little phaeton, which she had not sold because no one wanted it, and reflected that her good, brown horse could doubtless be bought back for a moderate sum, she almost wished that she had come home as poor as people thought she ought to be.

Now and then she ordered something done or spent some money in a way that excited the astonishment of Willy Croup—the sharper-witted Betty had gone home, for, of course, Mrs. Cliff could not be expected to be able to afford her company now. But in attempting to account for these inconsiderable extravagances, Mrs. Cliff was often obliged to content herself with admitting that while she had been abroad she might have acquired some of those habits of prodigality peculiar to our Western country. This might be a sufficient excuse for the new bottom step to the side door, but how could she account for the pair of soft, warm Californian blankets which were at the bottom of the trunk, and which she had not yet taken out even to air?

Matters had gone on in this way for nearly a month,—every day Mrs. Cliff had thought of some new expenditure which she could well afford, and every night she wished that she dared to put her money in the town bank and so be relieved from the necessity of thinking so much about door-locks and window-fastenings,—when there came a letter from Edna, informing her of the captain's safe arrival in Acapulco with the cargo of guano and gold, and inclosing a draft which first made Mrs. Cliff turn pale, and then compelled her to sit down on the floor and cry. The letter related in brief the captain's adventures, and stated his intention of returning for the gold.

"To think of it!" softly sobbed Mrs. Cliff, after she had carefully closed her bedroom door. "With this and what I am to get, I believe I could buy the bank, and yet I can only sit here and try to think of some place to hide this dangerous piece of paper."

The draft was drawn by a San Francisco house upon a Boston bank, and Edna had suggested that it might be well for Mrs. Cliff to open an account in the latter city. But the poor lady knew that would never do. A bank-account in Boston would soon become known to the people of Plainton, and what was the use of having an account anywhere if she could not draw from it? Edna had not failed to reiterate the necessity of keeping the gold discovery an absolute secret, and every word she said upon this point increased Mrs. Cliff's depression.

"If it were only for a fixed time, a month or three months, or even six months," the poor lady said to herself, "I might stand it. It would be hard to do without all the things I want, and be afraid even to pay the money I borrowed to go to South America, but if I knew when the day was certainly coming when I could hold up my head and let everybody know just what I am, and take my proper place in the community, then I might wait. But nobody knows how long it will take the captain to get away with that gold. He may have to make ever so many voyages. He may meet with wrecks, and dear knows what. It may be years before they are ready to tell me I am a free woman, and may do what I please with my own. I may die in poverty, and leave Mr. Cliff's nephews to get all the good of the draft and the money in my trunk up-stairs. I suppose they would think it came from Valparaiso, and that I had been hoarding it. It's all very well for Edna. She is going to Europe, where Ralph will be educated, I suppose, and where she can live as she pleases, and nobody will ask her any questions, and she need not answer them, if they should. But I must stay here, in debt, and in actual want of the comforts of life, making believe to pinch and to save, until a sea-captain thousands and thousands of miles away shall feel that he is ready to let me put my hand in my pocket and spend my riches."

CHAPTER XXIX
A COMMITTEE OF LADIES

It was about a week after the receipt of Edna's letter that Willy Croup came to Mrs. Cliff's bedroom, where that lady had been taking a surreptitious glance at her Californian blankets, to tell her that there were three ladies down in the parlor who wished to see her.

"It's the minister's wife, and Mrs. Hembold, and old Miss Shott," said Willy. "They are all dressed up, and I suppose they have come for something particular, so you'd better fix up a little afore you go down."

In her present state of mind, Mrs. Cliff was ready to believe that anybody who came to see her would certainly want to know something which she could not tell them, and she went down fearfully. But these ladies did not come to ask questions. They came to make statements. Mrs. Perley, the minister's wife, opened the interview by stating that, while she was sorry to see Mrs. Cliff looking so pale and worried, she was very glad, at the same time, to be able to say something which might, in some degree, relieve her anxiety and comfort her mind, by showing her that she was surrounded by friends who could give her their heartfelt sympathy in her troubles, and perhaps do a little more.

"We all know," said Mrs. Perley, "that you have had misfortunes, and that they have been of a peculiar kind, and none of them owing to your own fault."

"We can't agree exactly to that," interpolated Miss Shott, "but I won't interrupt."

"We all know," continued Mrs. Perley, "that it was a great loss and disappointment to you not to be able to get down to Valparaiso and settle your affairs there, for we are aware that you need whatever money is due you from that quarter. And we understand, too, what a great blow it was to you to be shipwrecked, and lose all your baggage except a hand-bag."

Miss Shott was about to say something here, but Mrs. Hembold touched her on the arm, and she waited.

"It grieves us very much," continued the minister's wife, "to think that our dear friend and neighbor should come home from her wanderings and perils and privations, and find herself in what must be, although we do not wish to pry into your private affairs, something of an embarrassed condition. We have all stayed at home with our friends and our families, and we have had no special prosperity, but neither have we met with losses, and it grieves us to think that you, who were once as prosperous as any of us, should now feel—I should say experience—in any manner the pressure of privation."

"I don't understand," said Mrs. Cliff, sitting up very straight in her chair. "Privation? What does that mean?"

"It may not be exactly that," said Mrs. Perley, quickly, "and we all know very well, Mrs. Cliff, that you are naturally sensitive on a point like this. But you have come back shipwrecked and disappointed in your business, and we want to show you that, while we would not hurt your feelings for anything in the world, we would like to help you a little, if we can, just as we would hope you would help us if we were in any embarrassment."

"I must say, however—" remarked Miss Shott; but she was again silenced by Mrs. Hembold, and the minister's wife went on.

"To come straight to the point," said she, "for a good while we have been wanting to do something, and we did not know what to do. But a few days ago we became aware, through Miss Willy Croup, that what was most needed in this house is blankets. She said, in fact, that the blankets you had were the same you bought when you were first married, that some of them had been worn out and given to your poorer neighbors, and that now you were very short of blankets, and, with cold weather coming on, she did not consider that the clothing on your own bed was sufficient. She even went so far as to say that the blankets she used were very thin, and that she did not think they were warm enough for winter. So, some of us have agreed together that we would testify our friendship and our sympathy by presenting you with a pair of good, warm blankets for your own bed; then those you have could go to Willy Croup, and you both would be comfortable all winter. Of course, what we have done has not been upon an expensive scale. We have had many calls upon us,—poor old Mrs. Bradley, for one,— and we could not afford to spend much money. But we have bought you a good pair of blankets, which are warm and serviceable, and we hope you will not be offended, and we do not believe that you will be, for you know our motives, and all that we ask is that when you are warm and comfortable under our little gift, you will sometimes think of us. The blankets are out in the hall, and I have no doubt that Miss Willy Croup will bring them in."

Mrs. Cliff's eyes filled with tears. She wanted to speak, but how could she speak! But she was saved from further embarrassment, for when Willy, who had been standing in the doorway, had gone to get the blankets, Miss Shott could be restrained no longer.

"I am bound to say," she began, "that, while I put my money in with the rest to get those blankets,—and am very glad to be able to do it, Mrs. Cliff,—I don't think that we ought to do anything which would look as if we were giving our countenances to useless extravagances in persons, even if they are our friends, who, with but small means, think they must live like rich people, simply because they happen to be travelling among them. It is not for me to allude to hotels in towns where there are good boarding-houses, to vestibule cars and fur-trimmed cloaks; but I will say that when I am called upon to help my friends who need it, I will do it as quick as anybody, but I also feel called upon by my conscience to lift up my voice against spending for useless things what little money a person may have, when that person needs that money for—well, for things I shall not mention. And now that I have said my say, I am just as glad to help give you those blankets, Mrs. Cliff, as anybody else is."

Every one in the room knew that the thing she would not mention was the money Mrs. Cliff had borrowed for her passage. Miss Shott had not lent any of it, but her brother, a retired carpenter and builder, had, and as his sister expected to outlive him, although he was twelve years younger than she was, she naturally felt a little sore upon this point.

Now Mrs. Cliff was herself again. She was not embarrassed. She was neither pale nor trembling. With a stern severity, not unknown to her friends and neighbors in former days, she rose to her feet.

"Nancy Shott," said she, "I don't know anything that makes me feel more at home than to hear you talk like that. You are the same woman that never could kiss a baby without wanting to spank it at the same time. I know what is the matter with you. You are thinking of that money I borrowed from your brother. Well, I borrowed that for a year, and the time is not up yet; but when it is, I'll pay it, every cent of it, and interest added. I knew what I was about when I borrowed it, and I know what I am about now, and if I get angry and pay it before it becomes due, he will lose that much interest, and he can charge it to you. That is all I have to say to you.

"As for you, Mrs. Perley, and the other persons who gave me these blankets, I want you to feel that I am just as grateful as if—just as grateful as I can be, and far more for the friendliness than for the goods. I won't say anything more about that, and it isn't necessary, but I must say one thing. I am ready to take the blankets, and to thank you from the bottom of my heart, but I will not have them unless the money Miss Shott put in is given back to her. Whatever that was, I will make it up myself, and I hope I may be excused for saying that I don't believe it will break me."

Now there was a scene. Miss Shott rose in anger and marched out of the house. Mrs. Perley and the other lady expostulated with Mrs. Cliff for a time, but they knew her very well, and soon desisted. Twenty-five cents was handed to Mrs. Perley to take the place of the sum contributed by Miss Shott, and the ladies departed, and the blankets were taken up-stairs. Mrs. Cliff gave one glance at them as Willy Croup spread them out.

"If those women could see my Californian blankets!" she said to herself, but to Willy she said, "They are very nice, and you may put them away."

Then she went to her own room and went to bed. This last shock was too much for her nerves to bear. In the afternoon Willy brought her some tea, but the poor lady would not get up. So long as she stayed in bed, people could be kept away from her, but there was nowhere else where she could be in peace.

All night she lay and thought and thought and thought. What should she do? She could not endure this condition of things. There was only one relief that presented itself to her: she might go to Mr. Perley, her minister, and confide everything to him. He would tell her what she ought to do.

"But," she thought, "suppose he should say it should all go to the Peruvians!" And then she had more thinking to do, based upon this contingency, which brought on a headache, and she remained in bed all the next day.

The next morning, Willy Croup, who had begun to regret that she had ever said anything about blankets,—but how could she have imagined that anybody could be so cut up at what that old Shott woman had said?— brought Mrs. Cliff a letter.

This was from Edna, stating that she and Ralph and the two negroes had just arrived in New York, from which point they were to sail for Havre. Edna wished very much to see Mrs. Cliff before she left the country, and wrote that if it would be convenient for that lady, she would run up to Plainton and stay a day or two with her. There would be time enough for this before the steamer sailed. When she read this brief note, Mrs. Cliff sprang out of bed.

"Edna come here!" she exclaimed. "That would be simply ruin! But I must see her. I must tell her everything, and let her help me."

As soon as she was dressed, she went down-stairs and told Willy that she would start for New York that very afternoon. She had received a letter from Mrs. Horn, and it was absolutely necessary to see her before she sailed. With only a small leather bag in her hand, and nearly all her ready money and her peace-destroying draft sewed up inside the body of her dress, she left Plainton, and when her friends and neighbors heard that she had gone, they could only ascribe such a sudden departure to the strange notions she had imbibed in foreign parts. When Plainton people contemplated a journey, they told everybody about it, and took plenty of time to make preparations; but South Americans and Californians would start anywhere at a moment's notice. People had thought that Mrs. Cliff was too old to be influenced by association in that way, but it was plain that they had been mistaken, and there were those who were very much afraid that even if the poor lady had got whatever ought to be coming to her from the Valparaiso business, it would have been of little use to her. Her old principles of economy and prudence must have been terribly shaken. This very journey to New York would probably cost twenty dollars!

When Mrs. Cliff entered Edna's room in a New York hotel, the latter was startled, almost frightened. She had expected her visitor, for she had had a telegram, but she scarcely recognized at the first glance the pale and haggard woman who had come to her.

"Sick!" exclaimed poor Mrs. Cliff, as she sank upon a sofa. "Yes, I am sick, but not in body, only in heart. Well, it is hard to tell you what is the matter. The nearest I can get to it is that it is wealth struck in, as measles sometimes strike in when they ought to come out properly, and one is just as dangerous as the other."

When Mrs. Cliff had had something to eat and drink, and had begun to tell her tale, Edna listened with great interest and sympathy. But when the good lady had nearly finished, and was speaking of her resolution to confide everything to Mr. Perley, Edna's gaze at her friend became very intent, and her hands tightly grasped the arms of the chair in which she was sitting.

"Mrs. Cliff," said she, when the other had finished, "there is but one thing for you to do: you must go to Europe with us."

"Now!" exclaimed Mrs. Cliff. "In the steamer you have engaged passage in? Impossible! I could not go home and settle up everything and come back in time."

"But you must not go home," said Edna. "You must not think of it. Your troubles would begin again as soon as you got there. You must stay here and go when we do."

Mrs. Cliff stared at her. "But I have only a bag and the clothes I have on. I am not ready for a voyage. And there's the house, with nobody but Willy in it. Don't you see it would be impossible for me to go?"

"What you need for the passage," said Edna, "you can buy here in a few hours, and everything else you can get on the other side a great deal cheaper and better than here. As to your house, you can write to that other lady to go there and stay with Miss Croup until you come back. I tell you, Mrs. Cliff, that all these things have become mere trifles to you. I dare say you could buy another house such as you own in Plainton, and scarcely miss the money. Compared to your health and happiness, the loss of that house, even if it should burn up while you are away, would be as a penny thrown to a beggar."

"And there is my new trunk," said Mrs. Cliff, "with my blankets and ever so many things locked up in it."

"Let it stay there," said Edna. "You will not need the blankets, and I don't believe any one will pick the lock."

"But how shall I explain my running away in such a fashion? What will they all think?"

"Simply write," said Edna, "that you are going to Europe as companion to Mrs. Horn. If they think you are poor, that will explain everything. And you may add, if you choose, that Mrs. Horn is so anxious to have you, she will take no denial, and it is on account of her earnest entreaties that you are unable to go home and take leave in a proper way of your friends."

It was half an hour afterwards that Mrs. Cliff said: "Well, Edna, I will go with you. But I can tell you this: I would gladly give up all the mountains and palaces I may see in Europe, if I could go back to Plainton this day, deposit my money in the Plainton bank, and then begin to live according to my means. That would be a joy that nothing else on this earth could give me."

Edna laughed. "All you have to do," she said, "is to be patient and wait awhile, and then, when you go back like a queen to Plainton, you will have had your mountains and your palaces besides."

CHAPTER XXX
AT THE HÔTEL BOILEAU

It was early in December,—two months after the departure of Edna and her little party from New York,—and they were all comfortably domiciled in the Hotel Boileau, in a quiet street, not far from the Boulevard des Italiens. This house, to which they came soon after their arrival in Paris, might be considered to belong to the family order, but its grade was much higher than that of the hotel in which they had lived in San Francisco. As in the former place, they had private apartments, a private table, and the service of their own colored men, in addition to that of the hotel servants. But their salon was large and beautifully furnished, their meals were cooked by a French chef, every one, from the lordly porter to the quick-footed chambermaid, served them with a courteous interest, and Mrs. Cliff said that although their life in the two hotels seemed to be in the main the same sort of life, they were, in reality, as different as an old, dingy mahogany bureau, just dragged from an attic, and that same piece of furniture when it had been rubbed down, oiled, and varnished. And Ralph declared that, so far as he knew anything about it, there was nothing like the air of Paris to bring out the tones and colorings and veinings of hotel life. But the greatest difference between the former and the present condition of this little party lay in the fact that in San Francisco its principal member was Mrs. Philip Horn, while in Paris it was Miss Edna Markham.

This change of name had been the result of nights of thought and hours of consultation. In San Francisco Edna felt herself to be Mrs. Horn as truly as if they had been married at high noon in one of the city churches, but although she could see no reason to change her faith in the reality of her conjugal status, she had begun to fear that Captain Horn might have different views upon the subject. This feeling had been brought about by the tone of his letters. If he should die, those letters might prove that she was then his widow, but it was plain that he did not wish to impress upon her mind that she was now his wife.

If she had remained in San Francisco, Edna would have retained the captain's name. There she was a stranger, and Captain Horn was well known. His agents knew her as Mrs. Horn, the people of the *Mary Bartlett* knew her as such, and she should not have thought of resigning it. But in Paris the case was very different. There she had friends, and expected to make more, and in that city she was quite sure that Captain Horn was very little known.

Edna's Parisian friends, were all Americans, and some of them people of consideration, one of her old schoolmates being the wife of a secretary of the American legation. Could she appear before these friends as Mrs. Captain Philip Horn, feeling that not only was she utterly unable to produce Captain Horn, but that she might never be able to do so? Should the captain not return, and should she have proofs of his death, or sufficient reason to believe it, she might then do as she pleased about claiming her place as his widow. But should he return, he should not find that she had trammelled and impeded his plans and purposes by announcing herself as his wife. She did not expect ever to live in San Francisco again, and in no other place need she be known as Mrs. Horn.

As to the business objects of her exceptional marriage, they were, in a large degree, already attained. The money Captain Horn had remitted to her in San Francisco was a sum so large as to astound her, and when she reached Paris she lost no time in depositing her funds under her maiden name. For the sake of security, some of the money was sent to a London banker, and in Paris she did not deposit with the banking house which Captain Horn had mentioned. But directions were left with that house that if a letter ever came to Mrs. Philip Horn, it was to be sent to her in care of Mrs. Cliff, and, to facilitate the reception of such a letter, Mrs. Cliff made Wraxton, Fuguet & Co. her bankers, and all her letters were addressed to them. But at Edna's bankers she was known as Miss Markham, and her only Parisian connection with the name of Horn was through Mrs. Cliff.

The amount of money now possessed by Edna was, indeed, a very fair fortune for her, without regarding it, as Captain Horn had requested, as a remittance to be used as a year's income. In his letters accompanying his remittances the captain had always spoken of them as her share of the gold brought away, and in this respect he treated her exactly as he treated Mrs. Cliff, and in only one respect had she any reason to infer that the money was in any manner a contribution from himself. In making her divisions according to his directions, her portion was so much greater than that of the others, Edna imagined Captain Horn sent her his share as well as her own. But of this she did not feel certain, and should he succeed in securing the rest of the gold in the mound, she did not know what division he would make. Consequently, this little thread of a tie between herself and the captain, woven merely of some hypothetical arithmetic, was but a cobweb of a thread. The resumption of her maiden name had been stoutly combated by both Mrs. Cliff and Ralph. The first firmly insisted upon the validity of the marriage, so long as the captain did not appear, but she did not cease to insist that the moment he did appear, there should be another ceremony.

"But," said Edna, "you know that Cheditafa's ceremony was performed simply for the purpose of securing to me, in case of his loss on that boat trip, a right to claim the benefit of his discovery. If he should come back, he can give me all the benefit I have a right to claim from that discovery, just as he gives you your share, without the least necessity of a civilized marriage. Now, would you advise me to take a step which would seem to force upon him the necessity for such a marriage?"

"No," said Mrs. Cliff. "But all your reasoning is on a wrong basis. I haven't the least doubt in the world—-I don't see how any one can have a doubt—that the captain intends to come back and claim you as his wife; and if anything more be necessary to make you such, as I consider there would be, he would be as ready as anybody to do it. And, Edna, if you could see yourself, not merely as you look in the glass, but as he would see you, you would know that he would be as ready as any of us would wish him to be. And how will he feel, do you suppose, when he finds that you renounce him and are going about under your maiden name?"

In her heart Edna answered that she hoped he might feel very much as she had felt when he did not come to see her in San Francisco, but to Mrs. Cliff she said she had no doubt that he would fully appreciate her reasons for assuming her old name.

Ralph's remarks were briefer, and more to the point.

"He married you," he said, "the best way he could under the circumstances, and wrote to you as his wife, and in San Francisco you took his name. Now, if he comes back and says you are not his wife, I'll kill him."

"If I were you, Ralph," said his sister, "I wouldn't do that. In fact, I may say I would disapprove of any such proceeding."

"Oh, you can laugh," said he, "but it makes no difference to me. I shall take the matter into my own hands if he repudiates that contract."

"But suppose I give him no chance to repudiate it?" said Edna. "Suppose he finds me Miss Edna Markham, and finds, also, that I wish to continue to be that lady? If what has been done has any force at all, it can easily be set aside by law."

Ralph rose and walked up and down the floor, his hands thrust deep into his pockets.

"That's just like a woman," he said. "They are always popping up new and different views of things, and that is a view I hadn't thought of. Is that what you intend to do?"

"No," said Edna, "I do not intend to do anything. All I wish is to hold myself in such a position that I can act when the time comes to act."

Ralph took the whole matter to bed with him in order to think over it. He did a great deal more sleeping than thinking, but in the morning he told Edna he believed she was right.

"But one thing is certain," he said: "even if that heathen marriage should not be considered legal, it was a solemn ceremony of engagement, and nobody can deny that. It was something like a caveat which people get before a regular patent is issued for an invention, and if you want him to do it, he should stand up and do it; but if you don't, that's your business. But let me give you a piece of advice: wherever you go and whatever you do, until this matter is settled, be sure to carry around that two-legged marriage certificate called Cheditafa. He can speak a good deal of English now, if there should be any dispute."

"Dispute!" cried Edna, indignantly. "What are you thinking of? Do you suppose I would insist or dispute in such a matter? I thought you knew me better than that."

Ralph sighed. "If you could understand how dreadfully hard it is to know you," he said, "you wouldn't be so severe on a poor fellow if he happened to make a mistake now and then."

When Mrs. Cliff found that Edna had determined upon her course, she ceased her opposition, and tried, good woman as she was, to take as satisfactory a view of the matter as she could find reason for.

"It would be a little rough," she said, "if your friends were to meet you as Mrs. Horn, and you would be obliged to answer questions. I have had experience in that sort of thing. And looking at it in that light, I don't know but what you are right, Edna, in defending yourself against questions until you are justified in answering them. To have to admit that you are not Mrs. Horn after you had said you were, would be dreadful, of course. But the other would be all plain sailing. You would go and be married properly, and that would be the end of it. And even if you were obliged to assert your claims as his widow, there would be no objection to saying that there had been reasons for not announcing the marriage. But there is another thing. How are you going to explain your prosperous condition to your friends? When I was in Plainton, I thought of you as so much better off than myself in this respect, for over here there would be no one to pry into your affairs. I did not know you had friends in Paris."

"All that need not trouble me in the least," said Edna. "When I went to school with Edith Southall, who is now Mrs. Sylvester, my father was in a very good business, and we lived handsomely. It was not until I was nearly grown up that he failed and died, and then Ralph and I went to Cincinnati, and my life of hard work began. So you see there is no reason why my friends in Paris should ask any questions, or I should make explanations."

"I wish it were that way in Plainton," said Mrs. Cliff, with a sigh. "I would go back there the moment another ship started from France."

So it was Miss Edna Markham of New York who took apartments at the Hotel Boileau, and it was she who called upon the wife of the American secretary of legation.

CHAPTER XXXI
WAITING

For several weeks after their arrival, the members of the little party had but one common object,—to see and enjoy the wonders and beauties of Paris,—and in their sight-seeing they nearly always went together, sometimes taking Cheditafa and Mok with them. But as time went on, their different dispositions began to assert themselves, and in their daily pursuits they gradually drifted apart.

Mrs. Cliff was not a cultivated woman, but she had a good, common-sense appreciation of art in its various forms. She would tramp with untiring step through the galleries of the Louvre, but when she had seen a gallery, she did not care to visit it again. She went to the theatre and the opera because she wanted to see how they acted and sang in France, but she did not wish to go often to a place where she could not understand a word that was spoken.

Ralph was now under the charge of a tutor, Professor Barré by name, who took a great interest in this American boy, whose travels and experiences had given him a precocity which the professor had never met with in any of his other scholars. Ralph would have much preferred to study Paris instead of books, and the professor, who was able to give a great deal of time to his pupil, did not altogether ignore this natural instinct of a youthful heart. In consequence, the two became very good friends, and Ralph was the best-satisfied member of the party.

It was in regard to social affairs that the lives of Edna and Mrs. Cliff diverged most frequently. Through the influence of Mrs. Sylvester, a handsome woman with a vivacious intelligence which would have made her conspicuous in any society, Edna found that social engagements, not only in diplomatic circles and in those of the American colony, but, to some extent, in Parisian society, were coming upon her much more rapidly than she had expected. The secretary's wife was proud of her countrywoman, and glad to bring her forward in social functions. Into this new life Edna entered as if it had been a gallery she had not yet visited, or a museum which she saw for the first time. She studied it, and enjoyed the study.

But only in a limited degree did Mrs. Cliff enjoy society in Paris. To be sure, it was only in a limited degree that she had been asked to do it. Even with a well-filled purse and all the advantages of Paris at her command, she was nothing more than a plain and highly respectable woman from a country town in Maine. More than this silks and velvets could not make her, and more than this she did not wish to be. As Edna's friend and companion, she had been kindly received at the legation, but after attending two or three large gatherings, she concluded that she would wait until her return to Plainton before she entered upon any further social exercises. But she was not at all dissatisfied or homesick. She preferred Plainton to all places in the world, but that little town should not see her again until she could exhibit her Californian blankets to her friends, and tell them where she got the money to buy them.

"Blankets!" she said to herself. "I am afraid they will hardly notice them when they see the other things I shall take back there."

With society, especially such society as she could not enjoy, Mrs. Cliff could easily dispense. So long as the shops of Paris were open to her, the delights of these wonderful marts satisfied the utmost cravings of her heart; and as she had a fine mind for bargaining, and plenty of time on her hands, she was gradually accumulating a well-chosen stock of furnishings and adornments, not only for her present house in Plainton, but for the large and handsome addition to it which she intended to build on an adjoining lot. These schemes for establishing herself in Plainton, as a wealthy citizen, did not depend on the success of Captain Horn's present expedition. What Mrs. Cliff already possessed was a fortune sufficient for the life she desired to lead in her native town. What she was waiting for was the privilege of going back and making that fortune known. As to the increase of her fortune she had but small belief. If it should come, she might change her plans, but the claims of the native Peruvians should not be forgotten. Even if the present period of secrecy should be terminated by the news of the non-success of Captain Horn, she intended to include, among her expenses, a periodical remittance to some charitable association in Peru for the benefit of the natives.

The Christmas holidays passed, January was half gone, and Edna had received no news from Captain Horn. She had hoped that before leaving South. America and beginning his long voyage across the Atlantic, he would touch at some port from which he might send her a letter, which, coming by steamer, would reach her before she could expect the arrival of the brig. But no letter had come. She had arranged with a commercial agency to telegraph to her the moment the Miranda should arrive in any French port, but no message had come, and no matter what else she was doing, it seemed to Edna as if she were always expecting such a message. Sometimes she thought that this long delay must mean disaster, and at such times she immediately set to work to reason out the matter. From Acapulco to Cape Horn, up through the South Atlantic and the North Atlantic to France, was a long voyage for a sailing-vessel, and to the time necessary for this she must add days, and perhaps weeks, of labor at the caves, besides all sorts of delays on the voyage. Like Ralph, she had an unbounded faith in the captain. He might not bring her one bar of gold, he might meet with all sorts of disasters, but, whenever her mind was in a healthy condition, she expected him to come to France, as he had said he would.

She now began to feel that she was losing a great deal of time. Paris was all very well, but it was not everything. When news should come to her, it might be necessary for her to go to America. She could not tell what would be necessary, and she might have to leave Europe with nothing but Paris to remember. There was no good objection to travel on the Continent, for, if the *Miranda* should arrive while she was not in Paris, she would not be so far away that a telegram could not quickly bring her back. So she listened to Mrs. Cliff and her own desires, and the party journeyed to Italy, by the way of Geneva and Bern.

Ralph was delighted with the change, for Professor Barré, his tutor, had consented to go with them, and, during these happy days in Italy, he was the preceptor of the whole party. They went to but few places that he had not visited before, and they saw but little that he could not talk about to their advantage. But, no matter what they did, every day Edna expected a message, and every day, except Sunday, she went to the banker's to look over the maritime news in the newspapers, and she so arranged her affairs that she could start for France at an hour's notice.

But although Edna had greatly enjoyed the Italian journey, it came to an end at last, and it was with feelings of satisfaction that she settled down again in Paris. Here she was in the centre of things, ready for news, ready for arrivals, ready to go anywhere or do anything that might be necessary, and, more than that, there was a delightful consciousness that she had seen something of Switzerland and Italy, and without having missed a telegram by being away.

The party did not return to the Hotel Boileau. Edna now had a much better idea of the Continental menage than she had brought with her from America, and she believed that she had not been living up to the standard that Captain Horn had desired. She wished in every way to conform to his requests, and one of these had been that she should consider the money he had sent her as income, and not as property. It was hard for her to fulfil this injunction, for her mind was as practical as that of Mrs. Cliff, and she could not help considering the future, and the probability of never receiving an addition to the funds she now had on deposit in London and Paris. But her loyalty to the man who had put her into possession of that money was superior to her feelings of prudence and thrift. When he came to Paris, he should find her living as he wanted her to live. It was not necessary to spend all she had, but, whether he came back poor or rich, he should see that she had believed in him and in his success.

The feeling of possible disaster had almost left her. The fears that had come to her had caused her to reason upon the matter, and the more she reasoned, the better she convinced herself that a long period of waiting without news was to be expected in the case of an adventure such as that in which Captain Horn was engaged. There was, perhaps, another reason for her present state of mind—a reason which she did not recognize: she had become accustomed to waiting.

It was at a grand hotel that the party now established themselves, the space, the plate-glass, the gilt, and the general splendor of which made Ralph exclaim in wonder and admiration.

"You would better look out, Edna," said he, "or it will not be long before we find ourselves living over in the Latin Quarter, and taking our meals at a restaurant where you pay a sou for the use of the napkins."

Edna's disposition demanded that her mode of life should not be ostentatious, but she conformed in many ways to the style of her hotel. There were returns of hospitality. There was a liveried coachman when they drove. There was a general freshening of wardrobes, and even Cheditafa and Mok had new clothes, designed by an artist to suit their positions.

If Captain Horn should come to Paris, he should not find that she had doubted his success, or him.

After the return from Italy, Mrs. Cliff began to chafe and worry under her restrictions. She had obtained from Europe all she wanted at present, and there was so much, in Plainton she was missing. Oh, if she could only go there and avow her financial condition! She lay awake at night, thinking of the opportunities that were slipping from her. From the letters that Willy Croup wrote her, she knew that people were coming to the front in Plainton who ought to be on the back seats, and that she, who could occupy, if she chose, the best place, was thought of only as a poor widow who was companion to a lady who was travelling. It made her grind her teeth to think of the way that Miss Shott was talking of her, and it was not long before she made up her mind that she ought to speak to Edna on the subject, and she did so.

"Go home!" exclaimed the latter. "Why, Mrs. Cliff, that would be impossible just now. You could not go to Plainton without letting people know where you got your money."

"Of course I couldn't," said Mrs. Cliff, "and I wouldn't. There have been times when I have yearned so much for my home that I thought it might be possible for me to go there and say that the Valparaiso affair had turned out splendidly, and that was how I got my money. But I couldn't do it. I could not stand up before my minister and offer to refurnish the parsonage parlor, with such a lie as that on my lips. But there is no use in keeping back the real truth any longer. It is more than eight months since Captain Horn started out for that treasure, and it is perfectly reasonable to suppose either that he has got it; or that he never will get it, and in either one of these cases it will not do any injury to anybody if we let people know about the money we have, and where it came from."

"But it may do very great injury," said Edna. "Captain Horn may have been able to take away only a part of it, and may now be engaged in getting the rest. There are many things which may have happened, and if we should now speak of that treasure, it might ruin all his plans."

"If he has half of it," said Mrs. Cliff, "he ought to be satisfied with that, and not keep us here on pins and needles until he gets the rest. Of course, I do not want to say anything that would pain you, Edna, and I won't do it, but people can't help thinking, and I think that we have waited as long as our consciences have any right to ask us to wait."

"I know what you mean," replied Edna, "but it does not give me pain. I do not believe that Captain Horn has perished, and I certainly expect soon to hear from him."

"You have been expecting that a long time," said the other.

"Yes, and I shall expect it for a good while yet. I have made up my mind that I shall not give up my belief that Captain Horn is alive, and will come or write to us, until we have positive news of his death, or until one year has passed since he left Acapulco. Considering what he has done for us, Mrs. Cliff, I think it very little for us to wait one year before we betray the trust he has placed in us, and, merely for the sake of carrying out our own plans a little sooner, utterly ruin the plans he has made, and which he intends as much for our benefit as for his own."

Mrs. Cliff said no more, but she thought that was all very well for Edna, who was enjoying herself in a way that suited her, but it was very different for her.

In her heart of hearts, Mrs. Cliff now believed they would never see Captain Horn again. "For if he were alive," she said to herself, "he would certainly have contrived in some way or other to send some sort of a message. With the whole world covered with post routes and telegraph-wires, it would be simply impossible for Captain Horn and those two sailors to keep absolutely silent and unheard of for such a long time—unless," she continued, hesitating even in her thoughts, "they don't want to be heard from." But the good lady would not allow her mind to dwell on that proposition; it was too dreadful!

And so Edna waited and waited, hoping day by day for good news from Captain Horn; and so Mrs. Cliff waited and waited, hoping for news from Captain Horn—good news, if possible, but in any case something certain and definite, something that would make them know what sort of life they were to lead in this world, and make them free to go and live it.

CHAPTER XXXII
A MARINER'S WITS TAKE A LITTLE FLIGHT

When Captain Horn, in the brig *Miranda*, with the American sailors Burke and Shirley, and the four negroes, left Acapulco on the 16th of September, he might have been said to have sailed "in ballast," as the only cargo he carried was a large number of coffee-bags. He had cleared for Rio Janeiro, at which port he intended to touch and take on board a small cargo of coffee, deeming it better to arrive in France with something more than the auriferous mineral matter with which he hoped to replace a large portion of discarded ballast. The unusual cargo of empty coffee-bags was looked upon by the customs officials as a bit of Yankee thrift, it being likely enough that the captain could obtain coffee-bags in Mexico much cheaper than in Rio Janeiro.

The voyage to the Peruvian coast was a slow one, the *Miranda* proving to be anything but a clipper, and the winds were seldom in her favor. But at last she rounded Aguja Point, and the captain shaped his course toward the coast and the Rackbirds' cove, the exact position of which was now dotted on his chart.

A little after noon on a quiet October day, they drew near enough to land to recognize the coast-line and the various landmarks of the locality. The negroes were filled with surprise, and afterwards with fright, for they had had no idea that they were going near the scene of their former horrible captivity. From time to time, they had debated among themselves the intentions of Captain Horn in regard to them, and now the idea seized them that perhaps he was going to leave them where he had found them. But, through Maka, who at first was as much frightened as the rest, the captain succeeded in assuring them that he was merely going to stop as near as possible to the cave where he had stayed so long, to get some of his property which it had been impossible to take away when the rest of the party left. Maka had great confidence in the captain's word, and he was able to infuse a good deal of this into the minds of the three other negroes.

Captain Horn had been in considerable doubt in regard to the best method of shipping the treasure; should he be so fortunate as to find it as he had left it. The cove was a quiet harbor in which the small boats could easily ply between the vessel and the shore, but, in this case, the gold must be carried by tedious journeys along the beach. On the other hand, if the brig lay too near the entrance to the caves, the treasure-laden boats must be launched through the surf, and, in case of high seas, this operation might be hazardous; consequently, he determined to anchor in the Rackbirds' cove and submit to the delay and inconvenience of the land transportation of the gold.

When the captain and Shirley went ashore in a boat, nothing was seen to indicate that any one had visited the spot since the last cargo of guano had been shipped. This was a relief, but when the captain had wandered through the place, and even examined the storehouse of the Rackbirds, he found, to his regret, that it was too late for him to visit the caves that day. This was the occasion of a night of wakefulness and unreasonable anxiety — unreasonable, as the captain assured himself over and over again, but still impossible to dissipate. No man who has spent weeks in pursuit of a royal treasure, in a vessel that at times seemed hardly to creep, could fail to be anxious and excited when he is compelled to pause within a few miles of that treasure.

But early in the morning the captain started for the caves. He took with him Shirley and Maka, leaving the brig in charge of Burke. The captain placed great confidence in Shirley, who was a quiet, steady man. In fact, he trusted every one on the ship, for there was nothing else to do. If any of them should prove false to him, he hoped to be able to defend himself against them, and it would be more than foolish to trouble his mind with apprehensions until there should be some reason for them. But there was a danger to be considered, quite different from the criminal cupidity which might be provoked by companionship with the heap of gold, and this was the spirit of angry disappointment which might be looked for should no heap of gold be found. At the moment of such possible disappointment, the captain wanted to have with him a man not given to suspicions and resentments.

In fact, the captain thought, as the little party strode along the beach, that if he should find the mound empty, — and he could not drive from his mind that once he had found it uncovered, — he wished to have with him some one who would back him up a little in case he should lower his lantern into a goldless void.

As they walked up the plateau in the path worn principally by his own feet, and the captain beheld the great stone face against the wall of rock, his mind became quieter. He slackened his pace, and even began to concoct some suitable remarks to make to Shirley in case of evil fortune.

Shirley looked about him with great interest. He had left the place before the great stone face had been revealed by the burning of the vines, and he would have been glad to stop for a minute and examine it. But although Captain Horn had convinced himself that he was in no hurry, he could not allow delay. Lighting a lantern, they went through the passageway and entered the great cave of the lake, leaving Maka rummaging around with eager delight through the rocky apartments where he had once been a member of a domestic household.

When they reached the mound, the captain handed his lantern to Shirley, telling him to hold it high, and quickly clambered to the top.

"Good!" he exclaimed. "The lid is just as I left it. Come up!"

In a moment Shirley was at his side, and the captain with his pocket-knife began to pick out the oakum which he had packed around the edges of the lid, for otherwise it would have been impossible for him to move it. Then he stood up and raised the lid, putting it to one side.

"Give me the lantern!" he shouted, and, stooping, lie lowered it and looked in. The gold in the mound was exactly as he had left it.

"Hurrah!" he cried. "Now you take a look!" And he handed the lantern to his companion.

Shirley crawled a little nearer the opening and looked into it, then lowered the lantern and put his head down so that it almost disappeared. He remained in this position for nearly a minute, and the captain gazed at him with a beaming face. His whole system, relieved from the straining bonds of doubt and fear and hope, was basking in a flood of ecstatic content.

Suddenly Shirley began to swear. He was not a profane man, and seldom swore, but now the oaths rolled from him in a manner that startled the captain.

"Get up," said he. "Haven't you seen enough?"

Shirley raised his head, but still kept his eyes on the treasure beneath him, and swore worse than before. The captain was shocked.

"What is the matter with you?" said he. "Give me the lantern. I don't see anything to swear at."

Shirley did not hand him the lantern, but the captain took it from him, and then he saw that the man was very pale.

"Look out!" he cried. "You'll slip down and break your bones."

In fact, Shirley's strength seemed to have forsaken him, and he was on the point of either slipping down the side of the mound or tumbling into the open cavity. The captain put down the lantern and moved quickly to his side, and, with some difficulty, managed to get him safely to the ground. He seated him with his back against the mound, and then, while he was unscrewing the top of a whiskey flask, Shirley began to swear again in a most violent and rapid way.

"He has gone mad," thought the captain. "The sight of all that gold has crazed him."

"Stop that," he said to the other, "and take a drink."

Shirley broke off a string of oaths in the middle, and took a pull at the flask. This was of service to him, for he sat quiet for a minute or two, during which time the captain brought down the lantern. Looking up at him, Shirley said in a weak voice:

"Captain, is what I saw all so?"

"Yes," was the reply, "it's all so."

"Then," said the other, "help me out of this. I want to get out into common air."

The captain raised Shirley to his feet, and, with the lantern in one hand, he assisted him to walk. But it was not easy. The man appeared to take no interest in his movements, and staggered and leaned upon the captain as if he were drunk.

As soon as they came out of the utter darkness and had reached the lighter part of the cave, the captain let Shirley sit down, and went for Maka.

"The first mate has been taken sick," said he to the negro, "and you must come help me get him out into the open air."

When the negro saw Shirley in a state of semi-collapse, he began to tremble from head to foot, but he obeyed orders, and, with a great deal of trouble, the two got the sailor outside of the caves and gave him another drink of whiskey.

Maka had his own ideas about this affair. There was no use telling him Mr. Shirley was sick—at least, that he was afflicted by any common ailment. He and his fellows knew very well that there were devils back in the blackness of that cave, and if the captain did not mind them, it was because they were taking care of the property, whatever it was, that he kept back here, and for which he had now returned. With what that property was, and how it happened to be there, the mind of the negro did not concern itself. Of course, it must be valuable, or the captain would not have come to get

The Adventures Of Captain Horn | 181

it, but that was his business. He had taken the first mate into that darkness, and the sight of the devils had nearly killed him, and now the negro's mind was filled with but one idea, and that was that the captain might take him in there and make him see devils.

After a time Shirley felt very much better, and able to walk.

"Now, captain," said he, "I am all right, but I tell you what we must do: I'll go to the ship, and I'll take charge of her, and I'll do whatever has got to be done on shore. Yes, and, what's more, I'll help do the carrying part of the business,—it would be mean to sneak out of that,—and I'll shoulder any sort of a load that's put out on the sand in the daylight. But, captain, I don't want to do anything to make me look into that hole. I can't stand it, and that is the long and short of it. I am sorry that Maka saw me in such a plight—it's bad for discipline; but it can't be helped."

"Never mind," cried the captain, whose high spirits would have overlooked almost anything at that moment. "Come, let us go back and have our breakfast. That will set you up, and I won't ask you to go into the caves again, if you don't want to."

"Don't let's talk about it," said Shirley, setting off. "I'd rather get my mind down to marlin-spikes and bilge-water."

As the captain walked back to the cove, he said to himself:

"I expect it struck Shirley harder than it did rest of us because he knew what he was looking at, and the first time we saw it we were not sure it was gold, as it might have been brass. But Shirley knew, for he had already had a lot of those bars, and had turned them into money. By George! I don't wonder that a poor fellow who had struggled for life with a small bag of that gold was knocked over when he saw a wagon-load of it."

Maka, closely following the others, had listened with eagerness to what had been said, and had been struck with additional horror when he heard Shirley request that he might not again be asked to look into that hole. Suddenly the captain and Shirley were startled by a deep groan behind them, and, turning, saw the negro sitting upon the sand, his knees drawn up to his face, and groaning grievously.

"What's the matter?" cried the captain.

"I sick," said Maka. "Sick same as Mr. Shirley."

"Get up and come along," said the captain, laughing. He saw that something was really ailing the black fellow, for he trembled from head to foot, and his face had the hue of a black horse recently clipped. But he thought it best not to treat the matter seriously. "Come along," said he.

"I am not going to give you any whiskey." And then, struck by a sudden thought, he asked, "Are you afraid that you have got to go into that cave?"

"Yes, sir," said Maka, who had risen to his feet. "It make me pretty near die dead to think that."

"Well, don't die any more," said the captain. "You sha'n't go anywhere that you have not been before."

The pupils of Maka's eyes, which had been turned up nearly out of sight, were now lowered. "All right, cap'n," said he. "I lot better now."

This little incident was not unpleasant to the captain. If the negroes were afraid to go into the blackness of the caves, it would make fewer complications in this matter.

CHAPTER XXXIII
THE "MIRANDA" TAKES IN CARGO

The next day the work of removing the treasure from the caves to the vessel began in good earnest. The Miranda was anchored not far from the little pier, which was found in good order, and Shirley, with one negro, was left on board, while the captain and Burke took the three others, loaded with coffee-bags, to the caves.

For the benefit of the minds of the black men, the captain had instructed Maka to assure them that they would not be obliged to go anywhere where it was really dark. But it was difficult to decide how to talk to Burke. This man was quite different from Shirley. He was smaller, but stout and strong, with a dark complexion, and rather given to talk. The captain liked him well enough, his principal objection to him being that he was rather too willing to give advice. But, whatever might be the effect of the treasure on Burke, the captain determined that he should not be surprised by it. He had tried that on Shirley, and did not want to try it again on anybody. So he conversed freely about the treasure and the mound, and, as far as possible, described its appearance and contents. But he need not have troubled himself about the effect of the sight of a wagon-load of gold upon Burke's mind. He was glad to see it, and whistled cheerfully as he looked down into the mound.

"How far do you think it goes down?" said he to the captain.

"Don't know," was the reply. "We can't tell anything about that until we get it out."

"All right," said Burke. "The quicker we do it, the better."

The captain got into the mound with a lantern, for the gold was now too low for him to reach it from above, and having put as many bars into a coffee-bag as a man could carry, he passed it up to Burke, who slid it down to the floor, where another lantern had been left. When five bags had been made ready, the captain came out, and he and Burke put each bag into another, and these were tied up firmly at each end, for a single coffee-bag was not considered strong enough to hold the weighty treasure. Then the two carried the bags into the part of the cave which was lighted by the great fissure, and called the negroes. Then, each taking a bag on his shoulder, the party returned to the cove. On the next trip, Shirley decided to go with the captain, for he said he did not care for anything if he did not have to look down into the mound, for that was sure to make him dizzy. Maka's place was taken by the negro who had been previously left in the vessel. Day by day the work went on, but whoever might be relieved, and whatever arrangements might be made, the captain always got into the mound and handed out the gold. Whatever discovery should be made when the bottom of the deposit was reached, he wanted to be there to make it.

The operations were conducted openly, and without any attempt at secrecy or concealment. The lid of the mound was not replaced when they left it, and the bags of gold were laid on the pier until it was convenient to take them to the vessel. When they were put on board, they were lowered into the hold, and took the place of a proportionate amount of ballast, which was thrown out.

All the negroes now spoke and understood a little English. They might think that those bags were filled with gold, or they might think that they contained a mineral substance, useful for fertilizer; but if by questioning or by accidental information they found out what was the load under which they toiled along the beach, the captain was content. There was no reason why he should fear these men more than he feared Burke and Shirley. All of them were necessary to him, and he must trust them. Several times when he was crouched down in the interior of the mound, filling a bag with gold, he thought how easy it would be for one of the sailors to shoot him from above, and for them, or perhaps only one of them, to become the owner of all that treasure. But then, he could be shot in one place almost as well as in another, and if the negroes should be seized with the gold fever, and try to cut white throats at midnight, they would be more likely to attempt it after the treasure had been secured and the ship had sailed than now. In any case, nothing could be gained by making them feel that they were suspected and distrusted. Therefore it was that when, one day, Maka said to the captain that the little stones in the bags had begun to make his shoulder tender, the captain showed him how to fold an empty sack and put it between the bags and his back, and then also told him that what he carried was not stones, but lumps of gold.

"All yourn, cap'n!" asked Maka.

"Yes, all mine," was the reply.

That night Maka told his comrades that when the captain got to the end of this voyage, he would be able to buy a ship bigger than the *Castor*, and that they would not have to sail in that little brig any more, and that he expected to be cook on the new vessel, and have a fine suit of clothes in which to go on shore.

For nearly a month the work went on, but the contents of the mound diminished so slowly that the captain, and, in fact, the two sailors, also, became very impatient. Only about forty pounds could be carried by each man on a trip, and the captain saw plainly that it would not do to urge greater rapidity or more frequent trips, for in that case there would be sure to be breakdowns. The walk from the cove to the caves was a long one, and rocky barriers had to be climbed, and although now but one man was left on board the vessel, only thirty bags a day were stored in its hold. This was very slow work. Consultations were held, and it was determined that some quicker method of transportation must be adopted. The idea that they could be satisfied with what they already had seemed to enter the mind of none of them. It was a foregone conclusion that their business there was to carry away all the gold that was in the mound.

A new plan, though rather a dangerous one, was now put into operation. The brig was brought around opposite the plateau which led to the caves, and anchored just outside the line of surf, where bottom was found at a moderate depth. Then the bags were carried in the boats to the vessel. A line connected each boat with the ship, and the negroes were half the time in the water, assisting the boats backward and forward through the surf. Now work went on very much more rapidly. The men had all become accustomed to carrying the heavy bags, and could run with them down the plateau. The boats were hauled to and from the vessel, and the bags were hoisted on board by means of blocks and tackle and a big basket. Once the side of the basket gave way, and several bags went down to the bottom of the sea, never to be seen again. But there was no use in crying over spilt gold, and this was the only accident.

The winds were generally from the south and east, and, therefore, there was no high surf; and this new method of working was so satisfactory that they all regretted they had not adopted it from the first, notwithstanding the risk. But the captain had had no idea that it would take so long for five men to carry that treasure a distance of two miles, taking forty pounds at a time.

At night everybody went on board the brig, and she lay to some distance from the shore, so as to be able to run out to sea in case of bad weather, but no such weather came.

It was two months since the brig had dropped anchor in the Rackbirds' cove when the contents of the mound got so low that the captain could not hand up the bags without the assistance of a ladder, which he made from some stuff on board the brig. By rough measurement, he found that he should now be near the level of the outside floor of the cave, and he worked with great caution, for the idea, first broached by Ralph, that this mass of gold might cover something more valuable than itself, had never left him.

But as he worked steadily, filling bag after bag, he found that, although he had reached at the outer edge of the floor of the mound what seemed to be a pavement of stone, there was still a considerable depth of gold in the centre of the floor. Now he worked faster, telling Shirley, who was outside, that he would not come out until he had reached the floor of the mound, which was evidently depressed in the centre after the fashion of a saucer. Working with feverish haste, the captain handed up bag after bag, until every little bar of gold had been removed from the mound.

The bottom of the floor was covered with a fine dust, which had sifted down in the course of ages from the inside coating of the mound, but it was not deep enough to conceal a bar of gold, and, with his lantern and his foot, the captain made himself sure that not a piece was left. Then his whole soul and body thrilled with a wild purpose, and, moving the ladder from the centre of the floor, he stooped to brush away the dust. If there should be a movable stone there! If this stone should cover a smaller cavity beneath the great one, what might he not discover within it? His mind whirled before the ideas which now cast themselves at him, when suddenly he stood up and set his teeth hard together.

"I will not," he said. "I will not look for a stone with a crack around it. We have enough already. Why should we run the risk of going crazy by trying to get more? I will not!" And he replaced the ladder.

"What's the matter in there?" called Shirley, from outside. "Who're you talking to?"

The captain came out of the opening in the mound, pulled up the ladder and handed it to Shirley, and then he was about to replace the lid upon the mound. But what was the use of doing that, he thought. There would be no sense in closing it. He would leave it open.

"I was talking to myself," he said to Shirley, when he had descended. "It sounded crack-brained, I expect."

"Yes, it did," answered the other. "And I am glad these are the last bags we have to tie up and take out. I should not have wondered if the whole three of us had turned into lunatics. As for me, I have tried hard to stop thinking about the business, and I have found that the best thing I could do was to try and consider the stuff in these bags as coal—good, clean, anthracite coal. Whenever I carried a bag, I said to myself, 'Hurry up, now, with this bag of coal.' A ship-load of coal, you know, is not worth enough to turn a man's head."

"That was not a bad idea," said the captain. "But now the work is done, and we will soon get used to thinking of it without being excited about it. There is absolutely no reason why we should not be as happy and contented as if we had each made a couple of thousand dollars apiece on a good voyage."

"That's so," said Shirley, "and I'm going to try to think it."

When the last bag had been put on board, Burke and the captain were walking about the caves looking here and there to take a final leave of the place. Whatever the captain considered of value as a memento of the life they had led here had been put on board.

"Captain," said Burke, "did you take all the gold out of that mound?"

"Every bit of it," was the reply.

"You didn't leave a single lump for manners?"

"No," said the captain. "I thought it better that whoever discovered that empty mound after us should not know what had been in it. You see, we will have to circulate these bars of gold pretty extensively, and we don't want anybody to trace them back to the place where they came from. When the time comes, we will make everything plain and clear, but we will want to do it ourselves, and in our own way."

"There is sense in that," said Burke. "There's another thing I want to ask you, captain. I've been thinking a great deal about that mound, and it strikes me that there might be a sub-cellar under it, a little one, most likely, with something else in it—rings and jewels, and nobody knows what not. Did you see if there was any sign of a trap-door?"

"No," said the captain, "I did not. I wanted to do it,—you do not know how much,—but I made up my mind it would be the worst kind of folly to try and get anything else out of that mound. We have now all that is good for us to have. The only question is whether or not we have not more than is good for us. I was not sure that I should not find something, if I looked for it, which would make me as sick as Shirley was the first time he looked into the mound. No, sir; we have enough, and it is the part of sensible men to stop when they have enough."

Burke shook his head. "If I'd been there," he said, "I should have looked for a crack in that floor."

When the brig weighed anchor, she did not set out for the open sea, but proceeded back to the Rackbirds' cove, where she anchored again. Before setting out, the next day, on his voyage to France, the captain wished to take on board a supply of fresh water.

CHAPTER XXXIV
BURKE AND HIS CHISEL

That night George Burke went off his watch at twelve o'clock, and a few minutes after he had been relieved, he did something he had never done before—he deserted his ship. With his shoes and a little bundle of clothes on his head, he very quietly slipped down a line he had fastened astern. It was a very dark night, and he reached the water unseen, and as quietly as if he had been an otter going fishing. First swimming, and then wading, he reached the shore. As soon as he was on land, he dressed, and then went for a lantern, a hammer, and a cold-chisel, which he had left at a convenient spot.

Without lighting the lantern, he proceeded as rapidly as possible to the caves. His path was almost invisible, but having travelled that way so often, he knew it as well as he knew his alphabet. Not until he was inside the entrance to the caves did he light his lantern. Then he proceeded, without loss of time, to the stone mound. He knew that the ladder had been left there, and, with a little trouble, he found it, where Shirley had put it, behind some rocks on the floor of the cave. By the aid of this he quickly descended into the mound, and then, moving the foot of the ladder out of the way, he vigorously began to brush away the dust from the stone pavement. When this was done, he held up the lantern and carefully examined the central portion of the floor, and very soon he discovered what he had come to look for. A space about three feet square was marked off on the pavement of the mound by a very perceptible crevice. The other stones of the pavement were placed rather irregularly, but some of them had been cut to allow this single square stone to be set in the centre.

"That's a trap-door," said Burke. "There can't be any doubt about that." And immediately he set to work to get it open.

There was no ring, nor anything by which he could lift it; but if he could get his heavy chisel under it, he was sure he could raise it until he could get hold of it with his hands. So he began to drive his chisel vigorously down into the cracks at various places. This was not difficult to do, and, trying one side after another, he got the chisel down so far that he could use it as a lever. But with all his strength he could not raise the stone.

At last, while working at one corner, he broke out a large piece of the pavement, eight or nine inches long, and found that it had covered a metal bar about an inch in diameter. With his lantern he carefully examined this rod, and found that it was not iron, but appeared to be made of some sort of bronze.

"Now, what is this?" said Burke to himself. "It's either a hinge or a bolt. It doesn't look like a hinge, for it wouldn't be any use for it to run so far into the rest of the pavement, and if it is a bolt, I don't see how they got at it to move it. I'll see where it goes to." And he began to cut away more of the pavement toward the wall of the dome. The pieces of stone came up without much trouble, and as far as he cut he found the metal rod.

"By George!" said he, "I believe it goes outside of the mound! They worked it from outside!"

Putting the ladder in place, he ran up with his lantern and tools, and descended to the outside floor. Then he examined the floor of the cave where the rod must run if it came outside the mound. He found a line of flat stones, each about a foot square, extending from the mound toward the western side of the cave.

"Oh, ho!" he cried, and on his knees he went to work, soon forcing up one of these stones, and under it was the metal rod, lying in a groove considerably larger than itself. Burke now followed the line of stones to the western side of the cave, where the roof was so low he could scarcely stand up under it. To make sure, he took up another stone, and still found the rod.

"I see what this means," said he. "That bolt is worked from clean outside, and I've got to find the handle of it. If I can't do that, I'll go back and cut through that bolt, if my chisel will do it."

He now went back to a point on the line of stones about midway between the side of the cave and the mound, and then, walking forward as nearly as possible in a straight line, which would be at right angles with the metal rod, he proceeded until he had reached the entrance to the passageway which led to the outer caves, carefully counting his steps as he went. Then he turned squarely about, entered the passage, and walked along it until he came to the door of the room which had once been occupied by Captain Horn.

"I'll try it inside first," said Burke to himself, "and then I'll go outside."

He walked through the rooms, turning to the right about ten feet when he came to the middle apartment,—for the door here was not opposite to the others,—but coming back again to his line of march as soon as he was on the other side. He proceeded until he reached the large cave, open at the top, which was the last of these compartments. This was an extensive cavern, the back part being, however, so much impeded by rocks that had fallen from the roof that it was difficult for him to make any progress, and the numbering of his steps depended very much upon calculation. But when he reached the farthest wall, Burke believed that he had gone about as great a distance as he had stepped off in the cave of the lake.

"But how in the mischief," thought he, "am I to find anything here?" He held up his lantern and looked about. "I can't move these rocks to see what is under them."

As he gazed around, he noticed that the southeast corner seemed to be more regular than the rest of the wall of the cave. In fact, it was almost a right-angled corner, and seemed to have been roughly cut into that shape. Instantly Burke was in the corner. He found the eastern wall quite smooth for a space about a foot wide and extending about two yards from the floor. In this he perceived lines of crevice marking out a rectangular space some six inches wide and four feet in height.

"Ha, ha!" cried Burke. "The handle is on the other side of that slab, I'll bet my head!" And putting down the lantern, he went to work.

With his hammer and chisel he had forced the top of the slab in less than two minutes, and soon he pulled it outward and let it drop on the floor. Inside the narrow, perpendicular cavity which was now before him, he saw an upright metal bar.

"The handle of the bolt!" cried Burke. "Now I can unfasten the trap-door." And taking hold of the top of the bar, he pulled back with all his force. At first he could not move it, but suddenly the resistance ceased, and he pulled the bar forward until it stood at an angle of forty-five degrees from the wall. Further than this Burke could not move it, although he tugged and bore down on it with all his weight.

"All right," said he, at last. "I guess that's as far as she'll come. Anyway, I'm off to see if I've drawn that bolt. If I have, I'll have that trap-door open, if I have to break my back lifting it."

With his best speed Burke ran through the caves to the mound, and, mounting by means of the stone projections, he was about to descend by the ladder, when, to his utter amazement, he saw no ladder. He had left it projecting at least two feet through the opening in the top of the mound, and now he could see nothing of it.

What could this mean? Going up a little higher, he held up his lantern and looked within, but saw no signs of the ladder.

"By George!" he cried, "has anybody followed me and pulled out that ladder?"

Lowering the lantern farther into the mound, he peered in. Below, and immediately under him, was a black hole, about three feet square. Burke was so startled that he almost dropped the lantern. But he was a man of tough nerve, and maintained his clutch upon it. But he drew back. It required some seconds to catch his breath. Presently he looked down again.

"I see," said he. "That trap-door was made to fall down, and not to lift up, and when I pulled the bolt, down it went, and the ladder, being on top of it, slipped into that hole. Heavens!" he said, as a cold sweat burst out over him at the thought, "suppose I had made up my mind to cut that bolt! Where would I have gone to?"

It was not easy to frighten Burke, but now he trembled, and his back was chilled. But he soon recovered sufficiently to do something, and going down to the floor of the cave, he picked up a piece of loose stone, and returning to the top of the mound, he looked carefully over the edge of the opening, and let the stone drop into the black hole beneath. With all the powers of his brain he listened, and it seemed to him like half a minute before he heard a faint sound, far, far below. At this moment he was worse frightened than he had ever been in his life. He clambered down to the foot of the mound, and sat down on the floor.

"What in the name of all the devils does it mean?" said he; and he set himself to work to think about it, and found this a great deal harder labor than cutting stone.

"There was only one thing," he said to himself, at last, "that they could have had that for. The captain says that those ancient fellows put their gold there keep it from the Spaniards, and they must have rigged up this devilish contrivance to work if they found the Spaniards had got on the track of their treasure. Even if the Spaniards had let off the water and gone to work to get the gold out, one of the Incas' men in the corner of that other cave, which most likely was all shut up and not discoverable, would have got hold of that bar, given it a good pull, and let down all the gold, and what Spaniards might happen to be inside, to the very bottom of that black hole. By George! it would have been a pretty trick! The bottom of that mound is just like a funnel, and every stick of gold would have gone down. But, what is more likely, they would have let it out before the Spaniards had a chance to open the top, and then, if the ancients had happened to lick the Spaniards, they could have got all that gold up again. It might have taken ten or twenty years, but then, the ancients had all the time they wanted."

After these reflections, Burke sat for a few moments, staring at the lantern. "But, by George!" said he again, speaking aloud, though in low tones, "it makes my blood run cold to think of the captain working day after day, as hard as he could, right over that horrible trap-door. Suppose he had moved the bolt in some way! Suppose somebody outside had found that slab in the wall and had fooled with the bar! Then, there is another thing. Suppose, while they were living here, he or the boy had found that bar before he found the dome, and had pulled out the concern to see what it was! Bless me! in that case we should all be as poor as rats! Bat I must not stop here, or the next watch will be called before I get back. But one thing I'll do before I go. I'll put back that lid. Somebody might find the dome in the dark, and tumble into it. Why, if a wandering rat should make a slip, and go down into that black hole, it would be enough to make a fellow's blood run cold if he knew of it."

Without much trouble Burke replaced the lid, and then, without further delay, he left the caves. As he hurried along the beach, he debated within himself whether or not he should tell Captain Horn what he had discovered.

"It will be mighty hard on his nerves," said he, "if he comes to know how he squatted and worked for days and weeks over that diabolical trap that opens downward. He's a strong man, but he's got enough on his nerves as it is. No, I won't tell him. He is going to do the handsome thing by us, and it would be mean for me to do the unhandsome thing by him. By George! I don't believe he could sleep for two or three nights if he knew what I know! No, sir! You just keep your mouth shut until we are safe and sound in some civilized spot, with the whole business settled, and Shirley and me discharged. Then I will tell the captain about it, so that nobody need ever trouble his mind about coming back to look for gold rings and royal mummies. If I don't get back before my watch is called, I'll brazen it out somehow. We've got to twist discipline a little when we are all hard at work at a job like this."

He left his shoes on the sand of the cove, and swam to the ship without taking time to undress. He slipped over the taffrail, and had scarcely time to get below and change his clothes before his watch was called.

CHAPTER XXXV
THE CAPTAIN WRITES A LETTER

On the afternoon of the next day, the Miranda, having taken in water, set sail, and began her long voyage to Rio Janeiro, and thence to France.

Now that his labors were over, and the treasure of the Incas safely stored in the hold of the brig, where it was ignominiously acting as ballast, Captain Horn seated himself comfortably in the shade of a sail and lighted his pipe. He was tired of working, tired of thinking, tired of planning—tired in mind, body, and even soul; and the thought that his work was done, and that he was actually sailing away with his great prize, came to him like a breeze from the sea after a burning day. He was not as happy as he should have been. He knew that he was too tired to be as happy as his circumstances demanded, but after a while he would attend better to that business. Now he was content to smoke his pipe, and wait, and listen to the distant music from all the different kinds of enjoyment which, in thought, were marching toward him. It was true he was only beginning his long voyage to the land where he hoped to turn his gold into available property. It was true that he might be murdered that night, or some other night, and that when the brig, with its golden cargo, reached port, he might not be in command of her. It was true that a hundred things might happen to prevent the advancing enjoyments from ever reaching him. But ill-omened chances threaten everything that man is doing, or ever can do, and he would not let the thought of them disturb him now.

Everybody on board the Miranda was glad to rest and be happy, according to his methods and his powers of anticipation. As to any present advantage from their success, there was none. The stones and sand they had thrown out had ballasted the brig quite as well as did the gold they now carried. This trite reflection forced itself upon the mind of Burke.

"Captain," said he, "don't you think it would be a good idea to touch somewhere and lay in a store of fancy groceries and saloon-cabin grog? If we can afford to be as jolly as we please, I don't see why we shouldn't begin now."

But the captain shook his head. "It would be a dangerous thing," he said, "to put into any port on the west coast of South America with our present cargo on board. We can't make it look like ballast, as I expected we could, for all that bagging gives it a big bulk, and if the custom-house officers came on board, it would not do any good to tell them we are sailing in ballast, if they happened to want to look below."

"Well, that may be so," said Burke. "But what I'd like would be to meet a first-class, double-quick steamer, and buy her, put our treasure on board, and then clap on all steam for France."

"All right," said the captain, "but we'll talk about that when we meet a steamer for sale."

After a week had passed, and he had begun to feel the advantages of rest and relief from anxiety, Captain Horn regretted nothing so much as that the *Miranda* was not a steamer, ploughing her swift way over the seas. It must be a long, long time before he could reach those whom he supposed and hoped were waiting for him in France. It had already been a long, long time since they had heard from him. He did not fear that they would suffer because he did not come. He had left them money enough to prevent anything of that sort. He did not know whether or not they were longing to hear from him, but he did know that he wanted them to hear from him. He must yet sail about three thousand miles in the Pacific Ocean, and then about two thousand more in the Atlantic, before he reached Rio Janeiro, the port for which he had cleared. From there it would be nearly five thousand miles to France, and he did not dare to calculate how long it would take the brig to reach her final destination.

This course of thought determined him to send a letter, which would reach Paris long before he could arrive there. If they should know that he was on his way home, all might be well, or, at least, better than if they knew nothing about him. It might be a hazardous thing to touch at a port on this coast, but he believed that, if he managed matters properly, he might get a letter ashore without making it necessary for any meddlesome custom-house officers to come aboard and ask questions. Accordingly, he decided to stop at Valparaiso. He thought it likely that if he did not meet a vessel going into port which would lay to and take his letter, he might find some merchantman, anchored in the roadstead, to which he could send a boat, and on which he was sure to find some one who would willingly post his letter.

He wrote a long letter to Edna—a straightforward, business-like missive, as his letters had always been, in which, in language which she could understand, but would carry no intelligible idea to any unauthorized person who might open the letter, he gave her an account of what he had done, and which was calculated to relieve all apprehensions, should it be yet a long time before he reached her. He promised to write again whenever there was an opportunity of sending her a letter, and wrote in such a friendly and encouraging manner that he felt sure there would be no reason for any disappointment or anxiety regarding him and the treasure.

Burke and Shirley were a little surprised when they found that the captain had determined to stop at Valparaiso, a plan so decidedly opposed to what he had before said on the subject. But when they found it was for the purpose of sending a letter to his wife, and that he intended, if possible, barely to touch and go, they said nothing more, nor did Burke make any further allusions to improvement in their store of provisions.

When, at last, the captain found himself off Valparaiso, it was on a dark, cloudy evening and nothing could be done until the next morning, and they dropped anchor to wait until dawn.

As soon as it was light, the captain saw that a British steamer was anchored about a mile from the *Miranda*, and he immediately sent a boat, with Shirley and two of the negroes, to ask the officer on duty to post his letter when he sent on shore. In a little more than an hour Shirley returned, with the report that the first mate of the steamer knew Captain Horn and would gladly take charge of his letter.

The boat was quickly hauled to the davits, and all hands were called to weigh anchor and set sail. But all hands did not respond to the call. One of the negroes, a big, good-natured fellow, who, on account of his unpronounceable African name, had been dubbed "Inkspot," was not to be found. This was a very depressing thing, under the circumstances, and it, almost counterbalanced the pleasure the captain felt in having started a letter on its way to his party in France.

It seemed strange that Inkspot should have deserted the vessel, for it was a long way to the shore, and, besides, what possible reason could he have for leaving his fellow-Africans and taking up his lot among absolute strangers? The crew had all worked together so earnestly and faithfully that the captain had come to believe in them and trust them to an extent to which he had never before trusted seamen.

The officers held a consultation as to what was to be done, and they very quickly arrived at a decision. To remain at anchor, to send a boat on shore to look for the missing negro, would be dangerous and useless. Inquiries about the deserter would provoke inquiries about the brig, and if Inkspot really wished to run away from the vessel, it would take a long time to find him and bring him back. The right course was quite plain to every one. Having finished the business which brought them there, they must up anchor and sail away as soon as possible. As for the loss of the man, they must bear that as well as they could. Whether he had been drowned, eaten by a shark, or had safely reached the shore, he was certainly lost to them.

At the best, their crew had been small enough, but six men had sailed a brig, and six men could do it again.

So the anchor was weighed, the sails were set, and before a northeast wind the *Miranda* went out to sea as gayly as the nature of her build permitted, which is not saying much. It was a good wind, however, and when the log had been thrown, the captain remarked that the brig was making better time than she had made since they left Acapulco.

CHAPTER XXXVI
A HORSE-DEALER APPEARS ON THE SCENE

When the brig *Miranda* was lying at anchor in the Rackbirds' cove, and Mr. George Burke had silently left her in order to go on shore and pursue some investigations in which he was interested, his departure from the brig had not been, as he supposed, unnoticed. The big, good-natured African, known as Inkspot, had been on watch, and, being himself so very black that he was not generally noticeable in the dark, was standing on a part of the deck from which, without being noticed himself, he saw a person get over the taffrail and slip into the water. He knew this person to be the second mate, and having a high respect and some fear of his superiors, he did not consider it his business to interfere with him. He saw a head above the water, moving toward the shore, but it soon disappeared in the darkness. Toward the end of his watch, he had seen Mr. Burke climb up the vessel's side as silently as he had gone down it, and disappear below.

When Inkspot went to his hammock, which he did very shortly afterwards, he reflected to the best of his ability upon what he had seen. Why did Mr. Burke slip away from the ship so silently, and come back in the same way? He must have gone ashore, and why did he want no one to know that he had gone? He must have gone to do something he ought not to do, and Inkspot could think of nothing wrong that Mr. Burke would like to do, except to drink whiskey. Captain Horn was very particular about using spirits on board, and perhaps Mr. Burke liked whiskey, and could not get it. Inkspot knew about the storehouse of the Rackbirds, but he did not know what it had contained, or what had been left there. Maka had said something about the whiskey having been poured out on the sand, but that might have been said just to keep people away from the place. If there were no whiskey there, why did Mr. Burke go on shore?

Now, it so happened that Inkspot knew a good deal about whiskey. Before he had gone into the service of the Rackbirds, he had, at different times, been drunk, and he had the liveliest and most pleasant recollections of these experiences. It had been a long time since he had had enough whiskey to make him feel happy. This had probably been the case with

Mr. Burke, and he had gone on shore, and most likely had had some very happy hours, and had come back without any one knowing where he had gone. The consequence of this train of thought was that Inkspot determined that he would go on shore, the next night, and hunt for whiskey. He could do it quite as well as Mr. Burke had done it, perhaps even better. But the *Miranda* did not remain in the cove the next night, and poor Inkspot looked with longing eyes upon the slowly departing spot on the sands where he knew the Rackbirds' storehouse was located.

The days and nights went on, and in the course of time the *Miranda* anchored in the harbor of Valparaiso; and, when this happened, Inkspot determined that now would be his chance to go on shore and get a good drink of whiskey—he had money enough for that. He could see the lights of El Puerto, or the Old Town, glittering and beckoning, and they did not appear to be very far off. It would be nothing for him to swim as far as that.

Inkspot went off his watch at midnight, and he went into the water at fifty minutes to one. He wore nothing but a dark-gray shirt and a pair of thin trousers, and if any one had seen his head and shoulders, it is not likely, unless a good light had been turned on them, that they would have been supposed to be portions of a human form.

Inkspot was very much at home in the water, and he could swim like a dog or a deer. But it was a long, long swim to those glittering and beckoning lights. At last, however, he reached a pier, and having rested himself on the timbers under it, he cautiously climbed to the top. The pier was deserted, and he walked to the end of it, and entered the town. He knew nothing of Valparaiso, except that it was a large city where sailors went, and he was quite sure he could find a shop where they sold whiskey. Then he would have a glass—perhaps two—perhaps three—after which he would return to the brig, as Mr. Burke had done. Of course, he would have to do much more swimming than had been necessary for the second mate, but then, he believed himself to be a better swimmer than that gentleman, and he expected to get back a great deal easier than he came, because the whiskey would make him strong and happy, and he could play with the waves.

Inkspot did find a shop, and a dirty one it was—but they sold whiskey inside, and that was enough for him. With the exception of Maka, he was the most intelligent negro among the captain's crew, and he had picked up some words of English and some of Spanish. But it was difficult for him to express an idea with these words. Among these words, however, was one which he pronounced better than any of the others, and which had always been understood whenever he used it,—whether in English or Spanish, no matter what the nationality might be of the person addressed,—and that word was "whiskey."

Inkspot had one glass, and then another, a third, and a fourth, and then his money gave out—at least, the man who kept the shop insisted, in words that any one could understand, that the silver the big negro had fished out of his dripping pockets would pay for no more drinks. But Inkspot had had enough to make him happy. His heart was warm, and his clothes were getting drier. He went out into the glorious night. It was dark and windy, and the sky was cloudy, but to him all things were glorious. He sat down on the pavement in the cosey corner of two walls, and there he slept luxuriously until a policeman came along and arrested him for being drunk in the street.

It was two days before Inkspot got out of the hands of the police. Then he was discharged because the authorities did not desire to further trouble themselves with a stupid fellow who could give no account of himself, and had probably wandered from a vessel in port. The first thing he did was to go out to the water's edge and look out over the harbor, but although he saw many ships, his sharp eyes told him that not one of them was the brig he had left.

After an hour or two of wandering up and down the waterside, he became sure that there was no vessel in that harbor waiting for him to swim to her. Then he became equally certain that he was very hungry. It was not long, however, before a good, strong negro like Inkspot found employment. It was not necessary for him to speak very much Spanish, or any other language, to get a job at carrying things up a gang-plank, and, in pay for this labor, he willingly took whatever was given him.

That night, with very little money in his pocket, Inkspot entered a tavern, a low place, but not so low as the one he had patronized on his arrival in Valparaiso. He had had a meagre supper, and now possessed but money enough to pay for one glass of whiskey, and having procured this, he seated himself on a stool in a corner, determined to protract his enjoyment as long as possible. Where he would sleep that night he knew not, but it was not yet bedtime, and he did not concern himself with the question.

Near by, at a table, were seated four men, drinking, smoking, and talking. Two of these were sailors. Another, a tall, dark man with a large nose, thin at the bridge and somewhat crooked below, was dressed in very decent shore clothes, but had a maritime air about him, notwithstanding. The fourth man, as would have been evident to any one who understood

Spanish, was a horse-dealer, and the conversation, when Inkspot entered the place, was entirely about horses. But Inkspot did not know this, as he understood so few of the words that he heard, and he would not have been interested if he had understood them. The horse-dealer was the principal spokesman, but he would have been a poor representative of the shrewdness of his class, had he been trying to sell horses to sailors. He was endeavoring to do nothing of the kind. These men were his friends, and he was speaking to them, not of the good qualities of his animals, but of the credulous natures of his customers. To illustrate this, he drew from his pocket a small object which he had received a few days before for some horses which might possibly be worth their keep, although he would not be willing to guarantee this to any one at the table. The little object which he placed on the table was a piece of gold about two inches long, and shaped like an irregular prism.

This, he said, he had received in trade from a man in Santiago, who had recently come down from Lima. The man had bought it from a jeweller, who had others, and who said he understood they had come from California. The jeweller had owed the man money, and the latter had taken this, not as a curiosity, for it was not much of a curiosity, as they could all see, but because the jeweller told him exactly how much it was worth, and because it was safer than money to carry, and could be changed into current coin in any part of the world. The point of the horse-dealer's remarks was, however, the fact that not only had he sold his horses to the man from Lima for very much more than they were worth, but he had made him believe that this lump of gold was not worth as much as he had been led to suppose, that the jeweller had cheated him, and that Californian gold was not easily disposed of in Chili or Peru, for it was of a very inferior quality to the gold of South America. So he had made his trade, and also a profit, not only on the animals he delivered, but on the pay he received. He had had the little lump weighed and tested, and knew exactly how much it was worth.

When the horse-dealer had finished this pleasant tale, he laughed loudly, and the three other men laughed also because they had keen wits and appreciated a good story of real life. But their laughter was changed to astonishment—almost fright—when a big black negro bounded out of a dark corner and stood by the table, one outstretched ebony finger pointing to the piece of gold. Instantly the horse dealer snatched his treasure and thrust it into his pocket, and almost at the same moment each man sprung to his feet and put his hand on his favorite weapon. But the negro made no attempt to snatch the gold, nor did there seem to be any reason to apprehend an attack from him. He stood slapping his thighs with his hands, his mouth in a wide grin, and his eyes sparkling in apparent delight.

"What is the matter with you?" shouted the horse-dealer. "What do you want?"

Inkspot did not understand what had been said to him, nor could he have told what he wanted, for he did not know. At that moment he knew nothing, he comprehended nothing, but he felt as a stranger in a foreign land would feel should he hear some words in his native tongue. The sight of that piece of gold had given to Inkspot, by one quick flash, a view of his negro friends and companions, of Captain Horn and his two white men, of the brig he had left, of the hammock in which he had slept—of all, in fact, that he now cared for on earth.

He had seen pieces of gold like that. Before all the treasure had been carried from the caves to the *Miranda*, the supply of coffee-bags had given out, and during the last days of the loading it had been necessary to tie up the gold in pieces of sail-cloth, after the fashion of a wayfarer's bundle. Before these had been put on board, their fastening had been carefully examined, and some of them had been opened and retied. Thus all the negroes had seen the little bars, for, as they knew the bags contained gold, there was no need of concealing from them the shape and size of the contents.

So, when, sitting in his gloomy corner, his spirits slowly rising under the influence of his refreshment, which he had just finished, he saw before him an object which recalled to him the life and friends of which he had bereft himself, Inkspot's nature took entire possession of him, and he bounded to the table in ecstatic recognition of the bit of metal.

The men now swore at Inkspot, but as they saw he was unarmed, and not inclined to violence, they were not afraid of him, but they wondered at him. The horse-dealer took the piece of gold out of his pocket and held it in his hand.

"Did you ever see anything like that before?" he asked. He was a shrewd man, the horse-dealer, and really wanted to know what was the matter with the negro.

Inkspot did not answer, but jabbered in African.

"Try him in English," suggested the thin-nosed man, and this the horse-dealer did.

Many of the English words Inkspot understood. He had seen things like that. Yes, yes! Great heaps! Heaps! Bags! Bags! He carried them! Throwing an imaginary package over his shoulder, he staggered under it across the floor. Heaps! Piles! Bags! Days and days and days he carried many bags! Then, in a state of exalted mental action, produced by his recollections and his whiskey, he suddenly conceived a scorn for a man who prized so highly just one of these lumps, and who was nearly frightened out of his wits if a person merely pointed to it. He shrugged his shoulders, he spread out the palms of his hands toward the piece of gold, he turned away his head and walked off sniffing. Then he came back and pointed to it, and, saying "One!" he laughed, and then he said "One!" and laughed again. Suddenly he became possessed with a new idea. His contemptuous manner dropped from him, and in eager excitement he leaned forward and exclaimed:

"Cap' 'Or?"

The four men looked at each other and at him in wonder, and asked what, in the name of his satanic majesty, the fellow was driving at. This apparent question, now repeated over and over again in turn to each of them, they did not understand at all. But they could comprehend that the negro had carried bags of lumps like that. This was very interesting.

CHAPTER XXXVII
THE "ARATO"

The subject of the labors of an African Hercules, mythical as these labors might be, was so interesting to the four men who had been drinking and smoking in the tavern, that they determined to pursue it as far as their ignorance of the African's language, and his ignorance of English and Spanish, would permit. In the first place, they made him sit down with them, and offered him something to drink. It was not whiskey, but Inkspot liked it very much, and felt all sorts of good effects from it. In fact, it gave him a power of expressing himself by gestures and single words in a manner wonderful. After a time, the men gave him something to eat, for they imagined he might be hungry, and this also helped him very much, and his heart went out to these new friends. Then he had a little more to drink, but only a little, for the horse-dealer and the thin-nosed man, who superintended the entertainment, were very sagacious, and did not want him to drink too much.

In the course of an hour, these four men, listening and watching keenly and earnestly, had become convinced that this black man had been on a ship which carried bags of gold similar to the rude prism possessed by the horse-dealer, that he had left that vessel for the purpose of obtaining refreshments on shore and had not been able to get back to it, thereby indicating that the vessel had not stopped long at the place where he had left it, and which place must have been, of course, Valparaiso. Moreover, they found out to their full satisfaction where that vessel was going to; for Maka had talked a great deal about Paris, which he pronounced in English fashion, where Cheditafa and Mok were, and the negroes had looked forward to this unknown spot as a heavenly port, and Inkspot could pronounce the word "Paris" almost as plainly as if it were a drink to which he was accustomed.

But where the vessel was loaded with the gold, they could not find out. No grimace that Inkspot could make, nor word that he could say, gave them an idea worth dwelling upon. He said some words which made them believe that the vessel had cleared from Acapulco, but it was foolish to suppose that any vessel had been loaded there with bags of gold carried on men's shoulders. The ship most probably came from California, and had touched at the Mexican port. And she was now bound for Paris. That was natural enough. Paris was a very good place to which to take gold. Moreover, she had probably touched at some South American port, Callao perhaps, and this was the way the little pieces of gold had been brought into the country, the Californians probably having changed them for stores.

The words "Cap' 'Or,'" often repeated by the negro, and always in a questioning tone, puzzled them very much. They gave up its solution, and went to work to try to make out the name of the vessel upon which the bags had been loaded. But here Inkspot could not help them. They could not make him understand what it was they wanted him to say. At last, the horse-dealer proposed to the others, who, he said, knew more about such things than he did, that they should repeat the name of every sailing-vessel on that coast of which they had ever heard—for Inkspot had made them understand that his ship had sails, and no steam. This they did, and presently one of the sailors mentioned the name *Miranda*, which belonged to a brig he knew of which plied on the coast. At this, Inkspot sprang to his feet and clapped his hands.

"*Miran'a! Miran'a.'*" he cried. And then followed the words, "Cap' 'Or! Cap' 'Or!" in eagerly excited tones.

Suddenly the thin-nosed man, whom the others called Cardatas, leaned forward.

"Cap'n Horn?" said he.

Inkspot clapped his hands again, and exclaimed:

"Ay, ay! Cap' 'Or! Cap' 'Or!"

He shouted the words so loudly that the barkeeper, at the other end of the room, called out gruffly that they'd better keep quiet, or they would have somebody coming in.

"There you have it!" exclaimed Cardatas, in Spanish. "It's Cap'n Horn that the fool's been trying to say. Cap'n Horn of the brig *Miranda*. We are getting on finely."

"I have heard of a Cap'n Horn," said one of the sailors. "He's a Yankee skipper from California. He has sailed from this port, I know."

"And he touched here three days ago, according to the negro," said Cardatas, addressing the horse-dealer. "What do you say to that, Nunez? From what we know, I don't think it will be hard to find out more."

Nunez agreed with him, and thought it might pay to find out more. Soon after this, being informed that it was time to shut up the place, the four men went out, taking Inkspot with them. They would not neglect this poor fellow. They would give him a place to sleep, and in the morning he should have something to eat. It would be very unwise to let him go from them at present.

The next morning Inkspot strolled about the wharves of Valparaiso, in company with the two sailors, who never lost sight of him, and he had rather a pleasant time, for they gave him as much to eat and drink as was good for him, and made him understand as well as they could that it would not be long before they would help him to return to the brig *Miranda* commanded by Captain Horn.

In the meantime, the horse-dealer, Nunez, went to a newspaper office, and there procured a file of a Mexican paper, for the negro had convinced them that his vessel had sailed from Acapulco. Turning over the back numbers week after week, and week after week, Nunez searched in the maritime news for the information that the *Miranda* had cleared from a Mexican port. He had gone back so far that he had begun to consider it useless to make further search, when suddenly he caught the name *Miranda*. There it was. The brig *Miranda* had cleared from Acapulco September 16, bound for Rio Janeiro in ballast. Nunez counted the months on his fingers.

"Five months ago!" he said to himself. "That's not this trip, surely. But I will talk to Cardatas about that." And taking from his pocket a little note-book in which he recorded his benefactions in the line of horse trades, he carefully copied the paragraph concerning the *Miranda*.

When Nunez met Cardatas in the afternoon, the latter also had news. He had discovered that the arrival of the *Miranda* had not been registered, but he had been up and down the piers, asking questions, and he had found a mate of a British steamer, then discharging her cargo, who told him that the *Miranda*, commanded by Captain Horn, had anchored in the harbor three days back, during the night, and that early the next morning Captain Horn had sent him a letter which he wished posted, and that very soon afterwards the brig had put out to sea. Cardatas wished to know much more, but the mate, who had had but little conversation with Shirley, could only tell him that the brig was then bound from Acapulco to Rio Janeiro in ballast, which he thought rather odd, but all he could add was that he knew Captain Horn, and he was a good man, and that if he were sailing in ballast, he supposed he knew what he was about.

Nunez then showed Cardatas the note he had made, and remarked that, of course, it could not refer to the present voyage of the brig, for it could not take her five months to come from Acapulco to this port.

"No," said the other, musing, "it oughtn't to, but, on the other hand, it is not likely she is on her second voyage to Rio, and both times in ballast.

That's all stuff about ballast. No man would be such a fool as to sail pretty nigh all around this continent in ballast. He could find some cargo in Mexico that he could sell when he got to port. Besides, if that black fellow don't lie,—and he don't know enough to lie,—she's bound for Paris. It's more likely she means to touch at Rio and take over some cargo. But why, in the devil's name, should she sail from Acapulco in ballast? It looks to me as if bags of gold might make very good ballast."

"That's just what I was thinking," said Nunez.

"And what's more," said the other, "I'll bet she brought it down from California with her when she arrived at Acapulco. I don't believe she originally cleared from there."

"It looks that way," said Nunez, "but how do you account for such a long voyage?"

"I've been talking to Sanchez about that *Miranda*," said Cardatas. "He has heard that she is an old tub, and a poor sailer, and in that case five months is not such a very slow voyage. I have known of slower voyages than that."

"And now what are you going to do about it?" asked Nunez.

"The first thing I want to do is to pump that black fellow a little more."

"A good idea," said Nunez, "and we'll go and do it."

Poor Inkspot was pumped for nearly an hour, but not much was got out of him. The only feature of his information that was worth anything was the idea that he managed to convey that ballast, consisting of stones and bags of sand, had been taken out of the brig and thrown away, and bags of gold put in their places. Where this transfer had taken place, the negro could not make his questioners understand, and he was at last remanded to the care of Sanchez and the other sailor.

"The black fellow can't tell us much," said Cardatas to Nunez, as they walked away together, "but he has stuck to his story well, and there can't be any use of his lying about it. And there is another thing. What made the brig touch here just long enough to leave a letter, and that after a voyage of five months? That looks as if they were afraid some of their people would go on shore and talk."

"In that case," said Nunez, "I should say there is something shady about the business. Perhaps this captain has slipped away from his partners up there in California, or somebody who has been up to a trick has hired him to take the gold out of the country. If he does carry treasure, it isn't a fair and square thing. If it had been fair, the gold would have been sent in the regular way, by a steamer. It's no crime to send gold from California to France, or any other place."

"I agree with you," said Cardatas, as he lighted his twenty-seventh cigarette.

Nunez did not smoke, but he mused as he walked along.

"If she has gold on board," said he, presently, "it must be a good deal."

"Yes," said the other. "They wouldn't take so much trouble for a small lot. Of course, there can't be enough of it to take the place of all the ballast, but it must weigh considerable."

Here the two men were joined by an acquaintance, and their special conversation ceased. That night they met again.

"What are you going to do about this?" asked Nunez. "We can't keep on supporting that negro."

"What is to be done?" asked the other, his sharp eyes fixed upon his companion's face.

"Would it pay to go over to Rio and meet that brig when she arrives there? If we could get on board and have a talk with her captain, he might be willing to act handsomely when he found out we know something about him and his ship. And if he won't do that, we might give information, and have his vessel held until the authorities in California can be communicated with. Then I should say we ought to make something."

"I don't think much of that plan," said Cardatas. "I don't believe she's going to touch at Rio. If she's afraid to go into port here, why shouldn't she be afraid to go into port there? No. It would be stupid for us to go to Rio and sit down and wait for her."

"Then," answered the other, a little angrily, "what can be done?"

"We can go after her," said Cardatas.

The other sneered. "That would be more stupid than the other," said he. "She left here four days ago, and we could never catch up with her, even if we could find such a pin-point of a vessel on the great Pacific."

Cardatas laughed. "You don't know much about navigation," said he, "but that's not to be expected. With a good sailing-vessel I could go after her, and overhaul her somewhere in the Straits of Magellan. With such a cargo, I am sure she would make for the Straits. That Captain Horn is said to be a good sailor, and the fact that he is in command of such a tub as the *Miranda* is a proof that there is something underhand about his business."

"And if we should overhaul her?" said the other.

"Well," was the reply, "we might take along a dozen good fellows, and as the *Miranda* has only three men on board,—I don't count negroes worth anything,—I don't see why we couldn't induce the captain to talk reasonably to us. As for a vessel, there's the *Arato*."

"Your vessel?" said the other.

"Yes, I own a small share in her, and she's here in port now, waiting for a cargo."

"I forget what sort of a craft she is," said Nunez.

"She's a schooner," said the other, "and she can sail two miles to the *Miranda's* one in any kind of weather. If I had money enough, I could get the *Arato*, put a good crew on board, and be at sea and on the wake of that brig in twenty-four hours."

"And how much money would be needed?" asked the other.

"That remains to be calculated," replied Cardatas. Then the two went to work to calculate, and spent an hour or two at it.

When they parted, Nunez had not made up his mind that the plan of Cardatas was a good one, but he told him to go ahead and see what could be done about getting the *Arato* and a reliable crew, and that he would talk further to him about the matter.

That night Nunez took a train for Santiago, and on his arrival there, the next morning, he went straight to the shop of the jeweller of whom had been obtained the piece of gold in his possession. Here he made some cautious inquiries, and found the jeweller very ready to talk about the piece of gold that Nunez showed him. The jeweller said that he had had four pieces of the gold in his possession, and that he had bought them in Lima to use in his business. They had originally come from California, and were very fine gold. He had been a little curious about it on account of the shape of the pieces, and had been told that they had been brought into the country by an American sea-captain, who had seemed to have a good many of them. The jeweller thought it very likely that these pieces of gold passed for currency in California, for he had heard that at one time the people there had had to make their own currency, and that they often paid for merchandise in so many penny-weights and ounces of gold instead of using coin. The jeweller was himself very glad to do business in this way, for he liked the feel of a lump of gold.

After explaining that his reason for making these inquiries was his fear that the piece of gold he had accepted in trade because he also liked the feel of lumps of gold, might not be worth what he had given for it, Nunez thanked the jeweller, left him, and returned to Valparaiso. He went straight to his friend Cardatas, and said that he would furnish the capital to fit out the *Arato* for the projected trip.

It was not in twenty-four hours, but in forty-eight, that the schooner *Arato* cleared from Valparaiso for Callao in ballast. She had a good set of sails, and a crew of ten men besides the captain. She also had on board a passenger, Nunez by name, and a tall negro, who doubtless could turn his hand to some sort of work on board, and whom it would have been very indiscreet to leave behind.

Once outside the harbor, the *Arato* changed her mind about going to Callao, and sailed southward.

CHAPTER XXXVIII
THE COAST OF PATAGONIA

For about ten days after the brig *Miranda* left Valparaiso she had good winds and fair weather, and her progress was satisfactory to all on board, but at the end of that time she entered upon a season of head winds and bad weather. The vessel behaved very well in the stormy days that followed, but she made very little headway. Her course was now laid toward the Gulf of Penas, after reaching which she would sail along the protected waterways between the chain of islands which lie along the coast and the mainland, and which lead into the Straits of Magellan.

When the weather at last changed and the sea became smoother, it was found that the working and straining of the masts during the violent weather had opened some of the seams of the brig, and that she was taking in water. She was a good vessel, but she was an old one, and she had had a rough time of it. The captain thanked his stars that she had not begun to leak before the storm.

The short-handed crew went to work at the pumps, but, after two days' hard labor, it was found that the water in the hold steadily gained upon the pumps, and there was no doubt that the *Miranda* was badly strained. According to a report from Burke, the water came in forward, aft, and midships. Matters were now getting very serious, and the captain and his two mates consulted together, while the three negroes pumped. It was plain to all of them that if the water kept on gaining, it would not be long before the brig must go to the bottom. To keep her afloat until they reached a port would be impossible. To reach the shore in the boats was quite possible, for they were not a hundred miles from land. But to carry their treasure to land in two small boats was a thing which need not even be considered.

All agreed that there was but one thing to be done. The brig must be headed to land, and if she could be kept afloat until she neared one of the great islands which lie along the Patagonian coast, she might be run into some bay or protected cove, where she could be beached, or where, if she should sink, it might be in water so shallow that all hope of getting at her treasure would not have to be abandoned. In any case, the sooner they got to the shore, the better for them. So the brig's bow was turned eastward, and the pumps were worked harder than ever. There was a good wind, and, considering that the *Miranda* was steadily settling deeper and deeper, she made very fair progress, and in less than two days after she had changed her course, land was sighted. Not long after, Captain Horn began to hope that if the wind held, and the brig could keep above water for an hour or so, he could double a small headland which now showed itself plainly a couple of miles away, and might be able to beach his vessel.

What a dreary, depressing hope it was that now possessed the souls of Captain Horn, of Burke and Shirley, and of even the three negroes! After all the hardships, the labor, and the anxieties, after all the joy of success and escape from danger, after all happy chances which had come in various ways and from various directions, after the sweet delights of rest, after the super-exultation of anticipation which no one on board had been able to banish from his mind, there was nothing left to them now but the eager desire that their vessel might keep afloat until she could find some friendly sands on which she might be run, or some shallow water in which she might sink and rest there on the wild Patagonian coast, leaving them far from human beings of any kind, far from help, far, perhaps, from rescue and even safety.

To this one object each man gave his entire energy, his mind, and his body. Steadily went the pumps, steadily the captain kept his eyes fixed upon the approaching headland, and upon the waters beyond, and steadily, little by little, the *Miranda* sunk lower and lower into the sea.

At last the headland was reached, and on its ocean side the surf beat high. Keeping well away to avoid shoals or a bar, the *Miranda* passed the southern point of the headland, and slowly sailed into a little bay. To the left lay the rocky ridge which formed the headland, and less than half a mile away could be seen the shining sands of the smooth beach. Toward this beach the *Miranda* was now headed, every sail upon her set, and every nerve upon her strung to its tightest. They went in upon a flood-tide. If he had believed that the brig would float so long, Captain Horn would have waited an hour until the tide was high, so that he might run his vessel farther up upon the beach, but he could not wait, and with a strong west wind he steered straight for the sands.

There was a hissing under the bows, and a shock which ran through the vessel from stem to stern, and then grinding and grinding and grinding until all motion ceased, and a gentle surf began to curl itself against the stern of the brig.

Every halliard was let go, and down came every sail by the run, and then the brig *Miranda* ended this voyage, and all others, upon the shore of a desolate Patagonian island.

Between the vessel and dry land there was about a hundred feet of water, but this would be much less when the tide went out. Beyond the beach was a stretch of sandy hillocks, or dunes, and back of these was a mass of scrubby thicket, with here and there a low tree, and still farther back was seen the beginning of what might be a forest. It was a different coast from the desolate shores of Peru.

Burke came aft to the captain.

"Here we are, sir," said he, "and what's to happen next?"

"Happen!" exclaimed the captain. "We must not wait for things to happen! What we've got to do is to step around lively, and get the gold out of this brig before the wind changes and drives her out into deep water."

Burke put his hands into his pockets. "Is there any good of it, captain?" said he. "Will we be any better off with the bags on that shore than we would be if they were sunk in this bay?"

"Good of it!" exclaimed the captain. "Don't talk that way, Burke. If we can get it on shore, there is a chance for us. But if it goes to the bottom, out in deep water, there is none. There is no time to talk now. What we must do is to go to work."

"Yes," said Burke, "whatever happens, it is always work. But I'm in for it, as long as I hold together. But we've got to look out that some of those black fellows don't drop over the bow, and give us the slip."

"They'll starve if they do," said the captain, "for not a biscuit, or a drop of water, goes ashore until the gold is out of the hold."

Burke shook his head. "We'll do what we can, captain," said he, "but that hold's a regular fishpond, and we'll have to dive for the bags."

"All right," said the captain, "dive let it be."

The work of removing the gold began immediately. Tackle was rigged. The negroes went below to get out the bags, which were hauled up to the deck in a tub. When a moderate boat-load had been taken out, a boat was lowered and manned, and the bags passed down to it.

In the first boat the captain went ashore. He considered it wise to land the treasure as fast as it could be taken out of the hold, for no one could know at what time, whether on account of wind from shore or waves from the sea, the vessel might slip out into deep water. This was a slower method than if everybody had worked at getting the gold on deck, and then everybody had worked at getting it ashore, but it was a safer plan than the other, for if an accident should occur, if the brig should be driven off the sand, they would have whatever they had already landed. As this thought passed through the mind of the captain, he could not help a dismal smile.

"Have!" said he to himself. "It may be that we shall have it as that poor fellow had his bag of gold, when he lay down on his back to die there in the wild desert."

But no one would have imagined that such an idea had come into the captain's mind. He worked as earnestly, and as steadily, as if he had been landing an ordinary cargo at an ordinary dock.

The captain and the men in the boat carried the bags high up on the beach, out of any danger from tide or surf, and laid them in a line along the sand. The captain ordered this because it would be easier to handle them afterwards—if it should ever be necessary to handle them—than if they had been thrown into piles. If they should conclude to bury them, it would be easier and quicker to dig a trench along the line, and tumble them in, than to make the deep holes that would otherwise be necessary.

Until dark that day, and even after dark, they worked, stopping only for necessary eating and drinking. The line of bags upon the shore had grown into a double one, and it became necessary for the men, sometimes the white and sometimes the black, to stoop deeper and deeper into the water of the hold to reach the bags. But they worked on bravely. In the early dawn of the next morning they went to work again. Not a negro had given the ship the slip, nor were there any signs that one of them had thought of such a thing.

Backward and forward through the low surf went the boat, and longer and wider and higher grew the mass of bags upon the beach.

It was the third day after they had reached shore that the work was finished. Every dripping bag had been taken out of the hold, and the captain had counted them all as they had been put ashore, and verified the number by the record in his pocket-book.

When the lower tiers of bags had been reached, they had tried pumping out the water, but this was of little use. The brig had keeled over on her starboard side, and early in the morning of the third day, when the tide was running out, a hole had been cut in that side of the vessel, out of which a great portion of the water she contained had run. It would all come in again, and more of it, when the tide rose, but they were sure they could get through their work before that, and they were right. The bags now lay upon the beach in the shape of a long mound, not more than three feet high, and about four rows wide at the bottom and two at the top. The captain had superintended the arrangement of the bags, and had so shaped the mass that it somewhat resembled in form the dunes of sand which lay behind it. No matter what might be their next step, it would probably be advisable to conceal the bags, and the captain had thought that the best way to do this would be to throw sand over the long mound, in which work the prevailing western winds would be likely to assist, and thus make it look like a natural sand-hill. Burke and Shirley were in favor of burial, but the consideration of this matter was deferred, for there was more work to be done, which must be attended to immediately.

Now provisions, water, and everything else that might be of value was taken out of the brig and carried to shore. Two tents were constructed out of sails and spars, and the little party established themselves upon the beach. What would be their next work they knew not, but they must first rest from their long season of heavy labor. The last days had been harder even than the days of storm and the days of pumping. They had eaten hurriedly and slept but little. Regular watches and irregular watches had been kept— watches against storm, which might sweep the brig with all on board out to sea, watches against desertion, watches against they knew not what. As chief watcher, the captain had scarcely slept at all.

It had been dreary work, unrelieved by hope, uncheered by prospect of success; for not one of them, from the captain down, had any definite idea as to what was to be done after they had rested enough to act.

But they rested, and they went so far as to fill their pipes and stretch themselves upon the sand. When night came on, chilly and dark, they gathered driftwood and dead branches from the thicket and built a camp-fire. They sat around it, and smoked their pipes, but they did not tell stories, nor did they talk very much. They were glad to rest, they were glad to keep warm, but that was all. The only really cheerful thing upon the beach was the fire, which leaped high and blazed merrily as the dried wood was heaped upon it.

CHAPTER XXXIX
SHIRLEY SPIES A SAIL

When the *Arato* changed her mind about going to Callao, and sailed southward some five days after the *Miranda* had started on the same course, she had very good weather for the greater part of a week, and sailed finely. Cardatas, who owned a share in her, had sailed upon her as first mate, but he had never before commanded her. He was a good navigator, however, and well fitted for the task he had undertaken. He was a sharp fellow, and kept his eyes on everybody, particularly upon Nunez, who, although a landsman, and in no wise capable of sailing a ship, was perfectly capable of making plans regarding any vessel in which he was interested, especially when such a vessel happened to be sailing in pursuit of treasure, the value of which was merely a matter of conjecture. It was not impossible that the horse-dealer, who had embarked money in this venture, might think that one of the mariners on board might be able to sail the schooner as well as Cardatas, and would not expect so large a share of the profits should the voyage be successful. But when the storms came on, Nunez grew sick and unhappy, and retired below, and he troubled the mind of Cardatas no more for the present.

The *Arato* sailed well with a fair wind, but in many respects she was not as good a sea-boat in a storm as the *Miranda* had proved to be, and she had been obliged to lie to a great deal through the days and nights of high winds and heavy seas. Having never had, until now, the responsibility of a vessel upon him, Cardatas was a good deal more cautious and prudent, perhaps, than Captain Horn would have been had he been in command of the *Arato*. Among other methods of precaution which Cardatas thought it wise to take, he steered well out from the coast, and thus greatly lengthened his course, and at last, when a clearing sky enabled him to take an observation, he found himself so far to the westward that he changed his course entirely and steered for the southeast.

Notwithstanding all these retarding circumstances, Cardatas did not despair of overhauling the *Miranda*. He was sure she would make for the

Straits, and he did not in the least doubt that, with good winds, he could overtake her before she reached them, and even if she did get out of them, he could still follow her. His belief that the *Arato* could sail two miles to the *Miranda's* one was still unshaken. The only real fear he had was that the *Miranda* might have foundered in the storm. If that should happen to be the case, their voyage would be a losing one, indeed, but he said nothing of his fears to Nunez.

The horse-dealer was now on deck again, in pretty fair condition, but he was beginning to be despondent. After such an awful storm, and in all that chaos of waves, what chance was there of finding a little brig such as they were after?

"But vessels sail in regular courses," Cardatas said to him. "They don't go meandering all over the ocean. If they are bound for any particular place, they go there on the shortest safe line they can lay down on the map. We can go on that line, too, although we may be thrown out of it by storms. But we can strike it again, and then all we have to do is to keep on it as straight as we can, and we are bound to overtake another vessel on the same course, provided we sail faster than she does. It is all plain enough, don't you see?"

Nunez could not help seeing, but he was a little cross, nevertheless. The map and the ocean were wonderfully different.

The wind had changed, and the *Arato* did not make very good sailing on her southeastern course. High as was her captain's opinion of her, she never had sailed, nor ever could sail, two miles to the *Miranda's* one, although she was a good deal faster than the brig. But she was fairly well handled, and in due course of time she approached so near the coast that her lookout sighted land, which land Cardatas, consulting his chart, concluded must be one of the Patagonian islands to the north of the Gulf of Penas.

As night came on, Cardatas determined to change his course somewhat to the south, as he did not care to trust himself too near the coast, when suddenly the lookout reported a light on the port bow. Cardatas had sailed down this coast before, but he had never heard of a lighthouse in the region, and with his glass he watched the light. But he could not make it out. It was a strange light, for sometimes it was bright and sometimes dull, then it would increase greatly and almost fade away again.

"It looks like a fire on shore," said he, and some of the other men who took the glass agreed with him.

"And what does that mean?" asked Nunez.

"I don't know," replied Cardatas, curtly. "How should I? But one thing I do know, and that is that I shall lie to until morning, and then we can feel our way near to the coast and see what it does mean."

"But what do you want to know for?" asked Nunez. "I suppose somebody on shore has built a fire. Is there any good stopping for that? We have lost a lot of time already."

"I am going to lie to, anyway," said Cardatas. "When we are on such business as ours, we should not pass anything without understanding it."

Cardatas had always supposed that these islands were uninhabited, and he could not see why anybody should be on one of them making a fire, unless it were a case of shipwreck. If a ship had been wrecked, it was not at all impossible that the *Miranda* might be the unfortunate vessel. In any case, it would be wise to lie to, and look into the matter by daylight. If the *Miranda* had gone down at sea, and her crew had reached land in boats, the success of the *Arato's* voyage would be very dubious. And should this misfortune have happened, he must be careful about Nunez when he came to hear of it. When he turned into his hammock that night, Cardatas had made up his mind that, if he should discover that the *Miranda* had gone to the bottom, it would be a very good thing if arrangements could be made for Nunez to follow her.

That night the crew of the Miranda slept well and enjoyed the first real rest they had had since the storm. No watch was kept, for they all thought it would be an unnecessary hardship. The captain awoke at early dawn, and, as he stepped out of the tent, he glanced over sea and land. There were no signs of storm, the brig had not slipped out into deep water, their boats were still high and dry upon the beach, and there was something encouraging in the soft, early light and the pleasant morning air. He was surprised, however, to find that he was not the first man out. On a piece of higher ground, a little back from the tents, Shirley was standing, a glass to his eye.

"What do you see?" cried the captain.

"A sail!" returned Shirley.

At this every man in the tents came running out. Even to the negroes the words, "A sail," had the startling effect which they always have upon ship-wrecked men.

The effect upon Captain Horn was a strange one, and he could scarcely understand it himself. It was amazing that succor, if succor it should prove to be, had arrived so quickly after their disaster. But not-withstanding the fact that he would be overjoyed to be taken off that desolate coast, he could not help a strong feeling of regret that a sail had appeared so soon. If they had had time to conceal their treasure, all might have been well. With the bags of gold buried in a trench, or covered with sand so as to look like a natural mound, he and his sailors might have been taken off merely as shipwrecked sailors, and carried to some port where he might charter another vessel and come back after his gold. But now he knew that whoever landed on this beach must know everything, for it would be impossible to conceal the contents of that long pile of bags, and what consequences might follow upon such knowledge it was impossible for him to imagine. Burke had very much the same idea.

"By George, captain!" said he, "it is a great pity that she came along so soon. What do you say? Shall we signal her or not? We want to get away, but it would be beastly awkward for anybody to come ashore just now. I wish we had buried the bags as fast as we brought them ashore."

The captain did not answer. Perhaps it might be as well not to signal her. And yet, this might be their only chance of rescue!

"What do you say to jumping into the boats and rowing out to meet them?" asked Burke. "We'd have to leave the bags uncovered, but we might get to a port, charter some sort of a craft, and get back for the bags before any other vessel came so near the coast."

"I don't see what made this one come so near," said Shirley, "unless it was our fire last night. She might have thought that was a signal."

"I shouldn't wonder," said the captain, who held the glass. "But we needn't trouble ourselves about going out in boats, for she is making straight for land."

"That's so," said Shirley, who could now see this for himself, for the light was rapidly growing stronger. "She must have seen our fire last night. Shall I hoist a signal?"

"No," said the captain. "Wait!"

They waited to see what this vessel was going to do. Perhaps she was only tacking. But what fool of a skipper would run so close to the shore for the sake of tacking! They watched her eagerly, but not one of the white men would have been wholly disappointed if the schooner, which they could now easily make out, had changed her course and gone off on a long tack to the southwest.

But she was not tacking. She came rapidly on before a stiff west wind. There was no need of getting out boats to go to meet her. She was south of the headland, but was steering directly toward it. They could see what sort of craft she was—a long schooner, painted green, with all sails set. Very soon they could see the heads of the men on board. Then she came nearer and nearer to land, until she was less than half a mile from shore. Then she shot into the wind; her sails fluttered; she lay almost motionless, and her head-sails were lowered.

"That's just as if they were coming into port," said Burke.

"Yes," said Shirley, "I expect they intend to drop anchor."

This surmise was correct, for, as he spoke, the anchor went down with a splash.

"They're very business-like," said Burke. "Look at them. They are lowering a boat."

"A boat!" exclaimed Shirley, "They're lowering two of them."

The captain knit his brows. This was extraordinary action on the part of the vessel. Why did she steer so straight for land? Why did she so quickly drop anchor and put out two boats? Could it be that this vessel had been on their track? Could it be that the Peruvian government—But he could not waste time in surmise as to what might be. They must act, not conjecture.

It was not a minute before the captain made up his mind how they should act. Five men were in each boat, and with a glass it was easy to see that some of them carried guns.

"Get your rifles!" cried he to Shirley and Burke, and he rushed for his own.

The arms and ammunition had been all laid ready in the tent, and in a moment each one of the white men had a rifle and a belt of cartridges. For the blacks there were no guns, as they would not have known how to use them, but they ran about in great excitement, each with his knife drawn, blindly ready to do whatever should be ordered. The poor negroes were greatly frightened. They had but one idea about the approaching boats: they believed that the men in them were Rackbirds coming to wreak vengeance upon them. The same idea had come into the mind of the captain. Some of the Rackbirds had gone back to the cove. They had known that there had been people there. They had made investigations, and found the cave and the empty mound, and in some way had discovered that the *Miranda* had gone off with its contents. Perhaps the black fellow who had deserted the vessel at Valparaiso had betrayed them. He hurriedly mentioned his suspicions to his companions.

"I shouldn't wonder," said Burke, "if that Inkspot had done it. Perhaps he could talk a good deal better than we thought. But I vow I wouldn't have supposed that he would be the man to go back on us. I thought he was the best of the lot."

"Get behind that wall of bags," cried the captain, "every one of you. Whoever they are, we will talk to them over a breastwork."

"I think we shall have to do more than talk," said Burke, "for a blind man could see that there are guns in those boats."

CHAPTER XL
THE BATTLE OF THE GOLDEN WALL

The five men now got behind the barrier of bags, but, before following them, Captain Horn, with the butt of his rifle, drew a long, deep furrow in the sand about a hundred feet from the breastwork of bags, and parallel with it. Then he quickly joined the others.

The three white men stationed themselves a little distance apart, and each moved a few of the top bags so as to get a good sight between them, and not expose themselves too much.

As the boats came on, the negroes crouched on the sand, entirely out of sight, while Shirley and Burke each knelt down behind the barrier, with his rifle laid in a crevice in the top. The captain's rifle was in his hand, but he did not yet prepare for action. He stooped down, but his head was sufficiently above the barrier to observe everything.

The two boats came rapidly on, and were run up on the beach, and the men jumped out and drew them up, high and safe. Then, without the slightest hesitation, the ten of them, each with a gun in his hand, advanced in a body toward the line of bags.

"Ahoy!" shouted the captain, suddenly rising from behind the barrier. "Who are you, and what do you want?" He said this in English, but immediately repeated it in Spanish.

"Ahoy, there!" cried Cardatas. "Are you Captain Horn?"

"Yes, I am," said the captain, "and you must halt where you are. The first man who passes that line is shot."

Cardatas laughed, and so did some of the others, but they all stopped.

"We'll stop here a minute to oblige you," said Cardatas, "but we've got something to say to you, and you might as well listen to it."

Shirley and Burke did not understand a word of these remarks, for they did not know Spanish, but each of them kept his eye running along the line of men who still stood on the other side of the furrow the captain had made in the sand, and if one of them had raised his gun to fire at their skipper, it is probable that he would have dropped. Shirley and Burke had been born and bred in the country; they were hunters, and were both good shots. It was on account of their fondness for sport that they had been separated from the rest of their party on the first day of the arrival of the people from the *Castor* at the caves.

"What have you to say?" said the captain. "Speak quickly."

Cardatas did not immediately answer, for Nunez was excitedly talking to him. The soul of the horse-dealer had been inflamed by the sight of the bags. He did not suppose it possible that they could all contain gold, but he knew they must be valuable, or they would not have been carried up there, and he was advising a rush for the low wall.

"We will see what we can do with them, first," said Cardatas to Nunez. "Some of us may be shot if we are in too great a hurry. They are well defended where they are, and we may have to get round into their rear. Then we can settle their business very well, for the negro said there were only three white men. But first let us talk to them. We may manage them without running any risks."

Cardatas turned toward the captain, and at the same time Burke said:

"Captain, hadn't you better squat down a little? You're making a very fine mark of yourself."

But the captain still stood up to listen to Cardatas.

"I'll tell you what we've come for," said the latter. "We are not officers of the law, but we are the same thing. We know all about you and the valuable stuff you've run away with, and we've been offered a reward to bring back those bags, and to bring you back, too, dead or alive, and here we are, ready to do it. It was good luck for us that your vessel came to grief, but we should have got you, even if she hadn't. We were sure to overhaul you in the Straits. We know all about you and that old hulk, but we are fair and square people, and we're sailors, and we don't want to take advantage of anybody, especially of sailors who have had misfortunes. Now, the reward the Californian government has offered us is not a very big one, and I think you can do better by us, so if you'll agree to come out from behind that breastwork and talk to us fair and square, your two white men and your three negroes,—you see, we know all about you,—I think we can make a bargain that'll suit all around. The government of California hasn't any claim on us, and we don't see why we should serve it any more than we should serve you, and it will be a good deal better for you to be content with half the treasure you've gone off with, or perhaps a little more than that, and let us have the rest. We will take you off on our vessel, and land you at any port you want to go to, and you can take your share of the bags ashore with you. Now, that's what I call a fair offer, and I think you will say so, too."

Captain Horn was much relieved by part of this speech. He had had a slight fear, when Cardatas began, that these men might have been sent out by the Peruvian government, but now he saw they were a set of thieves, whether Rackbirds or not, doing business on their own account.

"The Californian government has nothing to do with me," cried Captain Horn, "and it never had anything to do with you, either. When you say that, you lie! I am not going to make any bargain with you, or have anything to do with you. My vessel is wrecked, but we can take care of ourselves. And now I'll give you five minutes to get to your boats, and the quicker you go, the better for you!"

At this, Nunez stepped forward, his face red with passion. "Look here, you Yankee thief," he cried, "we'll give you just one minute to come out from behind that pile of bags. If you don't come, we'll—"

But if he said any more, Captain Horn did not hear it, for at that moment Burke cried: "Drop, captain!" And the captain dropped.

Stung by the insult he had received, and unable to resist the temptation of putting an end to the discussion by shooting Captain Horn, Cardatas raised his rifle to his shoulder, and almost in the same instant that the captain's body disappeared behind the barrier, he fired. But the bullet had scarcely left his barrel when another ball, from Shirley's gun, struck Cardatas under his uplifted left arm, and stretched him on the sand.

A shock ran through the attacking party, and instinctively they retreated several yards. So suddenly had they lost their leader that, for a few moments, they did not seem to understand the situation. But, on a shout from one of them to look out for themselves, every man dropped flat upon the beach, behind a low bank of sand scarcely a foot high. This was not much protection, but it was better than standing up as marks for the rifles behind the barrier.

The men from the *Arato* were very much surprised by what had happened. They had expected to have an easy job with the crew of the *Miranda*. As soon as the sailor Sanchez had seen the stranded brig, he had recognized her, and Cardatas, as well as the rest of them, had thought that there would be nothing to do but to go on shore with a party of well-armed men, and possess themselves of whatever treasure she had brought to this deserted coast. But to find her crew strongly intrenched and armed had very much amazed them.

Nunez's anger had disappeared, and his accustomed shrewdness had taken its place, for he now saw that very serious business was before them. He was not much of a soldier, but he knew enough to understand that in the plan proposed by Cardatas lay their only hope of success. It would be ridiculous to lie there and waste their ammunition on that wall of bags. He was lying behind the others, and raised his head just enough to tell them what they should do.

"We must get into their rear," he said. "We must creep along the sand until we reach those bushes up there, and then we can get behind them. I'll go first, and you can follow me."

At, this, he began to work himself along the beach, somewhat after the fashion of an earthworm. But the men paid no attention to him. There was little discipline among them, and they had no respect for the horse-dealer as a commander, so they remained on the sands, eagerly talking among themselves. Some of them were frightened, and favored a rush for the boats. But this advice brought down curses from the others. What were three men to nine, that they should run away?

Burke now became tired of waiting to see what would happen next, and putting his hat on a little stick, he raised it a short distance above the breastwork. Instantly one of the more excitable men from the *Arato* fired at it.

"Very good," said Burke. "They want to keep it up, do they? Now, captain," he continued, "we can see the backs and legs of most of them. Shall we fire at them? That will be just as good as killing them. They mean fight—that's easy to see."

But the captain was not willing to follow Burke's advice.

"I don't want to wound or maim them," he replied. "Let's give them a volley just over their heads, and let them see what we are prepared to do. Now, then, when I give the word!"

In a few moments three shots rang out from the intrenchment, and the bullets went whistling over the prostrate bodies of the men on the sand. But these tactics did not have the effect Captain Horn hoped for. They led to no waving of handkerchiefs, nor any show of an intention to treat with an armed and intrenched foe. Instead of that, the man Sanchez sprang to his feet and cried:

"Come on, boys! Over the wall and at them before they can reload!"

At this all the men sprang up and dashed toward the line of bags, Nunez with them. Somebody might get hurt in this wild charge, but he must reach the treasure as soon as the others. He must not fail in that. But Sanchez made a great mistake when he supposed that Captain Horn and his men fought with such arms as the muzzle-loading rifles and shot-guns which the *Arato's* men had thought quite sufficient to bring with them for the work they had to do. Captain Horn, when he had fitted out the *Miranda*, had supplied himself and his two white men with fine repeating rifles, and the *Arato's* men had scarcely crossed the line which had been drawn on the sand before there were three shots from the barrier, and three of the enemy dropped. Even the captain made a good shot this time.

At this the attacking party stopped, and some of them shouted, "To the boats!" Nunez said nothing, for he was dead. There had been much straggling in the line, and Shirley had singled him out as one of the leaders. Before one of them had turned or a retreat begun, Burke's rifle flashed, and another man fell over against a companion, and then down upon the sand. The distance was very short, and a bad shot was almost impossible for a good hunter.

Now there was no hesitation. The five men who had life and legs, turned and dashed for the boats. But the captain did not intend, now, that they should escape, and rifle after rifle cracked from the barricade, and before they reached the boats, four of the flying party had fallen. The fifth man stumbled over one of his companions, who dropped in front of him, then rose to his feet, threw down his gun, and, turning his face toward the shore, held up his hands high above his head.

"I surrender!" he cried, and, still with his arms above his head, and his face whiter than the distant sands, he slowly walked toward the barrier.

The captain rose. "Halt!" he cried, and the man stood stock-still. "Now, my men," cried the captain, turning to Burke and Shirley, "keep your eyes on that fellow until we reach him, and if he moves, shoot him."

The three white men, followed by the negroes, ran down to the man, and when they had reached him, they carefully searched him to see if he had any concealed weapons.

After glancing rapidly over the bodies which lay upon the sand, the captain turned to his men.

"Come on, every one of you," he shouted, "and run out that boat," pointing to the largest one that had brought the *Arato's* men ashore.

Shirley and Burke looked at him in surprise.

"We want that vessel!" he cried, in answer. "Be quick!" And taking hold of the boat himself, he helped the others push it off the sand. "Now, then," he continued, "Shirley, you and Burke get into the bow, with your rifles. Tumble in, you black fellows, and each take an oar. You," he said in Spanish to the prisoner, "get in and take an oar, too."

The captain took the tiller. Shirley and Burke pushed the boat into deep water, and jumped aboard. The oars dipped, and they were off, regardless of the low surf which splashed its crest over the gunwale as the boat turned.

"Tell me, you rascal," said the captain to the prisoner, who was tugging at his oar as hard as the others, "how many men are aboard that schooner?"

"Only two, I swear to you, Señor Capitan; there were twelve of us in all."

The men left on the schooner had evidently watched the proceedings on shore, and were taking measures accordingly.

"They've slipped their anchor, and the tide is running out!" shouted the captain. "Pull! Pull!"

"They're running up their jib!" cried Burke. "Lay to, you fellows, or I'll throw one of you overboard, and take his place!"

The captured man was thoroughly frightened. They were great fighters, these men he had fallen among, and he pulled as though he were rowing to rescue his dearest friend. The black fellows bent to their oars like madmen. They were thoroughly excited. They did not know what they were rowing: for they only knew they were acting under the orders of their captain, who had just killed nine Rackbirds, and their teeth and their eyes flashed as their oars dipped and bent.

CHAPTER XLI
THE "ARATO" ANCHORS NEARER SHORE

On went the boat, each one of the oarsmen pulling with all his force, the captain in the stern, shouting and encouraging them, and Shirley and Burke crouched in the bow, each with his rifle in hand. Up went the jib of the *Arato*. She gently turned about as she felt the influence of the wind, and then the captain believed the men on board were trying to get up the foresail.

"Are you sure there are only two of the crew on that schooner?" said the captain to the prisoner. "Now, it isn't worth while to lie to me."

"Only two," said the man. "I swear to it. Only two, Señor Capitan."

The foresail did not go up, for one of the men had to run to the wheel, and as the vessel's head got slowly around, it seemed as if she might sail away from the boat, even with nothing but the jib set. But the schooner gained headway very slowly, and the boat neared her rapidly. Now the man at the wheel gave up all hope of sailing away from his pursuers. He abandoned the helm, and in a few moments two heads and two guns showed over the rail, and two shots rang out. But the schooner was rolling, and the aim was bad. Shirley and Burke fired at the two heads as soon as they saw them, but the boat was rising and pitching, and their shots were also bad.

For a minute there was no more firing, and then one of the heads and one of the guns were seen again. Shirley was ready, and made his calculations, and, as the boat rose, he drew a bead upon the top of the rail where he saw the head, and had scarcely pulled his trigger when he saw a good deal more than a head, for a man sprung up high in the air and then fell backward.

The captain now ordered his men to rest on their oars, for, if the other man on board should show himself, they could get a better shot at him than if they were nearer. But the man did not show himself, and, on consideration of his probable tactics, it seemed extremely dangerous to approach the vessel. Even here they were in danger, but should they attempt to board her, they could not tell from what point he might fire down upon them, and some of them would surely be shot before they could get a chance at him, and the captain did not wish to sacrifice any of his men, even for a vessel, if it could be helped. There seemed to be no hope of safely gaining their object, except to wait until the man should become tired and impatient, and expose himself.

Suddenly, to the amazement of every one in the boat, for all heads were turned toward the schooner, a man appeared, boldly running over her deck. Shirley and Burke instantly raised their rifles, but dropped them again. There was a shout from Maka, and an exclamation from the prisoner. Then the man on deck stooped close to the rail and was lost to their sight, but almost instantly he reappeared again, holding in front of him a struggling pair of legs, feet uppermost. Then, upon the rail, appeared a man's head and body; but it only remained there for an instant, for his legs were raised still higher by the person behind him, and were then propelled outward with such force that he went headlong overboard. Then the man on deck sprang to the top of the rail, regardless of the rolling of the vessel in the gentle swell, and waved his hands above his head.

"Inkspot!" shouted the captain. "Pull away, you fellows! Pull!"

The tall, barefooted negro sprang to the deck from his perilous position, and soon reappeared with a line ready to throw to the boat.

In a few minutes they reached the vessel, and the boat was quickly made fast, and very soon they were on board. When he saw his old friends and associates upon the deck, Inkspot retired a little distance and fell upon his knees.

"You black rascal!" roared Burke, "you brought these cut-throat scoundrels down upon us! You—"

"That will do," said the captain. "There is no time for that sort of thing now. We will talk to him afterwards. Mr. Shirley, call all hands and get up sail. I am going to take this schooner inside the headland. We can find safe anchorage in the bay. We can sail over the same course we went on with the *Miranda*, and she drew more water than this vessel."

In an hour the *Arato*, moored by her spare anchor, lay in the little bay, less than two hundred yards from shore. It gave the shipwrecked men a wild delight to find themselves again upon the decks of a seaworthy vessel, and everybody worked with a will, especially the prisoner and Inkspot. And when the last sail had been furled, it became evident to all hands on board that they wanted their breakfast, and this need was speedily supplied by Maka and Inkspot from the *Arato's* stores.

That afternoon the captain went on shore with the negroes and the Chilian prisoner, and the bodies of the nine men who had fallen in the attack upon the wall of gold were buried where they lay. This was a very different climate from that of the Peruvian coast, where the desiccating air speedily makes a mummy of any dead body upon its arid sands.

When this work had been accomplished, the party returned to the *Arato*, and the captain ordered Inkspot and the prisoner to be brought aft to be tried by court martial. The big negro had been wildly and vociferously received by his fellow-countrymen, who, upon every possible occasion, had jabbered together in their native tongue, but Captain Horn had, so far, said nothing to him.

The captain had been greatly excited from the moment he had seen the sail in the offing. In his dire distress, on this almost desolate shore, he had beheld what might prove to be speedy relief, and, much as he had needed it, he had hoped that it might not come so soon. He had been apprehensive and anxious when he supposed friendly aid might be approaching, and he had been utterly astounded when he was forced to believe that they were armed men who were rowing to shore, and must be enemies. He had fought a terrible fight. He had conquered the scoundrels who had come for his life and his treasure, and, best of all, he had secured a vessel which would carry him and his men and his fortune to France. He had endeavored to keep cool and think only of the work that was immediately in hand, and he had no wish to ask anybody why or how things had happened. They had happened, and that was all in all to him. But now he was ready to make all necessary inquiries, and he began with Inkspot. Maka being interpreter, the examination was easily carried on.

The story of the negro was a very interesting one. He told of his adventures on shore, and how kind the men had been to him until they went on board the *Arato*, and how then they treated him as if he had been a dog—how he had been made to do double duty in all sorts of disagreeable work, and how, after they had seen the light on the beach, he had been put into the hold and tied hand and foot. While down there in the dark he had heard the firing on shore, and, after a long while, the firing from the deck, and other shots near by. All this had so excited him that he managed to get one hand loose from his cords, and then had speedily unfastened the rest, and had quietly crept to a hatchway, where he could watch what was going on without showing himself. He had seen the two men on deck, ready to fire on the approaching boat. He had recognized Captain Horn and the people of the *Miranda* in the boat. And then, when there was but one man left on deck, and the boat was afraid to come nearer, he had rushed up behind him and tumbled him overboard.

One thing only did Inkspot omit: he did not say that it was Mr. Burke's example that had prompted him to go ashore for refreshments. When the story had been told, and all questions asked and answered, the captain turned to Burke and Shirley and asked their opinions upon the case. Shirley was in favor of putting the negro in irons. He had deserted them, and had nearly cost them their lives by the stories he had told on shore. Burke, to the captain's surprise,—for the second mate generally dealt severely with nautical transgressions,—was in favor of clemency.

"To be sure," said he, "the black scoundrel did get us into trouble. But then, don't you see, he has got us out of it. If these beastly fellows hadn't been led by him to come after our money, we would not have had this schooner, and how we should have got those bags away without her,—to say nothing of ourselves,—is more than I can fathom. It is my belief that no craft ever comes within twenty miles of this coast, if she can help it. So I vote for letting him off. He didn't intend to do us any harm, and he didn't intend to do us any good, but it seems to me that the good he did do rises higher above the water-line than the harm. So I say, let him off. We need another hand about as much as we need anything."

"And so say I," said the captain. "Maka, you can tell him we forgive him, because we believe that he is really a good fellow and didn't intend any harm, and he can turn in with the rest of you on his old watch. And now bring up that Chilian fellow."

The prisoner, who gave his name as Anton Garta, was now examined in regard to the schooner *Arato*, her extraordinary cruise, and the people who had devised it. Garta was a fellow of moderate intelligence, and still very much frightened, and having little wit with which to concoct lies, and no reason for telling them, he answered the questions put to him as correctly as his knowledge permitted. He said that about two months before he had been one of the crew of the *Arato*, and Manuel Cardatas was second mate, and he had been very glad to join her on this last cruise because he was out of a job. He thought she was going to Callao for a cargo, and so did the rest of the crew. They did not even know there were guns on board until they were out at sea. Then, when they had turned southward, their captain and Señor Nunez told them that they were going in pursuit of a treasure ship commanded by a Yankee captain, who had run away with ever so much money from California, and that they were sure to overhaul this ship, and that they would all be rich.

The guns were given to them, and they had had some practice with them, and thought that Cardatas intended, should the *Miranda* be overhauled, to run alongside of her as near as was safe, and begin operations by shooting everybody that could be seen on deck. He was not sure that this was his plan, but they all had thought it was. After the storm the men had become dissatisfied, and said they did not believe it was possible to overhaul any vessel after so much delay, and when they had gone so far out of their course; and Señor Nunez, who had hired the vessel, was in doubt as to whether it would be of any use to continue the cruise. But when Cardatas had talked to him, Señor Nunez had come among them and promised them good rewards, whether they sighted their prize or not, if they would work faithfully for ten days more. The men had agreed to do this, but when they had seen the light on shore, they had made an agreement among themselves that, if this should be nothing but a fire built by savages or shipwrecked people of no account, they would not work the schooner any farther south. They would put Cardatas and Nunez in irons, if necessary, and take the *Arato* back to Valparaiso. There were men among them who could navigate. But when they got near enough to shore to see that the stranded vessel was the *Miranda*, there was no more insubordination.

As for himself, Garta said he was a plain, common sailor, who went on board the *Arato* because he wanted a job. If he had known the errand on which she was bound, he would never have approached within a league of her. This he vowed, by all the saints. As to the ownership of the vessel Garta could tell but little. He had heard that Cardatas had a share in her, and thought that probably the other owners lived in Valparaiso, but he could give no positive information on this subject. He said that every man of the boat's crew was in a state of wild excitement when they saw that long pile of bags, which they knew must contain treasure of some sort, and it was because of this state of mind, most likely, that Cardatas lost his temper and got himself shot, and so opened the fight. Cardatas was a cunning fellow, and, if he had not been upset by the sight of those bags, Garta believed that he would have regularly besieged Captain Horn's party, and must have overcome them in the end. He was anxious to have the captain believe that, when he had said there were only two men on board, he had totally forgotten the negro, who had been left below.

When Garta's examination had been finished, the captain sent him forward, and then repeated his story in brief to Shirley and Burke, for, as the prisoner had spoken in Spanish, they had understood but little of it.

"I don't see that it makes much difference," said Burke, "as to what his story is. We've got to get rid of him in some way. We don't want to carry him about with us. We might leave him here, with a lot of grub and a tent. That would be all he deserves."

"I should put him in irons, to begin with," said Shirley, "and then we can consider what to do with him when we have time."

"I shall not leave him on shore," said the captain, "for that would simply be condemning him to starvation; and as for putting him in irons, that would deprive us of an able seaman. I suppose, if we took him to France, he would have to be sent to Chili for trial, and that would be of no use, unless we went there as witnesses. It is a puzzling question to know what to do with him."

"It is that," said Burke, "and it is a great pity he wasn't shot with the others."

"Well," said the captain, "we've got a lot of work before us, and we want hands, so I think it will be best to let him turn in with the rest, and make him pay for his passage, wherever we take him. The worst he can do is to desert, and if he does that, he will settle his own business, and we shall have no more trouble with him."

"I don't like him," said Shirley. "I don't think we ought to have such a fellow going about freely on board."

"I am not afraid he will hurt any of us," said the captain, "and I am sure he will not corrupt the negroes. They hate him. It is easy to see that."

"Yes," said Burke, with a laugh. "They think he is a Rackbird, and it is just as well to let them keep on thinking so."

"Perhaps he is," thought the captain, but he did not speak this thought aloud.

CHAPTER XLII
INKSPOT HAS A DREAM OF HEAVEN

The next day the work of loading the *Arato* with the bags of gold was begun, and it was a much slower and more difficult business than the unloading of the *Miranda*, for the schooner lay much farther out from the beach. But there were two men more than on the former occasion, and the captain did not push the work. There was no need now for extraordinary haste, and although they all labored steadily, regular hours of work and rest were adhered to. The men had carried so many bags filled with hard and uneven lumps that the shoulders of some of them were tender, and they had to use cushions of canvas under their loads. But the boats went backward and forward, and the bags were hoisted on board and lowered into the hold, and the wall of gold grew smaller and smaller.

"Captain," said Burke, one day, as they were standing by a pile of bags waiting for the boat to come ashore, "do you think it is worth it! By George! we have loaded and unloaded these blessed bags all down the western coast of South America, and if we've got to unload and load them all up the east coast, I say, let's take what we really need, and leave the rest."

"I've been at the business a good deal longer than you have," said the captain, "and I'm not tired of it yet. When I took away my first cargo, you must remember that I carried each bag on my own shoulders, and it took me more than a month to do it, and even all that is only a drop in the bucket compared to what most men who call themselves rich have to do before they make their money."

"All right," said Burke, "I'll stop growling. But look here, captain. How much do you suppose one of these bags is worth, and how many are there in all? I don't want to be inquisitive, but it would be a sort of comfort to know."

"No, it wouldn't," said the captain, quickly. "It would be anything else but a comfort. I know how many bags there are, but as to what they are worth, I don't know, and I don't want to know. I once set about calculating it, but I didn't get very far with the figures. I need all my wits to get through with this business, and I don't think anything would be more likely to scatter them than calculating what this gold is worth. It would be a good deal better for you—and for me, too—to consider, as Shirley does, that these bags are all filled with good, clean, anthracite coal. That won't keep us from sleeping."

"Shirley be hanged!" said Burke, "He and you may be able to do that, but I can't. I've got a pretty strong mind, and if you were to tell me that when we get to port, and you discharge this crew, I can walk off with all the gold eagles or twenty-franc pieces I can carry, I think I could stand it without losing my mind."

"All right," said the captain, "If we get this vessel safely to France, I will give you a good chance to try your nerves."

Day by day the work went on, and at last the *Arato* took the place of the *Miranda* as a modern *Argo*.

During the reëmbarkation of the treasure, the captain, as well as Shirley and Burke, had kept a sharp eye on Garta. The two mates were afraid he might run away, but, had he done so, the captain would not have regretted it very much. He would gladly have parted with one of the bags in order to get rid of this encumbrance. But the prisoner had no idea of running away. He knew that the bags were filled with treasure, but as he could now do nothing with any of it that he might steal, he did not try to steal any. If he had thoughts of the kind, he knew this was no time for dishonest operation. He had always been a hardworking sailor, with a good appetite, and he worked hard now, and ate well.

The *Miranda's* stores had not been injured by water, and when they had been put on board, the *Arato* was well fitted out for a long voyage. Leaving the *Miranda* on the beach, with nothing in her of much value, the *Arato*, which had cleared for Callao, and afterwards set out on a wild piratical cruise, now made a third start, and set sail for a voyage to France. They had good weather and tolerably fair winds, and before they entered the Straits of Magellan the captain had formulated a plan for the disposition of Garta.

"I don't know anything better to do with him," said he to Shirley and Burke, "than to put him ashore at the Falkland Islands. We don't want to take him to France, for we would not know what to do with him after we got him there, and, as likely as not, he would swear a lot of lies against us as soon as he got on shore. We can run within a league of Stanley harbor, and then, if the weather is good enough, we can put him in a boat, with something to eat and drink, and let him row himself into port. We can give him money enough to support himself until he can procure work."

"But suppose there is a man-of-war in there," said Shirley, "he might say things that would send her after us. He might not know where to say we got our treasure, but he could say we had stolen a Chilian vessel."

"I had thought of that," said the captain, "but nothing such a vagrant as he is could say ought to give any cruiser the right to interfere with us when we are sailing under the American flag. And when I go to France, nobody shall say that I stole a vessel, for, if the owners of the *Arato* can be found, they shall be well paid for what use we have made of their schooner. I'll send her back to Valparaiso and let her be claimed."

"It is a ticklish business," said Burke, "but I don't know what else can be done. It is a great pity I didn't know he was going to surrender when we had that fight."

They had been in the Straits less than a week when Inkspot dreamed he was in heaven. His ecstatic visions became so strong and vivid that they awakened him, when he was not long in discovering the cause which had produced them. The dimly lighted and quiet forecastle was permeated by a delightful smell of spirituous liquor. Turning his eyes from right to left, in his endeavors to understand this unusual odor of luxury, Inkspot perceived the man Garta standing on the other side of the forecastle, with a bottle in one hand and a cork in the other, and, as he looked, Garta raised the bottle to his mouth, threw back his head, and drank.

Inkspot greatly disliked this man. He had been one of the fellows who had ill-treated him when the *Arato* sailed under Cardatas, and he fully agreed with his fellow-blacks that the scoundrel should have been shot. But now his feelings began to undergo a change. A man with a bottle of spirits might prove to be an angel of mercy, a being of beneficence, and if he would share with a craving fellow-being his rare good fortune, why should not all feelings of disapprobation be set aside? Inkspot could see no reason why they should not be, and softly slipping from his hammock, he approached Garta.

"Give me. Give me, just little," he whispered.

Garta turned with a half-suppressed oath, and seeing who the suppliant was, he seized the bottle in his left hand, and with his right struck poor

Inkspot a blow in the face. Without a word the negro stepped back, and then Garta put the bottle into a high, narrow opening in the side of the forecastle, and closed a little door upon it, which fastened with a snap. This little locker, just large enough to hold one bottle, had been made by one of the former crew of the *Arato* solely for the purpose of concealing spirits, and was very ingeniously contrived. Its door was a portion of the side of the forecastle, and a keyhole was concealed behind a removable knot. Garta had not opened the locker before, for the reason that he had been unable to find the key. He knew it had been concealed in the forecastle, but it had taken him a long time to find it. Now his secret was discovered, and he was enraged. Going over to the hammock, where Inkspot had again ensconced himself, he leaned over the negro and whispered:

"If you ever say a word of that bottle to anybody, I'll put a knife into you! No matter what they do to me, I'll settle with you."

Inkspot did not understand all this, but he knew it was a threat, and he well understood the language of a blow in the face. After a while he went to sleep, but, if he smelt again the odor of the contents of the bottle, he had no more heavenly dreams.

The next day Captain Horn found himself off the convict settlement of Punta Arenas, belonging to the Chilian government. This was the first port he had approached since he had taken command of the *Arato*, but he felt no desire nor need to touch at it. In fact, the vicinity of Punta Arenas seemed of no importance whatever, until Shirley came to him and reported that the man Garta was nowhere to be found. Captain Horn immediately ordered a search and inquiry to be made, but no traces of the prisoner could be discovered, nor could anybody tell anything about him. Burke and Inkspot had been on watch with him from four to eight, but they could give no information whatever concerning him. No splash nor cries for help had been heard, so that he could not have fallen overboard, and it was generally believed that, when he knew himself to be in the vicinity of a settlement, he had quietly slipped into the water and had swum for Punta Arenas. Burke suggested that most likely he had formerly been a resident of the place, and liked it better than being taken off to unknown regions in the schooner. And Shirley considered this very probable, for he said the man had always looked like a convict to him.

At all events, Garta was gone, and there was no one to say how long he had been gone. So, under full sail, the *Arato* went on her way. It was a relief to get rid of the prisoner, and the only harm which could come of his disappearance was that he might report that his ship had been stolen by the men who were sailing her, and that some sort of a vessel might be sent in pursuit of the *Arato,* and, if this should be the case, the situation would be awkward. But days passed on, the schooner sailed out of the Straits, and no vessel was seen pursuing her.

To the northeast Captain Horn set his course. He would not stop at Rio Janeiro, for the *Arato* had no papers for that port. He would not lie to off Stanley harbor, for he had now nobody to send ashore. But he would sail boldly for France, where he would make no pretensions that his auriferous cargo was merely ballast. He was known at Marseilles. He had business relations with bankers in Paris. He was a Californian and an American citizen, and he would merely be bringing to France a vessel freighted with gold, which, by the aid of his financial advisers, would be legitimately cared for and disposed of.

One night, before the *Arato* reached the Falkland Islands, Maka, who was on watch, heard a queer sound in the forecastle, and looking down the companionway, he saw, by the dim light of the swinging lantern, a man with a hatchet, endeavoring to force the blade of it into the side of the vessel. Maka quickly perceived that the man was Inkspot, and as he could not imagine what he was doing, he quietly watched him. Inkspot worked with as little noise as possible, but he was evidently bent upon forcing off one of the boards on the side of the forecastle. At first Maka thought that his fellow-African was trying to sink the ship by opening a seam, but he soon realized that this notion was absurd, and so he let Inkspot go on, being very curious to know what he was doing. In a few minutes he knew. With a slight noise, not enough to waken a sound sleeper, a little door flew open, and almost immediately Inkspot held a bottle in his hand.

Maka slipped swiftly and softly to the side of the big negro, but he was not quick enough. Inkspot had the neck of the bottle in his mouth and the bottom raised high in the air. But, before Maka could seize him by the arm, the bottle had come down from its elevated position, and a doleful expression crept over the face of Inkspot. There had been scarcely a teaspoonful of liquor left in the bottle. Inkspot looked at Maka, and Maka looked at him. In an African whisper, the former now ordered the disappointed negro to put the bottle back, to shut up the locker, and then to get into his hammock and go to sleep as quickly as he could, for if Mr. Shirley, who was on watch on deck, found out what he had been doing, Inkspot would wish he had never been born.

The next day, when they had an opportunity for an African conversation, Inkspot assured his countryman that he had discovered the little locker by smelling the whiskey through the boards, and that, having no key, he had determined to force it open with a hatchet. Maka could not help thinking that Inkspot had a wonderful nose for an empty bottle, and could scarcely restrain from a shudder at the thought of what might have happened had the bottle been full. But he did not report the occurrence. Inkspot was a fellow-African, and he had barely escaped punishment for his former misdeed. It would be better to keep his mouth shut, and he did.

Against the north winds, before the south winds, and on the winds from the east and the west, through fair weather and through foul, the *Arato* sailed up the South Atlantic. It was a long, long voyage, but the schooner was skilfully navigated and sailed well. Sometimes she sighted great merchant-steamers plying between Europe and South America, freighted with rich cargoes, and proudly steaming away from the little schooner, whose dark-green hull could scarcely be distinguished from the color of the waves. And why should not the captain of this humble little vessel sometimes have said to himself, as he passed a big three-master or a steamer:

"What would they think if they knew that, if I chose to do it, I could buy every ship, and its cargo, that I shall meet between here and Gibraltar!"

"Captain," said Shirley, one day, "what do you think about the right and wrong of this?"

"What do you mean?" asked Captain Horn.

"I mean," replied Shirley, "taking away the gold we have on board. We've had pretty easy times lately, and I've been doing a good deal of thinking, and sometimes I have wondered where we got the right to clap all this treasure into bags and sail away with it."

"So you have stopped thinking the bags are all filled with anthracite coal," said the captain.

"Yes," said the other. "We are getting on toward the end of this voyage, and it is about time to give up that fancy. I always imagine, when I am near the end of a voyage, what I am going to do when I go ashore, and if I have any real right to some of the gold down under our decks, I shall do something very different from anything I ever did before."

"I hope you don't mean going on a spree," said Burke, who was standing near. "That would be something entirely different."

"I thought," said the captain, "that you both understood this business, but I don't mind going over it again. There is no doubt in my mind that this gold originally belonged to the Incas, who then owned Peru, and they put it into that mound to keep it from the Spaniards, whose descendants now own Peru, and who rule it without much regard to the descendants of the ancient Peruvians. Now, when I discovered the gold, and began to have an idea of how valuable the find was, I knew that the first thing to do was to get it out of that place and away from the country. Whatever is to be done in the way of fair play and fair division must be done somewhere else, and not there. If I had informed the government of what I had found, this gold would have gone directly into the hands of the descendants of the people from whom its original owners did their very best to keep it, and nobody else would have had a dollar's worth of it. If we had stood up for our rights to a reward for finding it, ten to one we would all have been clapped into prison."

"I suppose by that," said Burke, "that you looked upon the stone mound in the cave as a sort of will left by those old Peruvians, and you made yourself an executor to carry out the intentions of the testators, as the lawyers say."

"But we can set it down as dead certain," interrupted Shirley, "that the testators didn't mean us to have it."

"No," said the captain, "nor do I mean that we shall have all of it. I intend to have the question of the ownership of this gold decided by people who are able and competent to decide such a question, and who will be fair and honest to all parties. But whatever is agreed upon, and whatever is done with the treasure, I intend to charge a good price—a price which shall bear a handsome proportion to the value of the gold—for my services, and all our services. Some of this charge I have already taken, and I intend to have a great deal more. We have worked hard and risked much to get this treasure—"

"Yes," thought Burke, as he remembered the trap at the bottom of the mound. "You risked a great deal more than you ever supposed you did."

"And we are bound to be well paid for it," continued the captain. "No matter where this gold goes, I shall have a good share of it, and this I am going to divide among our party, according to a fair scale. How does that strike you, Shirley?"

"If the business is going to be conducted as you say, captain," replied the first mate, "I say it will be all fair and square, and I needn't bother my head with any more doubts about it. But there is one thing I wish you would tell me: how much do you think I will be likely to get out of this cargo, when you divide?"

"Mr. Shirley," said the captain, "when I give you your share of this cargo, you can have about four bags of anthracite coal, weighing a little over one hundred pounds, which, at the rate of six dollars a ton, would bring you between thirty and forty cents. Will that satisfy you? Of course, this is only a rough guess at a division, but I want to see how it falls in with your ideas."

Shirley laughed. "I guess you're right, captain," said he. "It will be better for me to keep on thinking we are carrying coal. That won't bother my head."

"That's so," said Burke. "Your brain can't stand that sort of badger. I'd hate to go ashore with you at Marseilles with your pocket full and your skull empty. As for me, I can stand it first-rate. I have already built two houses on Cape Cod,—in my head, of course,—and I'll be hanged if I know which one I am going to live in and which one I am going to put my mother in."

CHAPTER XLIII
MOK AS A VOCALIST

It would have been very comfortable to the mind of Edna, during her waiting days in Paris, had she known there was a letter to her from Captain Horn, in a cottage in the town of Sidmouth, on the south coast of Devonshire. Had she known this, she would have chartered French trains, Channel steamers, English trains, flies, anything and everything which would have taken her the quickest to the little town of Sidmouth. Had she known that he had written to her the first chance he had had, all her doubts and perplexities would have vanished in an instant. Had she read the letter, she might have been pained to find that it was not such a letter as she would wish to have, and she might have grieved that it might still be a long time before she could expect to hear from him again, or to see him, but she would have waited—have waited patiently, without any doubts or perplexities.

This letter, with a silver coin,—much more than enough to pay any possible postage,—had been handed by Shirley to the first mate of the British steamer, in the harbor of Valparaiso, and that officer had given it to a seaman, who was going on shore, with directions to take it to the post-office, and pay for the postage out of the silver coin, and whatever change there might be, he should keep it for his trouble. On the way to the post-office, this sailor stopped to refresh himself, and meeting with a fellow-mariner in the place of refreshment, he refreshed him also. And by the time the two had refreshed themselves to their satisfaction, there was not much left of the silver coin—not enough to pay the necessary postage to France.

"But," said the seaman to himself, "it doesn't matter a bit. We are bound for Liverpool, and I'll take the letter there myself, and then I'll send it over to Paris for tuppence ha'penny, which I will have then, and haven't now. And I bet another tuppence that it will go sooner than if I posted it here, for it may be a month before a mail-steamer leaves the other side of this beastly continent. Anyway, I'm doing the best I can."

He put the letter in the pocket of his pea-jacket, and the bottom of that pocket being ripped, the letter went down between the outside cloth and the lining of the pea-jacket to the very bottom of the garment, where it remained until the aforesaid seaman had reached England, and had gone down to see his family, who lived in the cottage in Sidmouth. And there he had hung up his pea-jacket on a nail, in a little room next to the kitchen, and there his mother had found it, and sewed on two buttons, and sewed up the rips in the bottoms of two pockets. Shortly after this, the sailor, happening to pass a post-office box, remembered the letter he had brought to England. He went to his pea-jacket and searched it, but could find no letter. He must have lost it—he hoped after he had reached England, and no doubt whoever found it would put a tuppence ha'penny stamp on it and stick it into a box. Anyway, he had done all he could.

One pleasant spring evening, the negro Mok sat behind a table in the well-known beer-shop called the "Black Cat." He had before him a half-emptied beer-glass, and in front of him was a pile of three small white dishes. These signified that Mok had had three glasses of beer, and when he should finish the one in his hand, and should order another, the waiter would bring with it another little white plate, which he would put on the table, on the pile already there, and which would signify that the African gentleman must pay for four glasses of beer.

Mok was enjoying himself very much. It was not often that he had such an opportunity to sample the delights of Paris. His young master, Ralph, had given him strict orders never to go out at night, or in his leisure hours, unless accompanied by Cheditafa. The latter was an extremely important and sedate personage. The combined dignity of a butler and a clergyman were more than ever evident in his person, and he was a painful drawback to the more volatile Mok. Mok had very fine clothes, which it rejoiced him to display. He had a fine appetite for everything fit to eat and drink. He had money in his pockets, and it delighted him to see people and to see things, although he might not know who they were or what they were. He knew nothing of French, and his power of expressing himself in English had not progressed very far. But on this evening, in the jolly precincts of the Black Cat, he did not care whether the people used language or not. He did not care what they did, so that he could sit there and enjoy himself. When he wanted more beer, the waiter understood him, and that was enough.

The jet-black negro, gorgeously arrayed in the livery Ralph had chosen for him, and with his teeth and eyeballs whiter than the pile of plates before him, was an object of great interest to the company in the beer-shop. They talked to him, and although he did not understand them, or answer them, they knew he was enjoying himself. And when the landlord rang a big bell, and a pale young man, wearing a high hat, and sitting at a table opposite him, threw into his face an expression of exalted melancholy, and sang a high-pitched song, Mok showed how he appreciated the performance by thumping more vigorously on the table than any of the other people who applauded the singer.

Again and again the big bell was rung, and there were other songs and choruses, and then the company turned toward Mok and called on him to sing. He did not understand them, but he laughed and pounded his fist upon the table. But when the landlord came down to his table, and rang the bell in front of him, that sent an informing idea into the African head. He had noticed that every time the bell had been rung, somebody had sung, and now he knew what was wanted of him. He had had four glasses of beer, and he was an obliging fellow, so he nodded his head violently, and everybody stopped doing what they had been doing, and prepared to listen.

Mok's repertoire of songs could not be expected to be large. In fact, he only knew one musical composition, and that was an African hymn which Cheditafa had taught him. This he now proceeded to execute. He threw back his head, as some of the others had done, and emitted a succession of grunts, groans, yelps, barks, squeaks, yells, and rattles which utterly electrified the audience. Then, as if his breath filled his whole body, and quivering and shaking like an angry squirrel when it chatters and barks, Mok sang louder and more wildly, until the audience, unable to restrain themselves, burst into laughter, and applauded with canes, sticks, and fists. But Mok kept on. He had never imagined he could sing so well. There was only one person in that brasserie who did not applaud the African hymn, but no one paid so much attention to it as this man, who had entered the Black Cat just as Mok had begun.

He was a person of medium size, with a heavy mustache, and a face darkened by a beard of several days' growth. He was rather roughly dressed, and wore a soft felt hat. He was a Rackbird.

This man had formerly belonged to the band of desperadoes which had been swept away by a sudden flood on the coast of Peru. He had accompanied his comrades on the last marauding expedition previous to that remarkable accident, but he had not returned with them. He had devised a little scheme of his own, which had detained him longer than he had expected, and he was not ready to go back with them. It would have been difficult for him to reach the camp by himself, and, after what he had done, he did not very much desire to go, there as he would probably have been shot as a deserter; for Captain Raminez was a savage fellow, and more than willing to punish transgressions against his orders. This deserter, Banker by name, was an American, who had been a gold-digger, a gambler, a rough, and a dead shot in California, and he was very well able to take care of himself in any part of the world.

He had made his way up to Panama, and had stayed there as long as it was safe for him to do so, and had eventually reached Paris. He did not like this city half so well as he liked London, but in the latter city he happened to be wanted, and he was not wanted in Paris. It was generally the case that he stayed where he was not wanted.

Of course, Banker knew nothing of the destruction of his band, and the fact that he had not heard from them since he left them gave him not the slightest regret. But what did astonish him beyond bounds was to sit at a table in the Black Cat, in Paris, and see before him, dressed like the valet of a Spanish grandee, a coal-black negro who had once been his especial and particular slave and drudge, a fellow whom he had kicked and beaten and sworn at, and whom he no doubt would have shot had he stayed much longer with his lawless companions, the Rackbirds. There was no mistaking this black man. He well remembered his face, and even the tones of his voice. He had never heard him sing, but he had heard him howl, and it seemed almost impossible that he should meet him in Paris. And yet, he was sure that the man who was bellowing and bawling to the delight of the guests of the Black Cat was one of the African wretches who had been entrapped and enslaved by the Rackbirds.

But if Banker had been astonished by Mok, he was utterly amazed and confounded when, some five minutes later, the door of the brasserie was suddenly opened, and another of the slaves of the Rackbirds, with whose face he was also perfectly familiar, hurriedly entered.

Cheditafa, who had been sent on an errand that evening, had missed Mok on his return. Ralph was away in Brussels with the professor, so that his valet, having most of his time on his hands, had thought to take a holiday during Cheditafa's absence, and had slipped off to the Black Cat, whose pleasures he had surreptitiously enjoyed before, but never to such an extent as on this occasion. Cheditafa knew he had been there, and when he started out to look for him, it was to the Black Cat that he went first.

Before he had quite reached the door, Cheditafa had been shocked and angered to hear his favorite hymn sung in a beer-shop by that reprobate and incompetent Mok, and he had rushed in, and in a minute seized the blatant vocalist by the collar, and ordered him instantly to shut his mouth and pay his reckoning. Then, in spite of the shouts of disapprobation which arose on every side, he led away the negro as if he had been a captured dog with his tail between his legs.

Mok could easily have thrown Cheditafa across the street, but his respect and reverence for his elder and superior were so great that he obeyed his commands without a word of remonstrance.

Now up sprang Banker, who was in such a hurry to go that he forgot to pay for his beer, and when he performed this duty, after having been abruptly reminded of it by a waiter, he was almost too late to follow the two black men, but not quite too late. He was an adept in the tracking of his fellow-beings, and it was not long before he was quietly following Mok and Cheditafa, keeping at some distance behind them, but never allowing them to get out of his sight.

In the course of a moderate walk he saw them enter the Hotel Grenade. This satisfied the wandering Rackbird. If the negroes went into that hotel at that time of night, they must live there, and he could suspend operations until morning.

CHAPTER XLIV
MR. BANKER'S SPECULATION

That night Banker was greatly disturbed by surmises and conjectures concerning the presence of the two negroes in the French capital. He knew Cheditafa quite as well as he knew Mok, and it was impossible that he should be mistaken. It is seldom that any one sees a native African in Paris, and he was positive that the men he had seen, dressed in expensive garments, enjoying themselves like gentlemen of leisure, and living at a grand hotel, were the same negroes he had last seen in rags and shreds, lodged in a cave in the side of a precipice, toiling and shuddering under the commands of a set of desperadoes on a desert coast in South America. There was only one way in which he could explain matters, and that was that the band had had some great success, and that one or more of its members had come to Paris, and had brought the two negroes with them as servants. But of one thing he had no doubts, and that was that he would follow up the case. He had met with no successes of late, but if any of his former comrades had, he wanted to meet those dear old friends. In Paris he was not afraid of anything they might say about his desertion.

Very early in the morning Banker was in front of the Hotel Grenade. He did not loiter there; he did not wander up and down like a vagrant, or stand about like a spy. It was part of his business to be able to be present in various places almost at the same time, and not to attract notice in any of them. It was not until after ten o'clock that he saw anything worthy of his observation, and then a carriage drove up to the front entrance, and on the seat beside the driver sat Cheditafa, erect, solemn, and respectable. Presently the negro got down and opened the door of the carriage. In a few moments a lady, a beautiful lady, handsomely dressed, came out of the hotel and entered the carriage. Then Cheditafa shut the door and got up beside the driver again. It was a fine thing to have such a footman as this one, so utterly different from the ordinary groom or footman, so extremely *distingué*!

As the carriage rolled off, Banker walked after it, but not in such a way as to attract attention, and then he entered a cab and told the *cocher* to drive to the Bon Marché. Of course, he did not know where the lady was going to, but at present she was driving in the direction of that celebrated mart, and he kept his eye upon her carriage, and if she had turned out of the Boulevard and away from the Seine, he would have ordered his driver to turn also and go somewhere else. He did not dare to tell the man to follow the carriage. He was shaved, and his clothes had been put in as good order as possible, but he knew that he did not look like a man respectable enough to give such an order without exciting suspicion.

But the carriage did go to the Bon Marché, and there also went the cab, the two vehicles arriving at almost the same time. Banker paid his fare with great promptness, and was on the pavement in time to see the handsomely dressed lady descend and enter the establishment. As she went in, he took one look at the back of her bonnet. It had a little green feather in it. Then he turned quickly upon Cheditafa, who had shut the carriage door and was going around behind it in order to get up on the other side.

"Look here," whispered Banker, seizing the clerical butler by the shoulder, "who is that lady? Quick, or I'll put a knife in you."

At these words Cheditafa's heart almost stopped beating, and as he quickly turned he saw that he looked into the face of a man, an awfully wicked man, who had once helped to grind the soul out of him, in that dreadful cave by the sea. The poor negro was so frightened that he scarcely knew whether he was in Paris or Peru.

"Who is she?" whispered again the dreadful Rackbird.

"Come, come!" shouted the coachman from his seat, "we must move on."

"Quick! Who is she?" hissed Banker.

"She?" replied the quaking negro. "She is the captain's wife. She is—" But he could say no more, for a policeman was ordering the carriage to move on, for it stopped the way, and the coachman was calling impatiently. Banker could not afford to meet a policeman. He released his hold on Cheditafa and retired unnoticed. An instant afterward he entered the Bon Marché.

Cheditafa climbed up to the side of the driver, but he missed his foothold several times, and came near falling to the ground. In all Paris there was no footman on a carriage who looked less upright, less sedate, and less respectable than this poor, frightened black man.

Through the corridors and passageways of the vast establishment went Banker. But he did not have to go far. He saw at a counter a little green feather in the back of a bonnet. Quietly he approached that counter, and no sooner had the attendant turned aside to get something that had been asked for than Banker stepped close to the side of the lady, and leaning forward, said in a very low but polite voice:

"I am so glad to find the captain's wife. I have been looking for her."

He was almost certain, from her appearance, that she was an American, and so he spoke in English.

Edna turned with a start. She saw beside her a man with his hat off, a rough-looking man, but a polite one, and a man who looked like a sailor.

"The captain!" she stammered. "Have you—do you bring me anything! A letter?"

"Yes, madam," said he. "I have a letter and a message for you."

"Give them to me quickly!" said she, her face burning.

"I cannot," he said. "I cannot give them to you here. I have much to say to you, and much to tell you, and I was ordered to say it in private."

Edna was astounded. Her heart sank. Captain Horn must be in trouble, else why such secrecy? But she must know everything, and quickly. Where could she meet the man? He divined her thought.

"The Gardens of the Tuileries," said he. "Go there now, please. I will meet you, no matter in what part of it you are." And so saying, he slipped away unnoticed.

When the salesman came to her, Edna did not remember what she had asked to see, but whatever he brought she did not want, and going out, she had her carriage called, and ordered her coachman to take her to the Gardens of the Tuileries. She was so excited that she did not wait for Cheditafa to get down, but opened the door herself, and stepped in quickly, even before the porter of the establishment could attend to her.

When she reached the Gardens, and Cheditafa opened the carriage door for her, she thought he must have a fit of chills and fever. But she had no time to consider this, and merely told him that she was going to walk in the Gardens, and the carriage must wait.

It was some time before Edna met the man with whom she had made this appointment. He had seen her alight, and although he did not lose sight of her, he kept away from her, and let her walk on until she was entirely out of sight of the carriage. As soon as Edna perceived Banker, she walked directly toward him. She had endeavored to calm herself, but he could see that she was much agitated.

"How in the devil's name," he thought to himself, "did Raminez ever come to marry such a woman as this? She's fit for a queen. But they say he used to be a great swell in Spain before he got into trouble, and I expect he's put on his old airs again, and an American lady will marry anybody that's a foreign swell. And how neatly she played into my hand! She let me know right away that she wanted a letter, which means, of course, that Raminez is not with her."

"Give me the letter, if you please," said Edna.

"Madam," said Banker, with a bow, "I told you I had a letter and a message. I must deliver the message first."

"Then be quick with it," said she.

"I will," said Banker. "Our captain has had great success lately, you know, but he is obliged to keep a little in the background for the present, as you will see by your letter, and as it is a very particular letter, indeed, he ordered me to bring it to you."

Edna's heart sank. "What has happened?" said she. "Why—"

"Oh, you will find all that in the letter," said Banker. "The captain has written out everything, full and clear. He told me so himself. But I must get through with my message. It is not from him. It is from me. As I just said, he ordered me to bring you this letter, and it was a hard thing to do, and a risky thing to do. But I undertook the job of giving it to you, in private, without anybody's knowing you had received it."

"What!" exclaimed Edna. "Nobody to know!"

"Oh, that is all explained," said he, hurriedly. "I can't touch on that. My affair is this: The captain sent me with the letter, and I have been to a lot of trouble to get it to you. Now, he is not going to pay me for all this,—if he thanks me, it will be more than I expect,—and I am going to be perfectly open and honest with you, and say that as the captain won't pay me, I expect you to do it; or, putting it in another way, before I hand you the letter I brought you, I want you to make me a handsome present."

"You rascal!" exclaimed Edna. "How dare you impose on me in this way?"

It humiliated and mortified her to think that the captain was obliged to resort to such a messenger as this. But all sorts of men become sailors, and although her pride revolted against the attempted imposition, the man had a letter written to her by Captain Horn, and she must have it.

"How much do you want?" said she.

"I don't mind your calling me names," said Banker. "The captain has made a grand stroke, you know, and everything about you is very fine, while I haven't three francs to jingle together. I want one thousand dollars."

"Five thousand francs!" exclaimed Edna. "Absurd! I have not that much money with me. I haven't but a hundred francs, but that ought to satisfy you."

"Oh, no," said Banker, "not at all. But don't trouble yourself. You have not the money, and I have not the letter. The letter is in my lodgings. I was not fool enough to bring it with me, and have you call a policeman to arrest me, and take it for nothing. But if you will be here in two hours, with five thousand francs, and will promise me, upon your honor, that you will bring no one with you, and will not call the police as soon as you have the letter, I will be here with it."

"Yes," said Edna, "I promise."

She felt humbled and ashamed as she said it, but there was nothing else to do. In spite of her feelings, in spite of the cost, she must have the letter.

"Very good," said Banker, and he departed.

Banker had no lodgings in particular, but he went to a brasserie and procured writing materials. He had some letters in his pocket,—old, dirty letters which had been there for a long time,—and one of them was from Raminez, which had been written when they were both in California, and which Banker had kept because it contained an unguarded reference to Raminez's family in Spain, and Banker had thought that the information might some day be useful to him. He was a good penman, this Rackbird,—he was clever in many ways,—and he could imitate handwriting very well, and he set himself to work to address an envelope in the handwriting of Raminez.

For some time he debated within himself as to what title he should use in addressing the lady. Should it be "Señora" or "Madame"? He inclined to the first appellation, but afterwards thought that as the letter was to go to her in France, and that as most likely she understood French, and not Spanish, Raminez would probably address her in the former language, and therefore he addressed the envelope to "Madame Raminez, by private hand." As to the writing of a letter he did not trouble himself at all. He simply folded up two sheets of paper and put them in the envelope, sealing it tightly. Now he was prepared, and after waiting until the proper time had arrived he proceeded to the Gardens.

Edna drove to her hotel in great agitation. She was angry, she was astounded, she was almost frightened. What could have happened to Captain Horn?

But two things encouraged and invigorated her: he was alive, and he had written to her. That was everything, and she would banish all speculations and fears until she had read his letter, and, until she had read it, she must keep the matter a secret—she must not let anybody imagine that she had heard anything, or was about to hear anything. By good fortune, she had five thousand francs in hand, and, with these in her pocket-book, she ordered her carriage half an hour before the time appointed.

When Cheditafa heard the order, he was beset by a new consternation. He had been greatly troubled when his mistress had gone to the Gardens the first time—not because there was anything strange in that, for any lady might like to walk in such a beautiful place, but because she was alone, and, with a Rackbird in Paris, his lady ought never to be alone. She had come out safely, and he had breathed again, and now, now she wanted to go back! He must tell her about that Rackbird man. He had been thinking and thinking about telling her all the way back to the hotel, but he had feared to frighten her, and he had also been afraid to say that he had done what he had been ordered not to do, and had told some one that she was the captain's wife. But when he had reached the Gardens, he felt that he must say something— she must not walk about alone. Accordingly, as Edna stepped out of the carriage, he began to speak to her, but, contrary to her usual custom, she paid no attention to him, simply telling him to wait until she came back.

Edna was obliged to wander about for some time before Banker appeared.

"Now, then, madam," said he, "don't let us waste any time on this business. Have you the money with you?"

"I have," said she. "But before I give it to you, I tell you that I do so under protest, and that this conduct of yours shall be reported. I consider it a most shameful thing, and I do not willingly pay you for what, no doubt, you have been sufficiently paid before."

"That's all very well," said Banker. "I don't mind a bit what you say to me. I don't mind your being angry—in fact, I think you ought to be. In your place, I would be angry. But if you will hand me the money—"

"Silence!" exclaimed Edna. "Not another word. Where is my letter?"

"Here it is," said Banker, drawing the letter he had prepared from his pocket, and holding it in such a position that she could read the address. "You see, it is marked, 'by private hand,' and this is the private hand that has brought it to you. Now, if you will count out the money, and will hand it to me, I will give you the letter. That is perfectly fair, isn't it?"

Edna leaned forward and looked at it. When she saw the superscription, she was astonished, and stepped back.

"What do you mean?" she exclaimed, and was about to angrily assert that she was not Madame Raminez, when Banker interrupted her. The sight of her pocket-book within two feet of his hands threw him into a state of avaricious excitement.

"I want you to give me that money, and take your letter!" he said savagely. "I can't stand here fooling."

Edna firmly gripped her pocket-book, and was about to scream, but there was no occasion for it. It had been simply impossible for Cheditafa to remain on the carriage and let her go into the Gardens alone; he had followed her, and, behind some bushes, he had witnessed the interview between her and Banker. He saw that the man was speaking roughly to her and threatening her. Instantly he rushed toward the two, and at the very top of his voice he yelled:

"Rackbird! Rackbird! Police!"

Startled out of her senses, Edna stepped back, while Banker turned in fury toward the negro, and clapped his hand to his hip pocket. But Cheditafa's cries had been heard, and down the broad avenue Banker saw two gendarmes running toward him. It would not do to wait here and meet them.

"You devil!" he cried, turning to Cheditafa, "I'll have your blood before you know it. As for you, madam, you have broken your word! I'll be even with you!" And, with this, he dashed away.

When the gendarmes reached the spot, they waited to ask no questions, but immediately pursued the flying Banker. Cheditafa was about to join in the chase, but Edna stopped him.

"Come to the carriage—quick!" she said. "I do not wish to stay here and talk to those policemen." Hurrying out of the Gardens, she drove away.

The ex-Rackbird was a very hard man to catch. He had had so much experience in avoiding arrest that his skill in that direction was generally more than equal to the skill, in the opposite direction, of the ordinary detective. A good many people and two other gendarmes joined in the chase after the man in the slouch-hat, who had disappeared like a mouse or a hare around some shrubbery. It was not long before the pursuers were joined by a man in a white cap, who asked several questions as to what they were running after, but he did not seem to take a sustained interest in the matter, and soon dropped out and went about his business. He did not take his slouch-hat out of his pocket, for he thought it would be better to continue to wear his white cap for a time.

When the police were obliged to give up the pursuit, they went back to the Gardens to talk to the lady and her servant who, in such strange words, had called to them, but they were not there.

CHAPTER XLV
MENTAL TURMOILS

Edna went home faint, trembling, and her head in a whirl. When she had heard Cheditafa shout "Rackbird," the thought flashed into her mind that the captain had been captured in the caves by some of these brigands who had not been destroyed, that this was the cause of his silence, and that he had written to her for help. But she considered that the letter could not be meant for her, for under no circumstance would he have written to her as Madame Raminez—a name of which she had never heard. This thought gave her a little comfort, but not much. As soon as she reached the hotel, she had a private talk with Cheditafa, and what the negro told her reassured her greatly.

He did not make a very consecutive tale, but he omitted nothing. He told her of his meeting with the Rackbird in front of the Bon Marché, and he related every word of their short conversation. He accounted for this Rackbird's existence by saying that he had not been at the camp when the water came down. In answer to a question from Edna, he said that the captain of the band was named Raminez, and that he had known him by that name when he first saw him in Panama, though in the Rackbirds' camp he was called nothing but "the captain."

"And you only told him I was the captain's wife?" asked Edna. "You didn't say I was Captain Horn's wife?"

Cheditafa tried his best to recollect, and he felt very sure that he had simply said she was the captain's wife.

When his examination was finished, Cheditafa burst into an earnest appeal to his mistress not to go out again alone while she stayed in Paris. He said that this Rackbird was an awfully wicked man, and that he would kill all of them if he could. If the police caught him, he wanted to go and tell them what a bad man he was. He did not believe the police had caught him. This man could run like a wild hare, and policemen's legs were so stiff.

Edna assured him that she would take good care of herself, and, after enjoining upon him not to say a word to any one of what had happened until she told him to, she sent him away.

When Edna sat in council with herself upon the events of the morning, she was able to make some very fair conjectures as to what had happened. The scoundrel she met had supposed her to be the wife of the Rackbirds' captain. Having seen and recognized Cheditafa, it was natural enough for him to suppose that the negro had been brought to Paris by some of the band. All this seemed to be good reasoning, and she insisted to herself over and over again that she was quite sure that Captain Horn had nothing to do with the letter which the man had been intending to give her.

That assurance relieved her of one great trouble, but there were others left. Here was a member of a band of bloody ruffians,—and perhaps he had companions,—who had sworn vengeance against her and her faithful servant, and Cheditafa's account of this man convinced her that he would be ready enough to carry out such vengeance. She scarcely believed that the police had caught him. For she had seen how he could run, and he had the start of them. But even if they had, on what charge would he be held? He ought to be confined or deported, but she did not wish to institute proceedings and give evidence. She did not know what might be asked, or said, or done, if she deposed that the man was a member of the Rackbird band, and brought Cheditafa as a witness.

In all this trouble and perplexity she had no one to whom she could turn for advice and assistance. If she told Mrs. Cliff there was a Rackbird in Paris, and that he had been making threats, she was sure that good lady would fly to her home in Plainton, Maine, where she would have iron bars put to all the windows, and double locks to her doors.

In this great anxiety and terror—for, although Edna was a brave woman, it terrified her to think that a wild and reckless villain, purple with rage, had shaken his fist at her, and vowed he would kill Cheditafa—she could not think of a soul she could trust.

Her brother, fortunately, was still in Belgium with his tutor—fortunately, she thought, because, if he knew of the affair, he would be certain to plunge himself into danger. And to whom could she apply for help without telling too much of her story?

Mrs. Cliff felt there was something in the air. "You seem queer," said she. "You seem unusually excited and ready to laugh. It isn't natural. And Cheditafa looks very ashy. I saw him just a moment ago, and it seems to me a dose of quinine would do him good. It may be that it is a sort of spring fever which is affecting people, and I am not sure but that something of the kind is the matter with me. At any rate, there is that feeling in my spine and bones which I always have when things are about to happen, or when there is malaria in the air."

Edna felt she must endeavor in all possible ways to prevent Mrs. Cliff from finding out that the curses of a wicked Rackbird were in the air, but she herself shuddered when she thought that one or more of the cruel desperadoes, whose coming they had dreaded and waited for through that fearful night in the caves of Peru, were now to be dreaded and feared in the metropolis of France. If Edna shuddered at this, what would Mrs. Cliff do if she knew it?

As for the man with the white cap, who had walked slowly away about his business that morning when he grew tired of following the gendarmes, he was in a terrible state of mind. He silently raged and stormed and gnashed his teeth, and swore under his breath most awfully and continuously. Never had he known such cursed luck. One thousand dollars had been within two feet of his hand! He knew that the lady had that sum in her pocket-book. He was sure she spoke truthfully. Her very denunciation of him was a proof that she had not meant to deceive him. She hesitated a moment, but she would have given him the money. In a few seconds more he would have made her take the letter and give him the price she promised. But in those few seconds that Gehenna-born baboon had rushed in and spoiled everything. He was not enraged against the lady, but he was enraged against himself because he had not snatched the wallet before he ran, and he was infuriated to a degree which resembled intoxication when he thought of Cheditafa and what he had done. The more he thought, the more convinced he became that the lady had not brought the negro with her to spy on him. If she had intended to break her word, she would have brought a gendarme, not that ape.

No, the beastly blackamoor had done the business on his own account. He had sneaked after the lady, and when he saw the gendarmes coming, he had thought it a good chance to pay off old scores.

"Pay off!" growled Banker, in a tone which made a shop-girl, who was walking in front of him carrying a band-box, jump so violently that she dropped the box. "Pay off! I'll pay him!" And for a quarter of a mile he vowed that the present purpose of his life was the annihilation, the bloody annihilation, of that vile dog, whom he had trampled into the dirt of the Pacific coast, and who now, decked in fine clothes, had arisen in Paris to balk him of his fortune.

It cut Banker very deeply when he thought how neat and simple had been the plan which had almost succeeded. He had had a notion, when he went away to prepare the letter for the captain's wife, that he would write in it a brief message which would mean nothing, but would make it necessary for her to see him again and to pay him again. But he had abandoned this. He might counterfeit an address, but it was wiser not to try his hand upon a letter. The more he thought about Raminez, the less he desired to run the risk of meeting him, even in Paris. So he considered that if he made this one bold stroke and got five thousand francs, he would retire, joyful and satisfied. But now! Well, he had a purpose: the annihilation of Cheditafa was at present his chief object in life.

Banker seldom stayed in one place more than a day at a time, and before he went to a new lodging, that night, he threw away his slouch-hat, which he had rammed into his pocket, for he would not want it again. He had his hair cut short and his face neatly shaved, and when he went to his room, he trimmed his mustache in such a way that it greatly altered the cast of his countenance. He was not the penniless man he had represented himself to be, who had not three francs to jingle together, for he was a billiard sharper and gambler of much ability, and when he appeared in the street, the next morning, he was neatly dressed in a suit of second-hand clothes which were as quiet and respectable as any tourist of limited means could have desired. With Baedeker's "Paris" in his hand, and with a long knife and a slung-shot concealed in his clothes, he went forth to behold the wonders of the great city.

He did not seem to care very much whether he saw the sights by day or by night, for from early morning until ten or eleven o'clock in the evening, he was an energetic and interested wayfarer, confining his observations, however, to certain quarters of the city which best suited his investigations. One night he gawkily strolled into the Black Cat, and one day he boldly entered the Hotel Grenade and made some inquiries of the porter regarding the price of accommodations, which, however, he declared were far above his means. That day he saw Mok in the courtyard, and once, in passing, he saw Edna come out and enter her carriage with an elderly lady, and they drove away, with Cheditafa on the box.

Under his dark sack-coat Banker wore a coarse blouse, and in the pocket of this undergarment he had a white cap. He was a wonderful man to move quietly out of people's way, and there were places in every neighborhood where, even in the daytime, he could cast off the dark coat and the derby hat without attracting attention.

It was satisfactory to think, as he briskly passed on, as one who has much to see in a little time, that the incident in the Tuileries Gardens had not yet caused the captain's wife to change her quarters.

CHAPTER XLVI
A PROBLEM

It was a little more than a week after Edna's adventure in the Gardens, and about ten o'clock in the morning, that something happened—something which proved that Mrs. Cliff was entirely right when she talked about the feeling in her bones. Edna received a letter from Captain Horn, which was dated at Marseilles.

As she stood with the letter in her hand, every nerve tingling, every vein throbbing, and every muscle as rigid as if it had been cast in metal, she could scarcely comprehend that it had really come—that she really held it. After all this waiting and hoping and trusting, here was news from Captain Horn—news by his own hand, now, here, this minute!

Presently she regained possession of herself, and, still standing, she tore open the letter. It was a long one of several sheets, and she read it twice. The first time, standing where she had received it, she skimmed over page after page, running her eye from top to bottom until she had reached the end and the signature, but her quick glance found not what she looked for. Then the hand holding the letter dropped by her side. After all this waiting and hoping and trusting, to receive such a letter! It might have been written by a good friend, a true and generous friend, but that was all. It was like the other letters he had written. Why should they not have been written to Mrs. Cliff?

Now she sat down to read it over again. She first looked at the envelope. Yes, it was really directed to "Mrs. Philip Horn." That was something, but it could not have been less. It had been brought by a messenger from Wraxton, Fuguet & Co., and had been delivered to Mrs. Cliff. That lady had told the messenger to take the letter to Edna's salon, and she was now lying in her own chamber, in a state of actual ague. Of course, she would not intrude upon Edna at such a moment as this. She would wait until she was called. Whether her shivers were those of ecstasy, apprehension, or that nervous tremulousness which would come to any one who beholds an uprising from the grave, she did not know, but she surely felt as if there were a ghost in the air.

The second reading of the letter was careful and exact. The captain had written a long account of what had happened after he had left Valparaiso. His former letter, he wrote, had told her what had happened before that time. He condensed everything as much as possible, but the letter was a very long one. It told wonderful things—things which ought to have interested any one. But to Edna it was as dry as a meal of stale crusts. It supported her in her fidelity and allegiance as such a meal would have supported a half-famished man, but that was all. Her soul could not live on such nutriment as this.

He had not begun the letter "My dear Wife," as he had done before. It was not necessary now that his letters should be used as proof that she was his widow! He had plunged instantly into the subject-matter, and had signed it after the most friendly fashion. He was not even coming to her! There was so much to do which must be done immediately, and could not be done without him. He had telegraphed to his bankers, and one of the firm and several clerks were already with him. There were great difficulties yet before him, in which he needed the aid of financial counsellors and those who had influence with the authorities. His vessel, the *Arato*, had no papers, and he believed no cargo of such value had ever entered a port of France as that contained in the little green-hulled schooner which he had sailed into the harbor of Marseilles. This cargo must be landed openly. It must be shipped to various financial centres, and what was to be done required so much prudence, knowledge, and discretion that without the aid of the house of Wraxton, Fuguet & Co., he believed his difficulties would have been greater than when he stood behind the wall of gold on the shore of the Patagonian island.

He did not even ask her to come to him. In a day or so, he wrote, it might be necessary for him to go to Berlin, and whether or not he would travel to London from the German capital, he could not say, and for this reason he could not invite any of them to come down to him.

"Any of us!" exclaimed Edna.

For more than an hour Mrs. Cliff lay in the state of palpitation which pervaded her whole organization, waiting for Edna to call her. And at last she could wait no longer, and rushed into the salon where Edna sat alone, the letter in her hand.

"What does he say?" she cried, "Is he well? Where is he? Did he get the gold?"

Edna looked at her for a moment without answering. "Yes," she said presently, "he is well. He is in Marseilles. The gold—" And for a moment she did not remember whether or not the captain had it.

"Oh, do say something!" almost screamed Mrs. Cliff. "What is it? Shall I read the letter? What does he say?"

This recalled Edna to herself. "No," said she, "I will read it to you." And she read it aloud, from beginning to end, carefully omitting those passages which Mrs. Cliff would have been sure to think should have been written in a manner in which they were not written.

"Well!" exclaimed Mrs. Cliff, who, in alternate horror, pity, and rapture, had listened, pale and open-mouthed, to the letter. "Captain Horn is consistent to the end! Whatever happens, he keeps away from us! But that will not be for long, and—oh, Edna!"—and, as she spoke, she sprang from her chair and threw her arms around the neck of her companion, "he's got the gold!" And, with this, the poor lady sank insensible upon the floor.

"The gold!" exclaimed Edna, before she even stooped toward her fainting friend. "Of what importance is that wretched gold!"

An hour afterwards Mrs. Cliff, having been restored to her usual condition, came again into Edna's room, still pale and in a state of excitement.

"Now, I suppose," she exclaimed, "we can speak out plainly, and tell everybody everything. And I believe that will be to me a greater delight than any amount of money could possibly be."

"Speak out!" cried Edna, "of course we cannot. We have no more right to speak out now than we ever had. Captain Horn insisted that we should not speak of these affairs until he came, and he has not yet come."

"No, indeed!" said Mrs. Cliff, "that seems to be the one thing he cannot do. He can do everything but come here. And are we to tell nobody that he has arrived in France?—not even that much?"

"I shall tell Ralph," replied Edna. "I shall write to him to come here as soon as possible, but that is all until the captain arrives, and we know everything that has been done, and is to be done. I don't wish any one, except you and me and Ralph, even to know that I have heard from him."

"Not Cheditafa? Not the professor? Nor any of your friends?"

"Of course not," said Edna, a little impatiently. "Don't you see how embarrassing, how impossible it would be for me to tell them anything, if I did not tell them everything? And what is there for me to tell them? When we have seen Captain Horn, we shall all know who we are, and what we are, and then we can speak out to the world, and I am sure I shall be glad enough to do it."

"For my part," said Mrs. Cliff, "I think we all know who we are now. I don't think anybody could tell us. And I think it would have been a great deal better—"

"No, it wouldn't!" exclaimed Edna. "Whatever you were going to say, I know it wouldn't have been better. We could have done nothing but what we have done. We had no right to speak of Captain Horn's affairs, and having accepted his conditions, with everything else that he has given us, we are bound to observe them until he removes them. So we shall not talk any more about that."

Poor Mrs. Cliff sighed. "So I must keep myself sealed and locked up, just the same as ever?"

"Yes," replied Edna, "the same as ever. But it cannot be for long. As soon as the captain has made his arrangements, we shall hear from him, and then everything will be told."

"Made his arrangements!" repeated Mrs. Cliff. "That's another thing I don't like. It seems to me that if everything were just as it ought to be, there wouldn't be so many arrangements to make, and he wouldn't have to be travelling to Berlin, and to London, and nobody knows where else. I wonder if people are giving him any trouble about it! We have had all sorts of troubles already, and now that the blessed end seems almost under our fingers, I hope we are not going to have more of it."

"Our troubles," said Edna, "are nothing. It is Captain Horn who should talk in that way. I don't think that, since the day we left San Francisco, anybody could have supposed that we were in any sort of trouble."

"I don't mean outside circumstances," said Mrs. Cliff. "But I suppose we have all got souls and consciences inside of us, and when they don't know what to do, of course we are bound to be troubled, especially as they don't know what to tell us, and we don't know whether or not to mind them when they do speak. But you needn't be afraid of me. I shall keep quiet—that is, as long as I can. I can't promise forever."

Edna wrote to Ralph, telling him of the captain's letter, and urging him to come to Paris as soon as possible. It was scarcely necessary to speak to him of secrecy, for the boy was wise beyond his years. She did speak of it, however, but very circumspectly. She knew that her brother would never admit that there was any reason for the soul-rending anxiety with which she waited the captain's return. But whatever happened, or whatever he might think about what should happen, she wanted Ralph with her. She felt herself more truly alone than she had ever been in her life.

During the two days which elapsed before Ralph reached Paris from Brussels, Edna had plenty of time to think, and she did not lose any of it. What Mrs. Cliff had said about people giving trouble, and about her conscience, and all that, had touched her deeply. What Captain Horn had said about the difficulties he had encountered on reaching Marseilles, and what he had said about the cargo of the *Arato* being probably more valuable than any which had ever entered that port, seemed to put an entirely new face upon the relations between her and the owner of this vast wealth, if, indeed, he were able to establish that ownership. The more she thought of this point, the more contemptible appeared her own position—that is, the position she had assumed when she and the captain stood together for the last time on the shore of Peru. If that gold truly belonged to him, if he had really succeeded in his great enterprise, what right had she to insist that he should accept her as a condition of his safe arrival in a civilized land with this matchless prize, with no other right than was given her by that very indefinite contract which had been entered into, as she felt herself forced to believe, only for her benefit in case he should not reach a civilized land alive?

The disposition of this great wealth was evidently an anxiety and a burden, but in her heart she believed that the greatest of his anxieties was caused by his doubt in regard to the construction she might now place upon that vague, weird ceremony on the desert coast of Peru.

The existence of such a doubt was the only thing that could explain the tone of his letters. He was a man of firmness and decision, and when he had reached a conclusion, she knew he would state it frankly, without hesitation. But she also knew that he was a man of a kind and tender heart, and it was easy to understand how that disposition had influenced his action. By no word or phrase, except such as were necessary to legally protect her in the rights he wished to give her in case of his death, had he written anything to indicate that he or she were not both perfectly free to plan out the rest of their lives as best suited them.

In a certain way, his kindness was cruelty. It threw too much upon her. She believed that if she were to assume that a marriage ceremony performed by a black man from the wilds of Africa, was as binding, at least, as a solemn engagement, he would accept her construction and all its consequences. She also believed that if she declared that ceremony to be of no value whatever, now that the occasion had passed, he would agree with that conclusion. Everything depended upon her. It was too hard for her.

To exist in this state of uncertainty was impossible for a woman of Edna's organization. At any hour Captain Horn might appear. How should she receive him? What had she to say to him?

For the rest of that day and the whole of the night, her mind never left this question: "What am I to say to him?" She had replied to his letter by a telegram, and simply signed herself "Edna." It was easy enough to telegraph anywhere, and even to write, without assuming any particular position in regard to him. But when he came, she must know what to do and what to say. She longed for Ralph's coming, but she knew he could not help her. He would say but one thing—that which he had always said. In fact, he would be no better than Mrs. Cliff. But he was her own flesh and blood, and she longed for him.

CHAPTER XLVII
A MAN-CHIMPANZEE

Since the affair with the Rackbird, Cheditafa had done his duty more earnestly than ever before. He said nothing to Mok about the Rackbird. He had come to look upon his fellow-African as a very low creature, not much better than a chimpanzee. During Ralph's absence Mok had fallen into all sorts of irregular habits, going out without leave whenever he got a chance, and disporting himself generally in a very careless and unservant-like manner.

On the evening that Ralph was expected from Brussels, Mok was missing. Cheditafa could not find him in any of the places where he ought to have been, so he must be out of doors somewhere, and Cheditafa went to look for him.

This was the first time that Cheditafa had gone into the streets alone at night since the Rackbird incident in the Tuileries Gardens. As he was the custodian of Mok, and responsible for him, he did not wish to lose sight of him, especially on this evening.

It so happened that when Cheditafa went out of the hotel, his appearance was noticed by Mr. Banker. There was nothing remarkable about this, for the evening was the time when the ex-Rackbird gave the most attention to the people who came out of the hotel. When he saw Cheditafa, his soul warmed within him. Here was the reward of patience and steadfastness— everything comes to those who wait.

A half-hour before, Banker had seen Mok leave the hotel and make his way toward the Black Cat. He did not molest the rapidly walking negro. He would not have disturbed him for anything. But his watchfulness became so eager and intense that he almost, but not quite, exposed himself to the suspicion of a passing gendarme. He now expected Cheditafa, for the reason that the manner of the younger negro indicated that he was playing truant. It was likely that the elder man would go after him, and this was exactly what happened.

Banker allowed the old African to go his way without molestation, for the brightly lighted neighborhood of the hotel was not adapted to his projected performance. But he followed him warily, and, when they reached a quiet street, Banker quickened his pace, passed Cheditafa, and, suddenly turning, confronted him. Then, without a word having been said, there flashed upon the mind of the African everything that had happened, not only in the Tuileries Gardens, but in the Rackbirds' camp, and at the same time a prophetic feeling of what was about to happen.

By a few quick pulls and jerks, Banker had so far removed his disguise that Cheditafa knew him the instant that his eyes fell upon him. His knees trembled, his eyeballs rolled so that nothing but their whites could be seen, and he gave himself up to death. Then spoke out the terrible Rackbird.

What he said need not be recorded here, but every word of superheated vengeance, with which he wished to torture the soul of his victim before striking him to the earth, went straight to the soul of Cheditafa, as if it had been a white-hot iron. His chin fell upon his breast. He had but one hope, and that was that he would be killed quickly. He had seen people killed in the horrible old camp, and the man before him he believed to be the worst Rackbird of them all.

When Banker had finished stabbing and torturing the soul of the African, he drew a knife from under his coat, and down fell Cheditafa on his knees.

The evening was rainy and dark, and the little street was nearly deserted. Banker, who could look behind and before him without making much show of turning his head, had made himself sure of this before he stepped in front of Cheditafa. But while he had been pouring out his torrent of heart-shrivelling vituperation, he had ceased to look before and behind him, and had not noticed a man coming down the street in the opposite direction to that in which they had been going.

This was Mok, who was much less of a fool than Cheditafa took him for. He had calculated that he would have time to go to the Black Cat and drink two glasses of beer before Ralph was likely to appear, and he also made up his mind that two glasses were as much as he could dispose of without exciting the suspicions of the young man. Therefore, he had attended to the business that had taken him out of doors on that rainy night, and was returning to the hotel with a lofty consciousness of having done wrong in a very wise and satisfactory manner.

He wore india-rubber overshoes, because the pavements were wet, and also because this sort of foot-gear suited him better than hard, unyielding sole-leather. Had he had his own way, he would have gone bare-footed, but that would have created comment in the streets of Paris—he had sense enough to know that.

When he first perceived, by the dim light of a street lamp, two persons standing together on his side of the street, his conscience, without any reason for it, suggested that he cross over and pass by without attracting attention. To wrong-doers attention is generally unwelcome.

Mok not only trod with the softness and swiftness of a panther, but he had eyes like that animal, and if there were any light at all, those eyes could make good use of it. As he neared the two men, he saw that one was scolding the other. Then he saw the other man drop down on his knees. Then, being still nearer, he perceived that the man on his knees was Cheditafa. Then he saw the man in front of him draw a knife from under his coat.

As a rule, Mok was a coward, but two glasses of beer were enough to turn his nature in precisely the opposite direction. A glass less would have left him timorous, a glass more would have made him foolhardy and silly. He saw that somebody was about to stab his old friend. In five long, noiseless steps, or leaps, he was behind that somebody, and had seized the arm which held the knife.

With a movement as quick as the stroke of a rattlesnake, Banker turned upon the man who had clutched his arm, and when he saw that it was Mok, his fury grew tornado-like. With a great oath, and a powerful plunge backward, he endeavored to free his arm from the grasp of the negro. But he did not do it. Those black fingers were fastened around his wrist as though they had been fetters forged to fit him. And in the desperate struggle the knife was dropped.

In a hand-to-hand combat with a chimpanzee, a strong man would have but little chance of success, and Mok, under the influence of two glasses of beer, was a man-chimpanzee. When Banker swore, and when he turned so that the light of the street lamp fell upon his face, Mok recognized him. He knew him for a Rackbird of the Rackbirds—as the cruel, black-eyed savage who had beaten him, trodden upon him, and almost crushed the soul out of him, in that far-away camp by the sea. How this man should have suddenly appeared in Paris, why he came there, and what he was going to do, whether he was alone, or with his band concealed in the neighboring doorways, Mok did not trouble his mind to consider. He held in his brazen grip a creature whom he considered worse than the most devilish of African devils, a villain who had been going to kill Cheditafa.

Every nerve under his black skin, every muscle that covered his bones, and the two glasses of beer, sung out to him that the Rackbird could not get away from him, and that the great hour of vengeance had arrived.

Banker had a pistol, but he had no chance to draw it. The arms of the wild man were around him. His feet slipped from under him, and instantly the two were rolling on the wet pavement. But only for an instant. Banker was quick and light and strong to such a degree that no man but a man-chimpanzee could have overpowered him in a struggle like that. Both were on their feet almost as quickly as they went down, but do what he would, Banker could not get out his pistol.

Those long black arms, one of them now bared to the shoulder, were about him ever. He pulled, and tugged, and swerved. He half threw him one instant, half lifted the next, but never could loosen the grasp of that fierce creature, whose whole body seemed as tough and elastic as the shoes he wore.

Together they fell, together they rolled in the dirty slime, together they rose as if they had been shot up by a spring, and together they went down again, rolling over each other, pulling, tearing, striking, gasping, and panting.

Cheditafa had gone. The moment of Mok's appearance, he had risen and fled. There were now people in the street. Some had come out of their houses, hearing the noise of the struggle, for Banker wore heavy shoes. There were also one or two pedestrians who had stopped, unwilling to pass men who were engaged in such a desperate conflict.

No one interfered. It would have seemed as prudent to step between two tigers. Such a bounding, whirling, tumbling, rolling, falling, and rising contest had never been seen in that street, except between cats. It seemed that the creatures would dash themselves through the windows of the houses.

It was not long before Cheditafa came back with two policemen, all running, and then the men who lay in the street, spinning about as if moving on pivots, were seized and pulled apart. At first the officers of the law appeared at a loss to know what had happened, and who had been attacked.

What was this black creature from the Jardin des Plantes? But Banker's coat had been torn from his back, and his pistol stood out in bold relief in his belt, and Cheditafa pointed to the breathless bandit, and screamed: "Bad man! Bad man! Try to kill me! This good Mok save my life!"

Two more policemen now came hurrying up, for other people had given the alarm, and it was not considered necessary to debate the question as to who was the aggressor in this desperate affair. Cheditafa, Mok, and Banker were all taken to the police station.

As Cheditafa was known to be in the service of the American lady at the Hotel Grenade, the *portier* of that establishment was sent for, and having given his testimony to the good character of the two negroes, they were released upon his becoming surety for their appearance when wanted.

As for Banker, there was no one to go security. He was committed for trial.

* * * * *

When Ralph went to his room, that night, he immediately rang for his valet. Mok, who had reached the hotel from the police station but a few minutes before, answered the summons. When Ralph turned about and beheld the black man, his hair plastered with mud, his face plastered with mud, and what clothes he had on muddy, torn, and awry, with one foot wearing a great overshoe and the other bare, with both black arms entirely denuded of sleeves, with eyes staring from his head, and his whole form quivering and shaking, the young man started as if some afrit of the "Arabian Nights" had come at this dark hour to answer his call.

To the eager questions which poured upon him when his identity became apparent, Mok could make no intelligible answer. He did not possess English enough for that. But Cheditafa was quickly summoned, and he explained everything. He explained it once, twice, three times, and then he and Mok were sent away, and told to go to bed, and under no circumstances to mention to their mistress what had happened, or to anybody who might mention it to her. And this Cheditafa solemnly promised for both.

The clock struck one as Ralph still sat in his chair, wondering what all this meant, and what might be expected to happen next. To hear that a real, live Rackbird was in Paris, that this outlaw had threatened his sister, that the police had been watching for him, that he had sworn to kill Cheditafa, and that night had tried to do it, amazed him beyond measure.

At last he gave up trying to conjecture what it meant. It was foolish to waste his thoughts in that way. To-morrow he must find out. He could understand very well why his sister had kept him in ignorance of the affair in the Gardens. She had feared danger to him. She knew that he would be after that scoundrel more hotly than any policeman. But what the poor girl must have suffered! It was terrible to think of.

The first thing he would do would be to take very good care that she heard nothing of the attack on Cheditafa. He would go to the police office early the next morning and look into this matter. He did not think that it would be necessary for Edna to know anything about it, except that the Rackbird had been arrested and she need no longer fear him.

When Ralph reached the police station, the next day, he found there the portier of the hotel, together with Cheditafa and Mok.

After Banker's examination, to which he gave no assistance by admissions of any sort, he was remanded for trial, and he was held merely for his affair with the negroes, no charge having been made against him for his attempt to obtain money from their mistress, or his threats in her direction. As the crime for which he had been arrested gave reason enough for condign punishment of the desperado, Ralph saw, and made Cheditafa see, it would be unnecessary as well as unpleasant to drag Edna into the affair.

That afternoon Mr. Banker, who had recovered his breath and had collected his ideas, sent for the police magistrate and made a confession. He said he had been a member of a band of outlaws, but having grown disgusted with their evil deeds, had left them. He had become very poor, and having heard that the leader of the band had made a fortune by a successful piece of rascality, and had married a fine lady, and was then in Paris, he had come to this city to meet him, and to demand in the name of their old comradeship some assistance in his need. He had found his captain's wife. She had basely deceived him after having promised to help him, and he had been insulted and vilely treated by that old negro, who was once a slave in the Rackbirds' camp in Peru, and who had been brought here with the other negro by the captain. He also freely admitted that he had intended to punish the black fellow, though he had no idea whatever of killing him. If he had had such an idea, it would have been easy enough for him to put his knife into him when he met him in that quiet street. But he had not done so, but had contented himself with telling him what he thought of him, and with afterwards frightening him with his knife. And then the other fellow had come up, and there had been a fight. Therefore, although he admitted that his case was a great misdemeanor, and that he had been very disorderly, he boldly asserted that he had contemplated no murder. But what he wished particularly to say to the magistrate was that the captain of the Rackbirds would probably soon arrive in Paris, and that he ought to be arrested. No end of important results might come from such an arrest. He was quite sure that the great stroke of fortune which had enabled the captain's family to live in Paris in such fine style ought to be investigated. The captain had never made any money by simple and straightforward methods of business.

All this voluntary testimony was carefully taken down, and although the magistrate did not consider it necessary to believe any of it, the arrival of Captain Horn was thenceforth awaited with interest by the police of Paris.

It was not very plain how Miss Markham of the Hotel Grenade, who was well known as a friend of a member of the American legation, could be the wife of a South American bandit. But then, there might be reasons why she wished to retain her maiden name for the present, and she might not know her husband as a bandit.

CHAPTER XLVIII
ENTER CAPTAIN HORN

It was less than a week after the tumbling match in the street between Banker and Mok, and about eleven o'clock in the morning, when a brief note, written on a slip of paper and accompanied by a card, was brought to Edna from Mrs. Cliff. On the card was written the name of Captain Philip Horn, and the note read thus:

"He is here. He sent his card to me. Of course, you will see him. Oh, Edna! don't do anything foolish when you see him! Don't go and throw away everything worth living for in this world! Heaven help you!"

This note was hurriedly written, but Edna read it at a glance.

"Bring the gentleman here," she said to the man.

Now, with all her heart, Edna blessed herself and thanked herself that, at last, she had been strong enough and brave enough to determine what she ought to do when she met the captain. That very morning, lying awake in her bed, she had determined that she would meet him in the same spirit as that in which he had written to her. She would be very strong. She would not assume anything. She would not accept the responsibility of deciding the situation, which responsibility she believed he thought it right she should assume. She would not have it. If he appeared before her as the Captain Horn of his letters, he should go away as the man who had written those letters. If he had come here on business, she would show him that she was a woman of business.

As she stood waiting, with her eyes upon his card, which lay upon the table, and Mrs. Cliffs note crumpled up in one hand, she saw the captain for some minutes before it was possible for him to reach her. She saw him on board the *Castor*, a tall, broad-shouldered sailor, with his hands in the pockets of his pea-jacket. She saw him by the caves in Peru, his flannel shirt and his belted trousers faded by the sun and water, torn and worn, and stained by the soil on which they so often sat, with his long hair and beard, and the battered felt hat, which was the last thing she saw as his boat faded away in the distance, when she stood watching it from the sandy beach. She saw him as she had imagined him after she had received his letter, toiling barefooted along the sands, carrying heavy loads upon his shoulders, living alone night and day on a dreary desert coast, weary, perhaps haggard, but still indomitable. She saw him in storm, in shipwreck, in battle, and as she looked upon him thus with the eyes of her brain, there were footsteps outside her door.

As Captain Horn came through the long corridors and up the stairs, following the attendant, he saw the woman he was about to meet, and saw her before he met her. He saw her only in one aspect—that of a tall, too thin, young woman, clad in a dark-blue flannel suit, unshapely, streaked, and stained, her hair bound tightly round her head and covered by an old straw hat with a faded ribbon. This picture of her as he had left her standing on the beach, at the close of that afternoon when his little boat pulled out into the Pacific, was as clear and distinct as when he had last seen it.

A door was opened before him, and he entered Edna's salon. For a moment he stopped in the doorway. He did not see the woman he had come to meet. He saw before him a lady handsomely and richly dressed in a Parisian morning costume—a lady with waving masses of dark hair above a lovely face, a lady with a beautiful white hand, which was half raised as he appeared in the doorway.

She stood with her hand half raised. She had never seen the man before her. He was a tall, imposing gentleman, in a dark suit, over which he wore a light-colored overcoat. One hand was gloved, and in the other he held a hat. His slightly curling brown beard and hair were trimmed after the fashion of the day, and his face, though darkened by the sun, showed no trace of toil, or storm, or anxious danger. He was a tall, broad-shouldered gentleman, with an air of courtesy, an air of dignity, an air of forbearance, which were as utterly unknown to her as everything else about him, except his eyes—those were the same eyes she had seen on board the *Castor* and on the desert sands.

Had it not been for the dark eyes which looked so steadfastly at him, Captain Horn, would have thought that he had been shown into the wrong room. But he now knew there was no mistake, and he entered. Edna raised her hand and advanced to meet him.

He shook hands with her exactly as he had written to her, and she shook hands with him just as she had telegraphed to him. Much of her natural color had left her face. As he had never seen this natural color, under the sun-brown of the Pacific voyage, he did not miss it.

Instantly she began to speak. How glad she was that she had prepared herself to speak as she would have spoken to any other good friend! So she expressed her joy at seeing him again, well and successful after all these months of peril, toil, and anxiety, and they sat down near each other.

He looked at her steadfastly, and asked her many things about Ralph, Mrs. Cliff, and the negroes, and what had happened since he left San Francisco. He listened with a questioning intentness as she spoke. She spoke rapidly and concisely as she answered his questions and asked him about himself. She said little about the gold. One might have supposed that he had arrived at Marseilles with a cargo of coffee. At the same time, there seemed to be, on Edna's part, a desire to lengthen out her recital of unimportant matters. She now saw that the captain knew she did not care to talk of these things. She knew that he was waiting for an opportunity to turn the conversation into another channel,—waiting with an earnestness that was growing more and more apparent,—and as she perceived this, and as she steadily talked to him, she assured herself, with all the vehemence of which her nature was capable, that she and this man were two people connected by business interests, and that she was ready to discuss that business in a business way as soon as he could speak. But still she did not yet give him the chance to speak.

The captain sat there, with his blue eyes fixed upon her, and, as she looked at him, she knew him to be the personification of honor and magnanimity, waiting until he could see that she was ready for him to speak, ready to listen if she should speak, ready to meet her on any ground—a gentleman, she thought, above all the gentlemen in the world. And still she went on talking about Mrs. Cliff and Ralph.

Suddenly the captain rose. Whether or not he interrupted her in the middle of a sentence, he did not know, nor did she know. He put his hat upon a table and came toward her. He stood in front of her and looked down at her. She looked up at him, but he did not immediately speak. She could not help standing silently and looking up at him when he stood and looked down upon her in that way. Then he spoke.

"Are you my wife?" said he.

"By all that is good and blessed in heaven or earth, I am," she answered.

Standing there, and looking up into his eyes, there was no other answer for her to make.

* * * * *

Seldom has a poor, worn, tired, agitated woman kept what was to her a longer or more anxious watch upon a closed door than Mrs. Cliff kept that day. If even Ralph had appeared, she would have decoyed him into her own room, and locked him up there, if necessary.

In about an hour after Mrs. Cliff began her watch, a tall man walked rapidly out of the salon and went down the stairs, and then a woman came running across the hall and into Mrs. Cliff's room, closing the door behind her. Mrs. Cliff scarcely recognized this woman. She had Edna's hair and face, but there was a glow and a glory on her countenance such as Mrs. Cliff had never seen, or expected to see until, in the hereafter, she should see it on the face of an angel.

"He has loved me," said Edna, with her arms around her old friend's neck, "ever since we had been a week on the *Castor*."

Mrs. Cliff shivered and quivered with joy. She could not say anything, but over and over again she kissed the burning cheeks of her friend. At last they stood apart, and, when Mrs. Cliff was calm enough to speak, she said:

"Ever since we were on the *Castor!* Well, Edna, you must admit that Captain Horn is uncommonly good at keeping things to himself."

"Yes," said the other, "and he always kept it to himself. He never let it go away from him. He had intended to speak to me, but he wanted to wait until I knew him better, and until we were in a position where he wouldn't seem to be taking advantage of me by speaking. And when you proposed that marriage by Cheditafa, he was very much troubled and annoyed. It was something so rough and jarring, and so discordant with what he had hoped, that at first he could not bear to think of it. But he afterwards saw the sense of your reasoning, and agreed simply because it would be to my advantage in case he should lose his life in his undertaking. And we will be married to-morrow at the embassy."

"To-morrow!" cried Mrs. Cliff. "So soon?"

"Yes," replied Edna. "The captain has to go away, and I am going with him."

"That is all right," said Mrs. Cliff. "Of course I was a little surprised at first. But how about the gold? How much was there of it? And what is he going to do with it?"

"He scarcely mentioned the gold," replied Edna. "We had more precious things to talk about. When he sees us all together, you and I and Ralph, he will tell us what he has done, and what he is going to do, and—"

"And we can say what we please?" cried Mrs. Cliff.

"Yes," said Edna,—"to whomever we please."

"Thank the Lord!" exclaimed Mrs. Cliff. "That is almost as good as being married."

* * * * *

On his arrival in Paris the night before, Captain Horn had taken lodgings at a hotel not far from the Hotel Grenade, and the first thing he did the next morning was to visit Edna. He had supposed, of course, that she was at the same hotel in which Mrs. Cliff resided, which address he had got from Wraxton, in Marseilles, and he had expected to see the elderly lady first, and to get some idea of how matters stood before meeting Edna. He was in Paris alone. He had left Shirley and Burke, with the negroes, in Marseilles. He had wished to do nothing, to make no arrangements for any one, until he had seen Edna, and had found out what his future life was to be.

Now, as he walked back to his hotel, that future life lay before him radiant and resplendent. No avenue in Paris, or in any part of the world, blazing with the lights of some grand festival, ever shone with such glowing splendor as the future life of Captain Horn now shone and sparkled before him, as he walked and walked, on and on, and crossed the river into the Latin Quarter, before he perceived that his hotel was a mile or more behind him.

From the moment that the *Arato* had left the Straits of Magellan, and Captain Horn had had reason to believe that he had left his dangers behind him, the prow of his vessel had been set toward the Strait of Gibraltar, and every thought of his heart toward Edna. Burke and Shirley both noticed a change in him. After he left the Rackbirds' cove, until he had sailed into the South Atlantic, his manner had been quiet, alert, generally anxious, and sometimes stern. But now, day by day, he appeared to be growing into a different man. He was not nervous, nor apparently impatient, but it was easy to see that within him there burned a steady purpose to get on as fast as the wind would blow them northward.

Day by day, as he walked the deck of his little vessel, one might have thought him undergoing a transformation from the skipper of a schooner into the master of a great ship, into the captain of a swift Atlantic liner, into the commander of a man-of-war, into the commodore on board a line-of-battle ship. It was not an air of pride or assumed superiority that he wore, it was nothing assumed, it was nothing of which he was not entirely aware. It was the gradual growth within him, as health grows into a man recovering from a sickness, of the consciousness of power. The source of that consciousness lay beneath him, as he trod the deck of the *Arato*.

This consciousness, involuntary, and impossible to resist, had nothing definite about it. It had nothing which could wholly satisfy the soul of this man, who kept his eyes and his thoughts so steadfastly toward the north. He knew that there were but few things in the world that his power could not give him, but there was one thing upon which it might have no influence whatever, and that one thing was far more to him than all other things in this world.

Sometimes, as he sat smoking beneath the stars, he tried to picture to himself the person who might be waiting and watching for him in Paris, and to try to look upon her as she must really be; for, after her life in San Francisco and Paris, she could not remain the woman she had been at the caves on the coast of Peru. But, do what he would, he could make no transformation in the picture which was imprinted on the retina of his soul. There he saw a woman still young, tall, and too thin, in a suit of blue flannel faded and worn, with her hair bound tightly around her head and covered by a straw hat with a faded ribbon. But it was toward this figure that he was sailing, sailing, sailing, as fast as the winds of heaven would blow his vessel onward.

CHAPTER XLIX
A GOLDEN AFTERNOON

When Ralph met Captain Horn that afternoon, there rose within him a sudden, involuntary appreciation of the captain's worthiness to possess a ship-load of gold and his sister Edna. Before that meeting there had been doubts in the boy's mind in regard to this worthiness. He believed that he had thoroughly weighed and judged the character and capacities of the captain of the *Castor*, and he had said to himself, in his moments of reflection, that although Captain Horn was a good man, and a brave man, and an able man in many ways, there were other men in the world who were better fitted for the glorious double position into which this fortunate mariner had fallen.

But now, as Ralph sat and gazed upon his sister's lover and heard him talk, and as he turned from him to Edna's glowing eyes, he acknowledged, without knowing it, the transforming power of those two great alchemists,—gold and love,—and from the bottom of his heart he approved the match.

Upon Mrs. Cliff the first sight of Captain Horn had been a little startling, and had she not hastened to assure herself that the compact with Edna was a thing fixed and settled, she might have been possessed with the fear that perhaps this gentleman might have views for his future life very different from those upon which she had set her heart. But even if she had not known of the compact of the morning, all danger of that fear would have passed in the moment that the captain took her by the hand.

To find his three companions of the wreck and desert in such high state and flourishing condition so cheered and uplifted the soul of the captain that he could talk of nothing else. And now he called for Cheditafa and Mok—those two good fellows whose faithfulness he should never forget. But when they entered, bending low, with eyes upturned toward the lofty presence to which they had been summoned, the captain looked inquiringly at Edna. As he came in that afternoon, he had seen both the negroes in the courtyard, and, in the passing thought he had given to them, had supposed them to be attendants of some foreign potentate from Barbary or Morocco. Cheditafa and Mok! The ragged, half-clad negroes of the sea-beach—a parson-butler of sublimated respectability, a liveried lackey of rainbow and gold! It required minutes to harmonize these presentments in the mind of Captain Horn.

When the audience of the two Africans—for such it seemed to be—had lasted long enough, Edna was thinking of dismissing them, when it became plain to her that there was something which Cheditafa wished to say or do. She looked at him inquiringly, and he came forward.

For a long time the mind of the good African had been exercised upon the subject of the great deed he had done just before the captain had sailed away from the Peruvian coast. In San Francisco and Paris he had asked many questions quietly, and apparently without purpose, concerning the marriage ceremonies of America and other civilized countries. He had not learned enough to enable him, upon an emergency, to personate an orthodox clergyman, but he had found out this and that—little things, perhaps, but things which made a great impression upon him—which had convinced him that in the ceremony he had performed there had been much remissness—how much, he did not clearly know. But about one thing that had been wanting he had no doubts.

Advancing toward Edna and the captain, who sat near each other, Cheditafa took from his pocket a large gold ring, which he had purchased with his savings. "There was a thing we didn't do," he said, glancing from one to the other. "It was the ring part—nobody thought of that. Will captain take it now, and put it on the lady?"

Edna and the captain looked at each other. For a moment no one spoke. Then Edna said, "Take it." The captain rose and took the ring from the hand of Cheditafa, and Edna stood beside him. Then he took her hand, and reverently placed the ring upon her fourth finger. Fortunately, it fitted. It had not been without avail that Cheditafa had so often scanned with a measuring eye the rings upon the hands of his mistress.

A light of pleasure shone in the eyes of the old negro. Now he had done his full duty—now all things had been made right. As he had seen the priests stand in the churches of Paris, he now stood for a moment with his hands outspread. "Very good," he said, "that will do." Then, followed by Mok, he bowed himself out of the room.

For some moments there was silence in the salon. Nobody thought of laughing, or even smiling. In the eyes of Mrs. Cliff there were a few tears. She was the first to speak. "He is a good man," said she, "and he now believes that he has done everything that ought to be done. But you will be married to-morrow, all the same, of course."

"Yes," said Edna. "But it will be with this ring."

"Yes," said the captain, "with that ring. You must always wear it."

"And now," said Mrs. Cliff, when they had all reseated themselves, "you must really tell us your story, captain. You know I have heard nothing yet."

And so he told his story—much that Edna had heard before, a great deal she had not heard. About the treasure, almost everything he said was new to her. Mrs. Cliff was very eager on this point. She wanted every detail.

"How about the ownership of it?" she said. "After all, that is the great point. What do people here think of your right to use that gold as your own?"

The captain smiled. "That is not an easy question to answer, but I think we shall settle it very satisfactorily. Of course, the first thing to do is to get it safely entered and stored away in the great money centres over here. A good portion of it, in fact, is to be shipped to Philadelphia to be coined. Of course, all that business is in the hands of my bankers. The fact that I originally sailed from California was a great help to us. To ascertain my legal rights in the case was the main object of my visit to London. There Wraxton and I put the matter before three leading lawyers in that line of business, and although their opinions differed somewhat, and although we have not yet come to a final conclusion as to what should be done, the matter is pretty well straightened out as far as we are concerned. Of course, the affair is greatly simplified by the fact that there is no one on the other side to be a claimant of the treasure, but we consider it as if there were a claimant, or two of them, in fact. These can be no other than the present government of Peru, and that portion of the population of the country which is native to the soil, and the latter, if our suppositions are correct, are the only real heirs to the treasure which I discovered. But what are the laws of Peru in regard to treasure-trove, or what may be the disposition of the government toward the native population and their rights, of course we cannot find out now. That will take time. But of one thing we are certain: I am entitled to a fair remuneration for the discovery of this treasure, just the same as if I claimed salvage for having brought a wrecked steamer into port. On this point the lawyers are all agreed. I have, therefore, made my claim, and shall stand by it with enough legal force behind me to support me in any emergency.

"But it is not believed that either the Peruvian government, or the natives acting as a body, if it shall be possible for them to act in that way, will give us any trouble. We have the matter entirely in our own hands. They do not know of the existence of this treasure, or that they have any rights to it, until we inform them of the fact, and without our assistance it will be almost impossible for them to claim anything or prove anything. Therefore, it will be good policy and common sense for them to acknowledge that we are acting honestly, and, more than that, generously, and to agree to take what we offer them, and that we shall keep what is considered by the best legal authorities to be our rights.

"As soon as possible, an agent will be sent to Peru to attend to the matter. But this matter is in the hands of my lawyers, although, of course, I shall not keep out of the negotiations."

"And how much percentage, captain?" asked Mrs. Cliff. "What part do they think you ought to keep?"

"We have agreed," said he, "upon twenty per cent. of the whole. After careful consideration and advice, I made that claim. I shall retain it. Indeed, it is already secured to me, no matter what may happen to the rest of the treasure."

"Twenty per cent.!" exclaimed Mrs. Cliff. "And that is all that you get?"

"Yes," said the captain, "it is what I get—and by that is meant what is to be divided among us all. I make the claim, but I make it for every one who was on the *Castor* when she was wrecked, and for the families of those who are not alive—for every one, in fact, who was concerned in this matter."

The countenance of Mrs. Cliff had been falling, and now it went down, down, again. After all the waiting, after all the anxiety, it had come to this: barely twenty per cent., to be divided among ever so many people—twenty-five or thirty, for all she knew. Only this, after the dreams she had had, after the castles she had built! Of course, she had money now, and she would have some more, and she had a great many useful and beautiful things which she had bought, and she could go back to Plainton in very good circumstances. But that was not what she had been waiting for, and hoping for, and anxiously trembling for, ever since she had found that the captain had really reached France with the treasure.

"Captain," she said, and her voice was as husky as if she had been sitting in a draught, "I have had so many ups and so many downs, and have been turned so often this way and that, I cannot stand this state of uncertainty any longer. It may seem childish and weak, but I must know something. Can you give me any idea how much you are to have, or, at least, how much I shall have, and let me make myself satisfied with whatever it is? Do you think that I shall be able to go back to Plainton and take my place as a leading citizen there? I don't mind in the least asking that before you three. I thought I was justified in making that my object in life, and I have made it my object. Now, if I have been mistaken all this time, I would like to know it. Don't find fault with me. I have waited, and waited, and waited—"

"Well," interrupted the captain, "you need not wait any longer. The sum that I have retained shall be divided as soon as possible, and I shall divide it in as just a manner as I can, and I am ready to hear appeals from any one who is not satisfied. Of course, I shall keep the largest share of it—that is my right. I found it, and I secured it. And this lady here," pointing to Edna, "is to have the next largest share in her own right, because she was the main object which made me work so hard and brave everything to get that treasure here. And then the rest will share according to rank, as we say on board ship."

"Oh, dear! Oh, dear!" murmured Mrs. Cliff, "he never comes to any point. We never know anything clear and distinct. This is not any answer at all."

"The amount I claim," continued the captain, who did not notice that Mrs. Cliff was making remarks to herself, "is forty million dollars."

Everybody started, and Mrs. Cliff sprang up as if a torpedo had been fired beneath her.

"Forty million dollars!" she exclaimed. "I thought you said you would only have twenty per cent.?"

"That is just what it is," remarked the captain, "as nearly as we can calculate. Forty million dollars is about one fifth of the value of the cargo I brought to France in the *Arato*. And as to your share, Mrs. Cliff, I think, if you feel like it, you will be able to buy the town of Plainton; and if that doesn't make you a leading citizen in it, I don't know what else you can do."

CHAPTER L
A CASE OF RECOGNITION

Every one in our party at the Hotel Grenade rose very early the next morning. That day was to be one of activity and event. Mrs. Cliff, who had not slept one wink during the night, but who appeared almost rejuvenated by the ideas which had come to her during her sleeplessness, now entered a protest against the proposed marriage at the American legation. She believed that people of the position which Edna and the captain should now assume ought to be married in a church, with all proper ceremony and impressiveness, and urged that the wedding be postponed for a few days, until suitable arrangements could be made.

But Edna would not listen to this. The captain was obliged, by appointment, to be in London on the morrow, and he could not know how long he might be detained there, and now, wherever he went, she wished to go with him. He wanted her to be with him, and she was going. Moreover, she fancied a wedding at the legation. There were all sorts of regulations concerning marriage in France, and to these neither she nor the captain cared to conform, even if they had time enough for the purpose. At the American legation they would be in point of law upon American soil, and there they could be married as Americans, by an American minister.

After that Mrs. Cliff gave up. She was so happy she was ready to agree to anything, or to believe in anything, and she went to work with heart and hand to assist Edna in getting ready for the great event.

Mrs. Sylvester, the wife of the secretary, received a note from Edna which brought her to the hotel as fast as horses were allowed to travel in the streets of Paris, and arrangements were easily made for the ceremony to take place at four o'clock that afternoon.

The marriage was to be entirely private. No one was to be present but Mrs. Cliff, Ralph, and Mrs. Sylvester. Nothing was said to Cheditafa of the intended ceremony. After what had happened, they all felt that it would be right to respect the old negro's feelings and sensibilities. Mrs. Cliff undertook, after a few days had elapsed, to explain the whole matter to Cheditafa, and to tell him that what he had done had not been without importance and real utility, but that it had actually united his master and mistress by a solemn promise before witnesses, which in some places, and under certain circumstances, would be as good a marriage as any that could be performed, but that a second ceremony had taken place in order that the two might be considered man and wife in all places and under all circumstances.

The captain had hoped to see Shirley and Burke before he left Paris, but that was now impossible, and, on his way to his hotel, after breakfasting at the Hotel Grenade, he telegraphed to them to come to him in London. He had just sent his telegram when he was touched on the arm, and, turning, saw standing by him two police officers. Their manner was very civil, but they promptly informed him, the speaker using very fair English, that he must accompany them to the presence of a police magistrate.

The captain was astounded. The officers could or would give him no information in regard to the charge against him, or whether it was a charge at all. They only said that he must come with them, and that everything would be explained at the police station. The captain's brow grew black. What this meant he could not imagine, but he had no time to waste in imaginations. It would be foolish to demand explanations of the officers, or to ask to see the warrant for their action. He would not understand French warrants, and the quicker he went to the magistrate and found out what this thing meant, the better. He only asked time to send a telegram to Mr. Wraxton, urging him to attend him instantly at the police station, and then he went with the officers.

On the way, Captain Horn turned over matters in his mind. He could think of no cause for this detention, except it might be something which had turned up in connection with his possession of the treasure, or perhaps the entrance of the *Arato*, without papers, at the French port. But anything of this kind Wraxton could settle as soon as he could be made acquainted with it. The only real trouble was that he was to be married at four o'clock, and it was now nearly two.

At the police station, Captain Horn met with a fresh annoyance. The magistrate was occupied with important business and could not attend to him at present. This made the captain very impatient, and he sent message after message to the magistrate, but to no avail. And Wraxton did not come. In fact, it was too soon to expect him.

The magistrate had good reason for delay. He did not wish to have anything to do with the gentleman who had been taken in custody until his accuser, Banker by name, had been brought to this station from his place of confinement, where he was now held under a serious charge.

Ten minutes, twenty minutes, twenty-five minutes, passed, and the magistrate did not appear. Wraxton did not come. The captain had never been so fiercely impatient. He did not know to whom to apply in this serious emergency. He did not wish Edna to know of his trouble until he found out the nature of it, and if he sent word to the legation, he was afraid that the news would speedily reach her. Wraxton was his man, whatever the charge might be. He would be his security for any amount which might be named, and the business might be settled afterwards, if, indeed, it were not all a mistake of some sort.

But Wraxton did not appear. Suddenly the captain thought of one man who might be of service to him in this emergency. There was no time for delay. Some one must come, and come quickly, who could identify him, and the only man he could think of was Professor Barré, Ralph's tutor. He had met that gentleman the evening before. He could vouch for him, and he could certainly be trusted not to alarm Edna unnecessarily. He believed the professor could be found at the hotel, and he instantly sent a messenger to him with a note.

It took a good deal of time to bring the prisoner Banker to the station, and Professor Barré arrived there before him. The professor was amazed to find Captain Horn under arrest, and unable to give any reason for this state of things. But it was not long before the magistrate appeared, and it so happened that he was acquainted with Barré, who was a well-known man in Paris, and, after glancing at the captain, he addressed himself to the professor, speaking in French. The latter immediately inquired the nature of the charges against Captain Horn, using the same language.

"Ah! you know him?" said the magistrate. "He has been accused of being the leader of a band of outlaws—a man who has committed murders and outrages without number, one who should not be suffered to go at large, one who should be confined until the authorities of Peru, where his crimes were committed, have been notified."

The professor stared, but could not comprehend what he had heard.

"What is it?" inquired Captain Horn. "Can you not speak English?"

No, this Parisian magistrate could not speak English, but the professor explained the charge.

"It is the greatest absurdity!" exclaimed the captain. "Ralph told me that a man, evidently once one of that band of outlaws in Peru, had been arrested for assaulting Cheditafa, and this charge must be part of his scheme of vengeance for that arrest. I could instantly prove everything that is necessary to know about me if my banker, Mr. Wraxton, were here. I have sent for him, but he has not come. I have not a moment to waste discussing this matter." The captain gazed anxiously toward the door, and for a few moments the three men stood in silence.

The situation was a peculiar one. The professor thought of sending to the Hotel Grenade, but he hesitated. He said to himself: "The lady's testimony would be of no avail. If he is the man the bandit says he is, of course she does not know it. His conduct has been very strange, and for a long time she certainly knew very little about him. I don't see how even his banker could become surety for him if he were here, and he doesn't seem inclined to come. Anybody may have a bank-account."

The professor stood looking on the ground. The captain looked at him, and, by that power to read the thoughts of others which an important emergency often gives to a man, he read, or believed he did, the thoughts of Barré. He did not blame the man for his doubts. Any one might have such doubts. A stranger coming to France with a cargo of gold must expect suspicion, and here was more—a definite charge.

At this moment there came a message from the banking house: Mr. Wraxton had gone to Brussels that morning. Fuguet did not live in Paris, and the captain had never seen him. There were clerks whom he had met in Marseilles, but, of course, they could only say that he was the man known as Captain Horn.

The captain ground his teeth, and then, suddenly turning, he interrupted the conversation between the magistrate and Barré. He addressed the latter and asked, "Will you tell me what this officer has been saying about me?"

"He says," answered Barré, "that he believes you know nobody in Paris except the party at the Hotel Grenade, and that, of course, you may have deceived them in regard to your identity—that they have been here a long time, and you have been absent, and you have not been referred to by them, which seems strange."

"Has he not found out that Wraxton knows me?"

"He says," answered Barré, "that you have not visited that banking house since you came to Paris, and that seems strange also. Every traveller goes to his banker as soon as he arrives."

"I did not need to go there," said the captain. "I was occupied with other matters. I had just met my wife after a long absence."

"I don't wonder," said the professor, bowing, "that your time was occupied. It is very unfortunate that your banker cannot come to you or send."

The captain did not answer. This professor doubted him, and why should he not? As the captain considered the case, it grew more and more serious. That his marriage should be delayed on account of such a preposterous and outrageous charge against him was bad enough. It would be a terrible blow to Edna. For, although he knew that she would believe in him, she could not deny, if she were questioned, that in this age of mail and telegraph facilities she had not heard from him for nearly a year, and it would be hard for her to prove that he had not deceived her. But the most unfortunate thing of all was the meeting with the London lawyers the next day. These men were engaged in settling a very important question regarding the ownership of the treasure he had brought to France, and his claims upon it, and if they should hear that he had been charged with being the captain of a band of murderers and robbers, they might well have their suspicions of the truth of his story of the treasure. In fact, everything might be lost, and the affair might end by his being sent a prisoner to Peru, to have the case investigated there. What might happen then was too terrible to think of. He turned abruptly to the professor.

"I see that you don't believe in me," he said, "but I see that you are a man, and I believe in you. You are acquainted with this magistrate. Use your influence with him to have this matter settled quickly. Do as much as that for me."

"What is it that you ask me to do?" said the other.

"It is this," replied the captain. "I have never seen this man who says he was a member of the Rackbirds' band. In fact, I never saw any of those wretches except dead ones. He has never met me. He knows nothing about me. His charge is simply a piece of revenge. The only connection he can make between me and the Rackbirds is that he knew two negroes were once the servants of his band, and that they are now the servants of my wife. Having never seen me, he cannot know me. Please ask the magistrate to send for some other men in plain clothes to come into this room, and then let the prisoner be brought here, and asked to point out the man he charges with the crime of being the captain of the Rackbirds."

The professor's face brightened, and without answer he turned to the magistrate, and laid this proposition before him. The officer shook his head.

This would be a very irregular method of procedure. There were formalities which should not be set aside. The deposition of Banker should be taken before witnesses. But the professor was interested in Captain Horn's proposed plan. In an emergency of the sort, when time was so valuable, he thought it should be tried before anything else was done. He talked very earnestly to the magistrate, who at last yielded.

In a few minutes three respectable men were brought in from outside, and then a policeman was sent for Banker.

When that individual entered the waiting-room, his eyes ran rapidly over the company assembled there. After the first glance, he believed that he had never seen one of them before. But he said nothing; he waited to hear what would be said to him. This was said quickly. Banker spoke French, and the magistrate addressed him directly.

"In this room," he said, "stands the man you have accused as a robber and a murderer, as the captain of the band to which you admit you once belonged. Point him out immediately."

Banker's heart was not in the habit of sinking, but it went down a little now. Could it be possible that any one there had ever led him to deeds of violence and blood? He looked again at each man in the room, very carefully this time. Of course, that rascal Raminez would not come to Paris without disguising himself, and no disguise could be so effectual as the garb of a gentleman. But if Raminez were there, he should not escape him by any such tricks. Banker half shut his eyes, and again went over every countenance. Suddenly he smiled.

"My captain," he said presently, "is not dressed exactly as he was when I last saw him. He is in good clothes now, and that made it a little hard for me to recognize him at first. But there is no mistaking his nose and his eyebrows. I know him as well as if we had been drinking together last night. There he stands!" And, with his right arm stretched out, he pointed directly to Professor Barré.

At these words there was a general start, and the face of the magistrate grew scarlet with anger. As for the professor himself, he knit his brows, and looked at Banker in amazement.

"You scoundrel! You liar! You beast!" cried the officer. "To accuse this well-known and honorable gentleman, and say that he is a leader of a band of robbers! You are an impostor, a villain, and if you had been confronted with this other gentleman alone, you would have sworn that he was a bandit chief!"

Banker made no answer, but still kept his eyes fixed upon the professor. Now Captain Horn spoke: "That fellow had to say something, and he made a very wild guess of it," he said to Barré. "I think the matter may now be considered settled. Will you suggest as much to the magistrate? Truly, I have not a moment to spare."

Banker listened attentively to these words, and his eyes sparkled.

"You needn't try any of your tricks on me, you scoundrel Raminez," he said, shaking his fist at the professor. "I know you. I know you better than I did when I first spoke. If you wanted to escape me, you ought to have shaved off your eyebrows when you trimmed your hair and your beard. But I will be after you yet. The tales you have told here won't help you."

"Take him away!" shouted the magistrate. "He is a fiend!"

Banker was hurried from the room by two policemen.

To the profuse apologies of the magistrate Captain Horn had no time to listen; he accepted what he heard of them as a matter of course, and only remarked that, as he was not the man against whom the charges had been brought, he must hurry away to attend to a most important appointment. The professor went with him into the street.

"Sir," said the captain, addressing Barré, "you have been of the most important service to me, and I heartily acknowledge the obligation. Had it not been that you were good enough to exert your influence with the magistrate, that rascal would have sworn through thick and thin that I had been his captain."

Then, looking at his watch, he said, "It is twenty-five minutes to four. I shall take a cab and go directly to the legation. I was on my way to my hotel, but there is no time for that now," and, after shaking hands with the professor, he hailed a cab.

Captain Horn reached the legation but a little while after the party from the Hotel Grenade had arrived, and in due time he stood up beside Edna in one of the parlors of the mansion, and he and she were united in marriage by the American minister. The services were very simple, but the congratulations of the little company assembled could not have been more earnest and heartfelt.

"Now," said Mrs. Cliff, in the ear of Edna, "if we knew that that gold was all to be sunk in the ocean to-morrow, we still ought to be the happiest people on earth."

She was a true woman, Mrs. Cliff, and at that moment she meant what she said.

It had been arranged that the whole party should return to the Hotel Grenade, and from there the newly married couple should start for the train which would take them to Calais; and, as he left the legation promptly, the captain had time to send to his own hotel for his effects. The direct transition from the police station to the bridal altar had interfered with his ante-hymeneal preparations, but the captain was accustomed to interference with preparations, and had long learned to dispense with them when occasion required.

"I don't believe," said the minister's wife to her husband, when the bridal party had left, "that you ever before married such a handsome couple."

"The fact is," said he, "that I never before saw standing together such a fine specimen of a man and such a beautiful, glowing, radiant woman."

"I don't see why you need say that," said she, quickly. "You and I stood up together."

"Yes," he replied, with a smile, "but I wasn't a spectator."

CHAPTER LI
BANKER DOES SOME IMPORTANT BUSINESS

When Banker went back to the prison cell, he was still firmly convinced that he had been overreached by his former captain, Raminez; and, although he knew it not, there were good reasons for his convictions. Often had he noticed, in the Rackbirds' camp, a peculiar form of the eyebrows which surmounted the slender, slightly aquiline nose of his chief. Whenever Raminez was anxious, or beginning to be angered, his brow would slightly knit, and the ends of his eyebrows would approach each other, curling upward and outward as they did so. This was an action of the eyebrows which was peculiar to the Darcias of Granada, from which family the professor's father had taken a wife, and had brought her to Paris. A sister of this wife had afterwards married a Spanish gentleman named Blanquotè, whose second son, having fallen into disgrace in Spain, had gone to America, where he changed his name to Raminez, and performed a number of discreditable deeds, among which was the deception of several of his discreditable comrades in regard to his family. They could not help knowing that he came from Spain, and he made them all believe that his real name was Raminez. There had been three of them, besides Banker, who had made it the object of their lives to wait for the opportunity to obtain blackmail from his family, by threatened declarations of his deeds.

This most eminent scoundrel, whose bones now lay at the bottom of the Pacific Ocean, had inherited from his grandfather that same trick of the eyebrows above his thin and slightly aquiline nose which Banker had observed upon the countenance of the professor in the police station, and who had inherited it from the same Spanish gentleman.

The next day Banker received a visitor. It was Professor Barré. As this gentleman entered the cell, followed by two guards, who remained near the door, Banker looked up in amazement. He had expected a message, but had not dreamed that he should see the man himself.

"Captain," he exclaimed, as he sprang to his feet, "this is truly good of you. I see you are the same old trump as ever, and do not bear malice." He spoke in Spanish, for such had been the language in common use in camp.

The professor paid no attention to these words. "I came here," he said, "to demand of you why you made that absurd and malicious charge against me the other day. Such charges are not passed over in France, but I will give you a chance to explain yourself."

Banker looked at him admiringly. "He plays the part well," he said to himself. "He is a great gun. There is no use of my charging against him. I will not try it, but I shall let him see where I stand."

"Captain," said he, "I have nothing to explain, except that I was stirred up a good deal and lost my temper. I oughtn't to have made that charge against you. Of course, it could not be of any good to me, and I am perfectly ready to meet you on level ground. I will take back everything I have already said, and, if necessary, I will prove that I made a mistake and never saw you before, and I only ask in return that you get me out of this and give me enough to make me comfortable. That won't take much, you know, and you seem to be in first-class condition these days. There! I have put it to you fair and square, and saved you the trouble of making me any offers. You stand by me, and I'll stand by you. I am ready to swear until I am black in the face that you never were in Peru, and that I never saw you until the other day, when I made that mistake about you on account of the queer fashion of your eyebrows, which looked just like those of a man who really had been my captain, and that I now see you are two entirely different men. I will make a good tale of it, captain, and I will stick to it—you can rely on that. By all the saints, I hope those two fellows at the door don't understand Spanish!"

The professor had made himself sure that the guards who accompanied him spoke nothing but French. Without referring to Banker's proposed bargain, he said to him, "Was the captain of the bandits under whom you served a Spaniard?"

"Yes, you were a Spaniard," said Banker.

"From what part of Spain did he come?"

"You let out several times that you once lived in Granada."

"What was that captain's real name?" asked the professor.

"Your name was Raminez—unless, indeed," and here his face clouded a little, "unless, indeed, you tricked us. But I have pumped you well on that point, and, drunk or sober, it was always Raminez."

"Raminez, then, a Spaniard of my appearance," said the professor, "was your captain when you were in a band called the Rackbirds, which had its rendezvous on the coast of Peru?"

"Yes, you were all that," said Banker.

"Very well, then," said Barré. "I have nothing more to say to you at present," and he turned and left the cell. The guards followed, and the door was closed.

Banker remained dumb with amazement. When he had regained his power of thought and speech, he fell into a state of savage fury, which could be equalled by nothing living, except, perhaps, by a trapped wildcat, and among his objurgations, as he strode up and down his cell, the most prominent referred to the new and incomprehensible trick which this prince of human devils had just played upon him. That he had been talking to his old captain he did not doubt for a moment, and that that captain had again got the better of him he doubted no less.

It may be stated here that, the evening before, the professor had had a long talk with Ralph regarding the Rackbirds and their camp. Professor Barré had heard something of the matter before, but many of the details were new to him.

When Ralph left him, the professor gave himself up to reflections upon what he had heard, and he gradually came to believe that there might be some reason for his identification as the bandit captain by the man Banker.

For five or six years there had been inquiries on foot concerning the second son of Señor Blanquotè of Granada, whose elder brother had died without heirs, and who, if now living, would inherit Blanquotè's estates. It was known that this man had led a wild and disgraceful career, and it was also ascertained that he had gone to America, and had been known on the Isthmus of Panama and elsewhere by the name of Raminez. Furthermore, Professor Barré had been frequently told by his mother that when he was a boy she had noticed, while on a visit to Spain, that he and this cousin very much resembled each other.

It is not necessary to follow out the legal steps and inquiries, based upon the information which he had had from Ralph and from Banker, which were now made by the professor. It is sufficient to state that he was ultimately able to prove that the Rackbird chief known as Raminez was, in reality, Tomaso Blanquotè, that he had perished on the coast of Peru, and that he, the professor, was legal heir to the Blanquotè estates.

Barré had not been able to lead his pupil to as high a place in the temple of knowledge as he had hoped, but, through his acquaintance with that pupil, he himself had become possessed of a castle in Spain.

CHAPTER LII
THE CAPTAIN TAKES HIS STAND

It was now July, and the captain and Edna had returned to Paris. The world had been very beautiful during their travels in England, and although the weather was beginning to be warm, the world was very beautiful in Paris. In fact, to these two it would have been beautiful almost anywhere. Even the desolate and arid coast of Peru would have been to them as though it were green with herbage and bright with flowers.

The captain's affairs were not yet definitely arranged, for the final settlement would depend upon negotiations which would require time, but there was never in the world a man more thoroughly satisfied than he. And whatever happened, he had enough; and he had Edna. His lawyers had made a thorough investigation into the matter of his rights to the treasure he had discovered and brought to Europe, and they had come to a conclusion which satisfied them. This decision was based upon equity and upon the laws and usages regarding treasure-trove.

The old Roman law upon the subject, still adhered to by some of the Latin countries of Europe, gave half of a discovered treasure to the finder, and half to the crown or state, and it was considered that a good legal stand could be taken in the present instance upon the application of this ancient law to a country now governed by the descendants of Spaniards.

Whether or not the present government of Peru, if the matter should be submitted to it, would take this view of the case, was a subject of conjecture, of course, but the captain's counsel strongly advised him to take position upon the ground that he was entitled to half the treasure. Under present circumstances, when Captain Horn was so well prepared to maintain his rights, it was thought that the Peruvian authorities might easily be made to see the advisability of accepting a great advantage freely offered, instead of endeavoring to obtain a greater advantage, in regard to which it would be very difficult, if not impossible, to legally prove anything or to claim anything.

Therefore, it was advised that a commission should be sent to Lima to open negotiations upon the subject, with instructions to make no admissions in regard to the amount of the treasure, its present places of deposit, or other particulars, until the Peruvian government should consent to a satisfactory arrangement.

To this plan Captain Horn consented, determining, however, that, if the negotiations of his commission should succeed, he would stipulate that at least one half the sum paid to Peru should be devoted to the advantage of the native inhabitants of that country, to the establishment of schools, hospitals, libraries, and benefactions of the kind. If the commission should not succeed, he would then attend to the matter in his own way.

Thus, no matter what happened, he would still insist upon his claim to one fifth of the total amount as his pay for the discovery of the treasure, and in this claim his lawyers assured him he could be fully secured.

Other matters were in a fair way of settlement. The captain had made Shirley and Burke his agents through whom he would distribute to the heirs of the crew of the *Castor* their share of the treasure which had been apportioned to them, and the two sailors had already gone to America upon this mission. How to dispose of the *Arato* had been a difficult question, upon which the captain had taken legal advice. That she had started out from Valparaiso with a piratical crew, that those pirates had made an attack upon him and his men, and that, in self-defence, he had exterminated them, made no difference in his mind, or that of his counsellors, as to the right of the owners of the vessel to the return of their property. But a return of the vessel itself would be difficult and hazardous. Whoever took it to Valparaiso would be subject to legal inquiry as to the fate of the men who had hired it, and it would be, indeed, cruel and unjust to send out a crew in this vessel, knowing that they would be arrested when they arrived in port. Consequently, he determined to sell the *Arato*, and to add to the amount obtained what might be considered proper on account of her detention, and to send this sum to Valparaiso, to be paid to the owners of the *Arato*.

The thoughts of all our party were now turned toward America. As time went on, the captain and Edna might have homes in different parts of the world, but their first home was to be in their native land.

Mrs. Cliff was wild to reach her house, that she might touch it with the magician's wand of which she was now the possessor, that she might touch not only it, but that she might touch and transform the whole of Plainton, and, more than all, that with it she might touch and transform herself. She had bought all she wanted. Paris had yielded to her everything she asked of it, and no ship could sail too fast which should carry her across the ocean.

The negroes were all attached to the captain's domestic family. Maka and Cheditafa were not such proficient attendants as the captain might have employed, but he desired to have these two near him, and intended to keep them there as long as they would stay. Although Mok and the three other Africans had much to learn in regard to the duties of domestic servants, there would always be plenty of people to teach them.

* * * * *

In his prison cell Banker sat, lay down, or walked about, cursing his fate and wondering what was meant by the last dodge of that rascal Raminez. He never found out precisely, but he did find out that the visit of Professor Barré to his cell had been of service to him.

That gentleman, when he became certain that he should so greatly profit by the fact that an ex-brigand had pointed him out as an ex-captain of brigands, had determined to do what he could for the fellow who had unconsciously rendered him the service. So he employed a lawyer to attend to Banker's case, and as it was not difficult to prove that the accused had not even touched Cheditafa, but had only threatened to maltreat him, and that the fight which caused his arrest was really begun by Mok, it was not thought necessary to inflict a very heavy punishment. In fact, it was suggested in the court that it was Mok who should be put on trial.

So Banker went for a short term to prison, where he worked hard and earned his living, and when he came out he thought it well to leave Paris, and he never found out the nature of the trick which he supposed his old chief had played upon him.

The trial of Banker delayed the homeward journey of Captain Horn and his party, for Cheditafa and Mok were needed as witnesses, but did not delay it long. It was early in August, when the danger from floating icebergs had almost passed, and when an ocean journey is generally most pleasant, that nine happy people sailed from Havre for New York. Captain Horn and Edna had not yet fully planned their future life, but they knew that they had enough money to allow them to select any sphere of life toward which ordinary human ambitions would be apt to point, and if they never received another bar of the unapportioned treasure, they would not only be preeminently satisfied with what fortune had done for them, but would be relieved of the great responsibilities which greater fortune must bring with it.

As for Mrs. Cliff, her mind was so full of plans for the benefit of her native town that she could talk and think of nothing else, and could scarcely be induced to take notice of a spouting whale, which was engaging the attention of all the passengers and the crew.

The negroes were perfectly content. They were accustomed to the sea, and did not mind the motion of the vessel. They had but little money in their pockets, and had no reason to expect they would ever have much more, but they knew that as long as they lived they would have everything that they wanted, that the captain thought was good for them, and to a higher earthly paradise their souls did not aspire. Cheditafa would serve his mistress, Maka would serve the captain, and Mok would wear fine clothes and serve his young master Ralph, whenever, haply, he should have the chance.

As for Inkspot, he doubted whether or not he should ever have all the whiskey he wanted, but he had heard that in the United States that delectable fluid was very plentiful, and he thought that perhaps in that blessed country that blessed beverage might not produce the undesirable effects which followed its unrestricted use in other lands.

CHAPTER LIII
A LITTLE GLEAM AFAR

It was late in the autumn of that year, and upon a lonely moor in Scotland, that a poor old woman stood shivering in the cold wind. She was outside of a miserable little hut, in the doorway of which stood two men.

For five or six years she had lived alone in that little hut.

It was a very poor place, but it kept out the wind and the rain and the snow, and it was a home to her, and for the greater part of these years in which she had lived there alone, she had received, at irregular and sometimes long intervals, sums of money, often very small and never large, from her son, who was a sailorman upon seas of which she did not even know the name.

But for many months no money had come from this wandering son, and it was very little that she had been able to earn. Sometimes she might have starved, had it not been for the charity of others almost as poor as she. As for rent, it had been due for a long time, and at last it had been due so long that her landlord felt that further forbearance would be not only unprofitable, but that it would serve as a bad example to his other tenants. Consequently, he had given orders to eject the old woman from her hut. She was now a pauper, and there were places where paupers would be taken care of.

The old woman stood sadly shivering. Her poor old eyes, a little dimmed with tears, were directed southward toward the far-away vanishing-point of the rough and narrow road which meandered over the moor and lost itself among the hills.

She was waiting for the arrival of a cart which a poor neighbor had promised to borrow, to take her and her few belongings to the nearest village, where there was a good road over which she might walk to a place where paupers were taken care of. A narrow stream, which roared and rushed around or over many a rock, ran at several points close to the road, and, swelled by heavy rains, had overflowed it to the depth of a foot or more. The old woman and the two men in the doorway of the hut stood and waited for the cart to come.

As they waited, heavy clouds began to rise in the north, and there was already a drizzle of rain. At last they saw a little black spot upon the road, which soon proved to be a cart drawn by a rough pony. On it came, until they could almost hear it splashing through the water where the stream had passed its bounds, or rattling over the rough stones in other places. But, to their surprise, there were two persons in the cart. Perhaps the boy Sawney had with him a traveller who was on his way north.

This was true. Sawney had picked up a traveller who was glad to find a conveyance going across the moor to his destination. This man was a quick-moving person in a heavy waterproof coat with its collar turned up over his ears.

As soon as the cart stopped, near the hut, he jumped down and approached the two men in the doorway.

"Is that the widow McLeish?" he said, pointing to the old woman.

They assured him that he was correct, and he approached her.

"You are Mrs. Margaret McLeish?" said he.

She looked at him in a vague sort of way and nodded. "That's me," said she. "Is it pay for the cart you're after? If that's it, I must walk."

"Had you a son, Mrs. McLeish?" said the man.

"Ay," said she, and her face brightened a little.

"And what was his name?"

"Andy," was the answer.

"And his calling?"

"A sailorman."

"Well, then," said the traveller in the waterproof, "there is no doubt that you are the person I came here to see. I was told I should find you here, and here you are. I may as well tell you at once, Mrs. McLeish, that your son is dead."

"That is no news," she answered. "I knew that he must be dead."

"But I didn't come here only to tell you that. There is money coming to you through him—enough to make you comfortable for the rest of your life."

"Money!" exclaimed the old woman. "To me?"

The two men who had been standing in the doorway of the hut drew near, and Sawney jumped down from the cart. The announcement made by the traveller was very interesting.

"Yes," said the man in the waterproof, pulling his collar up a little higher, for the rain was increasing, "you are to have one hundred and four pounds a year, Mrs. McLeish, and that's two pounds a week, you know, and you will have it as long as you live."

"Two pounds a week!" cried the old woman, her eyes shining out of her weazened old face like two grouse eggs in a nest. "From my Andy?"

"Yes, from your son," said the traveller. And as the rain was now much more than a drizzle, and as the wind was cold, he made his tale as short as possible.

He told her that her son had died far away in South America, and, from what he had gained there, one hundred and four pounds a year would be coming to her, and that she might rely on this as long as she lived. He did not state—for he was not acquainted with all the facts—that Shirley and Burke, when they were in San Francisco hunting up the heirs of the Castor's crew, had come upon traces of the A. McLeish whose body they had found in the desert, lying flat on its back, with a bag of gold clasped to its breast— that they had discovered, by means of the agent through whom McLeish had been in the habit of forwarding money to his mother, the address of the old woman, and, without saying anything to Captain Horn, they had determined to do something for her.

The fact that they had profited by the gold her son had carried away from the cave, was the main reason for this resolution, and although, as Shirley said, it might appear that the Scotch sailor was a thief, it was true, after all, he had as much right to a part of the gold he had taken as Captain Horn could have. Therefore, as they had possessed themselves of his treasure, they thought it but right that they should provide for his mother. So they bought an annuity for her in Edinburgh, thinking this better than sending her the total amount which they considered to be her share, not knowing what manner of woman she might be, and they arranged that an agent should be sent to look her up, and announce to her her good fortune. It had taken a long time to attend to all these matters, and it was now late in the autumn.

"You must not stand out in the rain, Mrs. McLeish," said one of the men, and he urged her to come back into the hut. He said he would build a fire for her, and she and the gentleman from Edinburgh could sit down and talk over matters. No doubt there would be some money in hand, he said, out of which the rent could be paid, and, even if this should not be the case, he knew the landlord would be willing to wait a little under the circumstances.

"Is there money in hand for me?" asked the old woman.

"Yes," said the traveller. "The annuity was to begin with October, and it is now the first of November, so there is eight pounds due to you."

"Eight pounds!" she exclaimed, after a moment's thought. "It must be more than that. There's thirty-one days in October!"

"That's all right, Mrs. McLeish," said the traveller. "I will pay you the right amount. But I really think you had better come into your house, for it is going to be a bad afternoon, and I must get away as soon as I can. I will go, as I came, in the cart, for you won't want it now."

Mrs. McLeish stood up as straight as she could, and glanced from the traveller to the two men who had put her out of her home. Then, in the strongest terms her native Gaelic would afford, she addressed these two men. She assured them that, sooner than enter that contemptible little hut again, she would sleep out on the bare moor. She told them to go to their master and tell him that she did not want his house, and that he could live in it himself, if he chose—that she was going in the cart to Killimontrick, and she would take lodgings in the inn there until she could get a house fit for the habitation of the mother of a man like her son Andy; and that if their master had anything to say about the rent that was due, they could tell him that he had satisfied himself by turning her out of her home, and if he wanted anything more, he could whistle for it, or, if he didn't choose to do that, he could send his factor to whistle for it in the main street of Killimontrick.

"Come, Sawney boy, put my two bundles in the cart, and then help me in. The gentleman will drive, and I'll sit on the seat beside him, and you can sit behind in the straw, and—you're sure it's two pounds a week, sir?" she said to the traveller, who told her that she was right, and then she continued to Sawney, "I'll make your mother a present which will help the poor old thing through the winter, and I'm sure she needs it."

With a heavier load than he had brought, the pony's head was turned homeward, and the cart rattled away over the rough stones, and splashed through the water on the roadway, and in the dark cloud which hung over the highest mountain beyond the moor, there came a little glint of lighter sky, as if some lustre from the Incas' gold had penetrated even into this gloomy region.